Please return on or before the latest date above.
You can renew online at *www.kent.gov.uk/libs*
or by telephone 08458 247 200

* *The Wording in this book May offend some people.*

Kevin Maher was born and brought up in Dublin, moving to London in 1994 to begin a career in journalism. He wrote for the *Guardian*, the *Observer* and *Time Out* and was film editor of the *Face* until 2002, before joining *The Times* where for the last eight years he has been a feature writer, critic and columnist.

THE FIELDS

Dublin, 1984: Ireland is a divided country, the parish priest remains a figure of immense authority who commands absolute respect, and Jim Finnegan is thirteen years old, the youngest in a family of five sisters. Life for Jim consists of dealing with his rumbustious family, taking breakneck bike-rides with his best friend, and secretly coveting the local girls. But after a delicate rendition of 'The Fields of Athenry' at the Donohues' annual party, Jim attracts both the attention of the beautiful Saidhbh Donohue and the unwanted desires of the dangerous Father Luke O'Culigeen. Caught between his love for Saidhbh and abuse at the hands of O'Culigeen, Jim's life starts to unravel. And soon he is forced to find a solution to all his problems in some unusual places.

KEVIN MAHER

THE FIELDS

Complete and Unabridged

CHARNWOOD
Leicester

First published in Great Britain in 2013 by
Little, Brown
An imprint of
Little, Brown Book Group
London

First Charnwood Edition
published 2013
by arrangement with
Little, Brown Book Group
An Hachette UK Company
London

The moral right of the author has been asserted

A catalogue record for this book is available
from the British Library.

ISBN 978-1-4448-1700-3

Published by
F. A. Thorpe (Publishing)
Anstey, Leicestershire

Set by Words & Graphics Ltd.
Anstey, Leicestershire
Printed and bound in Great Britain by
T. J. International Ltd., Padstow, Cornwall

This book is printed on acid-free paper

For Thomas Francis Matthew Matthias

ONE

When Jack died I was real young, younger than I am now, and I said, in a temper, that I would never let it happen again. Jack was our cat. A dark brown Burmese fella, with nippy teeth, grabby scratchy claws and loud wheezy breaths that rattled through him in a strange sing-songy chorus as he tottered about on unsteady paws. He was also the first and only time that we tried, as a family, to have a pet. And when he arrived there was a big hullaballoo among the girls. They were all pulling and shoving each other, with a bit of scratching too, all desperate to have a go. Kissing and cuddling and yanking him under the covers, and chasing him round the couch until he hid in the corner and did a pee under the coffee table that drove Dad completely wild. That fecking cat! he said, gritting his teeth and pulling his fingers into a fist as if he was going to punch to death a six-week-old fluff bundle.

Jack's wheezing, from day one, got louder and louder, and by the end of the first week it had turned into full-on flu. The vet said that he possibly had it all along, that the breeder, an ancient fella from County Cavan, was probably a bit of a shark, and that Jack might actually die instead of getting better. This scared the girls no end. And that, combined with all the snotty green drippy stuff pouring from his eyes and nose, and the way he'd suddenly sneeze and

3

blast it outwards and right into your face, made them run like mad whenever he appeared in the room. And it made Dad want to kill him even more.

I was the youngest, and I was the one who kept nagging Mam for a pet in the first place, so it was my job to be the cat-nurse. Which meant chasing Jack up the stairs with some cotton buds, wiping all the mucus away, and then bringing him into the bathroom and holding him over a hot bath so that he could breathe in the steam that was supposed to clear away all the hardened snot in his lungs that was causing the trouble in the first place. He hated this bit. And no matter how many times we did it, and no matter how many times I finished it up with a cuddle in a towel and a treaty piece of squashed sardine from my fingertips, he always thought that I was doing it for the hell of it, or because I was mental vicious, and was going to chuck him into the boiling bathwater for a laugh. He'd go scrapey crazy on my hands, driving big gashy cuts into my wrists, often drawing enough blood to make a lone red drip that would plip into the bath while he was taking his last few steamy panicky breaths. But it didn't matter to me, because I was making him better again.

Jack recovered after two full weeks of the treatment. Everyone, even the vet himself, went all, Woo woo, do we have ourselves a budding Doctor Doolittle here, or wha? Even Dad said, Well done, son, before looking over at Mam and adding with a sigh, I still think he should've died. She told him with a jokey slap that he was an

4

awful man, and he chuckled back that he was just the way she liked him, and that she was to get out of the garden, which was an expression that meant, ah, feck off with yourself ye little who-er, which was also an expression, and it really meant that you fancied the person on the receiving end of it.

Jack became super fit, and fast, and spent weeks and weeks lashing round the house, and causing all kinds of funny chaos, like chasing after the shadow of the pogo stick down the full length of the slope, or fighting with his bendy brass reflection in the coal scuttle and covering the green sitting-room carpet in tiny black paw prints. He was killed on the road outside our door when he was just seven months old. No one saw it happen. The first we knew of it was Maura Connell from next door with a big sad look on her face, telling Mam that she should go down the slope and see what's on the road in front of our driveway. I was the only one of the kids at home, because I hadn't gone to big school yet, so when Mam brought Jack in, all squashed and red around the head, I had loads of time alone with him.

Mam said that we'd have a family funeral in the back garden for Jack when the girls got home, and she used one of her good kitchen towels to wipe away all the red and black gooey stuff that was pouring out of the side of Jack's head, mostly through his left ear hole and eye socket. She laid him out, next to the onion patch, real nice like, on a knitted blanket that Sarah had made in Home Ec, and then she ran up to the attic to find an old shoe box to use for a coffin.

I lay out beside him too, on the grass. And with no one around I stroked his still-warm coat, kissed the non-bloody side of his head and started crying like mad and telling him how much I loved him. I told him that he was such a good cat. I lied to him too. I pretended that I didn't remember all the scratches he'd given me, or the times that he'd put massive rips in Dad's armchair, or when he climbed all over the tray-bake pastry while Mam was on the phone. You're the best cat, I said, stroking and weeping. You're such a good cat. The best cat in all Ireland. All the others are jealous of you, Jack. Coz you're the fastest, and the cleverest, and the funniest, and the best there is and ever will be.

I kind of wound myself up after a while. And the tears turned into big bonkers screams. Mam had to come rushing out and pin me into her arms. I told her that it was wrong, and that Jack should still be alive, and that God had made a stupid mistake. Mam, who went to Mass every day at ten in the morning without fail, and did praying the way most people did breathing, flinched a little at this. Feeling angry, I continued. And so, if God wanted Jack dead, I said, still crying, then I wanted God dead. Mam pushed me away from her chest and gave me a right shake, and told me that I was out of my mind, and saying terrible, terrible things. But that just made me worse, more angry, more bold, and made me say that I'd swap Jack for God any day of the week.

6

Mam told me to go to my room, and that I wasn't to come down until the funeral. I turned away from her, marched back into the house and shouted as I did, loud enough for her to hear, the words, Fecking God!

And I wasn't messing either. I lay on my bed, mad head dug into the pillow, still crying, still angry, and I said to God that I'd had it with Him, and that killing Jack was the last straw. He was in trouble now. Big trouble.

Eventually, drowsy with tear-heat, wet-eyed and weak, I fell asleep arguing with Him in my head, and thinking of the joke that Aunty Una once told about the little Italian fella who's praying to God for a brilliant birthday present and, just to be sure, chucks a statue of the Virgin Mary in his drawer, locks it tight, and then says to God that if He ever wants to see His Mother again He'd better make sure that he gets a bike for his birthday. It's a gas joke, because the little fella is supposed to be acting like a Mafia man that you see on telly, but actually the really funny part of the joke is that you say it with your voice gone all Italian, like the Cornetto man, all eef-a you-a want-a see-a your-a mother-a again-a you-a better-a get-a me-a bike-a. Aunty Una told it one Christmas Eve and it became the joke of the season, and the whole family, all eight of us, any time we wanted a laugh, kept on sticking 'a' at the end of our words and pretending-a we-a were-a Italian-a. Even after New Year's.

I told God that He could do what He liked to me, but really, that was the last time he was to pull that killing trick while I was around. I didn't have a statue of the Virgin Mary to hide, but I told him anyway that as soon as my mam allowed me, I was going to stop going to Mass, and confession too.

I slept right through to the next day. Missed the funeral and everything. Mam said it was just as well. Would've been too upsetting. I think of him now, though, Jack. Right at this moment. Here in this kitchen. And I wonder if it could've been different.

1

Summer Loving

Helen Macdowell gets hit in the face with a hockey ball. That's how it starts. Yes. The beginning of the end. All downhill from there. Helen's beautiful. She's got this light brown wavy flowy hair that curls back from her forehead. Her face is round, and her nose is soft and slightly ski-slopey. Her lips are browny pink, but shiny with lipgloss. And her eyes, Jesus, her eyes are crystal blue, really clear blue, no dirty bits in the blue. She's beautiful and she's going to be a nurse, or an air hostess, or a private investigator. At least that's what my sister Fiona says, and she should know. Fiona and Helen used to knock around together before Helen became too beautiful to have friends. They were best buddies once upon a time, and used to cut their fingers and stick the bloody bits together and pretend that they were witches and all the rest. Then Helen got boobs, nice hair and beautiful skin, and stopped knocking round with anyone except herself.

So, she's standing there, the best-looking girl on the black gravel pitch, wearing make-up and everything. Bully one, bully two, bully three's all done, and the sun's streaking down, battering the hockey girls good and hard. They're sweating in their short slate-grey gym skirts and their tight light-blue aertex tops, and we're cheering from the sidelines.

Go on now, ye ride, get them off ye, ye sexy little who-ers!

The nuns are looking round, scowling, pointing fingers, and we're loving it.

School's out, summer lovin, havin a blast.

And Helen's just standing there. Centre of the pitch. Staring.

I don't notice it at first, but the lads do.

They say, all giddy, Ooooooh, Finnegan, she's looking at you!

Looking at me?! Bollocks!

Yeah, looking at your bollocks all right!

But it's obvious, yes, she's looking straight at me. I turn my face away and go puce. I count to five while looking at the sideline grass and thinking about my whole family getting squished through a giant mincer like in the song on telly. But the funny thing is, when I turn back I notice that she's not really looking *looking* at me. Not giving me the eye or anything. She's just kind of staring into space, but at me.

Even so, the lads are going wild, saying that she wants to ride me, and touch me mickey, and all that stuff, only I'm feeling a bit sick from her stare. Her lips are curled downish, and her crystal-blue eyes are fizzing fire at me. She looks sad too, like she's feeling sorry for me, like she wants to shake her head and say, 'You poor poor prat.' I feel dizzy. I need to stand up, shake my head and turn away again. I want to go home to my mam.

But before I can do anything, it happens.

THWACKRUNCH!

Holy fuckster! one of the lads yells, as everyone goes spare. Helen Macdowell has just got a hockey ball in the mouth. There's teeth-bits everywhere, red teeth-bits. She opens up her mouth in agony and you can see that her lips are all puffed and slit and stabbed with bits of red teeth. Her face swells up in front of us. Blood pours out of her mouth. Like she's getting sick, and instead of puke there's blood coming out. The girl who hit her, Mary Davit, a big bruiser of a thing, is sitting in a heap on the ground, crying. Helen isn't crying yet. She's pawing her face, trying to feel the outline of her lumps and bumps. She's surrounded by the nuns, like a flock of nervous magpies, who keep the girls away. The others are still sweating in their skirts and shirts, but they're mostly whispering to each other and comforting Mary Davit. Someone whispers, Stupid bitch, that'll teach her!

After tapping and tipping her face for a few seconds, Helen lets her head drop to her chest and just screams the whole hockey pitch to pieces. Really screams. Like when you're being chased down a dark alley by a fella with a big carving knife in a Halloween horror flick. That loud! And to prove it, she lashes out at the nuns and starts to run for her life. Seriously. She runs straight off the hockey pitch, through the long grass, and out the main school gates on to the Ballydown Road. Screaming all the time, that carving-knife-horror-flick scream. And running, not stopping.

Maura Connell saw her running full pelt past

11

Quinnsworth's at two o'clock that afternoon. Helen Macdowell, the most beautiful girl on the hockey team, with her browny wavy hair flowing away from her, her crystal eyes on fire, and her battered minced-meat face shiny with blood. Blood pouring down her neck from her slash-hole mouth, all over her aertex gym shirt.

The rumour going round The Rise says that Helen was eventually wrestled to the ground by two shopping centre security guards inside Murray's chemist shop. She was in deep shock, and trying her damnedest to buy a jumbo refill of lipgloss.

★ ★ ★

We'd never seen anything like that around our place before. Not right in front of our eyes. You always heard about it, though. Through friends of friends. Or when The Mothers got together for coffee mornings. They'd sit around in a steamy kitchen circle like four mad witches, and dip ginger-snaps into Maxwell House until they went wobbly warm, and take turns at saying, Jahear about so-and-so, Lord rest his soul, only thirty years old, poor creature!?

They were brilliant at it. Scaring the shite out of each other, grinning inside, but on the outside all sad, just breaking up the day between ironing, washing and making sausage, spuds and parsnip dinners for the dads on their way home from work with their newspapers and their tired faces.

Of course, they'd go all hushed if they saw one of us coming in from the telly room. They'd lean in together and start talking with their mouths closed, or speaking in code. But most of the time, sitting in silence on the floor with the telly on low and the door half open, we got the gist.

For instance, there was Kent Foster, died of skin cancer aged twenty, God rest his soul. Kent was mad into the sunbathing. Every summer, down there on the black tarmac behind the five-a-side pitch, in his brown speedos, lathered in sunflower oil, like a Malteser covered in spit.

English blood! The Mothers would say.

With that name!

Right you are, Maisie.

Then one summer Kent just disappeared. No one knew where. No one except The Mothers.

Jahear about Kent Foster? No? Well, poor soul's down in the gym, he spots a little black freckle on his thigh, and two months later he's stone dead. Cancer! Riddled with the stuff! Only twenty years old, God rest his soul!

Cancer, death, only twenty! It's music to their ears, like the sound of a starter gun.

And so, stories at the ready, champing at the bit, they're off.

Gary's mam is thinking, I can beat that one hands down!

Mozzo's mam is racking her brains, scratching her fag packet and trying to remember that recent tragedy she heard about from her brother-in-law in Finglas.

And Maisie O'Mally, the crinkly septuagenarian from number 43, is faking it, saying, Did you hear about what's his name, who fell into the river?

Luckily, Gary's mam, the old reliable, cuts her dead. Not as bad as Neil Cody! she says.

Neil Cody is this boy from Mount Merrion, only fifteen. He's a bit of a swat, and likes to read his daddy's newspaper every day. So one Sunday morning, still in his pyjamas, he grabs the paper, the *Indo*, hot off the kitchen table and, dead excited, brings it up to his bedroom for a good ole read. Half an hour goes by. No sound from above. An hour. Nothing.

Imagine it! says Gary's mam, Silence from upstairs, what do you think? He's fallen asleep with the papers, the little dote, yes?

Well, no one's heard a peep out of Neil in three hours, so his mam runs up the stairs, knocks on his door, goes into his room, and there he is, dead as a dodo, flat out on the bed, a stream of blood coming out of his nostrils and down on to the funnies. He's had a brain haemorrhage and died. Just like that!

The Mothers all bless themselves and mutter things about St Anthony and Jesus and the apostles. Gary's mam is feeling happy with herself, and everyone thinks that she's won the competition hands down when Mozzo's mam lights up a John Player and says, dramatically, And of course, you've all heard about poor June Shilaweh?

Gary's mam freezes and, furious, aware that she's going to be trumped, shakes her head.

Mozzo's mam nods gravely to herself, as if she's not sure whether she should continue.

My mam tells her to hurry up and put them out of their misery.

14

The Shilawehs, Mozzo's mam says, are an African family, black as night, who've moved to the Villas.

The Villas! everyone goes in unison, groaning at the thought of that long line of little boxy terraced houses down the back of the estate. To hell or to the Villas! They couldn't've picked a worse spot if they tried, the eejits. Worse than the bloody jungles they've come from.

The Mothers all laugh at this, though they hold their hands over their mouths as they do.

So, the Shilawehs are trying to settle into life in the Villas. They say, Hello, good morning, to all their neighbours, even the ones who say Fuck off nigger to their faces. They send their only daughter, June, to the local girls Catholic school, Mother of Sorrow, or just The Sorrows for short, which is the one that my sisters go to, and the one that Helen Macdowell went to before she lost her face. And Mr Shilaweh gets a job stacking envelopes at Ryan's post office. The one thing that's missing is a bike. Little June Shilaweh has never had a bike, and now that she's in the free world and out of the jungle she wants one.

Indeed, interrupts Maisie, what would you want a bicycle for in the jungle? It'd only get whipped by the monkeys!

The Mothers do their hand-covering-mouth laugh again.

Anyway, little June Shilaweh gets a bike from her dad, who's saved up all his post-office money to pay for it. She hasn't even had it a week when she cycles up Clannard Road, gets overtaken by

15

a juggernaut, swivels and turns, falls off the bike and goes right under the rear wheels. Crushed to death on the spot.

The Mothers all sigh in silence and avoid looking each other in the eye.

And you know the worse bit? says Mozzo's mam, teasing and toying. Johnno Mac, who works in Mangan's Hairdressers right outside the crash spot, Clannard Road said he had to clean up after the truck was gone. Said that little June had no head left, swear to God, it was popped like a pimple under the weight of the truck. Ambulance just dragged a headless corpse inside, and the poor Shilawehs had to identify their daughter by the handlebars that were still stuck into her innards when they arrived.

Mozzo's mam has gone too far. My mam shoots up, leans against the sink, and says that she's doing sprouts tonight and you know how long them feckers take to peel. Gary's mam says that she'll walk Maisie home, even though it's only four houses down. Mozzo's mam, quickly getting the message, stands up to leave.

She sticks her head into the telly room and tells me that Mozzo's coming back today and he'll be dying to see me.

Mam, Gary's mam and Maisie mess about with coats until Mozzo's mam is out the door, and then they agree that she's a lovely girl, but a bit crude.

The fella left her, of course, says Gary's mam, left her with that little animal!

Meaning Mozzo.

2

The Turnip Incident

I have known Mozzo for only two months and already we are best friends. His hair is long, jet black and deliberately messy, he has a tiny hint of a greasy moustache on his pale upper lip, and he's the first person I tell about Helen Macdowell. He sits on my bed with his legs crossed and his shiny thirty-two-hole docs tucked neatly under each thigh. He rocks back'n'forth, picks at his faded red Iron Maiden T-shirt and says Fuckin Jaysus! out loud when I describe the moment of impact. He's so impressed that I tell him again, straight away, only this time I add a little extra gore, just to see his eyes pop even more. I tell him the sound the ball made when it hit her mouth.

THWACKRUNCH!

I describe little splatlets of blood flying off into the air from her burst lips. I describe her head shooting back on her neck like a boxer's punch-ball. And I describe the blood. Buckets of it. Everywhere.

Mozzo's impressed. He rocks back'n'forth at the top of the bed, right under the poster of a parked Porsche, doors open.

Fuckin hell, Finno! he says, over and over again. Fuckin hell, Finno, that's mad!

My Toshiba boombox plays Survivor at full

volume. I am pleased.

Mozzo's normally the one telling the stories. He's good at it too. His dad was a fisherman who worked out of Dublin port and used to fish at night, and take drugs during the day. He beat Mozzo's mam, Janet, at least once a week and then left her to raise Mozzo alone. But before he left he did loads of things that Mozzo turned into great stories. Like the time he came in pissed from work and held a knife to Janet's throat. How does it feel, wagon? he said. How does it feel?

Or the time he set himself on fire in front of the telly and didn't even notice because he was too far gone on booze and drugs. Mad. Or the time he threw a gas cylinder through the neighbour's front window because they complained about the smell coming off his fish van.

I'll give ye fish, ye stuck-up bastards! he said, and then he threw a big black plastic bag of fish guts through the hole where the window used to be. Mozzo said it was mad. The police came and everything, and they had to move houses in the end.

Mozzo's real name is Declan Morrissey, but even his mam calls him Mozzo. Fellas like him are always called something-o. There's loads of them down in the Villas. And they all know each other. Micko, Macko, Johnno, Backo, Stapo, Ryano, Freyno, Gavvo, Devo, Rocko, Knocko, Dicko, Mallo, Heno, Feno, Hylo and so on. The first thing that Mozzo said when he met me was, Howsigoing, Finno? It was a good start.

★　★　★

When Mozzo moved into The Rise my mam said that I should be friendly to him because he hadn't had all the luck that I had.

What luck? I asked her.

He has no feckin father! she answered.

I shrugged, and agreed that she was right. My father has a big thick brown moustache, laughs a lot, and is always called A Right Charmer by everyone who meets him. He makes money selling office equipment and he's genius at his job.

He could sell sand to the Arabs.

That's what everyone says about him. In fact, when the Shilawehs moved into the Villas, Maura Connell winked at him and told him that this was his chance to sell sand to the Arabs. He winked back at her, told her not to be so stupid, that they weren't Arabs, they were coloureds.

I have five sisters, all older than me. And no brothers. My father jokes that he wouldn't stop trying till he got a boy. And usually, depending on who's around, he'll then say, But I settled for Jim instead!

Then everyone laughs and says to my face that my dad's a wild card. Mam then grabs me, rubs my hair and says, Leave the poor creature alone!

⋆   ⋆   ⋆

Mozzo's still reeling from the excitement of the Helen MacDowell story. He's still rocking back'n'forth, but now he's nodding his head too. He looks up at my boombox, tells me that Survivor's fuckin shite and that I should listen to

19

some real fuckin music! He points to his T-shirt when he says this. Then he continues nodding, like he's thinking about something interesting inside. Eventually, he spits it out.

Let's do it, Finno, he says. Let's do a fuckin Helen Macker on it!

I'm confused.

I've seen it in a flick once, he says. We'll get a big fuckin melon, stick it on a fuckin pole and take fuckin potshots at it with the fuckin hockey gear. First shot to hit, splat goes the melon! Be fuckin mad!

Mozzo says fuckin the whole time, more than any friend I've ever had. More than Gary anyway.

★　★　★

Until Mozzo arrived on The Rise, Gary Connell was my number one buddy. His dad's a pilot for Aer Lingus and is always bringing him the latest electronic gadgets from America. Gary is an only child and a Protestant to boot, and, so my mam says, his parents have loads of money to spend on him because they don't have to be dividing it up among six hungry children. Nearly every day that Gary walks down The Rise he has a new gadget. Pocket space invaders cum leather wallet. Baseball-cap radio with joke drinking straw. Joke windscreen-wiper sunglasses. Sweat-band with built-in digital watch. Transistor-radio tankard.

If an alien scouting party landed in The Rise and saw Gary Connell marching down the street, with all his electronic blinking, tweeting, and bleating gadgets attached, I'm sure they'd scarper straight back to space, convinced they had met a super-advanced cyborg civilisation.

Mozzo likes hanging out with Gary, mostly because of Gary's gadgets. Gary's mam, Maura, hates Mozzo, mostly because Mozzo made Gary stick his mickey in between two pillows and hump away on it like it was a woman. Gary's mam is very glamorous and always wears mini-skirts, see-through blouses and lipstick indoors. Mozzo calls her a Fuckin Ride, even in front of Gary. Mozzo knows much more about girls than me and Gary. He's always talking about fannies and arses and blowjobs and lickjobs and bum-ming and wanking.

Just had a great pull of me dick, I spunked everywhere! he'll say as he walks into the room. He'll grab his crotch and say, Fuckin lovely!

Me and Gary joke about our mickeys and our balls too. But mostly when Mozzo's around. We go, Oh yeah, I'd definitely ride her! every time a girl walks by. And then we look at Mozzo to see if he agrees. Mostly though, he tells us that we haven't got a hope in hell of getting any fanny until we stop looking and acting like two little benders.

So one day Mozzo and Gary are up in Gary's room playing with his remote-control R2-D2 alarm clock and Mozzo says that he had the most amazing wank ever last night. He says that he put his mickey in between two pillows and banged away for hours, and it was just like the real thing, and he'd know about the real thing because he'd done it twice with his cousin at

21

their Stephen's Day party.

I'm tellin ya, he says to Gary, two pillows jammed together, fuckin hell, exactly like riding a real fuckin fanny! And then he says, You should fuckin try it!

Now Gary's a little blond fella with lots of freckles and he doesn't want to embarrass himself in front of Mozzo, so he says yeah, but insists that Mozzo leave the room while he's riding the pillows.

Mozzo stands outside the door and has a good ole laugh to himself listening to Gary humping and bumping away on the pillows. But then Gary's mam, Maura, comes up the stairs with a big pile of clothes for the hot press. She sees Mozzo standing outside the door and goes charging inside to find her little Gary, trousers down, having sexual intercourse with the bed linen. Gary's mam is disgusted and kicks Mozzo out of the house. She then sits Gary down on the bed and tries to talk to him about what he was doing and how it could ruin him and ruin his experiences with girls in the future. Gary said to me that the whole thing was a big laugh, but his mam told my mam that Gary burst out crying and said that it was all Mozzo's fault and that he never wanted any other girl but his own mam. Gary's mam hugged him close to her blouse and told him that everything would be all right and that he was supposed to be feeling confused at his age and that he'd make some woman very happy some day as long as he stayed away from Mozzo.

22

My mam doesn't hate Mozzo as much as Gary's mam. She says that's because Maura's a Protestant and she's a Catholic, and Protestants don't have much time for people like Mozzo or Mozzo's mam Janet. But my mam's a Catholic and our Lord was a Catholic and he was always looking after those who were less fortunate than himself, so that's why Mozzo needs our help. Mam then told me that if she ever caught me riding my pillows like Gary Connell she'd call the Parish Priest.

If there's any trouble at home at all, Mam threatens to call the Parish Priest. It's one of her rules.

★ ★ ★

Mozzo, Gary and me are out in the back garden, and we've Sellotaped a turnip to the Swingball post because we couldn't find a watermelon in Mam's veg basket. The turnip has been covered in a big red lipstick mouth to remind us of Helen Macdowell. My mam will later go spare when she finds her favourite lippy worn down to the base. Mozzo kisses the turnip for ages and calls it Helen Macker the Little Ride, and me and Gary laugh.

Gary has been told the Helen MacDowell story too so he's all excited about the game Mozzo has in store for us, and is wearing his joke drinking-straw baseball cap especially for the occasion. Mozzo's holding my sister Sarah's

23

hockey stick in his hand and he's marching around the garden like he owns the place.

The last time Mozzo was here it was my sister Fiona's seventeenth birthday barbecue party. It was brilliant fun, thanks to Mozzo. When it started getting dark, he rounded up all the kids into three groups, called one of them The British, the other The Argentinians and the other The IRA. So the IRA and The Argentinians got together under Mozzo's orders, and chased The British all around the apple trees shouting, Get out of the Falklands, Brits! Some of the parents thought this was very funny, especially Saidhbh Donohue's father, who always likes to sing songs and cry late at night about the times when our potatoes were rotten and the British were killing us all. After a few rounds of the apple trees, The IRA and The Argentinians cornered The British in the onion beds and started thumping them. My dad ran up the garden with a temper on him because loads of his onions were broken at the stalks and would therefore be tiny little malformed things when they were born instead of huge great tear-makers.

After rooting around in Sarah's sports bag, joking about finding her knickers and wanking all over them, Mozzo produces a badly scuffed hockey ball. It's a big heavy thing, like a perfectly round lump of concrete. He places the ball on the grass, ten feet in front of the Swingball post, facing up the garden, away from the house and towards the two apple trees. He turns to us and says that the first person to hit the turnip with a single shot wins the Mary Davit award for being a vicious bastard. Mozzo then strolls up to the ball, stands beside it, steadies himself, swings, shoots hard and clatters the turnip on the very first shot. Of course, nothing happens to the turnip. It doesn't explode like Mozzo said he saw in the flick, but even so me and Gary cheer out loud. We can't believe it. First shot and he gets it, one in a million. We look at each other and then over at Mozzo, who's lapping the garden in triumph, his hair blown off his face, his loose red Iron Maiden T-shirt flowing behind him, and we think together that he's brilliant.

★ ★ ★

It takes me and Gary ages to hit the turnip. I manage it after nearly twenty or so goes. Mozzo's sitting on the grass at this stage, making comments about the state of our shots.

Swing, ye big fuckin girlies! he's saying. Fuckin bufties, hit the fucker!

He says things like that right out loud after every shot, and he's starting to make Gary nervous. Gary still hasn't hit the turnip, and in fact is getting worse instead of better with each swing. He's even missing the ball altogether, taking big chunks of mucky-green earth out of Dad's very carefully cut grass. Dad never wanted us to have Swingball in the first place, said it wears down the grass something rotten, but Mam made him put it up after they had a big fight one night about how Dad was becoming a real killjoy in his old age. It started out as a jokey one around the table, with a few chuckles and

25

proddings from Mam, but it continued onwards, on through the night, up the stairs, and eventually behind closed bedroom doors, with voices raised, with tears, with everything. A real barnstormer.

Suddenly Mozzo says, Bollocks to this! He stands up with a big grin on his face, and says that he has a better plan, and that he's raising the stakes goodo. He grabs the ball and stick from Gary, who's nearly crying at this stage, and he walks round to the other side of the Swingball post, the side facing my mam's kitchen window. He looks up and down the garden, then he places the ball on the ground, again about ten feet away from the post, and he twists the post around so that the turnip's on this side. He hands the hockey stick to Gary and says, Try it now, ye big fuckin girl!

Gary refuses the stick. He says no way, because if he misses he's going to smash my mam's window. He even says fuckin this time.

No fuckin way!

But Mozzo's having none of it. He's teasing Gary, saying that he couldn't hit the bog with his own piss, or his own shit for that matter. And that Gary's bathroom floor must be covered in pools of piss and lumps of shit from all the times he's missed the loo. I know I shouldn't, but I'm laughing my head off picturing Gary slipping off the loo and pissing and shitting everywhere.

I can see Gary's really upset now, and his chin is clenching up all tight like your arse when you're holding in a fart. Mozzo can see it too, so he goes all soft and puts his arm around Gary's shoulder. He speaks to Gary like a dad, and says that there's method to his madness and that the risk of smashing my mam's kitchen window is called motivation. He says that Gary knows deep down inside that he'll be in trouble if he hits my mam's window, so there's no way he'll miss the turnip. Instead he'll focus on it, swing back and hit it in one. Just like that. Gary looks like he's feeling better after hearing this, and his chin relaxes a bit. Then Mozzo says, out of the blue, right into his face, Now go on and hit it, ye little pillow-fucker!

I burst out laughing at this, and so does Mozzo. We think it's so funny that Gary must find it funny too. But he doesn't. He just goes all red-faced and hits the hockey ball straight through my mam's kitchen window. Everyone goes Fuckin Hell! out loud and Gary bursts out crying and runs off home, holding his drinking-straw baseball cap in his hand.

3

Enter O'Culigeen

The window pane smashes into a billion pieces, like in the *Cannonball Run* when a stolen car gets driven through the glass front of a big fancy showroom, yee-haw style. There's a billion deadly bits of glass everywhere, all over the kitchen, like shiny snowflakes, covering the sink, the washing rack, the oven top and all the chopping boards. Mam has left a big bowl of brown scone mix out on the bread board and that's covered in glass too. When she walks in she can't believe her eyes and starts to cry. Me and Mozzo are out in the garden at this stage. We didn't know what to do, so we started playing Hit the Helen Macker Turnip again, only facing the right direction this time.

After the first few tears Mam goes crazy and comes charging out to the garden, screaming, I'll call the Parish Priest, I'll call the Parish Priest! over and over again, while grabbing me by the scruff of the neck.

Mozzo, cool as a cucumber, just looks at her and says, Does he know anything about fixing windows?

Mam was always threatening to call the Parish Priest on us. My sister Fiona says that's because she grew up in a small town down the bog, called Ballaghaderreen, in County Roscommon.

And in a small town, like when Mam was a child and when our nan was her mam, everyone thought that the priest was brilliant. He could do anything for you, solve any problem. He was like Moses, or the old fella in *The Equalizer*. If your kids were fighting or, as in our nan's case, if your husband was too drunk for words and belting you all the time, you'd call the Parish Priest and he'd be there in a flash. He'd sort out the situation, no bother to him, over a nice cup of tea by a roaring turf fire.

And the funny thing is, according to Fiona, it didn't matter who the Parish Priest actually was, as long as he was called the Parish Priest it meant that he was brilliant. The Parish Priest was like Miss Ellie in *Dallas*: one minute she's the lovely old lady with the warm face and crinkly eyes, the next minute she's been transformed into some ole boot with too much make-up, but she's still called Miss Ellie. The Parish Priest was always the Parish Priest, no matter what.

So far, Mam has called the Parish Priest out to our house only twice. The first time was because Dad was selling too much office furniture and never coming home for his meals on time. Fr Lonnegan had to tell him that a marriage was like a plant that needed sunlight and water to grow and that although Mam was providing the water goodo, she needed more than the amount of sunlight that she was getting from Dad. We all listened, all six of us, from upstairs with breaths held and giddy stomachs. We thought that there'd be murder, but after a while Dad was

29

being a real charmer and everyone was laughing and Fr Lonnegan was drinking whiskey and all three of them were having a gas time. The next morning Dad sat out in the back garden having a big long smoke to himself and Mam lay in bed on her own for ages. Fiona said it was because they had being 'doing it' all night long.

The second time was worse. There'd been a massive row in the house coz Sarah had stayed out till three in the morning without telling Mam or Dad. Sarah's the eldest, she was born two and a half minutes before Siobhan and she says that makes her the Leader of the Clan. She's got long jet-black hair, a sharp pointy nose and big boobs, and now that she's become a woman she makes Dad's friends pull stupid faces when Dad's not in the room. They stare at her legs and at her boobs, and then they look at each other and make 'whoooo' faces, as if they're eating something that's burning the roofs of their mouths.

Mam and Dad both stayed awake downstairs by the fire with Mam praying and Dad saying things like Little Floozy under his breath. Sarah had been smoking pot with Dave Gallagher outside Castle Mount Youth Club till three in the morning. When she came in she giggled a bit and said that she was sorry but Dave's car had broken down. Mam hugged her and told her to go to bed, but Dad said nothing.

Mozzo says that when someone offers you pot at a party you're either in or you're out. You can't just say no and watch everyone else smoke it. You join in, or you leave.

The next day, we're all sitting round the table having our dinner, me, Susan, Claire, Fiona, Siobhan, Sarah and Mam, when Dad comes in from work like a bear in a china shop and shouts at Sarah really loud.

You could've been raped last night, do you know that? You could've been dragged off the road into the bushes, stripped naked and raped!

We all drop our forks and stare into our plates of lovely buttery potato-cakes, beans and sausages.

Mam tells Dad to cool it, but he's having none of it.

He plonks himself down into his chair, savages a pan-blackened sausage, and starts saying things like, A daughter of mine, out till that hour, and no fella to show her home! What would've happened if you'd been raped and killed last night, eh? What would've happened?

Dad's moustache is mostly brown, but there are flecks of grey in it. And they are spreading. Over the years he's been able to do great things with it, like rub it against our bellies when he's in the mood of a big giddy grabby tickle machine, or make a big show of smoothing it down with two fingers when he's talking to sales customers or pretty women at Christmas parties. But when he's all raging, like this, it makes him look meaner than ever, and turns his whole face into a weird blank ball with three short dark strokes across it — two for the eyes, one for the 'tache.

Sarah says nothing and this makes Dad even angrier.

You're nothing but a tart! he says, and

everyone gasps. We all know this is a bad thing to call your own daughter. Dad knows it too and starts to tremble at what he's saying. He wipes a fleck of his own spat butter from the 'tache. Mam starts to cry.

A disgrace, he continues, but pauses before saying it again, And a tart!

Susan's sitting beside me. She's only just turned fifteen, and is, says Mam, a very young fifteen, and a real softie without a hardened bone in her body, so she bursts out crying too. Opposite me is Siobhan, Sarah's twin, identical except for the boobs, the long hair and the constant stream of admiring fellas, and she too starts to whine out loud like a mad old woman from down the bog. Fiona and Claire aren't crying, but you can tell by their faces that they're upset too.

Yet Sarah herself is dead calm and sits back and says nothing.

Dad gets tired of saying tart and stops. As he does, Mam sniffles and tells him that it's all over now, and she wants no more of this around her table. But Dad wants to know from the horse's mouth.

Well? he says, looking over at Sarah. What do you have to say for yourself?

Sarah stands up, shoves her plate aside, looks straight into Dad's face and says, It's not off the stones that I licked it!

None of us have a clue what she means by that but Dad obviously does because he leaps out of his place and tries to grab both her and the bamboo cane in the corner, screaming the word

Bitch as he does. But Sarah's way too fast and she's already upstairs with the door slammed and the stereo playing 'La Isla Bonita' before Dad can even get a whiff of her. And you just know that he's thinking about following her up and into the room, and giving her a good smackabout for her troubles. But he wouldn't dare. Not with the door shut, slammed or otherwise. Because Sarah and Siobhan's door is like a magic science-fiction force-field when it's closed, and it means that no one can dare enter, on pain of death, because they could both be standing right behind it, at any minute of the day, in their bras and pants, and lathering themselves in Impulse like the woman on the telly who uses half a can in one spray even though she's only running for the bus. And being in their bras and pants gives Sarah and Siobhan the right to scream out loud, at anyone unlucky enough to be on the other side of the door, stuff like, Feck off! Feck off! We're in here, and our bodies are on show, and we're women!

Naturally, Mam calls the Parish Priest. Fr O'Culigeen, this time. The new one. A young one, with slick black hair and tanned skin and black leather driving gloves. A handsome man, O'Culigeen. Standing at our door in his black outfit and black leather driving gloves like Simon Templar from *The Saint*. O'Culigeen. He looks at me, calls me a grand lad and says that I'd be perfect for altar-boy duty, before asking if he could speak to me mam. As usual, Mam tells us all to wait upstairs until the Parish Priest has sorted it all out, only this time Dad has already

33

stormed off in the car. So Mam and O'Culigeen sit downstairs and drink a bucket of tea and eat about twenty brown scones each before Dad gets back.

O'Culigeen wasn't as good as Fr Lonnegan. He didn't drink any of Dad's whiskey and he didn't have that much of a laugh.

Instead he was very serious and gave them a joint lecture on teenagers and hormones and changing body organs. After he left, Mam and Dad said Amen to that, and had a cuddle on the couch.

★　★　★

Mam and Maura Connell get together over soggy bickies and they ban me and Gary from seeing Mozzo for the rest of the summer. Mam goes all serious and takes me to see Fr O'Culigeen, and there right in the corner of the churchyard, behind the railings, beside the back door where the coffins come in and the hangers-on doss about at Saturday evening Mass, Mam holds my hand tightly and with me staring at the holy water bowl she looks into Fr O'Culigeen's eyes and tells him that I want to become an altar boy. I know, deep down inside, that this is wrong. My mam is lying to a priest in order to turn me into a good boy. She wants me to become one of those little fellas on the altar with the tiny pinched mouths and thick bowl haircuts who kneel and bow in all the right places and swing the smoky sling-shot around when the bell goes and make their parents in the front row proud because they look like mini-priests.

O'Culigeen is still wearing his black leather driving gloves and he leans a hand over to me and gently tilts my head back by putting two fingers under my chin and calling me My Child. He looks at me as if he's sizing me up for a photo-shoot for *Jackie* magazine, and then he says that it's such a shame that they don't need me at the moment. They've got loads of lads at my age just dying to be altar boys. But if I come again next year, there'll definitely be an opening for me.

In the meantime My Child, he says, I'll be looking out for you.

He winks at Mam and she winks back and in their winking I think they're saying that I'll be a good lad now because O'Culigeen the Priest is going to keep his eye on me and make sure that I don't get into any more trouble.

★ ★ ★

On the way home from the church Mam walks dead quiet beside me. She's not normally this quiet. Usually she asks me my opinion on loads of subjects, from the weather, to the holidays so far, to my sisters, to the fellas that Sarah and Siobhan are hanging out with, right down to things like her new haircut, the colour of her new A-wear blouse or the shape of her new stretch denims. It's like she loves talking to me. She's brilliant like that. Brilliant at making you feel like what you're saying is the most important thing ever. But today she's dead quiet. She's taking deep breaths the whole way home, and sighing a lot too.

Eventually, just after we pass the small side-gate to the Protestant church on Bailiff-scourt Road, she says it.

Jim, love, what do you know about periods?

Before I have a chance to answer, she says, And masturbation? And intercourse too?

She says that she's been talking to Maura and she's sorry to ask me so many questions but she's never had to raise a boy before and she wants to make sure that I don't grow up to be a pillow fucker. She doesn't actually say the words Pillow Fucker, but she says she wants me to have good experiences with girls, which is what Gary's mam said to him. I tell her not to worry about all that stuff. I tell her that Fiona told me everything a couple of years ago.

Did she now? says Mam, relieved that she's not going to have to talk about my mickey out loud, but clearly furious with Fiona for stealing her thunder as a mam.

★　★　★

Even though she's way older, Fiona and me share the same room. This is because the twins have their own room coz Mam says that they're magically bonded together by the very fact that they're twins, even though most of the time Sarah's a complete cow to Siobhan and is always real loud when they go out and gets all the fellas and leaves Siobhan feeling mousy, flat-chested and unpretty. Claire and Susan have a room too.

They're not twins but they may as well be. They've the same browny blondey hair, although Susan has to spend ages curling hers just to make it as wavy as Claire's, they wear the same blue Penny's denims, the same leg warmers, and the same luminous pink sweatshirts. If it wasn't for the fact that Susan's a big old podger and Claire's dead skinny, they'd be more like twins than Sarah and Siobhan.

This leaves only one more bedroom in our house, not including Mam and Dad's, and that's the one that me and Fiona have. It's got two single beds shoved up against opposite walls, two thin plywood wardrobes that Dad got free from a work fella, four short rickety bookshelves, a make-up table for Fiona, and a fancy paisley rug down the middle of the floor for dirty clothes and dancing.

Fiona is brilliant. She doesn't mind my parked Porsche poster over my bed, or Survivor, and I don't say anything about her framed picture of the fella and girl kissing goodnight under the bridge in Paris. She listens to Chicago and Kim Carnes, and doesn't spend for ever doing her make-up like Sarah and Siobhan. She has bright red hair, ginger red, that she keeps dead short, and Mozzo says that although she's got a bit of a doggy face she's got a lovely arse, but I don't know about that. I think her face is great, all round, smiley and warm, and with light greenish eyes. Best of all, me and Fiona get on like a house on fire. We have deadly chats most mornings where I sneak into her bed and she tells me everything that happened the night before. Who snogged who, who Sarah was with, what Siobhan did, who was drinking naggins of vodka down the field, who started on who, who fancies Saidhbh Donohue, and who got caught in the school sports hall with their cacks round their ankles. I love all that stuff, and Fiona's brilliant at describing it.

Fiona told me all about periods and sex. I think it was coz she was always leaving her maxipads around and she was sick of saying that they were just girls' stuff, like they were part of her make-up kit. One morning, out of the blue, in the week after Jack the kitten died, she asks me did I know what a Fuck was. I said it was the same as a bastard and a bender, then she laughed and told me all about intercourse and periods. I was only a little fella at the time and most of the boys in school didn't have a clue what fucking was and had never heard of periods, so if I was ever feeling mean I'd say to Fiona that I was going to tell Mam that she told me about sex, meaning that she told me about sex when I was way too young to know. Fiona would go all whiny and grab me by the arm and say, Please, please don't, I'll be killed! When she had begged enough, I'd say that she was off the hook, just this once. She'd sigh and flop back down on the fancy paisley rug. Thing was, we both knew that I wasn't going to tell Mam, but it was good fun pretending.

★   ★   ★

Sharing with Fiona is all hunky-dory, but ever since the Mozzo turnip incident and the whole pillow-fucking thing, Dad keeps saying that they're going to have to get me out of that bedroom soon. He says that it's because I'm going to become all hairy and manly and he doesn't want me to get any funny ideas about my own sister. I hate it when he says that at the table, coz I'm surrounded by sisters. And I don't know where he thinks he's going to put me? He talks about moving Fiona in with Sarah and Siobhan, but all three of them just scream No Way! And that makes Claire and Susan immediately add their own scream of, Don't even think of shifting us! It's a big problem and it makes me feel like I'm a werewolf. Like I'm going to be lying there in bed, chatting away to Fiona about the knacker-drinkers in the park and the next thing I'm going to go all hairy and attack her to death.

And the way Dad says it too: Getting any funny ideas. With his hands folded in front of his mouth and his moustache scratching against his crossed thumbs. And the look in his eyes, like the night he made Mam stitch my initials into all my underpants before I went to summer camp. He wouldn't tell me why, just gritted his teeth, gave me a filthy look and said that there were some odd folks out in the world today, and that no one could steal my underpants if I had my initials on them, as if having initials meant that your jocks were fitted with burglar alarms. He looks at me the same way when he's warning me about my sisters. It like he's saying, If you want to get your hands on these girls you'll have to come through me first! I feel like telling him to get Mam to put some initials on the girls, and that'll keep them safe from harm.

He's never been this bad with me before. Even when I accidentally knocked Susan out with the thick wooden rolling pin, or when I was caught nicking three plastic rulers from Deveny's, or when I called Old Mrs Dolan a 'Fucker' for scaring us out of her garden, or even when I got all D's in my summer report. But now it's different. He can fly off the handle at the slightest thing. Just looking at me can set him going. Like when Deirdre Brown from work came for dinner last Sunday. Mam had spent all morning doing the chicken in a brand-new roasty way that she got from the papers, which meant cooking it upside down without any tinfoil, then turning it over at the last minute. Mam had to check it the whole time — open the oven, take it out, prod it, pour the juices over it, and slip it back in. And each time she took it out she told the whole house how it was getting drier and smaller by the minute and how this new fancy fella in the papers didn't have a clue about anything to do with cooking. Eventually, just as Deirdre Brown arrived, the chicken pops out like a tiny cremated pigeon, and Mam has to scrape all the meat she can on to a single dinner plate and pass it round us in a dead embarrassing silence. Deirdre Brown makes a joke about me being a growing boy so, to keep the chat going and to show her that she's dead right and that I'm growing like a monster a minute, I take loads of meat and pile it high on my plate, next to the potatoes. I dip a piece of breast meat into the gravy and pop it into my mouth with my fingers, but before I even have a single chew done there's a massive bang on the table. It's Dad's fist. And when I look up at him he's glaring at me, like he wants to run me through with a fork. 'Disgusting,' he says, hissing through his teeth.

Mam says that I've to be patient with Dad these days because he's so tired. She says that providing for six children and a wife with a keen eye for the fashions has taken it out of him. He sleeps any chance he can, anywhere he can, and it's never enough. Even on Dun Laoghaire walks, he'll stay in the car and have a nap, while we race to the pier and jump on to the big brassy cannon. Or when we go to Silver Strand in Wicklow, he'll lie down on the red check rug and spend the whole day asleep, and miss the rounders, and the swimming and the moat-digging on the sand. He'll just about rouse himself for cheese-and-tomato sangers, crisps and Lilt before another doze. He's even been to the doctor, but all they say is that he's a 'tough old Dub', and is working all the hours that God has given him. Which means that he's entitled to forty winks every now and then. Case closed.

Usually Mam breaks up the room-swap discussion by talking about the meal.

Lovely bit of pork, isn't it, folks?

Everyone, all seven of us, including Dad, nod and grunt and say, Yes, lovely.

Mam then says that Tom the Butcher's getting married.

Dad says, To who?

Mam says, To Moira Ni Kennedy's young one.

41

Then Sarah dramatically flicks her silky hair out of her eyes and goes, all shocked, Julie Kennedy?

Mam goes, Yes.

Then Sarah goes, Jesus, she was in my year in The Sorrows!

And then they're all at it, full pelt. Five sisters and Mam, bashing away, covering the Kennedy clan, the wedding dress, the extended families, the connections to who and who, where they met and who they know in common and why they ended up with each other. Sometimes, when it's going really loud, and they're all talking together, me and Dad look at each other and, joking, roll our eyes to heaven. It makes me feel brilliant, coz it's like we're part of a secret club. Like when we watch *Benny Hill* together and nearly wet ourselves with the laughing, especially in the one where he has the magic remote control, and can make the world stop and start at will, and keeps stopping it just so he can whip off nurses' skirts and things. Or like the times when I was younger and me and Dad would go for long beach walks on holiday in Cork. And I'd be his best boy, asking him loads of questions about science and about the universe, volcanoes, earthquakes and sharks, strictly natural history stuff, and he'd be able to answer them all, no matter how tricky they were.

Me: Are there killer sharks in Ireland?

Dad: No, only basking sharks and they don't kill people.

Me: Where are they?

Dad: Way out to sea, way beyond Galway Bay.

42

Me: Are they big?

Dad: Yes, around thirty feet long.

Me: How long is that?

Dad: As long as a small bus.

Me: Why don't they eat people?

Dad: Because they can only eat little fish.

Me: Why don't they eat bigger fish?

Dad: Because they have a tiny hole in their throats, and they swim around all day with their mouths open, straining all the little fish out of the water.

Me: So, if you were swimming in the water in Galway and a basking shark came by with his mouth wide open could you get swallowed up?

Dad: No, he'd probably choke on you before he swallowed you properly.

Me: But he'd kill you doing it?

Dad: Probably.

Me: I knew it.

4

Tainted Love

The ban on Mozzo is strictly enforced by Mam and Maura Connell. They both tell him, in no uncertain terms, that me and Gary are not coming out to play whenever he calls. They confer with each other on the phone and say things like, I've a good mind to go round there and plant her, meaning Mozzo's mam Janet, with the bill, only I know she couldn't pay it. Little cheeky pup, meaning Mozzo.

Mozzo soon gets the point, and stops calling. Me and Gary become best friends again and spend the rest of the summer cycling around on our bikes, spitting off the overpass on the Oakfield dual carriageway and watching the sweaty Sorrows hockey matches with the lads every Friday. But now, because of Helen Macdowell, the girls wear big thick gumshields, making them all look like Rocky. Shitty-Pants Sweeny, named after the day he came out with a big shite bulging out of the back of his pants, says it doesn't matter, as long as they still wear the short skirts he'll keep watching them play. No one says anything about Helen Macdowell, although Gary's mam heard that she'd gone mad and had to leave the country to try and start her life all over again, but this time as a scarface instead of the pretty one that everyone fancies.

When me and Gary come back from our cycling trips we sit in my and Fiona's room and listen to my boombox. There's Kim Wilde's 'Kids in America' or Soft Cell's 'Tainted Love' if we're in the mood for a bop. And we are. Gary's great like that, he doesn't laugh at your moves and I don't laugh at his. I just press play and the two of us stand up on the fancy rug and go for it, doing our thing while the fella from Soft Cell with the broken nose and bright lipstick screams 'Don't touch me PLEASE, I cannot stand the way you TEASE!' My moves are quite simple, I go from side to side, letting my head lead me each time, but when I'm totally relaxed I let my shoulders lead me too. My legs do their own thing. Gary's moves are dead complicated. He dances exactly like they do on the telly. Just like the Soft Cell fella, he's got all the hand moves, waves his arms about like he's trying to fling some slime off them, and nods his head brilliantly while mouthing the words, pretending that he's really on *Top of the Pops*, singing in front of everyone. You can tell he loves dancing, coz I'm always the one who has to call it quits.

If I want to slow the pace I slap on the tape of Foreigner, 'Waiting for a Girl Like You'. It's a real tape, one that I was given for Christmas, whereas Soft Cell and Kim Wilde are just songs that I taped off the Larry Gogan Top Twenty. I love taping things with my boombox. I sometimes tape films off the telly and listen to them when I'm lying in bed at night. Like *The Valley of Gwangi*. It's brilliant when you're under the covers and you're really sleepy and suddenly you hear Gwangi screaming his head off. I know video recorders mean you can tape the picture as well, but the only person on The Rise who has one is Gerry Butler who works for RTE and he doesn't have any kids. Mam can't stand the way he dresses and is always saying, He's a right queer fella, that Gerry!

She doesn't mean to be saying out loud to all of us that Gerry Butler is a bender. But inside she secretly thinks that he is a bender and so she's trying to say something different to bender without realising that she's actually saying that he is a bender. Coz between all the fellas in school, 'queer' is pretty much the same word as bender nowadays.

I once taped the thirty minutes of us all squashed around the table having Sunday dinner without anyone noticing. I was silent and a bit giggly, but it was brilliant getting Sarah saying that Dad was an Old Fogey, and Susan saying that Fiona was a bitch for nicking her gel, and Mam trying to get Dad to talk about the unemployment figures from the news. When I showed them all that I had been taping them they all screamed and went spare and then laughed loads when they listened to themselves back sounding all nasally and hollow. They said it was a great laugh, but any time I tried to do it after that they could spot it a mile away.

So, Foreigner's singing about their imaginary girlfriend, and how she's amazing at doing it, and how she's so brilliant at everything that she doesn't even exist. They go all woozy and sigh, 'It's more than a touch or a word can say, Only

46

in dreams could it be this way,' and me and Gary feel sad. We're still breathing heavy from the dancing, but now we're sitting on my bed underneath the big Porsche poster. The song is slow and sounds like the Foreigner boys are wishing their lives had turned out differently, and wishing that they actually had this girl in their arms instead of just dreaming about her. Me and Gary know all the words but we don't sing them out loud. We hum along all the same.

Halfway through the second verse I notice that Gary has stopped humming. He's frozen stiff, staring at the small straw bin beside Fiona's make-up table where she's dropped a maxi pad with blood on it and forgotten to cover it up with tissues, like she usually does. Gary's seen Fiona's maxi pads before, but always in packets, and never like this. He's asked about them too, but I told him that they were make-up stuff for girls, for wiping stuff. This is different. Gary is terrified of girls. He normally just lashes up the stairs to get to my room, and if Fiona is already in it he goes all red and doesn't say a word until she leaves. He's scared stiff of being left alone with Claire and Susan, and if he ever had to spend a minute with Sarah and Siobhan I think he'd faint.

I turn off Foreigner and I tell Gary about periods as best I can. He gets really upset when I tell him that all women have them, even his mam.

★ ★ ★

47

The summer bike route takes me and Gary out of The Rise and through the dark and bushy overhanging laneway that slopes steeply and for ever up towards Clannard Road. When we reach the top, after much hard-pushing, standing-up cycling, we always stop, catch our breaths, and stare down at the hazy grey hugeness of Dublin below, newly blanketed by all those shimmering twinkling house lights that've only just been switched on by tired parents who are looking sadly up at the sky and turning to each other and swearing, even in the midst of high summer, that they can sense the change in the evenings already, a slow drift from bright to dark blue, a hint of almost black.

We dash along Ash Lane, towards Kilcuman, past the twisty-turny pot-hole assault course outside Kilcuman Tyres and past the cop-shop where we make 'oink oink' noises for all the pigs inside, but not too loud, in case there's one of them outside crouched behind the back of his car, like he's on a stake-out, and could leap up at any moment and arrest us for slagging off the guards. We take a right down the main street, break as many lights as we can, head back again towards The Rise but this time only skirting along its edge, by the Villas and the five-a-side pitch, and out again on to the Ballydown Road. From there it's a lethal breakneck race through Belfield college grounds, blemming past the dog walkers and the strollers and the boozy students lying locked out of their boxes on the short grass by the artificial lake. Then it's up the Oakfield dual carriageway, past the front gates of our school, where we each hock back as much spit as we can muster and try to land a big stretchy greener on the front of the big wooden St Cormac's crest. And, laughing our heads off, we then whore down the Dunbarton Road, and back to the finish line at Gary's dad's automatic garage door.

It's an hour trip, all in, and it's brilliant fun, dead exciting, especially when you're head down, top speed, racing from light to light, seeing how many you can break without dying. Gary said his speedometer once showed that we were doing fifty miles an hour along the carriageway. I asked him to show me next time, but he says there's no point coz he'd have to slow down then. Occasionally we get a shout from the Gardaí, who roll up beside us and tell us to cycle in single file, but most of the time we just love the thrill of weaving in and out of traffic, dodging articulated lorries, and avoiding a good squashing like June Shilaweh.

Gary has a racer and so do I. Only mine's a yellow hand-me-down girl's bike with the crossbar pointing downwards so they don't get bashed in the fanny when they slip off the seat. It used to be Claire's, then Susan's, now it's mine. Gary's bike is brilliant, and his dad brought it over on the plane from the States. It has graphite wheel-rims and weighs a feather and is ten times better than mine and Gary knows this so he says that all bikes should be made like mine, with the crossbar pointing down so you don't damage your balls. I say that I'd rather damage my balls than cycle around on this lemon-yellow piece of shit.

Race you! he says, and we head off again, this time in no particular direction, but with Gary hoping that by losing to me on purpose I won't feel too bad about having such a crap bike.

And so it goes, all summer long, almost every night. We even go when it's raining, but then we wear thick plastic wet-gear that makes you look like a bender and makes you sweat like a bastard underneath. The only nights we don't go out are when we have visitors or when Gary's away on Freebies with his parents. Mam calls them Freebies because Gary's dad gets them dead cheap for being a pilot. Mam says that they're not like proper holidays that normal hard-working people go on. They're just little freebie trips. And when she says it, she makes them sound like something you'd get on the back of the cornflakes box, or something you might leave in your jocks drawer and forget about. Although when Maura, Bill and Gary come home covered in tan, looking dead glamorous, I can tell she wouldn't mind a few Freebies of her own, instead of one grey rainy bank holiday weekend trapped in a giant mobile home in West County Cork.

★　★　★

By late August, the nights are getting dark, and we've both got dynamo-powered lights that Gary's dad got in America attached to the frames of our bikes. The dynamos rub off the tyres and make a funny whiny whirring noise as we bomb down the road, making it sound like we're driving mini-motorbikes. We're absolutely tearing along the main street at full speed, at least fifty, and the dynamo lights are shining so hard that I think my bulb's going to blow. Gary's got the advantage of having lights on his head too. He's wearing a joke UFO headband that's like a normal headband John McEnroe would wear playing tennis, only it has loads of lights in it that make it flash and sparkle like a UFO. If you blur your eyes a bit, it looks like Gary's bike is cycling on its own and there's a small UFO hovering above it, travelling at exactly the same speed down towards the Villas.

It's Saturday night, and this is one of our last cycling trips before school starts again. We get as far as the five-a-side pitch when we see a group of lads all sprawled out behind the goals, some of them on the honkers, some of them standing, most of them lying around. They've got a tiny fire lighting in the middle of them, and it's hard to see their faces coz it's already pretty dark and the fire is turning most of them into shadows. We decide to steer clear of the five-a-side pitch because we don't want any trouble. But just as we're about to turn off to make the desperate dash on to the Ballydown Road we hear a voice.

'Finno! Oi, Finno! Finno, howsigoing??'

5

Saidhbh, Aka Mozzo Returns

I pull the brakes, slide forward off the saddle and stand there spreadeagled at the edge of the footpath with the bike still between my legs. Gary does the same, only he says Fuck Sake under his breath and tries not to damage his balls on the crossbar. Two figures, still in shadow, are walking away from the fire, crossing the five-a-side and coming towards us. They're wobbling a bit, half tripping each other. They're muttering things that we cannot hear. It's hard to tell but it looks like they've got their arms linked around each other. One of them is definitely Mozzo. I knew that from the minute he shouted my name. The other one's a girl.

They get closer. Mozzo's hair's pulled tight into a ponytail and he's wearing a leather jacket with loads of buckles and zips that clink and clank like a tinker's cart with each step and half stumble. The girl's got long hair that's straight and shiny and brown. They keep coming. Closer still, right off the pitch, feet away from us. She's wearing drainpipe jeans and a black bomber jacket plastered with those tiny button badges that usually say things like Madness, Ska Rules, Elvis Lives, and so on. Closest yet. They walk right up to our bikes. Her skin is brown, summer-tanned. Her eyes are brown too, like the toy eyes you get in teddy-bears.

And her lips are shiny with whitish lipstick, like Madonna in the 'Borderline' video. Her name is Saidhbh Donohue, she is a vision of pure beauty, and her arm is locked tight around Mozzo.

If Helen Macdowell was as nice as the Bionic Woman, then Saidhbh Donohue is all three of Charlie's Angels put together. In school, before the summer holiday, we were doing this poem about Helen of Troy and in it they say that she's got 'beauty like a tightened bow'. Our English teacher, Mr King, says that beauty like a tightened bow is the most amount of beauty you can ever imagine in someone, just before it snaps and breaks like a bow that's been tightened too hard. Saidhbh Donohue is that beautiful. She's so beautiful that if she gets any more beautiful she'll be ugly.

Mr King is into all that kind of stuff, romance and everything. He has a brown leather jacket and he plays the guitar in class at the end of the lesson, when we're writing with our heads down on the desks, and the music with no words is like a waking lullaby as we suck bits of spit in and out of our jumper sleeves. He's always promising to take us to the pub, or bring us out for chips, but he can never find the time. He's dead friendly with all the boys, and he had to fight tooth and nail to get us reading the Heathcliff book, at our age, even though we won't be doing it till Leaving Cert. He does all the actions when he's reading it, and he goes on and on about Heathcliff and Cathy and life on the moors, which is the English version of the bog. His favourite bit of the book is when Heathcliff has to go out and bang his head against a knotty tree trunk, because he loves Cathy so much even though she's dead. Heathcliff's all like, Ah Jaysus, she's bleedin dead! Feck's sake! Cathy! Feckin no!!!

And Mr King then puts down the book and looks around the room and asks us to imagine loving a girl so much that we'd want to bash our own heads off a knotty tree trunk for her, even though she was dead. All the GAA lads snort at this, and say things like, She can knot my trunk any day of the week! Which is totally stupid and doesn't mean anything, but gets everyone laughing and kind of makes Mr King stare into space and dream about a time when he might be teaching real-life boys and not a load of complete fecking eejits.

★ ★ ★

Saidhbh's name is pronounced Sive, like hive, but her father's dead proud of being Irish so he always wears thick jumpers and makes his kids spell their names with as many 'bh's and 'dh's as possible. This is so everyone will always know that they're Irish, no matter what country they're in, even though the Donohues never go abroad coz Mr Donohue, Taighdhg (pronounced tie-g), always says that there's so many beautiful places to visit in Ireland why would you want to be going to some awful ole hot foreign place when you have all the riches you could want right here

54

in front of you? Sometimes Saidhbh hangs around with Fiona, but she never comes into our house or up to Fiona and mine's room. She's kind of floaty like that. Loses track of what you're saying and is off in her own head somewhere. Fiona says that Saidhbh is great fun and a real giggler when you get to know her. She's dead religious too, and goes to confession every fortnight, and is a real Mass-head. In fact, Fiona once met Saidhbh up in Kilcuman, stumbling out of the church on Good Friday, with tears streaming down her face. Fiona asked her what was wrong and Saidhbh said, It's the Passion, I just find it so moving.

And yet, she's crazy too. She's always being caught drinking in Belfield with the college boys, and smoking in the shopping centre, and in school too. Fiona says that there's a joke going round that this is why Saidhbh has to do so much confession, but actually it's because she has 'issues' with her parents. Samuel Foster, Kent Foster's younger brother, spilt the beans after their big religious retreat at school. Said that Saidhbh had a breakdown during one of the heavy group sessions, and cried in front of everyone about how her dad's a bit of an alkie, and only ever pays her attention when he's shouting at her to put on a longer skirt, or take off some make-up. They've called the Parish Priest too at theirs, loads of times. But he stopped coming after Taighdhg told him to 'fuck off' for saying that the whole family had 'issues' and that they needed to go on a religious sing-songy holiday in Connemara for Goddy people, called Camp Generation.

Saidhbh doesn't go to The Sorrows. Taighdhg sends her to an all-Irish-speaking school in Oakfield called Coláiste Mhuire ni Bheatha where he teaches history and everyone speaks Irish all day long and you can get expelled for speaking English. Fiona says that the teachers there, including Mr Donohue, are all mad. The men teachers have all got beards and belt you for talking out of place, and the women are worse and they carry sticks and hit the kids if they can't recite the national anthem backwards by the time they're in fifth class. Maura Connell thinks Coláiste Mhuire ni Bheatha is an awful place and one night, after the London burger bombings were on the news, she was over in our house talking to Dad about it and she mentioned the school and called it 'a Hotbed of Republicanism'. Later, when he was tucking me into bed, I asked Dad what she meant by that and he said that it means a place where you love things like flags and history books more than you love people.

Fiona says that there's a whole world of mental whispers and giddy gossip sprung up around the teachers in Coláiste Mhuire ni Bheatha, and that Samuel Foster told her, during a Spandau Ballet slow set, and after drinking a whole jam jar of gin at the Sorrow's summer disco, that half of them are in the IRA itself, and that there's a rumour going round school that Saidhbh's dad once allowed two IRA fellas to sleep on the floor in the family sitting room for a whole month when they were on the run from the British Army and the guards because of a shootout over in London. The rumour also says that all Taighdhg Donohue has to do is make one phone call and he can get straight through to The Movement. No sweat. And you don't call it the IRA when you're as close as Taighdhg. It's simply The Movement.

Fuckin Hell, Finno, how the fuck are you, haven't seen ya in fuckin ages! That's how he starts.

And you too, Gary, where you been hiding?

Gary doesn't answer. Mozzo never puts an O on to Gary's name, even though it would be easy — Garro, or Conno would do. Mozzo's holding a can of HCL in the hand that isn't attached to Saidhbh. She has one too. HCL is what everyone buys when they're going knacker-drinking. No one knows what HCL stands for but Steven Casey says it means High Content Lager. Content means how quickly it can get you pissed.

We've been around, I say. Just cycling.

And you wouldn't go fuckin cycling with me? What's fuckin wrong with me, do I have fuckin BO?

Now that I'm this close I can see that there's real fire in Mozzo's eyes. He looks like he could kill you on the spot. His upper lip is curled into his gums, his nostrils are all wrinkled and his bottom lip is tight and wet. Like the fella in *An American Werewolf in London*, when he's in the early stages of changing, before he turns totally into the doggy creature.

Saidhbh can see that I'm shitting bricks and I

don't know what to say to Mozzo so she butts in and says that Mozzo is an awful tease. He bursts out laughing and says sorry to me and Gary, says he knows the score that it was our mams that made us stay away because of the broken window. He looks at Gary and winks and says, And the other thing! Saidhbh giggles a bit and Gary goes puce. Imagine, the most beautiful girl on the planet knows that you shoved two pillows together and stuck your mickey in between them and pretended that they were a woman?

You're Fiona's little brother, aren't you? says Saidhbh, looking me right in the eyes, like she's trying to melt me there and then.

I say nothing, because I think that if I open my mouth I'll get sick.

Fiona's brother? she says again, slower this time, like she's talking to an old wan.

I nod. I remember you, she says, in your Spider Man pyjamas, following the big girls around all night.

I still don't know what to say.

Well, you're with the big boys now, says Mozzo, all macholike. Come over and meet the gang.

I freeze. The way Mozzo has said it means that I'm the one who's invited and Gary can come along too, if he likes. Mozzo and Saidhbh move straight away as if it's a done deal, but I just shuffle a bit on my bike so as not to look like I'm not going. But I'm not, coz Gary isn't having any of it. Gary is facing the ground and won't even look at me. It's like he's waiting for me to run off with Mozzo and Saidhbh.

58

Look, I say out loud to everyone, I better drop the bike off first.

Mozzo and Saidhbh just wander off and Mozzo shouts back, Don't worry we're not going to nick it.

Me and Gary stand there, spreadeagled over our bikes, arguing for ages as the night gets darker and darker about why we should or shouldn't follow them over to the fire. Gary is saying that we should just get on with our cycle, go back to my and Fiona's room, listen to some boppy music and not be messing with that crowd from the Villas. I'm saying that it might be a laugh if we give it a try, but I'm lying. What I should say is, Please Gary, come over with me so I can sit down next to Saidhbh Donohue.

We argue like this for about half an hour, while all the time in the background Mozzo is passing comments and shouting out things like, Come on, girls, we won't bite you! And, There's no pillows over here for you, Gary.

Gary says that there's no way he's going over for more of THAT. He tells me that I can do whatever I want and he jumps back up on to his saddle. He cycles away into the night with his bike whining and his flying saucer headband blipping away brightly, disappearing into the shadows of The Rise like a teeny-tiny space machine.

★ ★ ★

I wheel my bike over to the five-a-side fire. I'm shitting it. It's totally dark now, and for all I know Mozzo's probably gone off with Saidhbh Donohue to show her all the things he knows about lickjobs and fannies. And I'm thinking that I'll be left with all the lads from the Villas who'll slap me about and ask me for lunch money and call me a little posh queer even though I'm a knacker just like them compared to someone as well-off as Gary.

Nice bike, bufty! is the first thing I hear as I close in on the fire, but before I have time to mount up and leg it I hear Mozzo saying really angrily, Shut the fuck up, Heno!

Mozzo's sitting on the grass, right up against the flames, looking all orange and glowy. He's got his leather jacket open with Saidhbh still glued to his armpit. He pulls a can of HCL from his six-pack stash and offers it to me while introducing the four lads, Heno, Macko, Hylo and Stapo, sprawled around the fire.

The lads all have sharp faces. Tight split lips, bony battered cheeks, tiny beady slit eyes, and smooth skinheads. If they even looked at you cross you'd give 'em your boombox and your entire Soft Cell collection straight away. Still, they nod and call me Finno, which makes me feel kind of tough.

I grab the HCL, crack it open and take a decent slug, as if I do this all the time. Saidhbh and Mozzo are looking at me. They're waiting for me to go all red and cough and splutter like in the westerns when they give a glass of whiskey to a youngfella and he spits it all out and acts like it's red-hot poison. But I know that's the game, so I hold my back teeth together and push

60

it, all the fizzy mank, right down my throat, using my tongue as a sweeper, and I don't make the slightest noise or funny face. Instead I go Ahhh, a good long Ahhh, like when you've had a drink of lemonade after playing Swingball for an hour.

Mozzo nudges Saidhbh and then says, He's a madser all right!

This, I guess, is a good thing.

I have tasted drink before, a sip of leftover beer here, a glug of Christmas sherry there, but this is my first proper bout of knacker-drinking. Dad says that it's illegal for me to drink until I'm sixteen and that the booze is a terrible curse, but all the same he's always punching me in the shoulder and saying that he can't wait for the day when he can take me across to The Ballydown Inn and buy me my first pint. The way he says 'pint' makes it sound like something special. A decent ole Pint! A quick Pint! A lovely juicy Pint!

Even though Sarah and Siobhan are nineteen he doesn't think it's right that they drink and go into pubs. Mam agrees with him on this one.

At your age, going into pubs! she says. If my father ever caught me, or Grace for that matter, in a pub at nineteen, he would've lost his reason. We would've been the scandal of Ballaghaderreen!

Aunty Grace is Mam's younger sister, who was meant to be a bit wild when she was young, but now lives far away in London, right next to Buckingham Palace, and has a huge house, a flash car, and runs her own business. She might well have been caught in pubs at nineteen, but Mam certainly wouldn't. Because Mam is a

Pioneer and has never ever had a drink of drink, except for communion wine and the hot whiskies she has when she's got the flu. Being a Pioneer means that you always ask for fizzy orange at parties, you pretend to be enjoying yourself when everyone's getting all sweaty and stupid, and you pray every night to the Sacred Heart of Jesus and ask him not to send you to any more stupid parties. Mam has a little laminated card with the Pioneer's prayer printed on it. She keeps it tucked into her missal. The prayer is all, Give me strength for this and Help me offer it up for that and Don't let me fail and all that stuff. But the best thing is that right above the words there's this brilliant picture of the Sacred Heart of Jesus. It's got Jesus, looking calm and clean, opening his cloak and bam! There, right in the centre of his chest is a red heart floating out from his body, hovering in space! The heart itself is wrapped in thorns which are making it bleed, and it's got a crucifix jammed into the top of it, and it's on fire and the whole thing is glowing like mad.

And every night before she goes to bed, Mam says a prayer to the glowing, bleeding, burning heart and asks it to help her not to drink.

Mam says that she has been blessed with faith. She believes. Believes in everything. Heaven, Hell, Limbo, God, Angels, Spirits, Pixies, Banshees, Leprechauns. The whole kit and caboodle, as Dad would say. He says that country people are really wild pagans who got converted to Catholics and pretend to be civilised but are pagans underneath it all. He says that he's a Dub, true and

62

true, and that makes him more sophisticated and civilised and less likely to believe in all that stuff.

In what stuff? Mam says, getting a little angry.

All them special tribes of spirits and spooks that look after your special causes, he answers, not so sure of himself now. Instead of just the one God Almighty who looks down from heaven and cares for us all.

He says this last bit with a smile, as if he's trying to please her, showing her that he knows what's what when it comes to God in heaven. But the way he says it makes you think that he's not convinced about that either.

Mam wanted me to be a Pioneer too, but Dad told her to let me enjoy a decent pint when the law says it's time. To make her happy I took The Pledge, which is like being a mini-Pioneer. It's like a licence-not-to-drink that runs out when you're sixteen, but I break it the whole time when I sneak little slugs of booze from half-empty party glasses making their way into the sink.

★ ★ ★

After two cans of HCL the atmosphere down by the fire is brilliant. Mozzo, me and Saidhbh are in our own little gang talking about everything — about school and about our mams — while the four lads are playing dares, seeing who can walk over the fire slowest without burning their balls on the flames. When I tilt my head to the side the whole of the pitch seems to zoom in the opposite direction, and if I give it a little shake the world goes all blurry. Mozzo's talking about his dad, telling the story of how he smashed the neighbour's window and threw the bag of fish guts inside. Only this time he's adding extra details, saying that him and his mam were standing out in the street in their pyjamas and bare feet at the time, and that they were both crying and holding on to each other for dear life, and shouting and screaming, begging his dad to stop and come inside so they could have tea together by the fire and chat about the day and be a real family for once. We go quiet for a second, the three of us, and then Saidhbh says that there's loads of people in school that she'd love to cover in fish guts. We all start to giggle, and then we laugh out loud. Me and Mozzo look over at Saidhbh like she's all our mothers and more wrapped up into one lovely girl.

I say to Mozzo, Ah sure that's nothing, and then I start to tell him about the time Dad came home drunk from The Downs with Mam and couldn't get into the house. It was one night in winter, the girls were all out and Mam and Dad had just nipped over the pub for a quickie with the Connells, leaving me in charge, totally on my own. Mam had warned me to keep all the doors locked because there was an escaped loony from Kilcuman Central Mental about. There must have been a lot of breakouts from the Central Mental because she said that a lot, any time they left us home alone, even if Siobhan or Sarah was in charge, there was always a loony on the loose. But I wasn't going to take any chances coz I was the only one in our family who overheard

Dad talking on the phone about a Kilcuman mentaller he met on his business rounds to the Hospital. This particular fella was a shy country boy who was always reading about ghosts and vampires and the devil and stuff, and who used to make some spare change by babysitting for this really nice respectable family down the road. And then one night, while he's babysitting, he just flips out and performs a black pagan Mass, which is the opposite of a Catholic Mass, and sacrifices the family baby by stabbing it to death on an altar he's made from an old Subbuteo table.

Saidhbh goes, Jesus, that's disgusting! and turns her head further into Mozzo's chest. He rubs her head like a dad, smiles and tells me to go on.

So anyway, I've got the doors locked good and tight, I've finished watching *The Greatest American Hero* and I'm actually getting sleepy. The thing about being allowed stay up as late as you want is that it sounds much more fun than it is. I was wrecked. So I go to bed, and I'm not even ten minutes asleep when I . . .

Come on, lads, we're going to kick some fucking queer arse!

Heno is leaping up and down like a madman, with Macko, Hylo and Stapo behind him, zipping up their bombers, doing shadow kicks and boxes, looking like they're ready for some serious action. Heno is spitting and raging, and he tells Mozzo that tonight's the fuckin night, that he's had enough fuckin messing about, and now they're definitely going to fuckin do it.

Right fuckin now! He kicks the air to make his point. Mozzo stands straight up and says dead serious that he'll drop Saidhbh home and then he'll follow them on. I stop telling my story and gradually wobble to my feet. I ask Mozzo what's up. He says nothing, but Saidhbh takes me aside to explain.

She says that there's two fellas on motorbikes hanging out in the school grounds at The Sorrows, right at the back near the long grass and the canal. According to Heno, they're both queers who wear leather motorcycle gear and sit in the bushes every night waiting for youngfellas to pass. They then leap out of the grass, still in their gear, with their helmets on, drag the youngfella inside, rip off his cacks, play with his mickey, and then speed off again on their motorbikes. Saidhbh says that the lads are going to wait for them to come and then kick the living shit out of their queer arses, especially Heno, coz his younger brother, Basho, came home three weeks ago with no cacks on and wouldn't say anything to anyone about how he lost them except that he lost them in The Sorrows. But Heno knows it's the gay bikers that did it.

After Saidhbh's explanation, Mozzo turns to me, still dead seriously, and asks, You in? I tell him that I'd love to help him kick the queers to shit, but I'm already really late and will be lucky if I'm ever allowed out again. Mozzo grunts and turns to leave with Saidhbh. Before she goes she lays her gorgeous hand on my wrist and says that her dad's having a big hoolie tomorrow night to celebrate the last free day before school starts.

She says that I should come. Mozzo agrees. They both say it'll be brilliant, with loads of booze, and they'll tell me then how the queer-bashing went.

★ ★ ★

Twenty minutes of painfully uncoordinated on-again-off-again pedal-slipping zigzagging later, I wheel my lemon yellow hand-me-down bike casually through the garage door. Dad is there, bent over Siobhan's brand-new racer trying to fix the timing on her shimano gears. It's late, and he's wheezing and sighing to himself, more tired than ever. There's sweat on his forehead, and I'm guessing that it takes every bit of strength he has in his body not to just collapse over the upturned bike and fall fast asleep on the dirty concrete floor in front of him.

I pass him and say, really gently, Night night. Straight away he sniffs the air and barks, Have you been boozing?!

I ignore him and march quickly into the kitchen, right over to the press where Mam keeps the biscuits. Dad follows.

I'm asking you a question, have you been out boozing like a common tramp?

Still silent, I bend down, pull out the biscuit tin and shove a handful of jammy dodgers into my mouth, hoping to disguise any booze fumes with the thick wheaty smell of biscuit juice. It's at this point that I answer. It's the best excuse I can think of, but it's totally thick. I say that I've been down with Saidhbh Donohue and I've been drinking Cidona fizzy apple drink all night. I say this because Dad always says that Cidona smells like booze whenever we drink it, and then he makes jokes about rearing a whole family of underage alkies.

Either he believes me or he's just too tired to take it any further, but Dad nods, grunts, and then shuffles with another wheeze and a sigh back out to the garage to fix Siobhan's bike, like a man going to the gallows.

6

The Last Supper

It begins with the thum thum thum of *Hooked on Classics*. It's Dad's favourite record and it has all the best classical songs ever made squashed together on to one big song that's got this thum thum thum drumbeat banging through it. And every Sunday, after Mam, Dad, me, Claire and Susan get home from Mass, Dad slaps it on at full volume. Then, usually after about ten minutes, either Sarah or Siobhan, who've both been out at Blinkers nightclub in Leopardstown till really late the night before, start banging down on the floor coz their bedroom is right above the sitting room where the stereo lives. Fiona's also been out at Blinkers, but she never bangs down even though she can hear it too. If things are really bad, sometimes Sarah will come charging down the stairs in the old skanky T-shirt she wears to bed and with Sudocrem all over her forehead and around her chin to stop spots growing. And, like a mad Comanche in warpaint, she'll stand inside the sitting-room door and demand that Dad turns his *Hooked on Classics* down. She'll never actually go as far as the stereo, coz she knows that would be breaking the rules, but she'll stand and holler from the door all the same.

Dad just sits there, half-reclined on the couch

behind his *Sunday Independent*, and grumbles to himself. Says that if they wanted sleep the girls shouldn't have been out carousing with boys till four in the morning. It's like the *Hooked on Classics* is his way of getting back at them for being girls. Or for being girls who are messing about with boys.

Sarah mutters Nazi under her breath and charges back upstairs. Dad doesn't do anything because he doesn't mind being called a Nazi because he thinks that in the war they were wrong and they were mad and evil, but the Nazis were respected and that's all he wants. In fact, he wants respect so much that it's become one of his trademark jokes — every year we ask him what he wants for his birthday and every year he says, Just a bit of respect. But he says it in a soft, smiley way.

Mam shouts up after Sarah that it's time she was getting up anyway and that dinner's almost ready, and that Sarah is to tell that rip, meaning Fiona, to come down immediately! Sarah snaps back, Jeeeeeesus!

Sarah and Siobhan have both got Leaving Certs and they do job interviews every week with different firms, but haven't got anything proper yet, except for some part-time work in Dad's office. Now that they're becoming real women they either love Mam or they hate her. They sit on her bed late at night with the door closed, and have private chats for hours about fellas and things and who fancies who and what that bitch called this bitch and so on. Or else they just walk in the garage door, see her there, up to her elbows at the sink, and hate her on the spot. One time when Sarah shouted out that Mam was such an old cow, Mam responded by saying this little poem that she has memorised off by heart. It goes, *As you are now, so once I was. As I am now, so you will be.* Mam always says that she was thick in school and that she never did Irish and never got further than her Inter Cert, but when she wants to she can really pull it out of the bag.

The kitchen's getting busy. Mam has thrown off her glamorous church outfit and is down to a tracksuit top and jeans while quickly making a melon-balls starter by scraping a butter-ball scooper through a melon. When she says the words, 'melon-balls', Mam adds the phrase, 'saving your presence', which means that she doesn't want you to think of the rudeness in the word 'balls' when she says it. But by saying it she actually does, so it's a joke. Claire and Susan are both in stiff Sunday-best blouses and pleated skirts. Their hair-dos are neatly pulled back from their faces with metal clips and they're sitting on opposite sides of the table annoying each other.

Claire is trying to make origami animals out of the eight paper napkins on the table. Susan is picking at the folds in her skirt and in a big huffy mood because she wasn't allowed to go and stay at the Joyces last night. The Joyces are posh family friends with a giant house in Ballinteer. Claire slept over there last night in the same room as Brenda Joyce and she keeps talking about how they played dares and Girl's World all night and it's driving Susan mad. Susan's also annoyed because Claire wore her favourite

71

luminous deely boppers, the ones that she'd been saving up for some night when she's actually asked to go somewhere, anywhere.

Eventually, after about twenty minutes of *Hooked on Classics*, stair-thumping, shouting and pan-bashing, Sarah, Siobhan and Fiona come trudging down to the table. Even though it's only Sunday lunchtime, and not a disco, Sarah's hair is filled with mousse and gone all curly and she's wearing a denim miniskirt and a wrap-around top with no bra. Siobhan's wearing a secondhand black silk blouse, black drainpipes and cowboy boots, and Fiona's in a baggy grey tracksuit, with a thin blue scarf on her head that makes her look like a pirate but is used to flatten down the bits of red hair that got badly stuck up during the night's short kip.

The kitchen table has two foldable wings on either side, so normally it looks like it can hold about six of us, but when you flip out both wings it can hold the full eight at a squeeze. Sarah and Siobhan sit at the far end, near the door — this is useful for Sarah, so she can call Dad a senile old twit during the meal and dash straight up to her room before he gets a chance to squeeze out of his seat. Dad and Susan sit with their backs to the radiator. This is good for Susan, because it makes her feel like Dad's special girl. Mam sits opposite Dad and Susan, with her back to the kitchen presses and with Claire on her right-hand side. And me and Fiona sit opposite Sarah and Siobhan, with our backs to the big kitchen window, the one that Gary smashed with the hockey ball.

The meal starts with Mam marching inside and turning off *Hooked on Classics*. Dad doesn't make a sound about this. He just keeps his head slung low in his hands, staring down at the empty plate in front of him. He's tired again. Super-tired. It's like all that heavy-duty paper-reading has taken it out of him completely. He wouldn't dare argue with Mam about the music anyway, because her face is red and sweaty from preparing a meal for eight, and this gives her a licence to do just about anything she wants for the rest of the day.

Mam pours Dad a big glass of red wine, offers it to Sarah and Siobhan, who refuse, then gets us all to say the grace-before-meals. She does this by saying, Let's say grace.

And, even though it's as tired as old boots, every day without fail one of us will say out loud the word 'Grace' as a joke. No one laughs, it's not supposed to be dead funny, but it's just what you do.

This time I do it. I say, Grace! and Dad glares at me through his fingers. Mam leads the grace, which is a nice little prayer about blessing everyone around the table and blessing the food we're about to eat and blessing, especially, the hands that made the food. When she says, 'the hands that made the food', someone usually points to her hands, or if say Claire has had a big part in making the meal, like peeling the spuds, she'll point to her own hands as well. After that, the melon balls, saving your presence, hit the table and we're off!

Mam's the first one in.

She says, Well, how was Blinkers?

Sarah and Siobhan can't decide whether they're in a love her or hate her mood so they just twiddle with bits of loose hair and mumble things like OK, ah, the usual.

Fiona nudges me and says she's sure that Dave Gallagher wouldn't call what he got last night a bit of the usual.

What's that? snaps Sarah, glaring at Fiona.

Who's Dave Gallagher? asks Mam.

Hello! sings Fiona, launching into a mock version of Lionel Richie's hit song. She gets as far as the punchline, 'Are you somewhere feeling Davy or is Davy feeling you?' when Sarah cuts her short with loud sarcastic haw haw haws and everyone else has a giggle about 'feeling' except Dad who's still got his head in his left hand while using the other one to scoop the melon balls into his mouth.

Everyone notices this, but no one comments. Instead Claire tells Sarah that she should've seen Brenda Joyce's bedroom, that it was massive and had a whole make-up table just for Girl's World. Susan picks at her hairclips and starts to whine and Mam tells Claire not to be rubbing it in. Claire tells Mam to 'leave off' and then looks over at Sarah for a reaction. Claire is always trying to impress Sarah. It's like she wants to be Sarah when she grows up and have all the fellas getting a good feel out of her in Blinkers. When you think of it, it's like Claire wants to be Sarah, and so does Siobhan. Susan wants to be Claire. But no one wants to be me and Fiona.

You obviously weren't listening to young Fr

O'Culigeen's sermon then, Mam adds, looking at Claire.

No response.

Were you?

Was it something about love? chances Claire.

No, it was about honouring thy father and mother!

Holy God, says Sarah, sneering. Here we go again.

Oh, it's well you may scoff, answers Mam, seeing as I can't remember the last time you darkened the Parish doorstep.

I told you, says Sarah, head down, looking at Mam through her long black fringe, I go to Saturday evening Mass.

Psshhhhh, hisses Fiona.

Sometimes, adds Sarah.

Well, says Mam, young Fr O'Culigeen spoke eloquently and magnificently about juvenile crime and the savage breakdown of moral order, and how it stems from disregarding the Ten Commandments and especially not honouring thy father and mother!

A bit of respect! says Dad, piping up for the first time.

Glory be to the hokey, says Mam. And the dead arose and spoke to many!

Dad fakes a smile and we all giggle with relief. He's back! I'm so relieved I do a bit from Jesus of Nazareth, and say, Arise, Lazarus!

Dad doesn't think this is funny. He looks down at me and then says to the whole table, You know this one came in reeking of drink last night!

There's a moment of silence as everyone registers what Dad just said.

I stand up and start to clear the melon-ball dishes. As I do I say, It was Cidona! I was with Saidhbh Donohue!

Luckily, all the women around the table are far more interested in Saidhbh than they are in the reek of drink.

Saidhbh Donohue! gasps Sarah through a mouthful of mashed melon, as if I had just said I was out with Jane Fonda or Bo Derek.

Yeah, I say, trying to be casual, trying to aim the story away from the danger zones of Mozzo and HCL. Met her down the road with Gary and she just wanted a chat over some fizzies.

I hear she's going out with Declan Morrissey now, says Susan, bluntly whacking my story into the red.

That little pup? says Mam, getting edgy on her own seat, What's a smasher like her see in that savage? He wasn't there last night, was he?

She's not so great herself, says Claire, thankfully cutting in. Thinks she's above us all, little snooty wagon. All those Mhuire ni Bheatha girls are the same. Little Irish princesses.

Pretty Irish Girls, says Susan, which is a coded way of saying PIGs.

I've heard her dad's a right Provo, says Siobhan, adjusting the collar of her blouse and trying to stir things up.

That would be right, adds Dad, second comment of the day. Down at the British Embassy protesting about Bobby Sands whenever he gets the chance, with all his Provo buddies.

Jason Davit said that he runs a summer school in Galway, says Susan, where everyone does IRA target practice and learns how to make bombs.

Jason Davit's a gobshite, says Fiona.

Fiona! snaps Mam.

All I'm saying, says Claire, like a real know-all, is that Saidhbh Donohue isn't the little princess that everyone thinks she is!

Loverboy obviously does, says Sarah, smiling over at me, sensing a weakness.

They all start to sing, at the same time, the song about me and Saidhbh being up a tree, k-i-s-s-i-n-g. I turn my back to them and scrub the melon-ball bowls in the sink, but I know my ears have gone as red as my cheeks, giving my feelings for Saidhbh away.

Mam's confused, and sounds like she's a bit hurt. She's too old for you, pet!

And a Provo! adds Sarah, loving my pain.

And if you want to know, bursts in Claire excitedly, simply unable to contain herself, I've heard she's on the pill!

What's the pill? says Susan.

Mind your mouth! shouts Dad at Susan, his best girl, whose bottom lip immediately starts to wobble.

Sarah'll tell you what the pill is, teases Fiona.

Sarah's eyes pop, and she glares at Fiona.

Mam catches the glare and looks shocked.

Dad's got his head back in his hands.

I feel that there's no point in waiting for a better time to ask, and since we're on the subject I say, Saidhbh has invited me to a party in the Donohues' tonight, am I allowed to go?

★ ★ ★

There's a joke that Dad tells a lot, when he's being a wildcard, and stroking his moustache at the ladies. It's about the Queen, and she's touring a hospital in Dublin, and wants to see the baby ward. Now in this particular hospital the Protestant and the Catholic wards are separated. So the Queen visits the Catholic ward first. She walks up to a woman lying in bed with her baby and she says, and for this bit Dad puts on a deadly posh accent, And hew menny childreen does yew heeve et heme?

The woman in the bed says that she has six others at home, and the Queen, not shocked at all, says, Gewd Catholic femily.

The Queen then moves on to the Protestant ward. Again, she walks up to a woman, lying in bed with her baby and reading the *Irish Times* and she asks, And hew menny childreen does yew heeve et heme?

The Protestant woman says that she has three others waiting for her at home, and to this the Queen says, Randy Bitch!

Then everyone bursts out laughing, especially Dad, who thinks it's the funniest thing in the world, and when he's telling it with the Connells around, like at a party, he pretends that it actually happened to Maura Connell and Mam, coz they're Protestants and Catholics. And at the climax he says, Randy Bitch, Randy Bitch! How do you like that Maura, Randy Bitch?! Maura Connell then usually tells him to go away with himself, and that he's an awful man. Mam's always dead embarrassed coz she doesn't like jokes about Catholics and Protestants in the first place, and especially not now with all the killings and things.

★   ★   ★

Mam says we'll think about it, and everyone goes ballistic. Susan can't believe that I'm younger than her and I'm getting to go out on a Sunday night, and the last night before school and everything. Claire pipes up and demands to be allowed to invite Brenda Joyce around, since I'm going to a party. Sarah mutters that Saidhbh is a tart, Fiona barks back that it takes one to know one, Dolly, meaning Dolly Parton, and Siobhan says Provo-Tart to boot. Even Dad throws in his tuppence worth with something about the smell of booze and me becoming an alkie before my time, as if there is a proper age to become an alkie.

In school, when the teachers find out that I have five sisters, all older than me, they say that I must be so spoilt, being the only boy. Centre of attention. Apple of everyone's eye. Man of the house. Little Lord what's his name. I look around the table at all the angry girly faces snapping at me like the hungry crocodiles in *Live and Let Die* and I think, Bollocks to that.

★   ★   ★

Mam's already had enough of the arguing and of everyone moaning about me going to Saidhbh Donohue's party. She hasn't been slaving over a hot stove all day to have her Sunday roast ruined by a pack of bickering brats.

Nice melon balls, didn't you think, Matt? she says, deciding to make it her mission to bring Dad out of his daily exhaustion and post-paper slump. Saving your presence.

She knows that if she starts with him, there's a good chance that the rest will follow.

Dad says, Nice, while looking down at his empty plate.

Matt! Mam says sharply. A bit of eye-contact wouldn't go astray!

Dad lifts his head up and says, Nice melon balls, Devida.

She's smiling at him, beaming widely, full on, doing her best to bring him back to life. He notices this, so he gives her a polite half-smile in return.

She pounces on it.

Look at that, girls! It smiles. The beast smiles! Oh, I made a great choice there, marrying such a smiler. Praise the Lord, lucky me, what a happy man I married!

Now, this is a dangerous game she's playing, and we all know it. It's like she's messing with nitro. Coz it can either bring him into the glory of wildcard happiness, or it can send him over the edge and he'll storm out and go over to The Downs or out for a long drive and not come back until it's night and we're all in bed, wide awake.

But this time the gamble works.

And I got permanent rays of sunshine with you!! he says, a wicked grin beginning to break over his face. The fastest floozy in all of the bog!

Oh, Matt, you're awful! Mam says, mission accomplished, standing up and going over to the oven to pull out a freshly spitting chicken the size of an elephant.

I don't know what you're talking about, she says, continuing it on, like panto.

What's a floozy? says Susan, even though she knows what it is, coz Fiona's always calling Sarah one.

Will I tell 'em about the knocks? says Dad to Mam, but winking at us as the chicken hits the table in front of him with a carving knife and carving fork rammed into its chest.

Oh, now, none of your knocks, Mam protests.

Yeah, the knocks, says Siobhan, tell us about the knocks!

It was when your mam brought fellas back to the house in Ballaghaderreen, says Dad, as if he's presenting *Jackanory*. If it was late at night they were never allowed inside the building because there'd be no one up to keep everything above board. He winks to us all when he says this.

So, your mam would chat to her fellas outside the house, by the door, which was right below her father's bedroom. And if the conversation ever stopped, which meant that things between your mam and the fellas were getting just a little bit too quiet for their own good, her father'd give his window pane a decent few knocks to shake things up and get the conversations flowing again. You see, a right little bogwoman floozy, he says, his face beaming. A floozy!

Those were more innocent times, says Mam,

dropping the sprouts, parsnips and spuds down on to the table while we all imagine her getting a feel under Grandad's window, like Sarah at Blinkers last night.

Speaking of which, says Dad, seemingly back in wildcard mode, firing on all cylinders while jabbing away at the elephant chicken in front of him, Jahear the one about the woman breastfeeding on the bus?

Oh, Matt, says Mam, that's as old as the hills!

Dad ignores her and continues. The baby's screaming, it won't take any of its mammy's milk and so she says, Ah shut up or I'll give it to the bus conductor!

Mam and Dad both burst out laughing at this. It's not that they think it's the best thing ever, it's more like it's a joke from when they were young, when they first started courting, and that's why they like it.

Or the blind man, says Mam, serving out eight separate portions of the three different veg, who comes to the convent, knocks on the door and says, It's the blind man here! And the nun, who's nude from the shower, opens the door and says, Can I help you, my child? And he says, Nice boobs, wheredya want the blinds?

They both hoot with laughter at this one, and even though Sarah folds her arms to cover up her braless top, it kind of becomes infectious. I see Fiona's shoulder jigging about beside me. I hear her giggles, and find myself joining in too. Just watching Mam and Dad red-faced and hooting together is enough to get the giggles going.

Or the youngfella, says Dad, with the marks down his face!

They burst out laughing and Dad even has to stop carving now. He's kind of snotting into the chicken with laughter and can't finish the joke. Claire, Susan and Siobhan are giggling like mad too, and even Sarah is smiling at this stage.

You're both just so crude, she says, snorting to herself.

The doctor asks him what happened to his face, and he says that it's from drinking milk!

Dad's laughing like mad, and has got the joke all wrong, but he makes his best stab at it.

What do you mean, drinking milk? asks the doctor. Well, on my school lunchbreak I go up to the railings where I get a drink of milk from me mammy outside!

Dad laughs again, and this time he explains, with light tears on his lids, She's been breastfeeding him! And the lines down his face are from leaning into the railings to get a mouthful!

They laugh away, about the joke itself and about old times. Sarah joins in with a recent gag of her own, pulling the skin on her face back tightly from the cheeks and saying, Mammy mammy I think you tied my pigtails too tight!

Claire says, pretending to be a dad, How did you get that green line through your hair, son? Then she says, pretending to be the son too, I dunno, while rubbing her hand from her nose right over the top of her head, like she's wiping an imaginary load of snot into her hair, unknown to herself.

Mam has done her job well. And for a while there, right at the table, in front of chicken, veg and a bucket of gravy, we're all laughing at the same time. But we're not laughing coz the jokes are funny. We're laughing coz we're laughing.

And if I could get my hands on Benny Hill's magic remote control I'd use it right there and then. I'd press pause, and freeze us all for ever, just as we are, sitting round the table, giggling and shaking, and cracking crap jokes, and happy to be there, and giving each other quiet yet monumental looks of love.

And then I'd smash it.

★　★　★

The rest of the meal goes smooth as eggs, and Mam's so happy that she even allows Sarah to put some ELO on in the background. There's lots of chat during the main course. About Pat Shine's new skin-tight trousers which'll ruin his chances of having babies. About how the town of Navan is actually called a palindrome, which means it can be written forwards and backwards. And about the life and death of Princess Grace. The dessert pavlova comes and goes, and all the while we get Mam and Dad's sunburnt honeymoon, Claire's Inter Cert, Brenda Joyce's back garden, and why teachers, like Taighdhg Donohue, are all cute whores because they get so much holidays and are really well paid but always complain about having to work hard.

There's a lull at the end and, feeling that the coast is definitely clear by now, I lean over to

Mam and say, dead seriously, Can I go to the party? Just for a bit.

Fiona winks at Mam and says, Go on, Mam, last chance to see his love before school separates them for good.

Shut up, I say, pucking her in the arm.

I look across the table of empty pavlova bowls and see Sarah reaching into the back pocket of her mini and pulling out twenty Rothmans. She passes one to Siobhan, offers one to Dad, who accepts, and they all light up and start puffing away, like three disco smoke machines in the corner of the room.

Mam rubs me on the head and says, All right, loverboy, you're on.

I lean back in my chair and have to stop myself from going red with excitement. I let my shoulders drop, take a deep breath of hot kitchen air and gulp down the comforting choke of thick tobacco smoke circling the room.

★ ★ ★

Mam gets Saidhbh's number from Fiona and rings Mr Donohue just to make sure that everything's above board. I'm dead embarrassed but it's worth it. I hear Mam being polite first, saying that she heard he was having a party and that I'd got it into my head that I was invited. She giggles for a bit, like she's sharing a private joke with Mr Donohue, and then says, Of course, I will indeed send the wee fella down to you. That means me. She giggles some more and says thanks a million but sadly she can't, too many uniforms to iron and sandwiches to prepare. Mr Donohue has obviously invited her too, but she's said no. Lucky.

She puts down the phone and I leap out from my eavesdropping place at the top of the stairs and say, Well?

Kick-off's at seven, she says, before adding with a wink, Bring your own Cidona.

★ ★ ★

I'm normally not that fussy about clothes, but when it comes to this party I really want to knock 'em all dead. I want to walk into the room, like a cowboy coming into the smoky saloon through the swing doors, and have everyone stop talking and stop playing the piano and just look at me and go hushed. So, after my shower, Fiona and me sit down with Olivia Newton-John playing on the boombox, and me still in my towel, and we decide what to wear.

All the clothes I own in the world are spread out on my bed. I feel good choosing my outfit with Fiona because she knows Saidhbh's tastes and can tell me what to wear better than anyone. I never actually say, Would Saidhbh like me in this? But Fiona gets the message.

I have four pairs of trousers, not including the old stuff that doesn't fit me. Two pairs of blue jeans, a pair of black slacks for Mass and school, and a pair of grey denims with black herringbone stitching that I wore on Easter Sunday and for Fiona's seventeenth barbecue. I had a pair of white denims too, but Mam made me take them back to Penny's for a refund coz they were too tight. I told her that they were drainpipes and they were supposed to be that way, but when I walked into the kitchen with them on Dad just went spare and nearly killed me. He shot out of his seat and told me to take them off right away. I said no way and fuck sake, and then ran out of the room half crying. He chased me upstairs with the bamboo cane, hit me on the arse three times, then grabbed me by the waist and practically ripped the trousers off me, saying that no son of his was going to be seen walking around The Rise like a gombeen in sprayed-on trousers.

I cried for ages after that, and wouldn't come downstairs. When I told Fiona about it she said that Dad was jealous, and he wanted me to look like a square because that's what he was like when he was a fella.

Olivia Newton-John sings, 'Physical, I wanna get physical,' and Fiona and me both agree that I should wear the herrings. Dead classy. I've already decided outright that I'm wearing my black slip-ons with grey socks to match the herrings, so all that remains is the shirt. I'm rooting through my shirts — seven of them, three flowery, one plain yellow, one pink, one blue, and a school white — when Fiona says that she has just the thing for me. She reaches into her side of the wardrobe and pulls out her grey grandad shirt. She says that it's time I started wearing this, and she was sick of it anyway. Now this is breaking with the normal rules of family hand-me-downs. Coz Fiona should, according to

87

tradition, offer it to Claire first, then Susan, and only then, if they've both refused it, can she offer it to me.

Fiona says that Claire and Susan have more than enough gear of their own, without taking this shirt too. And besides, she says, they aren't going out on hot dates tonight.

Fiona turns her back, and I fling off the towel and get dressed. I stand in front of the full-length mirror, and I'm a vision in grey.

Stunning, says Fiona, hugging me. That's the one, the heart-breaker!

She lets me use some of her spray to flatten down my brown springy hair and when I look at myself again I'm pleased. My legs are too skinny, my herrings are a bit too short, and Fiona's shirt is way too big and flaps about around my waist even though miles of it is already tucked in, bundled all around me, making it look like I'm wearing a nappy. But even so, the overall impression is quite slick, and the spray-flattened hair is the icing on the cake.

Saidhbh, Saidhbh, Saidhbh.

7

Pre-Party Tips

There are two types of songs: Drinking Songs and Rebel Songs. In most parties, when the music gets going, and the booze is doing its job, everyone starts singing Drinking Songs. These are songs about coming into the parlour and having a drink on the house and generally having a laugh and getting drunk. They're fast songs and you clap along to them or stamp your feet. Mam and Dad only ever have Drinking Songs at their parties. Same with Maura Connell, Maisie O'Mally and most of the other adults on our road. But every now and then you hear about a party where they started singing Rebel Songs. These are songs about being Irish and fighting the English and never giving up the struggle. Mam and Dad were at a party once where everyone started singing Rebel Songs. Mam made Dad ask for their coats and they walked out in disgust.

This is not because Mam and Dad don't like being Irish. It's because, says Mam, there's singing, and there's killing, and they're two different sports altogether. Her father was in the IRA before they became burger-bombers, so she should know.

If you're at a party and someone starts singing a Rebel Song, it's as if they're smoking pot in front of you.

You're either in or you're out.

8

Party Time

Donohues' is already packed when I arrive. Saidhbh's brother Eaghdheanaghdh (pronounced Ay-anna) comes to the door in a Billy Idol T-shirt and grunts at me. He says nothing about my outfit, because for all he knows I could wear the Vision in Grey look all week long. Instead, he grabs the bottle of fizz out of my hand and sends me straight inside, right into the thick of things.

The Donohues' hallway is tiny and the door into the sitting room is wide open, so once you're inside their front door you're pretty much into the heart of the house itself.

Their sitting room is jammed with men and women standing, discussing, chatting and making jokes. The air is thick with cigarette smoke and tastes like booze. James Last and His Orchestra are banging away on the stereo. Taighdhg Donohue's beard is trimmed and he's wearing a new brown jumper. He has prime place in the centre of the room and is deep in discussion with some other beardy fella who's scratching the side of his face with concentration.

Yes fuckin way, I'm taking this right up to the Dáil, the fella's saying. They're fuckin chancers, the lot of them!

Taighdhg is nodding, and scratching his own beard in return, while at the same time keeping one eye out around the room and patting and shaking hands and making quick comments with various people who squash past him on their way to the kitchen for a refill.

Good man, Taighdhg! Right you are, Mick! Saw the Cats were on top today! Should fuckin hope so! How's she cutting, Taighdhg? Up the middle like a plough, Dick!

Taighdhg's wife Sinead is standing at the kitchen door, handing out drinks and wearing a big pink shimmery plungy dress that shows off her loose and leathery low-hanging boobs.

Go on, ya, get this down ya, warm ya up, hairs on your chest, cut a hole in it, murder it, go on, ya boyo ya, for the day that's in it, more power to your elbow.

Mutton dressed up as lamb, is what Mam calls Sinead Donohue. She's called her this ever since she arrived late for midnight Mass with newly dyed hair, thick make-up, ski-pants and a big bag of booze clanking around her ankles. Mam knows Sinead to see, and they might even pass an odd comment to each other out on the road, but they're not friends. Sinead is a Dublin tour guide in her real life, which means that day in and day out she brings buckets of foreigners around Trinity College so that they can see the Book of Kells and hear how Ireland is the best country in the world, and how when everyone else in Europe was going mad with the plague and biting each other's heads off, everyone in Ireland was like, Ah sorry, love, I can't come to bed yet because I haven't finished illustrating this here magical gospel manuscript. Or else she

91

takes them to Kilmainham Gaol and shows them the very spot where the Brits had to tie poor ole rebel hero James Connolly to a chair and shoot him dead, because he was already wounded to bits from the glorious battles of Easter 1916, and because the Brits are savage fecking bastards. And if there are any Brit tourists in her group on that day she'll make it all into a big joke thing and say, Present company excluded!

Being a tour guide means that Sinead is kind of a bit famous and full of herself. Which puts all the other mams' noses out of joint no end.

Sinead is doling out cans of Harp and kissing everyone that comes into the party. She looks like she's had a few Harps already, coz her eyes are blank and she's smiling a lot at nothing much. Standing just in front of her, leaning below the massive pride of place painting of mountains and sheep, is Fr O'Culigeen, still dressed in his black priest's outfit, not wearing his Simon Templar gloves, but with his hair even more slicked back than ever. O'Culigeen is sipping orange juice out of a small glass with his tiny tight mouth. He's swaying back'n'forward from his waist up, using his hips as if they were a see-saw, and he's talking to Kent Foster's mam, Joy.

Well, I've read that he does all his own stunts, the chancer's saying to her, all serious, and I'd believe it too. The fittest man in Hollywood, they call him!

The only other people I recognise in the crowd are Mozzo's mam Janet, who knows Taighdhg from doing adult Irish classes at Coláiste Mhuire

92

ni Bheatha, and Barry O'Driscoll, father to Liam O'Driscoll from the Villas. Liam's in school with me and gets driven from home to class and back again, including lunch trips, every day of term. The world and his wife think that Barry smothers his son. You'd swear the lad was made of glass, they say. He won't break! But the story from The Mothers' coffee mornings goes that Barry O'Driscoll's younger brother, Garrett, was drowned as a child and Barry never got over it, and is terrified that anything bad might happen to Liam.

Master Jim Finnegan! comes a roar out of Taighdhg, making everyone stop for a second. Come over to me here and let me shake your hand!

Some of the adults move aside and let me through. Taighdhg crunches my hand, grabs my shoulders, squeezes me a bit, says that I'll make a fine footballer and then tells me that Saidhbh and Mozzo are inside helping with the grub. I say, Thank you Mr Donohue, and edge my way over towards the kitchen door, where Sinead Donohue is still standing sentry, kissing everyone in sight while holding a bowl of KP peanuts in one hand and a can of Harp in the other. She sees me straightaway and lunges down to my height, sloppy kissing me roughly on the eye with her big wet lipstick mouth.

For God's sake leave him alone, Mam, comes a voice from inside the kitchen. You'll traumatise the poor fella!

I peek around Mrs Donohue's shimmering body and see Saidhbh, leaning against the sink, dressed in a black mini and baggy white blouse with the top button done up, and a silver chain with a tiny Jesus cross on it hanging round her neck. Her hair is tied back in a ponytail and her dark eyes are as gorgeous as ever.

Look at you, she says, nodding me up and down. A real spiv!

Inside I'm giddy and thrilled that the Vision in Grey look has done the trick.

So, I say, dead cool, what's up?

Just waiting for the vol-au-vents, Saidhbh says, pointing to the oven and then to the massive mound of cocktail sausages sitting in the bowl in front of her, waiting to be delivered to the party-goers.

Cool, I answer.

Saidhbh looks over at her turned-away mam, carefully reaches behind the sausage bowl, pulls out a can of Harp and tilts it towards me saying, You want some?

Can't, I whisper, it's the breath! Dad'll test me later!

Understanding, she nods, and offers me a glass of Crazy Prices lemonade instead.

I take a slug, go ahhhh, as usual, and then stare ahead of me, snatching tiny looks at Saidhbh.

She says nothing, but when I look at her I see that she's smiling.

She breaks the silence with, Sausage? shunting the massive pile of sausages in my direction.

Thanks, I say and grab one of the pre-stabbed sausages by its cocktail stick and take a bite.

Lovely, I say, after a few chews.

They're from Tom the Butchers, says Saidhbh.
You know he's marrying Julie Kennedy?
I do, she says.
Funny, I say.

★   ★   ★

The back door opens and Mozzo, wearing a long black shirt, black combats and black Docs, walks in from the garage playing with his fly and making contented noises.

What a slash! he says out loud, loud enough for Mrs Donohue to hear. Hit the spot!

Oh, Moz, you're a gas man, she says, as if the word 'slash' was the funniest thing in the world.

We aim to please, he says in her direction, before stopping in his tracks when he sees me holding a cocktail sausage and talking to Saidhbh. He acts like they do in Abbot and Costello when they see a ghost — he stays frozen, with his mouth wide open for around ten seconds. He then says, And who the hell have you come as?! and bursts out laughing at his own joke and runs over and punches me in the shoulder.

Glad you could make it, Finno, great hoolie, eh?

He doesn't wait for a reply but reaches over to the crate of Harp behind Mrs Donohue and, plain as day, pulls himself a can and cracks it open, right so she can hear it. She turns around, gives him one of her 'gas man' looks and goes back to kissing the guests.

★   ★   ★

Mozzo's swinging out of Saidhbh, his arm hooked heavily around her neck.

And how's my own little dirtbird? he says, nuzzling into her and winking over at me while doing licky signs with his tongue.

Your dirtbird is talking to our guest, answers Saidhbh, stiff as a board, elbowing him off her shoulders.

Oh, I see, says Mozzo, standing to attention, and looking a bit annoyed at me. Well, did we tell 'Our Guest' that me and the lads did none other than catch one of them fuckin queer bikers last night? And did you tell 'Our Guest' how we gave him a good fuckin kicking for his money?

Saidhbh throws her eyes up to heaven and shakes her head at the same time.

You're such a prick, Declan, she says and storms out of the kitchen.

In her flowers, he says turning to me, glugging back fully on his can.

How did you catch him? I ask.

Who?

The queer.

Surprise attack! says Mozzo, and he mock punches me in the balls, soft enough to be a mock punch, but hard enough to wind me.

★ ★ ★

Taighdhg and all his teacher friends from Coláiste Mhuire ni Bheatha are ganging up together and trying to get a quiz going, but Sinead is having none of it.

Quiz me arse! she says real tough like, and

96

everyone except Fr O'Culigeen hoots with laughter at her being so rude. One of the younger teacher fellas gets down on his knees, pretends his can of Harp is a microphone and starts quizzing Sinead's bum.

So, tell me, Mrs Donohue's Arse, he says, what's it like down there?

Everyone hoots again, coz this really is rude. O'Culigeen is morto, and turns back to Joy Foster and tries to talk to her about Burt Reynolds some more.

Taighdhg pretends he hasn't heard the rude jokes, and goes over and starts jostling O'Culigeen, asking him to be quizmaster.

Come on, Father, he's saying, you're the only man for the job. And we can even call you Bunny if you like!

Taighdhg is referring to Bunny Carr, the presenter of top quiz show *Quicksilver*, who happens to have a wife with polio who's stuck in a big iron lung like a criminal mastermind. Mam calls Bunny Carr a Great Man. Patience of a saint, she says, with a poor wife like that. Can have all the success in the world, and where does it get you? I know neither the hour nor the day!

Yeah, says Janet Morrissey, stop the Lights, Father!

Everyone hoots at this too, coz it's the expression that people use on *Quicksilver* when they want to skip a go.

O'Culigeen licks the bits of spit from the slit corners of his mouth and says that in theory he'd like nothing better than to be quizmaster. He then hums and haws and tries to be polite, but he can see that Sinead has Eaghdheanaghdh's guitar in her hands and is waving it in front of Barry O'Driscoll, who's meant to be gift at it, so he says that he doesn't want to upset the lady of the manor.

I'll always defer to the ladies, he says, sounding like some fancy eejit from the telly. And he's talking rubbish too, coz you can see that he's dying to be quizmaster and have everyone think that he knows everything, and be all-important.

Listen to the Father! barks Sinead, before nudging Barry O'Driscoll, Now come on, Barry, let's be having you! Play away!

Barry toys with the guitar, but doesn't do much. He can see that Taighdhg is still gagging for a quiz, and that the whole thing is starting to become a big deal between him and Sinead. Taighdhg and Sinead can sense this, so they decide to show everyone that it's a jokey big deal by flicking vol-au-vent lids at each other in a friendly way while Taighdhg's gang chant, Quiz, Quiz, Quiz at the top of their lungs. I sit on the couch, a vision in grey with my glass of lemonade, next to Eaghdheanaghdh, who's so moody he's practically dumb, and watch as everyone makes arguments for which is better, quizzes or sing-songs. Mozzo's still knocking back Harp in the kitchen and Saidhbh hasn't appeared since she called him a prick.

★ ★ ★

Because Taighdhg and his gang are teachers, they love having quizzes. They love knowing the answers to every single question in every single round, nodding to each other and patting each other and smiling to themselves when they remember the names of the two girls in Brotherhood of Man, or what Bagatelle means, or the capital of this place in Africa, or the year when some youngfella got himself tortured for Ireland. Mam says it's because that's their job, knowing things like that. It would be like Dad being told to stand up in public and tell everyone about office furniture and get a free bottle of whiskey for his troubles. He'd love it. And he'd charm them all, and probably sell a few honey maple bookcases into the bargain. On the other hand, Sinead Donohue, who's mostly in tour-guide mode even when she's not being a tour guide, wants everyone singing and clapping and banging and stamping all night long so we can all go home with scratchy voices and say what a brilliant old-fashioned hoolie they had at Donohue's last night. Just like the old days back down the bog when Red Rocks Farrell and Clops Connelly would have you in tears with 'Danny Boy' at four in the morning.

★ ★ ★

In the end, thanks to the busy-body go-betweening of Fr O'Culigeen, a compromise is reached. Taighdhg and his lot are allowed to organise a rapid-fire round of quiz questions. While Barry O'Driscoll is told to tune the guitar and get ready for a right ole sing-song.

We'll put 'em to shame with their quizzes, says

Sinead out loud to no one. And we'll bate them stupid at that too!

Everyone thinks that having a quick quiz followed by a sing-song is a genius decision, and O'Culigeen stands there, grinning away, proud as punch, getting orange juice and compliments shovelled in his direction.

Like Solomon cutting the baby in half, says a little specky runt, gumming for a sniff.

I wouldn't go that far, says O'Culigeen, but not really meaning it.

★　★　★

The whole party is split up into two teams, captained by Taighdhg and Sinead, and we shout out any answers we think are right while O'Culigeen, with the *Quicksilver Quiz Book* before him, tots up the scores on the spot. It's tough going, with Taighdhg's gang arguing over every little detail of every question asked, and Sinead's team shouting out any sort of interference they can think of.

Does it mean the last 'living' American president, or just the last president?

Shut up, Donohue, and write the fecker down!

Watch it, Walsh, or I'll book you in for ten of the best!

You, and your wife!

Next!

More gargle for Team Atrixo, we're running dry.

No chance, O'Driscoll's strictly on fumes till his big performance!

100

Were you referring to an official rebellion, or any local revolt?

What's the difference?

The peasants are revolting!

Aren't they always?

But at least I'll be sober in the morning!

Sober me arse!

Sinead!

Is that Greece or the whole Greek empire?

Give us a break, Daly, fuck sake!

Language, Timothy!

If you must know, the full title is *ET: The Extra-Terrestrial*, and not just *ET*!

The extra testicle!

Dream on, Bazzer.

You wouldn't know what to do with it.

And you would?

Three balls is a lot of gear to carry around in your jocks!

Come on, lads, for the love of God, says O'Culigeen, finally snapping and crumpling a page in temper. Can we please keep it clean!!

The quiz goes dead quiet and serious after this, like school. Mozzo, who's on Sinead's team, sneaks over beside me and says that Saidhbh, who still hasn't appeared since the prick outburst, wants to speak to me upstairs in her room.

What about you? I say, smelling a rat straightaway.

Mozzo shrugs, and says real sad, I dunno, I just think the better man won in the end. He then stands up and slinks out of the room, looking hurt as hell.

Over the next couple of rounds I think about it. And after each shouty question, it makes more and more sense.

Where was *The Quiet Man* filmed?

Just wants a chat.

What was Bing Crosby's real name?

Like Fiona in the mornings, wants to talk about stuff.

How many brothers in the Kennedy clan?

Talk things through. Yes.

Who wrote the theme tune to *Wanderly Wagon?*

Has heard from Fiona that I'm a good chatter and wants to put me to the test.

What's Mike Murphy's wife's maiden name?

Yes.

I squeeze my way out of the room during the final round, which is O'Culigeen's very own made-up Biblical Characters questions round. He sees me darting for the door and, in front of everyone, gives me a right sneer.

I see you're like the bishops, he says, pouting his slitty mouth like an old woman. They've heard it all before!

Some of the partygoers give a little polite laugh, to make him feel like he's funny, but it doesn't bother me. I don't even go red. I've more important business going on than to be worrying about offending O'Culigeen's big greasy head.

★　★　★

I get to the top of the stairs and stop at the open linen basket that smells of crunchy underwear and mansweat. I look left and right along the landing, hoping for signs of Saidhbh's room. A girly sticker on the door, a fancy name-tag, a hunky muscly fella poster, anything. The toilet door on my right swings wide open and some ole codger with a big belly and red eyes comes out, fiddles with his fly, mumbles as he passes me and treads gingerly back down the stairs. For a moment everything from below is quiet. O'Culigeen must be loving the attention, asking the 64,000-dollar question about the name of the tax collector who fell out of the tree or the age of the fella who Jesus brought back from the dead.

I listen carefully in the silence and can clearly hear, coming from the end of the landing, the sound of Saidhbh crying her poor heart out. I follow the noise past the bathroom to the nearest bedroom door, where a postcard of a monkey asleep in the zoo says, My Get Up and Go Just Got Up and Went. I take a deep breath and tap the door gently with my fingertip, just below the postcard. I don't want to storm in, but I want to let her know that I'm here for her. I give it another tap. Nothing. Just more whining. I give the door a light push and stick half my head, from the top of my gelled hair right down to the middle of my nose, into the open crack.

The room is dark enough, with a tiny bit of light coming from a small bedside lamp. Even so, I can make out the bed, a chair, a desk, a mirror and a giant *Chicago* poster right next to one of Jesus lying dead in his mother Mary's arms. But when my eyes get used to it, and when I look, really look, instead of seeing Saidhbh lying on the bed in tears, I see that she's lying beside the bed and on the floor. And she's sprawled out underneath Mozzo. He's all over her, in black, like a vampire, and he's got his hands rushing around her miniskirt and he's rubbing her everywhere he can. And her, she's whining away with her head tilted back like they do in the foreign films when they're having intercourse.

Straight away, dead quiet, but like a robot, not thinking, I reverse the top half of my head gently out of the open door-crack and tiptoe downstairs again. Still not thinking, not feeling, barely breathing, I sit quietly back on the couch, re-taking my place on Taighdhg's team. I stare ahead of me into space and try to stop my bottom lip from wobbling and my throat from going tight. O'Culigeen, who's counting the scores in silence, gives me a dirty look, as if to say, You're in big trouble, boyo!

I look right back at him, right into the eyes, real cheeky like, nothing to lose, nothing left for me, as if to say, Go on, try it, you bucko priest gobshite!

★　★　★

Mozzo and Saidhbh, smiley and spring-fresh, come prancing into the sitting room, casual as anything, just in time for the sing-song. Sinead Donohue sees them and tries to get a teasing chorus of 'We know what you're up to!' going, but most of the party-goers are only interested in hoovering back John Players and guzzling down Harp with whiskey chasers in order to pluck up

104

enough courage to sing a song in public. O'Culigeen, however, sober as a judge, gives Saidhbh a real evil eye, as if to say that she'll be telling him all about it the next time he sees her pretty face in confession. Saidhbh, not bothered, sits down beside me and ruffles my hair like I'm a shaggy dog, while Mozzo leans around her shoulders and gives me an evil wink.

The room has got dead hot since the excitement of the quiz, and all the windows are open to try and stop the sweating. Barry O'Driscoll, down to his shirtsleeves, has taken O'Culigeen's place in the quizmaster chair, and is tuning Eaghdheanaghdh's guitar like a real pro — head bowed, no nonsense. Since his team won *Quicksilver*, Taighdhg's prize is that he gets to sing the first song of the night. Some of the teachers, still giddy from their victory, are shouting up suggestions like, 'The Fields'! Give us 'The Fields'! and, 'Kevin Barry'! and, 'Galway Bay'! but Taighdhg silences them all with a calm wave of his hand. He strokes his beard like a wise man and then whispers something into O'Driscoll's ear, who nods and smiles and starts strumming the guitar real fast. Everyone claps or stamps in time to the beat and they're all waiting with bated breath to see what song Taighdhg has in mind. He lifts his head up high, takes a deep breath and begins.

I'll tell me Ma when I go home ... He's barely got the first word out when the whole place explodes with claps and cheers. This is a popular choice. I know this song, coz Mam has it on a Clancy Brothers record at home, and there's a line that goes, 'They pull me hair and stole me comb,' and we think it's dead funny to sing, 'They pull me hair and pinch me bum!' Most people join in on the chorus in a very shouty way, 'She is handsome, she is pretty,' but I just sit there and give my knee the odd tap. Mozzo and Saidhbh are loving it, and nudge each other when they sing, 'She is a courting, one, two, three!'

Taighdhg gets a big cheer when he finishes and he does three more songs before it becomes party-piece time. This is where, one by one, each person in the room stands up and sings their own party-piece. But even though you're singing on your own everyone usually joins in to help you along, especially if your voice is crap.

Sinead does the first party-piece by singing 'The Wild Rover'. We learnt this song in school and I know all the lyrics off by heart, but I don't do anything, don't join in, don't clap in the right places or anything. No one notices coz they're having such a good time, holding their cans of Harp in the air and bellowing, 'And it's no, nay, never! DRINK UP YOUR BEER!' After Sinead, Janet Morrissey, well locked, finds the courage to sing a song I don't recognise about whiskey. Then one of the old fellas gets everyone going mad with excitement by singing 'McNamara's Band', which we have at home on Perry Como's *Greatest Hits*.

The party-pieces are going clockwise around the room, and after eleven songs it's Mozzo's turn to sing. He makes a big deal about it and says that he's lost his voice. Then, dramatically, he stands up and pretends to try three different songs in this mock hoarse voice that he's really putting on, and everyone laughs at him and lets him away with it because he's been a good sport and made a fool of himself. After Mozzo, Saidhbh gets up and sings 'Danny Boy' with her hands folded in the centre of her miniskirt, her silver crucifix shining, and her big brown eyes looking up to the ceiling as if she's singing to someone upstairs on the floor of her bedroom. Taighdhg whispers that Saidhbh is head of the Mhuire ni Bheatha choir, and when she gets to the high bit in the middle she's probably the only one in the room who hits the right note. Everyone else together sounds like a mouldy bag of cats getting electrocuted. 'Tis I'll be heeeeeeeaaaarrrrrrrrrr!

When she finishes Saidhbh gets a massive round of applause, but without cheers because the mood has got a bit sad after such a brilliant performance. Taighdhg Donohue, with red bloodshot eyes and sweat pouring off his forehead, turns to me, deadly serious, and says, Come on, Master Finnegan, out with it. I freeze for a second and, like a gobshite, I think about singing 'Tainted Love', but it wouldn't suit the new mood. The only other song I know that's as sad as 'Danny Boy' is called 'The Fields of Athenry', or 'The Fields' for short. But 'The Fields' is a Rebel Song, and I'm not sure if this is the right time to start singing Rebel Songs. I know this song word for word coz I've written it out, the whole thing, seven times in my jotter for making fun of it during civics. Me and Gary

Connell kept singing, 'You stole Trevelyn's cornflakes' instead of his 'corn' and our teacher Mr Graham said we were making a mockery of our sacred past.

I'm standing up, looking down at Saidhbh and Mozzo on the couch, their hands hidden and holding under the cushion, and, furious, I decide to give it a shot. I sing it as best I can and try not to go off-key like Paul Garvy in school whose voice has been breaking since he was ten. The song is about a fella and a girl in the old days singing to each other from different sides of a prison wall. He's inside coz he stole corn, not cornflakes, from the landlord and he's about to be sent to Australia for his troubles, and she's outside saying what a mess everything is.

I can tell straight away that this is a good choice. Coz from the minute I sing, 'By a lonely prison wall' in my high Aled Jones voice, everyone goes all hushed and serious, like they're in Mass. The song works a treat, with the whole place joining in the chorus and swaying from side to side like they're at a real concert, moaning softly about how annoying it is when you're madly in love with some youngfella and he gets taken away from you and you're left down the bog with nothing but stoney mucky fields for company. I'm cruising my way through it, note perfect, and I get to the last verse. It's the bit where the youngfella, getting angry now, sings back across the wall about how he actually did nothing wrong when you think about it, except fight the Brits and try and whip up some grub for his starving family, but because of that he'll never be able to see his kid again, and that's some whopping injustice. And with that Kent Foster's mam, Joy, stands up and walks right out of the room, and right out of the house altogether, not even stopping to get her coat or say her goodnights. This could be either because her husband was English and she didn't like the bit about fighting the Brits, or because her son got skin cancer and died, and she too has to face the injustice of never being able to see him again, or it could be both. I'm not sure which, but I stop singing and look around at the door that Joy's slammed behind her.

Don't mind that! bellows one of the old fellas guzzling Powers over at the window sill. Don't stop for that wan! says another. Get on with it!

I look at Taighdhg, who nods at me, and I finish the last verse and chorus. I don't get much of a clap at the end, coz everyone's kind of thinking about Joy Foster, but some of the women say that I did myself proud, as if I've just won a boxing match.

After that, it's as if 'The Fields of Athenry' has opened up the Rebel Song floodgates. They all come pouring out. Now that Joy Foster's gone and there's no one with English relatives left in the room, it's full steam ahead. Eaghdheanaghdh Donohue opens his mouth and whips the crowd up into a sweaty frenzy with 'God save Ireland cry the heroes', then everyone leaps to their feet in excitement when Taighdhg's beardy teacher friend sings about the IRA making the Brits 'run like hell away'. It's totally mad, and everyone's dropping their drinks and looking at each other with wild giddy faces, like they can't believe what's going on, can't believe what they're doing, like their own bodies are out of control, singing about the IRA burger-bombers as if they're super-heroes. And loving it too!

England prepare to fight or die, la da da da da, true Irish soldiers are here, la da dada da, poor weeping Ireland no more, la di da di da, our day will come again!

★　★　★

Now, during all this O'Culigeen has been hovering behind the couch, trying to get himself picked for his party-piece. Thing is, he was originally sitting over by the door that Joy Foster slammed, but the minute the party-pieces began going clockwise around the room he knew that he'd be last to sing, and by then we'd all be bored or worse, the party-pieces might've fizzled out altogether. Finally he gets so desperate that he muscles in through the crowd and perches on the couch armrest and gives Taighdhg the eye during one of the other teachers' version of 'Turn My Plough into a Rifle and the Brits Will Pay in Blood'. When the song finishes and we're clapping and getting a bit bored, Taighdhg asks us all to pray silence and give a warm welcome to a man of the cloth, a quizmaster, and a bloody good gentleman — Fr Luke O'Culigeen!

Most people whoop and cheer. Sinead Donohue wolf-whistles. Mozzo's got his arm fully round Saidhbh, in full view of the whole room now, so he just stamps a few times with his big black Docs. Saidhbh, drowsy from the booze, is silent, and stuck deep inside Mozzo's armpit. I remain sitting on my own single couch cushion, clapping quietly but politely for the performance to come.

After the clapping stops, O'Culigeen stands up slowly and runs his hand through his greasy black hair-do. He puts his other hand, the clean one, softly on Barry's shoulder and whispers the name of his party-piece. He then drops his head down like he does at Mass after the 'Lord I am not worthy to receive you' bit. He doesn't start for ages, and the silence is making us all nervous. You can't even see if he's breathing or not, but suddenly this deep deep voice, like a long foghorn, comes out of nowhere. O'Culigeen looks up and his eyes are already glassy with tears. 'When boyhood's fire was in my blood,' he thunders, while O'Driscoll hammers away on the guitar, 'I read of ancient freemen!' I've never heard this song before, but already I like it. There's no instant whoops or cheers this time. Just silence, and eyes shut and mouths hanging open. Like we're all getting communion.

O'Culigeen booms away about the Greeks and the Romans and how they fought for their freedom, and then he sings of how he prays that some day he'll see our chains torn in two, but instead of 'two', he sings 'Twain'. He uses this because it rhymes with the next line, which is the big one, 'And Ireland, long a province, be a nation once again!' He repeats this line again and again, with tears just about creeping out of his eyes.

A nation once again! A nation once again! And Ireland long a province be a nation once again!

We all love the sound of this, and tap along goodo. It's like every history lesson in school rolled up into one brilliant song. We get the gist of the chorus straightaway and are quick enough to sing the last 'Nation once again'. We love it. And we can't wait for the next chorus. But O'Culigeen knows what he's doing. He slows it down just enough when singing about special lights watching from overhead and the voices of angels. Then he really puts the boot down when he gets back to the good stuff — 'And righteous men must make our land a nation once again!'

We do the chorus, all three 'nation once again's perfect. And this time with feeling too, shouting it out like we mean it, our eyes flashing with pride, reminding ourselves of all the poor youngfellas being killed every day in the North just coz they want the same jobs as the Proddy Brit-loving bastards. We love it, and we're shifting around in our seats with excitement. Saidhbh has woken up and is kneeling on the couch beside Mozzo, who's not trying to be cool any more, but instead is glued to the sight of O'Culigeen at work. Most of the rest of the room are on their feet anyway, but they're lepping from side to side, in time with the music, holding their hands to their chests like they're swearing an oath in court.

O'Culigeen does the last verse dead slow with his eyes shut tight and pain on his forehead, like he's dying inside. He sings that he's not a boy any more, he's a man. And he has a hope, but he hopes it's not a hope in vain. And when we hear the word 'vain' we all know what's coming. We're nearly crying for the fever of it.

'When my dear country will be made a nation once again!'

The final chorus is bedlam. We all, everyone, the whole room, from the old whiskey-drinking codgers in the corner to stumbling Sinead by the door to Taighdhg on the floor to the rowdy teachers to the giddy women at the back to Mozzo and Saidhbh on the couch, and to me, we all boom along together, with our voices cracking and our teeth on show. A nation once again! And we mean it, we really mean it. A nation once again! We want to run out in the streets and shout out A Nation Once Again and fight all the Brits who ever came over here and tied poor ole James Connolly to a chair before shooting him and all those bastards on the BBC who make jokes about the Irish and all those poshies singing 'Rule Britannia' every year in the big concert, and we want to knock down Joy Foster's door and tell her to fuck off back to England and blow up every burger bar in London and tell them all to watch their fuckin mouths because the Irish are back in town and the Irish are fuckin magic!

The last line, 'And Ireland long a province be . . . ' me, Mozzo and Saidhbh are standing up on the couch itself, interlocking our arms, I've got mine around Saidhbh and she's got hers around Mozzo, whose arm is long enough to go round her shoulder and touch the back of my neck. ' . . . A nation once again!!' we all scream

113

in triumph and jump up and down. It's like New Year's Eve, with everyone running around hugging each other and crying for Ireland. Mozzo reaches round and pulls me into a three-person hug with Saidhbh and him, and we jump up and down and go wooooowooowooo! Saidhbh gives me a little peck on the cheek and Mozzo looks at me and smiles a 'no hard feelings' smile. I jump off the couch and think that this is the best party in the best country in the world.

O'Culigeen is shattered. He's sat himself down on Barry O'Driscoll's *Quicksilver* chair and is rubbing the sweat from his forehead back into his black hair, like the fella in the snot joke. He wipes his cheeks with his arm, mushing the tears and sweat into his black sleeve. He breathes heavily like he's just crossed the Dublin City Marathon finish line. We're all queuing up to pat him on the back and tell him that it was the best party-piece we've ever heard.

I leave Mozzo and Saidhbh and walk right up to him, just like all the other adults. I touch him on the shoulder and I say, 'That was really nice.'

He looks into my eyes with a real sadness about him and says calmly, 'Glad you liked it, my child.'

★   ★   ★

There's a few streaks of late-night light coming in from the street lamps on The Rise, but otherwise everything's dark. I lie in bed with my arms sticking out over my Ernie and Bert

114

turndown and tell Fiona everything about the party. Saidhbh's mini, Sinead's boobs, the Harp, the quiz, the songs, O'Culigeen, the works. Fiona says that there was murder when I left coz Susan went all hysterical and cried for two hours non-stop about being older than me but not being allowed to go anywhere.

She was so mad that she started kicking the sides of the baking press in temper. And when Mam tried to stop her, she threw a Sindy pencil case right at Mam's head and told her that she hated her guts. She said she wished she had been born in Brenda Joyce's house and not in this stinking place. Dad had to run in from the telly room, clear everyone out of the kitchen and sit Susan down at the table for a lecture. He told her that the rules were different for boys coz boys couldn't get into as much 'trouble' as girls. Sarah, who was listening from the hall, went mad and burst into the kitchen and said that it was men like Dad who were keeping Irish women in the Stone Age. A long all-night full-family argument followed about who was better, men or women.

Dad's main point was that, at the end of the day, boys couldn't get 'into trouble' so that's why they got special treatment. Sarah said it was pathetic that he couldn't even say the word 'pregnant'. Mam told her to hush, and nodded towards Susan and Claire like they were little toddlers who still believed in Santy and fairies.

A boy'll never come back into the house and shame you, said Dad, before angrily adding, He'll never get PREGNANT!

Fiona says that Mam really threw the cat among the pigeons by asking Dad what he'd do if one of his five daughters came home pregnant. He said that from that moment on they would no longer be a daughter of his. Sarah screamed and said that she'd love to get pregnant just to put him to the test.

Off ye go, he says, put me to the test!

Fiona laughed out loud at this and everyone glared at her, especially Sarah.

During the whole argument, no matter what anyone said, no matter where the discussion went — to single mothers, or contraception, or sexism in schools and politics — Dad kept coming back to his original point. He said that he was not technically wrong because it was a fact of science that no one could deny that his son, meaning me, could never walk in the door pregnant! And therefore, because of this, plain as day, an extra bit of leeway is given to his son's, my, activities.

Fiona says that all the girls were pulling their hair out at the end, telling him that he was completely missing the point.

Secretly, deep down inside, I like the idea of Dad standing up for me while the whole world is against him.

Gas, I say, and shut my eyes and sing the chorus of 'A Nation Once Again' five times in a row, until Fiona throws her pillow at me and tells me to shut my gob.

9

The End

First day back is always a tough one. We trudge down to breakfast in our uniforms, like sad little soldiers. The table doesn't have its wings out at breakfast time, so we have our food in shifts. We look out, up into the garden at the Swingball post glinting in the sun and we curse the fact that we're going back to school when the weather still thinks it's summer. We eat porridge from a huge steel pot that Mam has prepared the night before. And then we have Brennan's bread toasted and covered in Chivers marmalade or homemade raspberry jam. Mam went through a phase of making us have a chunky vitamin C pill with our breakfast but the pills became too expensive so she stopped.

The relay shifts are always the same. Mam and Susan first. Mam pulls up the blinds and turns on all the knobs and switches, including the Gay Byrne radio show, or Gaybo for short — everyone calls him Gaybo, or Uncle Gaybo for a laugh, coz he's like a good-looking uncle that you wish you had, and if you're from down the bog you'd spend your life savings to get a ticket for his television show so you could go all nervous in front of the camera and read out a poem or sing a little ditty that you'd written that very day about being excited to be up in the big

117

city, in a big television studio, just a matter of mere inches away from Uncle Gaybo himself, who would laugh real hard all the way through your poem or your song, and look at you like you were a mentaller on day release and due back down the bog at any minute.

Mam sits down opposite Susan and asks her all about the school day ahead while they eat their grub. Susan normally has a small bowl of porridge, but eats diet Ryvita crackers instead of toast, on account of her weight. Next is Claire, followed closely by me. Claire is a bit of a brain-box and is always giddy when it comes to school, no matter what time of the year, and usually has some scandal concerning this teacher and that pupil that's got her all excited.

When I come down I'm expecting a right grilling over last night's party, especially coz of the big argument they had over me going in the first place. But I walk into the room and the only thing that happens is Mam says casually that Gary Connell called for me last night and was annoyed that I hadn't told him about the party. Otherwise, Claire ignores me and chats away about Sister Ursula's bad breath while I fiddle with my super-stiff shirt collar and spoon out some porridge. I go to St Cormac's Secondary School in Oakfield, and their uniform is black shoes, grey slacks, black jumper, blue-and-red tie, and white shirt. This year's white shirt is new, bought from the back-to-school section in Dunnes Stores, and the collar is tight, rough and sharp, like rusty steel around my neck.

Susan's standing over by the dishrack with her

back to me drying up her porridge bowl. She says nothing but doodles around behind me, picking up letters and biros from the countertop as she makes her way around the room. She gets as far as the kitchen door and she finally has to say it.

So, how was last night?

I stop buttering my toast and look up at her, and her face seems really sad, hurt, ashamed and interested all at the same time. I want to stand up from my place, run over and give her the biggest hug ever and tell her that I love her and that being a boy is rubbish too.

Yeah, I say, it wasn't bad, lots of singing. And we did a quiz.

What type of quiz? she says, her sad eyes wide.

Quicksilver, I say.

Stop the Lights! shouts Claire, then adds, Bunnnnnnny Carrrrrrrr! in a way that means she's making fun of his name.

Oh, you could do a lot worse than Bunny Car, interrupts Mam. Poor man, with that wife of his. All the riches in the world can't buy you health. I know neither the hour nor the day!

Fiona is the next to arrive. She's doing her Leaving Cert this year, so that makes her top dog in school, which means she can bend the rules if she likes and be late for everything and wear a crappy version of The Sorrows uniform — black shoes, white socks, grey skirt, blue jumper, blue shirt, blue tie. This morning she's not bothering with the tie. She walks silently through the kitchen, flicks me on the ear and says, Out of my seat, loverboy!

I laugh at this because it's funny.

Dad's office is only down the road in Kilcuman, so he'll be the last of this shift to arrive at the table, if he can manage to fight the tiredness and pull himself out of bed. He used to be full of chat in the mornings, about the work ahead and the contracts that'll be 'signed, sealed, and delivered' by the end of the day. He'd skip the porridge, have a mouthful of toast and then dash out the door looking all flash and manly in his navy suit, black tie and dead neat moustache. If he was in the mood he used to even do some machine-gun kissing. This is when he pretends his mouth is a machine-gun and makes a 'mu-mu-mu-mu-mu' sound while running past us all, even the older ones, kissing us on the forehead or making us giggle by rubbing his moustache against our bare necks, and covering us in the sweet smell of aftershave. These days we're lucky if he makes it down in time to grunt at us gruffly before propping his sleepy head up on the table and trying to stop it from flopping forward, Laurel and Hardy style, into the steaming bowl below him.

God knows when the twins'll appear. Without any interviews, they could be in bed till lunchtime.

When we're all gone and the kitchen is nice and quiet, with only Uncle Gaybo murmuring away to himself in the background, Mam'll sit down with two separate pieces of paper and make two lists — one, of all the jobs like hoovering and cooking and clothes-washing that she has to do over the course of the day, and two, of all the things like cream crackers and washing powder that she has to buy with Dad's housekeeping money from Quinnsworth's in Kilcuman shopping centre.

Then, after about an hour of making the beds and cleaning the kitchen, the other Mothers will come knocking for a coffee morning and a chat.

⋆ ⋆ ⋆

When I arrive into school I'm chirpier than normal for a first-day-backer. This is because I'm meeting Saidhbh and Mozzo after tea. Even though it's a school day, we're going to the canal at the back of The Sorrows and Mozzo's going to show us both how and where they caught the queer biker on Saturday night. We're already a small three-person gang. Like the Hardy Boys and Nancy Drew.

⋆ ⋆ ⋆

Gary ignores me in class. We normally sit together in our double-desk for everything except languages, coz he does German and I do French, but today he's decided to sit down the back and leave an empty space beside me.

What's wrong, says Martin Higgins, pucking me on the shoulder from behind, you two getting divorced?

Higgins is a big hairy fella with a prickly half-beard inching down from his ears. Him and all the GAA lads think that me and Gary are right benders coz we always sit together, do our homework and don't play hurling. The GAA lads, on the other hand, are real dossers and jokers. They love farting in class and flicking spit from the back of their biros, and they never do their homework coz they're always out training or off on the bus to an away game on the Northside of the city. The teachers don't mind that the GAA lads are messers, coz playing GAA is meant to be a very important thing that brings pride to the school and turns you into a man at one and the same time. The GAA lads all have showers together after training and flick each other with their towels on their nude arses and joke about each other's mickeys.

There are two other types of non-GAA people in our class. These are the Mods, who get into trouble for wearing shiny slip-ons and scraping 'The Specials' into their desks with compass ends. And there's the Benders, who are everyone else, including me, Steven Casey, Shitty-Pants Sweeny and Gary.

St Cormac's is run by 'brothers', who are like monks or pretend priests, but the teachers themselves are actually half and half, ordinary men who love banging blackboards with their dusters and screaming their heads off at terrified young boys. There's a couple of actual priests too, but these ones are just blow-ins, like Fr Jason, who's good fun and a real brain-box, but only swings by for special visits or when it's time to run one of the yearly retreats. The school itself is an ancient old redbrick building that holds, on a good day with no mitching, around four hundred fellas.

It can be difficult growing up and living with five sisters and a mother and then being surrounded by four hundred fellas all day. In fact, sometimes, when the fellas are belching and farting and punching and being thick on purpose and smelling something rotten I feel like there's been a terrible mistake and I'm in the wrong uniform and someone should slap a skirt on me and send me over to The Sorrows to be with all the girls who are clean and interesting and kind. Fiona says that all babies are girls at first, when they're in the mothers' wombs. It's just a cruel trick of fate when suddenly, after only three or four weeks of being a womb blob, some of them grow a mickey. She says that Sister Janine showed them a video all about it, but the video wasn't only about babies with mickeys but was actually about how babies are real live human beings from the very moment they stop being an egg and get covered in sperm. The video said that there was no greater evil in this world than to kill a baby that was still inside its mother. And then Sister Janine added, after the show was over and the blinds ripped open, that anyone who kills a baby in the womb goes straight to hell when they die, but even before that they'll spend their every remaining day on earth in an actual living hell of indescribable pain and torment. Enough to drive them completely insane and eventually into full-on suicide. Abortion, in short, was not a good thing.

Coz he's an only child and doesn't have any brothers either, Gary feels the same way about the St Cormac's boys as I do. Which is why we're such good friends and why the GAA lads call us benders. They call Gary a Proddy Bender if they really want to hurt him, coz he's the only Prod in the class. Mam says the Connells could've sent Gary to any school they wanted, Proddy or Catholic, but they sent him to St Cormac's coz it had such a good reputation. And because it was free. And Proddies are known to be good with their money.

I try to talk to Gary during our Eleven break, but he's having none of it.

Sorry, he says, when I ask him how's it going, but you must be mistaking me for the great Declan Morrissey.

At least fuckin sit beside me! I say, making sure to add the 'fuckin' bit to sound hard, in case Higgins is listening.

Sorry again, says Gary, flicking his soft blond hair out of his eyes, but no Mozzos here!

Mozzo goes to Kilcuman Tech to do metalwork and carpentry whenever he feels like it. Gary knows he's hardly going to turn up here.

★ ★ ★

The classes themselves are dead easy. Each teacher says the same ole thing, even Mr King. First day back, blah, blah, time for a new beginning, blah, blah, your Inter Cert in two years, blah, blah, buckle under now and you'll fly through it later, blah, blah, most important time of your lives, blah, blah, decide your future right here, right now.

The only one who gives a real class is Spits

McGee, who jumps straight into a physics lesson on the easy-peasy parallax experiment we'll be doing in the science lab on Friday. McGee is a little fella by any standards, but he used to be a boxer in his youth, before he went out to work for the priests in Africa, and so he still has to prove himself by beating up at least one youngfella every day of term. And so, halfway through the lesson, just as he's at the board describing how we'll be gently pushing our blocks of wood across an inclined platform, Spits swivels around on his heel, charges between the desks and gives Steven Casey a decent wallop on the ear. Casey's good at art and has been drawing pictures of nude women on Shitty-Pants Sweeny's copybook. His head makes a pop sound when Spits slaps. Open palm on the ear, deafen you for the day. Sweeny goes red and says nothing while Spits walks back up to the board saying, That'll teach you, dirty brat.

⋆   ⋆   ⋆

I try to talk to Gary again at lunchbreak, but he just whizzes off past me on his bike, out the gates and towards the shopping centre with the rest of the benders.

⋆   ⋆   ⋆

By final bell Gary still hasn't warmed up. He's ignored me right through Maths and Civics, and now he's slipped by me in the cloakroom and straight out into the bike sheds. I've had

125

enough, so I run across the yard after him screaming, Gary! Gary! while Higgins and the GAA
lads do high-pitched imitations of me.

Gary! Gary! they squeak. You left your rubber
johnnies in my bag!

When I finally catch up with him he's about to
whizz off again on his bike, so I have to grab his
back carrier and pull with all my strength to stop
him leaving.

Fuck off, he says, traitor!

What the fuck are you talking about? I say
back to him.

Just fuck off, will ye? He lashes out at me, as if
to hit me in the face, but making sure he doesn't.

You fuck off! I say, being just as tough back to
him.

I will if you fuckin let go! He tries to pedal,
but my heels are dug into the ground and he's
not moving.

I will if you fuckin tell me! I say.

Fuckin traitor!

Fuckin what?

He gets off his saddle. You and fuckin Mozzo!

It was Saidhbh's party, I explain, not Mozzo's.

Big fuckin deal, he says, looking away.

And you weren't invited! I add. I pause. And
then, Sorry!

Gary's still furious. I don't give a shite about
that fuckin party, he says. Or that fuckin Saidhbh
slutbag Donohue!

I want to give him a belt for the slutbag thing,
but I shake his bike instead, shouting, Then
what's your fucking problem?

He's not interested. Just let me fuckin go!

Three of the GAA lads pass on their racers and shout out that Gary's been having an affair with Spits McGee, and that's why we're fighting.

But I thought we were getting married! they squeak, before adding, in their real voices, Fuckin queers!

Let me go, says Gary, please!

I see that he's starting to cry and I don't know what to do.

Jesus, Gary, I say softly, I was only holding your bike. Sorry.

You and fuckin Mozzo, he says, on the edge of bawling, fuckin bastards!

Gary starts sobbing his heart out, no shame at all, right there in the yard. To save us both from a massive slagging, I rush him round the back of the bike sheds, wheeling his bike with one hand and kind of guiding him with my free elbow. After bawling for ages and gagging on his snot and mucus, he eventually says that Mozzo and the Villas gang mugged him on Saturday night. He says that they dragged him from his bike and gave him the biggest wedgie he'd ever had, ripping his pants elastic right off and hurting his balls like nothing on earth. A few of them then kicked him in the ribs and told him that he was a fuckin biker queer.

But you went home? I say. I saw you leave.

Gary says that he didn't go home but instead did a loop round the estate and came back and spied on us sitting round the fire, drinking HCL. And when Mozzo's gang went queer-bashing he followed them, thinking that I was still with them, thinking that I might need some help. He followed them right down to the long grass by The Sorrows canal where they turned round and jumped him.

★ ★ ★

When I get home Mam is hopping with excitement, saying that she has some great news. She sits me down and says that she met Fr O'Culigeen in the shopping centre and that he had nothing but the highest praise for me. He said that I had the voice of an angel and had done my country proud at Donohue's hoolie.

A voice of an angel, she repeats, and looks at me while shaking her head lightly like she can't believe she's so lucky to have such a son. I shrug, but don't say anything coz I'm still thinking about Mozzo and Saidhbh and what I'm going to do at our meeting tonight. I move to get up out of the kitchen chair when Mam says, even more excitedly than before, And there's more!

I sit back down.

It seems that Fr O'Culigeen is considering me for a place in the church choir.

Can you believe it? Mam says. Not just an altar boy but part of the choir itself!

Cool, I say, flatly, and rise out of my seat.

I get as far as the kitchen door when Mam says, And he wants to see you tonight, straight after tea!

Siobhan buzzes through the kitchen holding an empty plate covered in cake crumbs.

Nice going, Aled Jones, she says.

My plan is this. I will cycle to Saidhbh's house, and sit down in front of her and Mozzo and ask them both, straight up, if the Gary story is true. I've hugged you both, I'll say. We've sang songs together and jumped around the room. We're like the Hardy Boys and Nancy Drew. So tell me now, is it true?

Then, depending on their answers, I'll go along with them to see where the queer biker was done, after which I'll dash off, full speed, just in time to audition for O'Culigeen.

★ ★ ★

It's getting dark, and I'm speeding down The Rise on my yellow racer with no lights. I'm out of my uniform and back into the stunning Vision in Grey. Fiona made a big deal about it when I was leaving the house, asking me in front of everyone if I was going to see my lover, Saidhbh Donohue. Mam answered for me and said that I was, in fact, dressed up to see Fr O'Culigeen.

Is that right? said Fiona, winking at me on the sly.

I turn the blind corner up into The Avenue and see Mozzo sitting on the wall outside Saidhbh's house. Straight away I smell a rat.

He's wearing his long red Iron Maiden T-shirt and black combats. His legs are dangling down, he's kicking his Doc heels against the brickwork and he's slugging from a can of HCL, bold as brass in front of anyone who wants to have a

129

look. He sees me coming, leaps off the wall and takes about five strides towards me, blocking me from getting to Saidhbh's house.

What's up? I say, breathless.

Nothing, he says, smiling at me like a charmer. He swigs back the dregs, shoves the can down behind the Donohues' hedge and says, Let's go!

I look over his shoulder towards the house. What about Saidhbh? I ask.

He smiles again, but not like a charmer, and repeats my question in a boozy whisper, What about Saidhbh?

I shrug casually, She's coming with us?

No, says Mozzo, really cold, but she asked me to pass this on to you.

And with that he holds out his middle finger, and pushes it towards my nose.

Go on, he says, have a sniff! It's fresh!

What is it? I ask.

Fanny juice, he says, shoving it right against my lips. Sniff!

I look at him, I think of Saidhbh and her miniskirt, and I know I shouldn't, but I sniff it anyway. Just to check.

Mozzo's finger stinks of ciggies. He bursts out laughing.

Ye little fuckin pervert, I never knew you had it in ye. Fuckin perv! He punches me on the shoulder and tells me to hurry up coz we don't have all night.

But what about . . . ? I say, nodding towards Saidhbh's house.

Grounded, he says, marching off down the road. Smoking in the jacks!

I follow Mozzo's gallop, wheeling my bike beside me, trying not to chop my shins against the pedals. I'm nervous, but still I ask him right then, no messing, about Gary's story. Mozzo's cool as anything. He pulls on his hair and says that yes, they did bump into Gary late on Saturday night. But that Gary ran off crying when Mozzo joked in front of everyone that Gary was a pillow-fucker.

I'm telling ya, he says, like it's a crying shame, that fella needs to get a fuckin sense of humour. Eh? And as he says it he nudges me with his elbow as if to say, Not like you and me coz we've got one!

I think it over for a second, and then I agree. I feel relieved that Mozzo isn't a mugger. In fact, I'm so relieved I tell him about Gary crying his heart out in the yard today. Mozzo shakes his head like it's still a shame and says, That's just the sort of bollocks I'm talking about.

I know, I say, you shoulda seen him. All over the fuckin place!

I'll bet he was, says Mozzo, resting a hand on my bike.

★　★　★

Mozzo has me pinned down to the ground with his hand around my neck. We're in the long grasses by the canal and he's kneeling on my chest. His teeth are flashing, his nose is wrinkled back and his eyes are kind of mad-like.

Think you're too fuckin good for me, he says, squeezing my throat. Is that it, little fuckin

131

queer?!! He's gritting his teeth and he looks like he's going to take a bite out of me. Little posh queer!! He's screaming out loud and I'm sure he can be heard for miles.

Heno, Macko, Hylo and Stapo are jumping around us like mad rabbits in bomber jackets.

Go on, says Heno, give him a fuckin dig!! Little bollix! Fuckin queer bollix!

My grey denims are covered in grass stains. Fiona's grey grandad shirt is wet. Mam is going to kill me. I am late for Fr O'Culigeen.

Mozzo has me pinned good and tight to the ground.

Too good for me, are you? But ye want me bird? he says, leaning right into my face, close enough so I can gag on his boozie-ciggies breath. Is that it?

But he's a fuckin queer! says Hylo, confused and excited at the same time.

That's right he's a fuckin queer, says Mozzo. So what'ya want with my fuckin bird? Eh?

I am silent because I am terrified. But I manage to say, I just, I just, I just.

You just what? says Mozzo, like Spits McGee when he's taking no shit from Steven Casey. You're just a fuckin little posh queer who thinks he's too good for the likes of me but wants to ride me bird to show you're not a queer, is that it?

I just, I just. I'm like a record stuck.

Or maybe he wants to ride YOU, Mozzo! says Stapo, adding fuel to the flames.

You want to ride me? says Mozzo pushing himself away from my face as he says it, but squeezing harder with his hand as he does so.

You want to fuckin ride me, queer? Is that fuckin it? Bender boy?

Go on, shouts Heno, thrilled, give him a fuckin dig!

Mozzo lifts his fist up and back as if to dig me and I flinch. They laugh together, Heno, Macko, Stapo, Hylo and Mozzo.

See, says Mozzo to the lads, too fuckin easy!

Wedgie! shouts Hylo. Fuckin wedgie him! Rip his fuckin cacks off!!

You want your cacks ripped off, do you? says Mozzo. Is that it, queer? Is it a wedgie you want, queer?

★ ★ ★

Mozzo had barely said a word the whole way to the canal. When we arrived at the back of the school the Villas lads were already there guzzling HCL. They started crowding in around me and making me nervous with their blank smiles and winks and nudges. Mozzo had more booze and told me to relax and stop worrying about the time. He brought me to the place where they caught the last biker queer, and there hanging from the bushes, with a last few pale bleeps left in it yet, was Gary's UFO sweat-band. It was at that point that everyone started shouting queer and pulling me down to the ground.

★ ★ ★

Mozzo decides that I'm going to get the biggest most painful wedgie of my life. Normally you get

133

wedgies in school on your birthday. What happens is that someone finds out early in the morning that it's your birthday. Then, for the rest of the day you're followed around by groups of three and four lads together with mad expressions on their faces. They're always looking at you, sneaking peeks over their shoulders, trying to get the perfect time when there's no teachers about. When they finally get that time, maybe just before afternoon classes, they scream Wedgie! at the tops of their voices. Then anyone who can lend a hand pushes you up against the wall and grabs at your waist. There's hands coming in from all sides, pulling at your belt and at your buttons, scraping at your skin. Eventually some lucky fella will catch hold of your underpants elastic and pull it high above your trousers. From here on it's pretty easy for everyone else to grab their own private bit of elastic, and before you know it there's about eight sets of hands all holding on to your jocks, all reefing them up high, trying to stretch them over your head while the tough piece of material in between your arse-cheeks turns to cheese-wire.

As they're giving you the wedgie, the fellas, who are red-faced with excitement, are going happy birthday, happy birthday, happy birthday!

If you get a wedgie when it's not your birthday then you can get a few digs on top of everything just for being a bollocks. This is the type of wedgie Mozzo wants to give me.

Still kneeling on my chest, he leans back and reaches behind, trying to grab my underpants in one swift move under my belt. Luckily, Fiona's grey grandad shirt is so long that there's miles of it tucked down inside my trousers, so Mozzo's really struggling to get a hold of anything useful.

Fuck sake! shouts Heno. Stop fuckin feelin his mickey and give him a fuckin wedgie!

Up on your feet! he says, furious at Heno but barking at me as if he's a soldier and I'm his prisoner of war.

He lets go of my neck, rolls off my chest, and stands back to let me get up.

There's a gap between Heno and Hylo.

I run for it.

★　★　★

It's dark, and the long grass is up to my knees, trying to trip me, grabbing me by the ankles, but I know where I'm going. Away from the canal and across the hockey pitches, down towards the back gate that opens out on to the Ballydown Road. I can hear Mozzo thumping along behind me as I break free from the long grass and hit the gravel pitches. He's screaming, I'll kill ya, ye bollix! while he's running.

I can't hear anyone else. No other footsteps, no shouts and taunts. Heno, Stapo, Hylo and Macko couldn't be arsed. They'd much rather crack open some more cans and smash my bike to bits.

I'm running as fast as I can, head down, legs pumping away like Steve Austin, and have nearly cleared both hockey pitches when I suddenly notice that Mozzo's paces have faded far behind me. I can barely believe that he's given up already, and am reluctant to slow down. I think that it must be my unbeatable bionic pace that's put him off. Either that, or the car that's revving away loudly by the gate.

★ ★ ★

I stop dead in my tracks and look behind me. Mozzo is gone. If I squint hard I think I can see his shady outline limping towards the canal and into the safety of darkness. I look over at the gate and see a familiar car, lights on, engine revving, passenger door half open.

My mind freezes, jammed between relief and confusion. Like the gears on a bike when the chain sticks between two cogs on the back wheel. Now that he's gone, and now that I know I'm safe, I feel like I'm in total shock. My brain isn't working. I don't know if I can move my aching legs. There is only one thing going through my head, and this thing is whizzing around again and again like a strange taped voice on a mad deafening loop. And what it's saying is that I'm on the exact spot where Helen MacDowell was standing when she got hit in the face by the hockey ball.

THWACKRUNCH!

★ ★ ★

I'm still in a bit of a trance when I make it over to the car. O'Culigeen reaches over from the driver seat and pushes the passenger door fully open.

You're late, he says, inviting me into his flash red Capri. And look at the cut of you!

I get into the car and kind of grunt at him as he speeds off down the road, gripping the steering wheel with his leather driving gloves and sending gravel bullets flying in all directions.

We had an appointment, he says, as we whore along the dark and deserted Ballydown Avenue and on to the main street, straight up past the shopping centre.

I got mugged, I say, thinking of Gary and not knowing how to make it up to him.

Is that what they call it nowadays? he answers, winking at me and dead proud of himself for making a crap joke.

Hmmm, I say, the best I can muster. I know that my face is covered in sweat and that my heart is still beating like a bastard, but I feel cold. I look down at my grey but now mainly green-grass-stained denims and try to replay what happened in my head.

O'Culigeen does the final homeward sprint at around eighty. He passes Murray's chemist, Hagan's newsagents, and Foley's hardware shop in one roaring blur. He pulls into his driveway and comes to a stop by skidding dramatically along the loose pebbles, right up to his garage door.

How's your singing voice? he says, suddenly all businesslike, as if we're about to have a board meeting. Are you up for a quick performance?

I don't answer. Instead, I think for a second.

How d'you know where I was? I ask, suddenly confused.

O'Culigeen says that when I hadn't turned up he phoned Mam to see what had happened. She was shocked and told him that I had gone ages ago. He pauses and tells me that, by the way, I'm in big trouble when I get home.

He then says that he remembered 'accidentally' overhearing Mozzo tell me about The Sorrows' canal at Donohue's hoolie, so he thought he'd take a spin down there to see if everything was all right.

Lucky for you I came when I did, eh? he says, pointing to my filthy gear.

Yeah, lucky me.

O'Culigeen steps out of the car and looks around him and then over to the greybrick church building which is next to his tiny brown house. He gives the building a floppy salute, from his forehead, and says, Goodnight Lord, sleep tight!

He ducks his head back down inside the car and says to me, Come on, let's see what you can do!

★　★　★

I'm still in a daze when I find myself in O'Culigeen's study.

The sitting room next door is lovely and warm, with a real fire and soft fluffy rugs, but he says that we can't go in there coz I'll dirty it with my scruffy clothes.

And it's funny, coz this is when his voice starts to change. Telling me I'll dirty everything, as if I'm dripping with mud.

138

No, we don't want your dirt everywhere, do we, he says, suddenly sounding like Spits McGee or one of the St Cormac's boyos.

Don't want you rubbing your filth everywhere.

He guides me into the study, pushing me in like he's in a rush to get the last sliced pan in Quinnsworth's. His study smells of old socks and has light blue walls. There's a picture of the Pope on the wall behind his desk and one of those paintings of mountains, big green fields and sheep on the opposite wall. There's a lovely red leather chair in the corner, but O'Culigeen makes me stay standing, facing his desk, which has only got writing paper and a jar of biros on it.

Come on, he says, pacing around me like a lion tamer, let's hear it.

Hear what? I say.

Your voice, he snaps back.

I'm still shaking from my mugging and I don't like the way this is going either, so I'm not sure if I can even manage a note. But before I can tell him that my legs are weak and that I need a glass of water, he fuckin belts me in the centre of the back and shouts, 'The Fields', give us the fucking 'Fields'!

This is completely out of order, hitting me and saying 'fucking'. And normally I would've been out that door in full bionic mode, but I'm so shocked by the belt that my stupid fuckin brain actually thinks about giving 'The Fields of Athenry' a go!

Well, he says, grabbing both my shoulders and shaking me from side to side, like I'm a rag doll.

139

Do your best, ye filthy little pup.

He has decided, right then and there, that I am a filthy little pup, and he can't stop saying it.

Sing, ye pup, sing! Ye filthy little pup!

He's still pacing around me, giving me the odd puck in the arm, but now he takes off his jacket and throws it on the chair, as if he really means business and is going to belt me to blazes.

I don't want to find out so give the first line my best shot.

'By a lonely prison wall, I heard a young girl calling . . . '

This works a treat.

Oh, yes, he says, like the cat who got the cream. Would ye listen to the voice on that little pup!

It's as if he's talking to someone else in the room, maybe the Pope.

Voice of an angel, that's what ye have, he's saying, breathing his stale cheese breath on me. But you're a pup, and you'll always be a pup.

Next, it gets really fecking weird.

O'Culigeen takes out his mickey. Serious. He's behind me, but I can hear his trousers zipping apart while I'm singing about stealing Trevelyn's corn.

He starts stroking my head, calling me angel and pup one after the other, but I can feel his mickey bobbing about behind me, prodding me in the side, rubbing off me leg.

It's right at this point that I notice myself, me, who I am, shift over a couple of feet to the left of where I'm actually standing, without moving my body. From this new position I can see

140

everything happen clearly. O'Culigeen's trousers are completely off, and he's just in his black shirt and he's rubbing my body madly and humping up and down on my leg like he's a fuckin Jack Russell.

I get to the last verse of the song and stop singing. It's been such a mad night, and now this. I start to have a little cry.

O'Culigeen is not happy.

Sing! he says, belting me across the back of the head. Sing, ye dirty little pup! And as he's ordering me, he starts reefing off my grey denims.

The chorus of 'The Fields of Athenry' goes, 'Low lie the fields of Athenry, where once we watched the small free birds fly'. But all I can manage is a very long and really shaky version of, 'Low lie'. That's all I can sing, and I do it over and over again. Low lie, low lie, low lie.

O'Culigeen doesn't seem to be bothered by this coz he's too busy calling me a filthy pup and feeling me all over something vicious. He starts slobbing all over my shoulders and grunting and poking his mickey about in my arse.

In myself, with superhuman strength, me, who I am, I, take a massive four or five feet jump away from the table, but again, without actually bringing my body with me. It's mad, like I'm sitting up by the picture of green mountains and sheep while I watch him rut away at me. At one point I think, That's it, he's fecking riding me! Fr Luke O'Culigeen, man of the cloth, quizmaster, and bloody good gentleman is riding my arse! How mad is this?!

141

I'm hoping that this is as bad as it gets, but O'Culigeen is in a savage mood tonight. He can't stop calling me little filthy pup, even when he's banging away, and every time he says it he slaps me, or punches me.

Filthy little pup, he says, all the trouble you cause. Pup. Your mother. Pup. Your poor father. Pup. And me, pup, look what you've done to me, pup, look what you've made me do!

Somehow, in the midst of all this, he decides that squeezing me round the neck will teach me not to be a little pup any more. It's a tight squeeze, a hundred times worse than Mozzo, who it turns out was clearly messing compared to this.

So, O'Culigeen is riding me against his desk, squeezing me by the neck and calling me filthy little pup. He's squeezing and banging away to his heart's content when all of a sudden, bam!

★   ★   ★

It's that simple. I come flying off the wall and zooming back into my body like I'm attached to myself with a superstrong elastic band. For a brief moment I feel everything that's happening to me, and I'm on fire. It feels like O'Culigeen's driving a Yorkie Juggernaut right into me, and like my skull is packed to bursting with barbed-wire stuffing. I have a couple of seconds of this and then nothing. I'm out of the game. I fall forward on to the table, bounce my head off O'Culigeen's biro jar and flop back on to the floor.

Naturally, O'Culigeen, the big gobshite, goes mental. He thinks I'm dead. He's slapping me on the face and shaking me and crying and kissing me on the cheek and hugging me and bawling saying Jesus this, and Jesus that, and Lord have mercy and God knows what. He holds me there in his sweaty arms on that stinking smelly socks floor for an age and says that he's sorry and he loves me and he never meant to hurt me. I want to say Bollocks to that and give him a right slap for his troubles, but I'm having trouble speaking, and just putting all my energies into getting a few decent breaths down my mangled throat.

★　★　★

I lose track of time. Passing in and out. I get snatches of O'Culigeen pacing about above me, and talking gibberish to himself.

Jesus Lord, mea culpa, what to do, desperate hours, this is me, my hour, help me Lord, what do I do, mea culpa, what to do?

He then drags me in zigzags around the study. It's as if he's looking for a little cubbyhole to hide me in. Eventually he lets go of me, falls to his knees and starts praying really hard. His lids are squeezed closed and his hands clasped in a vicious double fist up against his mouth. He doesn't say a word out loud, but I can tell he's trying really hard coz there's tears flowing out of the cracks of his tight-shut eyes.

★　★　★

143

A full hour later I'm up on my feet again. Well, sitting actually, in the red leather armchair in the corner of the study. O'Culigeen's made me a pot of super-sugary tea and is pouring it down my throat, along with a whole plate of custard creams. He's covered the gash on my forehead with a huge waterproof plaster and, by home time, he's already washed my entire outfit and dried it by the fire next door.

He says nothing during all this, and just points me into rooms, through doors, and eventually back into his car. He drops me home, a little before midnight. As I get ready to leave him and crack open the car door, a light pings on above both our heads and he says sorry, and promises me that it'll never happen again. He then leans in and kisses me on the cheek, and says that if I mention this to anyone I know, alive or dead, he'll bring down upon me the wrath of the Lord God Himself.

TWO

1

Smalltown Boy

You're a disgrace! A disgusting disgrace!

Dad says this over and over again, and thumps the door in between each insult. He says that he's not leaving, and that I have two choices. Come out now, and get a belt of the cane for my troubles. Or stay inside and wait for nothing less than an everlasting downpour of hell almighty.

Naturally, I don't move. I am dressed in an open-necked monkey suit, badly creased and mildly stained from the Debs dance the night before, and I am inside our stand-alone toilet with the bluebird wallpaper. Most people on The Rise have bathrooms with a toilet attached on the inside, so that you can do all your washing and cleaning and bodily stuff at the same time and in the same place. But we have a separate toilet, in an upstairs room, a little bird-blue cell, all of its own. Dad says that he was given the choice, but asked the builder to keep it separate, because growing up in hard-knock centre-city Dublin you always had 'the jacks' outside the building, and he couldn't imagine anything worse than brushing your teeth and fixing your hair while the stink of fresh plop rides up through your nostrils. Mam agrees, and has loads of stories about lashing to the outhouse in small-town Ballaghaderreen during dangerous

147

thunderstorms and midnight snow freezes. She says that indoor toilets give her the collywobbles. You might as well do it right there on the carpet.

Our stand-alone toilet cell is narrow, with room enough only for the toilet itself, a few spare rolls of Jacks paper, and a tiny boxy window up at the top, to let the smells out. Dad says that the tiny window is the one design flaw in the whole house, because although it's good at letting the smell of plop out, it can also let crafty criminals in. When Mam jokes that she hasn't seen any midget burglars running round Dublin these days, Dad comes up with a whole big story about how the real Dublin criminals, like the tough ones he knew growing up, use small children to climb in through tiny windows and let their bosses in through the front door. He's seen it himself, as a kid, loads of times, and he's so convinced that there are indeed burglar children on every corner of our own suburban estate that he eventually decides to weld a thick metal bar on to the middle of the small boxy window, to allow the smell of plop to escape while the only thing from the Dublin underworld with a chance of getting in is a tiny trained criminal monkey.

The stand-alone toilet room is so narrow that you bash your arms, knuckles and elbows off the walls when you try any manoeuvre other than a straight honest to goodness man pee i.e. walk in, pee, flush, reverse, out. Anything that involves turning, or wiping of any sort, is instant clatter territory. My room, which used to be me and Fiona's room, sits right next to the stand-alone toilet room, and you get a right earful of everything that's going on. The clatter is just a small part of the sound picture that's painted every day for the unfortunate listener. It's really manky, and most of the time you ram your fingers hard in your ears the minute you hear the click of the door. But you're not always quick enough, or paying enough attention to the comings and goings outside your room, and soon, and against your better instincts, you get to recognise everyone in your whole family just by the noises, the bangs, and the unholy symphony of plops and splatters that constitutes their most private moments of business just three feet away from you at the edge of your bed, separated only by a rubbish plywood wall.

Dad's the biggest clatterer, and he seems to hit the walls with every part of his body as he gets up and down, and cartwheels around for a wiping session. And the splatters too. With him it's like someone's firing a super-charged sub-machine gun straight into the bowl. Dreadful stuff. With Sarah, there's constant moaning and pushing, like she's having a baby every time, even if it's only a pee. A big production. Claire and Susan are hard to tell apart, although Susan usually pulls the paper holder to pieces before she's even sat down. Siobhan can't stand the fact that I can hear everything, so she tries to do all her business outside the house, in public loos, in restaurants, anywhere. Mam's super silent. And Fiona's not thick, so she tells me to blare up the boombox every time she heads inside. And if it's not loud

149

enough she'll bang on the wall until the sound of Jimmy Somerville screeching 'Smalltown Boy' has managed to drown out her heaves and hos.

The best thing, however, about the stand-alone toilet is the lock. It's by far the best lock in the house. It's a proper lock. Not a little brass effort for decoration, like the bathroom lock, which is a shiny thin horseshoe thing you could push open with a decent shoulder shove and is only there to let you know that there's someone on the other side of it that's probably naked in the bath. No, the toilet lock is a big silver-grey Chubb thing that lives half-inside the door itself and could only be broken down with the aid of some serious sledgehammers. It's designed to give the person inside the loo the ultimate in privacy, which, considering the rubbish plywood walls and the subsequent plop family hits, is a bit dim. No matter, though, it's still the perfect lock to stop a rampaging father, despite 'his condition', from smashing in on top of you and skinning you alive for being a disgusting disgrace.

Things have not been good between me and Dad for ages now. Mam calls it a right across-the-board clash, which is nevertheless aggravated by Dad's condition. For a start, for instance, there's school. Here, I have become, through no deliberate plan of my own, totally rubbish at everything that happens inside of St Cormac's Secondary School for Boys. A complete failure. Sent down the back by Spits McGee most days. Kept in for detention by Mr King on Saturday mornings. And extra homework on Thursdays after Brother

Seamus's civics class. I stare into space a lot. I forget homework. I have entire sessions where the world stops in my head and everything around me goes blurry and I'm like the fella who wakes up in his bedroom at night and has no clue on earth as to where he actually is. I hear voices too. I see things. Clips, images. Moments and snatches of things gone by, and puzzling pictures that make no sense. Voices and noises, sizzling and burning inside me, like Helen Macker's eyes. Teachers don't like this. And it's worse for Dad. Because Dad's children, his girls at least, have always done well in tests and exams, and debating and camogie, and netball and hockey. So when it's my turn to finally start winning stuff and getting gold stars and proving myself in secondary school as Dad's finest offspring by totally dominating the rest of the boyos, it comes as something of a shock to him to find out that I can only achieve a performance level that's just a tiny rung below total fecking shite.

Me becoming an altar boy meant nothing to him either. He had big rows with Mam about it late into the night. Telling her that my immortal soul didn't matter two fecks if I was going to spend the rest of my life on the streets because I failed my Leaving Cert. Once I swore that I could hear him crying his head off in the loo. He asked Mam what in feck's name had happened to me, and how I had gone from a normal happy-go-lucky steady-Eddie who liked homework and doing physics experiments to a moody silent fella who could barely lift a pencil and hadn't even bothered to put protective brown paper wrapping

151

on this year's textbooks even though we were already well into winter.

The altar-boy thing, of course, was O'Culigeen's doing. It took him about two minutes to renege on his promise to the Lord God Almighty to be an honest non-raping man-of-the-cloth.

Instead, he arrives up to our house, barely three days after the attack, and pours some thick priesty talk into Mam's ear about maintaining the purity of my soul and the quietly divine influence of the Holy Mass. The upshot of it all is that, after one cup of Tetleys and three dipped ginger snaps, it is decided that instead of joining the church choir I can do one better — I am finally ready to become an altar boy. This is a bad thing. Mam calls me down from the bedroom and tells me to run out to O'Culigeen in his car and to thank him. He rolls down the window and winks at me through his sunglasses. Just before he whizzes off, *Knight Rider* style, he tells me that he's sorted out my little problem. Declan Morrissey, he says, when I blank him, and then adds, You won't be hearing from that young pup again!

I do Thursday evening Mass, and Vigil Mass on Saturdays. Twice a week, every week without fail. And before each Mass, when we're supposed to be preparing and praying, and getting all solemn like, O'Culigeen can't help but find himself in his giddy element. Oh, my boy this, my child that, come here to me, me little child, and so on. And then he checks the clock, makes sure that the others are busy on pew plaque duty, fighting over the Mr Sheen, and hustles me

152

into sacristy, mostly with a lock on the door, and gets busy raping.

On the plus side, he eventually stops doing the choking thing, which is a relief all round. And, instead of crying and praying after it, he loads me up with chockies and chewing gum, and sometimes, when he runs out of them, even money. It's gas. He's like, here's your fifty pence, which is like a tenner to me, and thanks for that. As if I've just bob-a-jobbed the windscreen on his jammer, or weeded the flower beds near the side entrance. And he stops blaming me too, stops acting like I'm filling him full of voodoo magic against his will. Instead, after it, while he's pulling himself back together and I'm lying there in a heap, dead to the world, without a tear in my eye or a feeling in my heart, he's all buddy buddy. Acting like we were two big benders together, me and him against the world, with a big secret between us about how we love getting dirty with our pants off. I hate that bit the most. At least the other bit is just him being Luke O'Culigeen the Rapist Priest. And I can understand that, and blank it out, and blank myself out, and go, and be gone. Whereas this bit, where he pretends that we're the bender version of *The Two Ronnies*, makes me want to cry till my stomach blows up inside me and spews guts out of my ears.

At home I spend more and more time alone in my bedroom making giant megamix tapes on C90s, of wall to wall Jimmy Somerville, because I'm done with Soft Cell and because Fiona's into Bronski Beat and she has much better taste than

153

me and is usually right about these things. It's my bedroom now, without Fiona, strictly on Dad's orders. He made her share with Susan and Claire because he was offering me, on Mam's instruction, the carrot rather than the stick. Being in my own room, on my own, was supposed to make me a super student who studies maths and biology and becomes friendly again, instead of a quiet fella who stares into space and looks moody and only comes alive when he's dancing to his boombox, spinning round in circles on the spot, into dizzy oblivion, singing 'Run away, turn away, run away, turn away, run away!' at the top of his voice.

I dress like Jimmy too, with tight jeans and an even tighter haircut. And I write the words Bronski Beat in wavy writing, like on the 'Smalltown Boy' twelve-inch cover, in Tippex on the back of my denim jacket. The jacket is ancient, and far too short for me, but this is actually perfect because it sits just above my belly button when I wear it with the sleeves up, like Jimmy on *Top of the Pops*.

Mam bought the jacket for me years ago, when I was a little fella, and still into the *Six Million Dollar Man*. I thought it made me look like Steve Austin in the giant life-size poster that used to sit on the entire back bedroom wall, and made Aunty Jane jump when she nipped in to check the path of her lipstick in the mirror during our annual New Year's Day bash. Aunty Jane is Dad's sister, and a Dublin spinster who never had any man action and always wore a big red splodge of lipstick that bled all over the

154

corners of her mouth and made her look like the Joker, from telly's *Batman*, but in a silky blue A-wear blouse. So when she told everyone the story about jumping at the sight of a handsome bionic man in the mirror most people felt that the joke was extra funny and extra sad at the same time. Like she was stupid for jumping at the sight of a man from a poster, but that part of her was really hoping that Steve Austin was actually alive and standing dead still in the running pose, just waiting for her to come into my room so he could start moving again and take her away from this boring old man-less life that had landed so unfairly on top of her.

Mam, of course, doesn't mind the new haircut, because in her mad golden-oldies rule book, a short haircut means you're neat, respectable, dead honest and good marriage material. And in altar-boy vestments she says that I look positively saintly. The shorter the better, as far as she's concerned. She tells Dad that I'm just going through a blip at school, and that he's to cast his mind back and remember how bad Siobhan was when Sarah started winning everything, and Siobhan had to get used to being second place, but only after an entire term of mitching and shoplifting.

Dad isn't convinced. He's bothered by the lot. A right-across-the-board clash. The haircut, the jacket, the music, the spinning, the school, the detention and the staring. What bothers him the most, though, and the reason that he has finally, right now, on the morning after my very first Debs Dance, and after months of simmering smouldering rage, worked up the energy, in spite of his condition, to chase me right up the stairs and into the loo, is none other than Saidhbh Donohue herself.

2

Early Days

Saidhbh and I are, officially, boyfriend and girlfriend. I know. It's mad. Considering the four-year age gap, and the fact that she's the heart-stoppingly fantastic Saidhbh Donohue, with pale lipstick, glossy brown hair, button badges and drainpipe jeans, and I'm someone who cycles a lot and wears Spider Man pyjamas and hovers around in the background at family hoolies, especially when she's in the foreground, or upstairs on the floor getting felt by a fella in thirty-two-hole Docs. It's mad. And normally her religious beliefs wouldn't allow it, and all the priests in the world would call her a filthy fecking cradle snatcher for coming anywhere near me with romance in mind. But she makes an exception this time, just for me.

It starts, of course, on the very first day after the very first O'Culigeen attack. She's heard all about the night's excitement from Mozzo, who first comes crashing into her house in a big teary fit, saying that his mam's been offered a gig, that very morning, a real bolt from the blue, as church caretaker in a parish right over on the Northside, and that they're going to have to move to Clontarf, and live far away from The Rise. He's looking for sympathy from Saidhbh, and is in full-on floods. Hasn't even put his Docs on or anything. And he's staring into her eyes, holding on to her bomber jacket, begging her to think of something, to come up with a plan. He says that he's not going anywhere. And that he'll sleep on the floor of Saidhbh's bedroom if she'll let him. She says, making light of it, that the Northside's not so bad, and that Mozzo can borrow my bike, and cycle over to visit her whenever he likes. This makes him go mental and he tells her not to mention my name, and that he's already showed me what's what by beating the crap out of my little arse down by the canal, and letting me know exactly whose bird belongs to what fella.

Naturally, at this, Saidhbh goes mental in return, and calls Mozzo a huge prat, leaves him sitting alone on the side of her bed, and comes rushing up to the house to see if I am OK. Mam sends her upstairs to me, and says that I've been quiet all day, with barely a word out of me about how I lost my bike and ended up coming home from Father's at God knows what hour.

And true, thanks to O'Culigeen's first night of meddling, I'm in a total state when Saidhbh arrives, and she says that she feels super guilty, imagining that it's her fault that she's found me here, on the bed, mousy and quiet and wondering what's become of my world. She sits there for ages. Looks around. Picks some of my school books off the floor and tells me that *Peig* is agony, even when you're in a school where they speak Irish all day. *Peig* is this book you do in Irish class, because it's written in full-on Irish, with no English at all, and is a real-life story of

158

this aul wan who lived down the bog and had a million children, half of whom emigrated, the other half died of being bog-Irish disease, and at the time of writing she's ancient and smokes a pipe and generally moans a lot about how tough it is to be an aul wan down the bog with a load of bad memories rattling around inside her skull. Everyone in school is forced to read it, and if you don't you can't pass your Leaving Cert, which makes everyone hate it even more. We can't stand this moany old bag, and her stories of the old days when you had to eat nettles out of cow dung to stay alive. Most of us do mad graffiti on the word 'Peig' and change it to 'Bog' or 'Bag'. However, Shitty-Pants Sweeny did the best one. He changed it to 'Bitch'.

She's dead patient, Saidhbh, and at first we begin as just friends. We go to *Police Academy II* in the Ambassador in town and we think it's rubbish except for the bits when the black fella makes all the electronic noises with his mouth. The Ambassador is a massive old cinema that smells of Bazooka Joe sweet wrappers and pee. It's right at the far end of O'Connell Street, which is full of corner boys and drug addicts who live in blocks of flats on the Northside and who have horses for pets and who'd kill you for half the price of a morning fix. It would normally be a big deal for me to go there on my own, without a big sister to protect me from knife-wielding junkies (although I never understood what exactly my sisters were supposed to do on my behalf if set upon by the knackers, other than to dazzle them into momentary blindness with the ultra-glowy multicoloured power of their Ton Sur Ton sweatshirts). But when Saidhbh calls up to collect me she gets the nod from Mam which says, Look after him, I trust you, you're like his mam for the day now.

And we don't do that much talking at first, me and Saidhbh. We barely say a word on the bus on the way in. Which is a bit weird, because the windows are all steamed up and foggy from the meeting of poxy cold and wet Dublin weather with the choky smoky heat of the bus's indoor radiators, so we could be driving around in circles for all we know, and it's not like there's much for us to look at and distract us. Instead I draw a face in the misty window, using my little finger as a pen — for neater lines. It's a standard screamy face with fangs. I start doing them a lot around then. And I can't decide whether it's because I've seen *An American Werewolf in London* at the school video club or because it's, like, some mad voice of terror screaming from deep within me. Either way, I'm pretty good at it, and Saidhbh is impressed.

Saidhbh's best skill is art, so she should know. She's gotten As in every art class she's ever attended since she was a toddler. She doesn't want to do art as a real job though. She wants to be a teacher, like her father before her. She says that she'll probably use her art most when she's retired from teaching. She'll do green paintings of landscapes then, and make loads of money by selling them around St Stephen's Green every summer to rich American tourists who want to always remember what Ireland looks like when

160

they're back in the US of A.

She nudges me in the side and calls me a little artist. I nudge her back and say, 'Gir wan owra tha!' Which means, 'Get on out of that' but spoken like an ole fella whose family have lived in Dublin for a thousand years and who thinks it's the best city on the planet, and loves Guinness and being funny, and having a pot belly.

We do lots of nudging, Saidhbh and me. In fact, sometimes we do more nudging than talking. After the first month, I don't dare ask her about Mozzo, because I don't want to hear that he's still her boyfriend, and that he's travelling every day from Clontarf to see her. And she doesn't dare mention him.

The cinema thing goes on for ages, all the way through the first school term, and right into the icy days of early December. *Short Circuit, Three Amigos, Jumpin' Jack Flash* and *Down and Out in Beverly Hills.* We do them all. Although for that last one, Saidhbh has to pretend to the manager that she's my legal guardian, because it's an over sixteens, and has this scene in it where the man of the house nips into the Mexican maid's room and lies underneath her groaning and sweating while she wriggles and writhes in a silky white nightie right on top of his mickey. Me and Saidhbh turn to statues during this scene. We barely breathe while it's on the screen. It's not like we were holding hands before it, or anything. But you can tell, when it's on, that both of us are staring straight ahead, not moving a single muscle, not even our eyes. Just

161

frozen in reaction, and in nervous thought.

I think about the fellas in school, like Shitty-Pants Sweeny and Steven Casey, and realise that this is exactly the sort of thing that would drive them crazy on a Monday morning, making them do humpety-hump signs with their hips and finger-through-the-round-hole signs with their hands. And for a while I think about how I'm going to bring it up, before Tech-drawing class, in the queue to get into the chilly prefab with the T-squares and tilted desks. I imagine nodding, and doing the old something's-burnt-the-roof-of-my-mouth face, and telling the fellas that Mexican women are fecking amazing. And I imagine watching their faces, and wondering if any of them will tell me to shut up and go back to being the big bender boy that I am. But mostly I think about how sad the scene makes me feel. And I wonder if Saidhbh and Mozzo have done wriggling and writhing like this. And if Saidhbh has a silky white nightie. And I feel bad about how things have turned out for me in the humpety-hump department, and especially about how the hell I ended up playing a sweaty Mexican maid to Fr O'Culigeen's randy man of the house.

Saidhbh and I don't discuss the wriggling and writhing on the way home. We say that the film was a real laugh and that we loved the beardy fella falling into the swimming pool. And then, in the silences between us, I sing. I do this a lot. It's a habit, like so many things, that has developed in me around then. It's not fully blown belting it out either. Not me turning to Saidhbh and launching into 'Oh, What a Beautiful Mornin''

162

from *Oklahoma!* (a Finnegan Family Favourite). No, it's much quieter than that. I just find myself, sometimes without even noticing it, launching softly into a few bars of Jimmy in the same way that other people would begin a conversation. So Saidhbh and I are walking from the bus stop on the Ballydown Road back through the villas and I start going, super high-pitched but soft too, 'You leave in the morning with everything you own in a little black case!'

I usually do a few more lines, probably to the end of 'Mother will never understand . . . ' and then I just stop, and start all over again. Sixteen paces down Rosemount Lane 'Alone on a platform the wind and the rain . . . ' Another twenty to the corner of Clannard Crescent. 'On a sad and lonely face.' And then another thirty-five to the laneway into Castle Mount Road. 'Mother will never understand . . . '

The best bit of all is that Saidhbh doesn't seem to mind. In fact, she kind of likes it. At times she just walks quietly beside me, listening to my singing, super-high Jimmy-style. And at others, she hums along too, also super-high, but doing the keyboard bits as well. 'Do, do, do-do, diw, do, do, do-do, diw, do, do, do-do.' And every now and then, she does the singing too, except she changes the words a teensy bit, just because she can. 'On YOUR sad and lonely face!'

Again, it's not like *Oklahoma!* or *Annie Get Your Gun,* or any of the other FFFs that clog up our telly every Christmas on BBC2. It's softer than that, and sometimes even hard to hear. And

163

yet, in these moments, while winding our way home to our wet winter houses, along cold concrete roads, but singing in what Dad would call, in his boasty posh voice, sweet simpatico, I believe, if only for a moment, that there is purity and beauty in the world. And that I can have some part of it all to myself.

And then we reach the black-and-white metal gates of Saidhbh's house. Mostly the farewells are dead simple, and Saidhbh takes the lead. She'll call me a little madser, and do something sisterly like give me pinch on the upper arm while swooping down to give me peck on the cheek and tell me nicely to get lost. But this time, and I'd swear it's the Mexican maid in the silky nightie clunking around in the back of both of our minds, everything feels a bit weird. I'm waiting for her to call me madser, or Finno, or even, at a push, for a joke, Jimbo, but she doesn't. She stands there in front of me, takes a few breaths, as if she's about to start ten different sentences, but doesn't.

We're standing before the gate, blocked from the front window of the house by an enormous overgrown evergreen hedge. No spying view at all for know-all dad Taighdhg, or mute brother Eaghdheanaghdh. Saidhbh is wearing denim dungarees over Doc Martens, and one of Taighdhg's old brown sports jackets that she's reinvented and made look cool again with her trademark button badges of Madness and The Clash. Her brown hair is pulled away from her face in a loose, last-minute ponytail. And even in the middle of winter her skin is somehow a touch

164

tanned, which makes her whitish lipstick look all the more magical. She is perfect.

The silence between us goes on for ever. Just standing there, like two lemons. I can't bear it any more so I burst out suddenly with, 'You leave in the morning with everything you own in a little black case!' She's clearly had enough of Jimmy today so, cutting me dead short, tells me to get lost and bends down for the little cheek-peck. When I say, 'bends down' I actually mean 'leans a bit forward, yet in a downwardly direction' — we're kind of the same height, even with the age difference, although she's always in heels — not dressy spiky things, but the healthy two inches that a decent pair of Docs will give you on a good day.

Anyway, she leans in for the cheek-peck and, for reasons known only to me and the creators of *Down and Out in Beverly Hills*, I suddenly, at the last minute, flick my head round to the front and make full contact, on the lips, kissy-kissy style.

For a nanosecond, just on that point of the clumsy, and cheaty, contact, I'm thinking, This is it. This is the moment when it all begins! When my life changes for the better! At last! But then she shoots her head back and says, What the feck!? And she looks at me like she's just kissed a great big steaming lump of plop. She puts her hand up to her mouth, does a little half-wipe (as if I was the one wearing the lipstick), and then heads into the house, shaking her head.

★ ★ ★

That's it for another age. Right through Christmas '84, through January, and into the second week of February. Right until 6.45 p.m. on the night of my fourteenth birthday, to be exact. Not a word. Not a phonecall. Not a single Hollywood comedy. Nothing. The shutters, officially, come down. All because of one misfired peck.

As a result, Christmas is rubbish. Everyone gives me the wrong presents. They have me pinned for ever in the kiddie zone. With no idea of what's going on inside or outside of me.

On the day itself I don't say anything. I just tear off the wrapping paper and go, Wow! Boba Fett! And, again, Wow! I've always wanted a snow trooper with backpack accessories! The sisters all give each other clothes and earrings and Thompson Twins CDs and Paul Young posters. Mam gives Dad a load of practical stuff, like wipey things for the car windscreen, and clip-on things to stick in the boot, that can hold the wipey things. Everyone looks at him when it's his turn to give her a present, and we all think, because he's a dad, and because he's still struck down with the dead-tired disease, that he's forgotten, or he doesn't quite have the energy to buy her one, let alone wrap it. But he goes all quiet and giggly and disappears out of the room and comes back with a huge box, big enough for a tumble drier to fit inside.

Mam, we all know, wants a tumble drier, and has wanted one for over a year, ever since she saw Maura Connell's in action. Maura's husband Tim took a break from being a pilot for

166

ten minutes and went into Clery's in town and bought it for her on the sly. Had it delivered and everything. It was a big deal when the Clery's van turned up. Everyone acted like it was the Pope himself, just dropping by to say Hi to Maura and bring her a gift from God. So now every day that Mam's out in the garden, hanging up and pulling down the damp manky clothes off the orange ropy line that Dad has rigged up for her, she enviously spies Maura's back door, where a thick black pipe is belching out wet smoky refuse from her tumble drier — hinting at the soft, feather-dry clothes inside, just waiting to be effortlessly picked and plumped into a perfect fold, and happily plonked on to the family beds.

Straight away, sadly, Mam spots that it's not a tumble drier, because Dad can practically carry the box above his head with one hand. He plonks it down in front of her, says Happy Christmas, and tries not to laugh. She half laughs, in sympathy with him, and to hide her disappointment, and begins opening the box. After one layer of wrapping paper she knows the score. As we all do. This is Dad's favourite trick. To get a tiny present and wrap it a million times until it's the size of a house. He does this every year, either at Christmas or at one of our birthdays. He thinks it's hilarious, like there is nothing funnier on planet Earth than watching someone peel back wrapping paper and look vaguely disappointed.

Thing is, once Mam gets over the annoyance of not having a new tumble drier, she kind of gets in on the joke. After every layer of paper she goes, Oh, Matt, you're an awful man! And this makes him go even gigglier than ever, right red in the face, like he's watching the best *Benny Hill* ever. After a while, of course, it gets totally stupid, and Mam is right down to a package the size of a tennis ball, with mounds of old ripped-up newspapers around her (Dad stops using wrapping paper about three layers down and switches to old copies of the *Irish Independent*). The present is eventually revealed to be either earrings or a chain necklace — not cheap, but not too expensive — and Mam goes overboard, saying it's totally glamorous and straight out of *Dynasty*. She turns to us all, and we coo and gawp in unison, but we're all just happy that she got to the end of the papers, and happy too that Dad has managed to break out of his sleepy funk long enough to get a present and turn it into a signature comedy showcase.

Mam then asks the girls to help her gather up the mess into plastic bags, and turns to me specifically and tells me to hurry up. It's Christmas Day, after all, she says. And you don't want to be late for Fr O'Culigeen!

No, I think quietly, I don't. So I gather up my *Star Wars* action figures, and carry them in my arms into my bedroom, and let them scatter down on the still-unmade mattress. I take some of them out of their packets. Boba Fett and Luke in Hoth costume. I kneel down before them, like I did for so many years of before, and set them up for a big adventure. Usually, I play games that have nothing to do with the *Star Wars* films, and instead make my action figures run ahead of a giant tidal wave (my blanket) and leap, at the last minute, off a cliff (my bed head) and into a raging blue torrent (my carpet). But today, on this Christmas Day, I just look at them. It's like my head, the one that made up all the stories, has become a megamix that's stuck in pause mode.

Mam comes rushing into my room, makes me put on my smartest Christmas clothes, which is a brown suit jacket with matching trousers, and then drops me down to the church, right to O'Culigeen's door, a whole forty-five minutes before Mass is due to start.

O'Culigeen nearly wets his pants when he sees me. He tells me that I look divine, and that I'm the best Christmas present that any priest could ever ask for.

3

The Retreat

The run-up to my fourteenth is just as bad. January is a nightmare. School is back on. And I'm a mess. Can't concentrate on anything. Not even Mr King's showy turn at the top of the room as King Lear, or my once favourite coefficient of static friction versus co-efficient of dynamic friction experiment in Spits McGee's Physics — which is basically pushing a block of wood along a slippy surface and seeing how much effort it takes to keep it from stopping. All the teachers think I've gone into messer mode and am trying to defy them, so they start putting me down to the back of the class, and out the door. This buys me some credibility with the GAA boys, who think that I may be a Bronski bender, but I'm a tough sonofabitch Bronski bender all the same. They like it especially when Fats Madigan has to kick me out of Geography because I can't answer the same question three times in a row.

He's asking me about glacial erosion. Really simple stuff, paternoster lakes and the like. And I see his big spitty lips moving, but something's stopping me from hearing the question. He's going, blah blah, mountain or low-lying? And all I'm doing is staring at his spitty lips. He marches down to me the first time, stands right beside me

170

and says, Well? And the only thing I can do is look at him and go, I dunno. He then gives it another shot, right into my face this time. Blah blah mountain or low-lying, and which region in France? Again, it just isn't getting through. The spitty lips are too powerful, and right next to my face they're almost impossible to ignore. He pucks me this time, right in the shoulder. Grabs my jumper and begins to shake me from side to side. His face is bright red now, and he bellows, full blast, Blah blah fecking blah, paternoster fecking lakes, blah mountainous fecking region, blah low-lying? But he might as well be saying, Look at my big spitty lips, shooting flecky foam right in your face. You like, no?

I shrug, and say, once more, I dunno, and he reefs me by the collar and marches me out of class, throwing me against the coat racks, telling me not to test his patience ever again, and to think about my life while I'm out there. It gets worse, however, because outside patrolling the corridor is Jack Downs, our civics teacher and newly appointed year head. Jack is a failed hurley player with a scar on his left temple that he got from being in a tractor crash down the bog when he was a toddler. He was a big cheese in the hurley world, but ever since he got fired from the Kerry squad and became a teacher, his favourite activity has been beating schoolboys to a pulp. Any excuse, any time, any place possible, he loves it. And not just little pucks on the shoulder here and there. No, he does the works. Big dramatic smackdowns from the top of the class to the bottom, with a slow-motion lecture

171

intermingled with the blows. Usually about what sort of animals this country is rearing these days. Except he'll say, What, bang, sort, bang, of animals, bang bang, is this country, bang, rearing, bang, these days. The bangs are when he's punching in the flat of the back, or smacking on the side of the head.

He does me on the Fats Madigan day, brings me back into the class and asks Fats why I'm out there. When he finds out that I've been silently insolent to a geography teacher he goes mental, and does the speechy hitting thing right the way up and down the class, only this time the hitty question is directed at me. You won't, bang, answer, bang, me now, bang, will ye, bang?

Normally, the fella getting the hitty speech beating would be in floods by now, but the way things have gone for me recently I just kind of dance along with Downs, all around the class-room till it's over. Not really feeling the punches or the slaps, not really hearing the words. Only the tiniest part of me, the smallest flickering light inside, wondering, like Downs himself, what sort of animals is the country rearing these days, when all they can do is beat, punch, and rape their own children.

It's not all bad though. The GAA lads think I'm like the Rocky Balboa of benders after this, and they re-imagine the beating with Downs as Apollo Creed and me as Rocky, getting thwacked and bashed but refusing to go down. Just staring blankly with that kind of brain-damaged Stallone look. They still call me a bender every time I wear my Jimmy jacket to school, but that's about

172

it. They don't even call me and Gary husband and wife any more. Plus I get sent on a religious retreat because of my bad behaviour. Which is better than it sounds.

The retreats happen twice a year up in the monastery on the hill at the back of the school. The monastery is where the brothers live when they're not teaching, and where they do a lot of gardening, praying, being silent and feeding grass to the two knackered ponies that live in the gardens (they were saved from tinkers in Tallaght, and have huge burn marks down near their hooves, where they were set fire to). The monastery sounds much grander than it is, and in fact calling it a monastery makes it seem all fifteenth-century and stony and mossy and candley, and a bit horror film. Whereas, in fact, it's dead modern, flat and cream-coloured, not more than fifty years old, and probably got planted there on top of the hill when the brothers who teach in the school got bored with travelling every day from a castle in God knows where just to smack some kids for a couple of hours before getting back on the bus.

The brothers, naturally, are the ones who choose the kids for the retreat, and they never pick more than twenty each time, out of an entire school of four hundred fellas. Everyone, of course, wants to get on their list, because you miss a whole two days of classes if they choose you, but no one knows exactly how. They go for a pretty random cross-section, choosing a few of the brainiest fellas as well as a few of the toughest and cheekiest. The brainy ones are

173

there because, and so the theory goes, if they fully turn to the Lord and become super-holy after their two days with the brothers it'll be a great result for the God squad. The toughies are there, I guess, because they're on the brink of going to hell, and only sudden intervention on behalf of their souls will save them.

Best of all, no one who goes on the retreats ever really spills the beans on what goes on up there. They come back two days later looking all sheepish and wonky-eyed, sometimes hanging out together in a group of twenty, smiling quietly to each other, whispering little jokes and sometimes, really, even hugging each other out of the blue. Like they're sharing something completely over the top.

So, of course, when I get picked for this one (that was always going to happen — I practically have a big red 'Soul in Danger' sign flashing over my head every time I walk past the staffroom), and bearing in mind my run-in with Downs and my twice-weekly O'Culigeen sessions, I can barely imagine the sort of bonkers hell-pain that awaits both me and the other luckless nineteen as we slip through the doors of the monastery. I'm thinking, best-case scenario, just full-on total rape for two days — with a load of foreign monks jetting in from around the world to place bets on us in some mad twisted poke-to-the-death spunk-a-thon. Worst case is, like, being forced to skewer each other with red-hot anal intruders while the brothers make us eat steaming plates of tortured Tallaght pony poo.

Imagine my relief, then, when the first priestly

174

figure we see inside, supping on a cuppa and clutching a fistful of Rich Tea, is Fr Jason himself. Immediately, my shoulders drop, and I'm like, ace, we're in for a goodie now.

And I'm not wrong either. Fr Jason is in total control for the two days. Cool as ice throughout. He starts the ball rolling by giving us all tea and bickies (which is probably why they choose twenty — they only just have enough cups), and then getting us to sit round him on the floor in a big circle in a darkened room that has thick carpets, chairs up against the wall and three or four candles lighting. He tells us about being an alcoholic, about how he ruined his life, about how he was once a family man long ago in his old non-priesty life, and how he once gave his wife a right belt in the mouth, and how he stole money from his own kids to pay for booze and even drugs.

And then, he says, one day, at his lowest ebb, with sick all down his filthy rags, right smack in the centre of Dublin, he stumbles past a church. The door is half open, and for some reason, unknown to himself, instead of toddling on past, or pissing in the corner, up against a bin, which he was fond of doing, he made a sharp left and went inside. The church is empty and the story ends with him lying prostrate in front of the altar, flat out on the floor, arms extended so that he's in the shape of the cross. And he cries, really bawls his head off, and screams big angry tears at God, saying things like, I'm here, you fucker! I'm finally here! Fr Jason actually uses the word 'fucker', which blows us all away, considering he's a priest, and he's talking about being in a church, and talking to God himself, and he's talking to schoolboys who normally never hear anything worse than 'corner boys' from teachery types in the curse department. But anyway, he says, I'm here, you fucker! I'm finally here! And I'm a worthless piece of shit, so fucking kill me! Come on! Fucking kill me!

And he's waiting and he's waiting, and he's begging to be killed. He hates himself so much, and he hates what he's done to his brilliant wife, and his amazing kids, that he just wants to die. Come on, you sick bastard, he's saying to the altar, up on his knees now, with tears and everything. Kill me.

And then, maddest of all, he sees a figure coming towards him from the behind the altar. And the figure isn't a priest, or a man, or an angel. It's everyone and no one. A presence, and a light. And the figure doesn't say much to Fr Jason. But he says enough. Just three words that change his life for ever, and turn him from a dirty drunken puke-addled alkie to a man of God. And the words? 'You are loved.'

Now, as Fr Jason's telling this story, his eyes in the candlelight are filling with tears. I don't look around at any of the other fellas, but mine are filling up too. Because, right then and there, I want to be Fr Jason back down on the floor, covered in rags in that church, and I want to know that I am loved. And loved in that way, by a magical force from above that knows everything about me, and all about my life, and yet remains all loving and all knowing and only

176

wants to scoop me up with enormous floaty cotton-wool arms and cuddle me close and kiss me on the place where my forehead ends and my hair begins and breathe heavenly breaths down slowly upon me, and tell me that I am safe.

It's a knockout beginning to a knockout two days. Fr Jason has set the standard and doesn't let up for an instant. Day one kicks off with a couple of prayers, a lap of the rosary, and then, for three hours straight, we do a brilliant game of chit-chat called, 'The Best Day of My Life and the Worst Day of My Life'. In this one Fr Jason goes around the circle, fella by fella, and asks us to tell the group about the one time we felt the worst in the world, and then to take a quick break and a deep breath, and tell us about the best time. Pretty simple. But brilliant all the same.

Now, the little fellas, from first and second class, are brutal at this. But in a funny way. A tiddler called Shaymo, who's deadly at football and sure to be a school star, says that the worst day in his life was when he missed a penalty for his local under nines side, the Dunbarton Kestrals, in the league final, and the best day of his life was when he was told the family were taking a summer holiday trip to Liverpool, to see Anfield. He added that they never actually went on the holiday, because his mam one day suddenly insisted that they put all the holiday money in the Trocaire box instead, for the starving Cambodians. Which, Shaymo adds, just after his turn has passed along the line, makes it probably as bad as the day he missed the peno.

Some of the little ones do get it, though. An angelic-looking midget in specs called Pilibeen, who wears an Irish dancing medal on the outside of his jacket, and sounds like he should be going to Coláiste Mhuire ni Bheatha, says that the worst day of his life was when his granny died. This immediately makes everyone go all hushed, and makes Pilibeen's cheeks go puce red. He says that he was at his dinner table, making mash-potato mountains and sausage trains through the middle, when the phone went and it was his uncle Billy. He knew it was his uncle Billy because his mam answered the phone and went, 'Oh, Billy noooooooo!!!!' Like they do in the movies when someone's about to shoot the one you love in slow motion. Pilibeen says that he loved his grandma loads, and that it was a terrible terrible day, but as he's speaking the little midge doesn't look all that gutted. So Fr Jason, who's on the ball, and like a friendly priest version of a TV copper, asks Pilibeen a few super-clever questions about how he felt exactly on that day, the answers to which eventually steer Pilibeen into admitting that what made the day so sad was seeing his own mother in a mess, and not the fact that his old granny — who he saw only once a month and was pretty boring because she was deaf and a bit smelly — was dead.

Fr Jason was amazing like that. He said that he was just looking for the truth in every situation. Because the truth is God. And only God can set you free. None of us have a clue what this means, but it sounds fecking brilliant.

Next he's on to the oldies, and this is where it really starts cooking. For it quickly transpires that we're all, basically, a bit mad. Daryl McDonagh, a real quiet fella from all three of my main classes, says, for instance, that the worst day of his life was when his father left the family home. Nothing surprising there. Everyone nods along in silence. But then he starts to go all red-faced and watery-eyed, and he says the best day of his life was that day too, and that his father was a complete bastard. He's allowed to say bastard because we're in, says Fr Jason, a safe space, and because calling your dad a bastard isn't half as bad as calling God a fucker. Turns out that Daryl's dad was a real bastard, and probably a bit of a fucker too. And not in the old-fashioned way. Not in the sense that he ever smacked Daryl around the place, Jack Downs-y style. No, he was weirder than that. Real head-messing stuff. Daryl explains that if he left any veg or skins on the plate, his da could suddenly go mad, tell everyone to leave the kitchen and load up Daryl's plate big time with all the scraps he could find. Then, and this is the weird bit, he'd make Daryl fetch a full-length mirror that was held in the garage for just such occasions, and he'd make him eat all the shitty scraps — bits of gristle from his brothers' plates, the tops and tails from uncooked veg, even the odd boiled egg shell — and he'd have to do so while staring at his increasingly on-the-verge-of-puking face in front of the mirror.

Now, naturally, Daryl's crying his head off when he's telling us this, and we all kind of feel a

179

bit sick while we're listening. Partly because it's a sick-making story, but also because by listening to it we all know we're crossing a line, and heading into uncharted waters where anything from any of us is likely to come spewing out.

And it does. And it keeps on coming. Justin Rafferty, one of the star swats from the Leaving Cert class, says that his best day was when he got his Inter Cert results, eight As and two Bs. He talks about being taken to Blakes in Oakfield, and having two helpings of everything, even two knickerbocker glories, and getting his picture taken with all the family members, uncles, aunts, the works. He jokes, at first, and says that the worst day of his life hasn't happened yet, and is going to be the day before his Leaving Cert results, just in case he doesn't do as well as in the Inter. Everyone laughs and we think he's going to get away with it when Fr Jason asks him if he's sure that's it. And then, like a fecking meteorite of filth, right out of nowhere, he goes, no, actually, the worst day of my life was when I licked out my cousin.

We're all looking at each other, like, What in feck's name?!!! And you just know the little ones, including and especially Pilibeen, are going, Licked out? But Fr Jason is cool as ice, and tells him to continue. We get the whole set-up, how he's bessie mates with his cousin Gemma, and how on her confirmation day, after another big pig-out in Blakes, he locks her in his room and forces her to let him lick her out because he was sick of being called a swat and a virgin by the other Leaving Cert hard men. Pilibeen's eyes, I can see at this stage, are out on stalks. Fr Jason is nodding. And Justin continues about the guilt, about Gemma crying all the way through, and about never again being able to look her in the eye, or speak to her parents — his once favourite aunty and uncle. Of course, he's bawling while he's telling us all this, and still sobbing when Fr Jason turns to me and says it's my go.

Before I've even started talking I can feel my legs shaking. In my head I'm thinking, fecking hell, how in God's name am I supposed to top all these totally bonkers stories?!! But in my heart I know what I have to tell them. I start with the best day of my life, and I tell them that there's been many, and that all mainly revolve around my mam telling the bus conductor breastfeeding joke around the table, and my whole family bursting out laughing. I look around, and even in the candlelight I can see that everyone's super-disappointed. Besides the mention of the word breast, this is perhaps the most boring thing that's been said all morning. Fr Jason, however, is pleased, and smiles and even half bows, and tells me that it's good to hear me speaking so readily from my heart. And the worst day? he says, beaming, hoping for a real humdinger. It's now when my breathing goes totally haywire.

I find it hard to catch my breath, but no one really notices. Plus the shakes in my legs have started to move up into my stomach. My fingers start to wriggle madly, as if I'm playing an invisible piano on the spot and I feel like I want to stand up and sit down a thousand times in a second. I can't actually make properly formed sentences, but I fire ahead as best I can and for some reason, I find myself starting with Helen Macdowell and the hockey ball. I don't make much sense. My words are coming out in either short sharp repetitive bursts, or else a big nonsensical tumble. I say that it was Helen Macdowell getting hit in the mouth with a hockey ball that ruined it all for me. I keep on repeating the five words, It was the hockey ball, like some complete looney, for about a minute, before Fr Jason asks if I'm OK. He does this because some of the fellas have started to laugh.

Fr Jason puts his hand on my shoulder and presses down hard, pushing me into the carpet. The pressure helps a little bit, and I can explain that Helen Macker saw it coming, and she looked inside me and saw it coming, saw the very spot I'd be standing on when it all went pear-shaped, and when He came along.

Who's He? says Fr Jason. I say the words, It was Father. It was Father. It was Father. It was Father. But I can't finish it. It's too much, even in this safe space, even with the lick-outs and the mad mirror-eating. It's too much, and I start to spaz again, only worse. Like the shakes in my legs suddenly rush up into my whole body and become concentrated madly right in the centre of my chest. I begin to flop about on the spot with the pain of it all. I fall forward on to the ground and have a fit of sorts, flipping and flopping like the fresh summer trout that Dad caught in Connemara on our last family holiday together. We were out in a tiny rowing boat that managed to fit all eight of us at a push, even though Mam said it was illegal and would get us all arrested if we didn't drown first. Dad was being all bold, and gamey, like a GAA lad, and rocking the boat on purpose just to make everyone, including Mam, cry for fun. When he caught the fish he flicked it down into the boat and told me to kill it. Back of the head! he kept barking, back of the head off the side of the boat!

Back of the head? I could barely hold its flippy whippy body in my hand for a micro-second, let alone manage a pin-point thwack of its head against a single wooden slat. In the end Dad battered it viciously with the handle of the oar and said, with a wink, Ask a boy to do a man's job, eh?!

The boys all freak. They stop laughing and Pilibeen nearly pisses himself. I can definitely hear him crying. Fr Jason, though, and true to character, is untroubled, and just stands over me, telling the fellas to make space. He starts by acting as if nothing is happening, and continues with my Worst Day story, saying, And what did Father do to you? What did he do? I can hear this in my state, but I can't quite believe it. My chest is about to explode outwards in a grenade blast of gore, like yer man in *Alien*, and my teeth are chattering like mad and there's not a chance in hell of getting anything out, let alone the story of how I was taken back to O'Culigeen's evil lair, and how I was demolished therein.

Fr Jason eventually gets this, and says that it's all good, and he holds my hand and raises his head up to face the ceiling and begins praying.

Although it's not like any praying I know. It's all gobbledegook. A few words here, a few words there, mixed up with lots of nonsense words, like Jabba the Hutt in *Return of the Jedi*. Pa-ees-ka-chung-cow-a-wookie!!!

He tells the boys not to be afraid, that what he's doing is called speaking in tongues, and that he's simply asking the Holy Spirit directly to help me in my hour of need. I feel dead embarrassed at this stage, and I still can't stop the shaking. Fr Jason is kneeling now, on both knees, right next to me, his hand just hovering on my head. I feel warm, hot even. And I remember my bible stories, and the one where Jesus casts out the spirit of Satan from some mad old fecker who's having a monster fit in the middle of the market square. In the TV show *Jesus of Nazareth* the fella goes from being a complete rag-tag rattle-boned mess to being a normal guy with gratitude in his eyes in ten seconds. I wonder if this is how he felt. Was he, maybe, not possessed by the spirit of Satan, but actually a victim of some ancient desert priest who picked him up on his camel and then raped him in the dunes. And maybe that's why he needed Jesus, the super-priest, to sort him out. And while I'm thinking this, and wondering if Fr Jason would've made a better Jesus than Robert Powell, I notice that the shakes are slowing down, and that things are beginning to calm around me.

Another minute and I stop completely. The fellas hold their breaths. Fr Jason picks me up with both his arms around me and lifts me on to my feet. He says I've done very well today, and that he's looking forward to see how I'll progress over the next twenty-four hours.

I get home late that evening and Mam asks me how was the retreat. I tell her that it was fine, and that nothing special happened. I don't have dinner that night, and instead I lie in bed feeling bad that everyone at the retreat thinks that my father is now the most hideous man on the planet and has done something so unspeakable that it would turn his own son into a mumbling whimpering flippy-floppy spazzer.

4

Dry Crying

I spend most of the night awake. Crying. Not real crying, though. Dry crying, where it's coming from your mouth only, and not really connected to your throat, or your stomach, much less your heart. Mam and Dad are having the Connells round at the time, for a chat, a drink and to show off the new brown sanger bread that's come directly from Quinnsworth's that evening. It's not like the brown bread that Grandma, Mam's mam, makes and has been passed down from family to family from the wilds of Ballaghaderreen and was probably the same brown bread that they were eating when St Patrick first came over on the slave boat with a bottle of holy water and a fistful of shamrock. That one is, basically, a load of nuts and seeds mixed up into a big brown paste that somehow comes out of the oven tasting brilliant, especially when lathered in melted butter and strawberry jam. Dad says, though, that he wouldn't touch it at room temperature because he values his teeth too much.

No, this new Quinnsworth's bread is like regular sliced Brennan's white bread, only it's coloured brown. Mam first got it over in Aunty Una's in Rathfarnham, wrapped around a couple of slices of cucumber. It was a big talking point for the night, and Aunty Una was dead proud when she arrived out with the sanger plate and no one could believe their eyes. Mam kept pucking Dad all night in the arm, asking him to agree with her that it was totally amazing that the bread tasted just like white bread, only it was brown. Una told her that it was much better for her, because it was brown, and then all the uncles and aunts got chatting about how they could barely keep up with the changes in Ireland, and how modern it was all getting. It's all cholesterol this, and roughage that, and women's lib this, and gay that, and divorce this. In these types of chats Dad normally tries to make a big joke of it, especially if he's had a drink or two, and he'll say things like, 'You should be so lucky' when Mam mentions divorce. But she usually gets annoyed and says, 'Oh, it's well you may laugh!' And then gives him, and whoever's listening, a lecture about the country going to the dogs before her very eyes and how her entire Christmas was ruined by that filthy song.

The filthy song is 'The Power of Love' by Frankie Goes to Hollywood, and it made Mam write to both the BBC in London and the *Irish Indo* letters page. It was the same letter to both. She read it out to us a million times, and in it she described how she had been enjoying a pre-Christmas tea of scones and sandwiches (white bread) with her entire family when the number one song, with its video, came on *Top of the Pops*, and how she had enjoyed the opening few bars and the Nativity theme of

187

the video until she was hit — and it was an assault, she wrote — with the chorus, and specifically with the words that invoked the listener, very explicitly, to make love.

She said that this might be the sort of thing that suffices for a Christmas message in heathen England, but in Catholic Ireland we have a tradition of wholesome family Christmases, where sex and filth are the last things on anyone's mind. Especially during Christmas songs. Plus the confusing of the Nativity theme with the very idea of making love was the most wicked sin of all, and a blasphemy that spoke volumes about the morals of the pop group Frankie Goes to Hollywood and of its lead singer Holly Johnson (she had to look that bit up in Susan's *Jackie*), and spoke even less about the makers of *Top of the Pops* itself, and the powers in Ireland who agreed to broadcast it in the first place. She signed it, Worried, from Eire.

Thankfully, the letter didn't get printed in the *Indo*, and she got no reply from the BBC, but Mam didn't tire of reciting its contents and telling anyone she could about how that filthy song had ruined her Christmas, and how she had lost track of the amount of times she had to dive across the kitchen floor when it came on the radio, in order to switch it off before the first chorus.

Tonight's different, though. The chat from below is more the low-level murmur-murmur of discussion than the whine and the bark of lecture and complaint. From my position in bed, over the kitchen and to the right of the sitting room, I

188

can tell that although the brown bread may indeed have gone down a storm, they have nonetheless moved on to more serious things. Fiona tells me that they're talking about Dad's always-tired disease, and how to beat it. She heard Tim Connell, the Aer Lingus pilot, saying that everyone's tired in the States, and that Dad just needs to go on a course of multi-vitamins and take up jogging with a Sony Walkman. He even offers to bring him back a Walkman from his next US flight. With the dollar only worth fifty pence it's a steal, he says. Dad asks what would he listen to on the Walkman and Tim tells him not to be such an old square, and that one of Dad's daughters can surely whip him together a jogging mix tape. Dad asks if you can get *Hooked on Classics* on tape, and Tim laughs.

Fiona does this a lot nowadays. She slips into the room, for old times' sake, and flops down on the floor where her bed used to be, and picks up my old discarded *Star Wars* figures, and fills me in on all the goss. The first time she did it, she managed to get into the room without me knowing it, and crawled on her hunkers, commando style, all the way under my bed and, just as I was falling asleep, kneed me very slowly in the base of the mattress, from below. Naturally, I freaked, and shouted out for Mam, and could only think that a ghost, or a burglar, was under the bed, and Fiona giggled like mad for the rest of the night, even when she was back in Claire and Susan's room.

She doesn't stay long tonight. Mostly because I'm not much to chat to. I grunt a lot, and barely take my eyes off the ceiling. She's only gone ten minutes when the crying starts. I don't know why. It's brutal stuff. Really fake. But I can't stop it. Waa-haa-haa. She comes shooting back into the room and tells me that I'm mad, and that the Connells will be able to hear me if I don't shut up. But I can't stop. I just keep going, like I'm being driven to it. Waa-haa-haa. Eventually Mam comes up and cuddles me and calls me her old-segosha, and asks me what's wrong, and if anything happened at the retreat today. I say nothing, but turn to the side and keep going. Waa-haa-haa.

Eventually, at last, Dad appears. My father. He sits down on the bed beside me and lays a huge hand on my back, just below my neck. He calls me his son, and asks me if he's going to have to phone for an ambulance. I continue. Waa-haa-haa. He leans in closer, and kisses the back of my head. I can feel his moustache grazing my ear. There's booze on his breath. He is a giant. His huge hand moves over on to my shoulder and he gives it a squeeze and says that I'm a good lad.

I close my eyes tight for the first time that night, and imagine him dropping down to his knees beside the bed and crooning 'The Power of Love' into my ear. I'll protect you from the hooded claw, he begins, half singing, half speaking, somewhere between Frankie Goes to Hollywood's Holly Johnson and Fr Jason's cuddly altar-floating non-God. He does it all note perfect, and with real feeling, just like in the video, and he cruises straight through, with his hands clasped and close to his heart, right up to the final shouty bit about always being around, no matter what, because he's driven by nothing less than his undying and death defying love.

The next thing I know, it's morning. And time, again, for the retreat.

5

The Retreat, Part Two

After all the shenanigans on day one, hopes are high for the second part of the retreat. We begin with a few prayers of thanks in the candle-lit sacred space, before Fr Jason moves us next door to a smaller antechamber, promising us a special surprise. Here, in a room little bigger than a box bedroom, and with strip lighting and grass-green carpets, is apparently where the real transformation is going to take place. Fr Jason dramatically drops a large navy-blue paperback bible in the centre of the room, kneels down upon it, looks up to the ceiling, then around to each one of us, and announces that this is where we are going to learn how to speak in tongues.

Naturally, we all nearly crap our pants. Daryl McDonagh immediately asks if it's going to hurt. Fr Jason ignores him, claps his hands, and calls out for 'Jacko' and 'Fenzer'. Two junior priests suddenly appear at his side, with sleeves rolled up, black shirts unbuttoned at the neck, and no sign of white priestly dog collars. Fr Jason turns to Daryl and says that he'll certainly feel his head warm up, as the Holy Spirit is entering him from above, but it shouldn't be too traumatic. Then he turns his face up towards one of the juniors and says, 'Not unless you've got the devil inside you. Then we're in for a real battle, eh,

Jacko?' He winks at Jacko as he says this, to let us know that it's kind of a joke and kind of serious at the same time.

Fr Jason decides that Daryl should go first, just to put him out of his misery. He asks him to kneel, right down on the bible, and then tells us all to leave the room, and to line up neatly along the corridor outside, and in the order in which we fancy being done. I take my time, and am the last to leave. The final glimpse I get of Daryl is of his shaking frame kneeling dutifully on the navy-blue bible cover, while Fr Jason, Jacko and Frenzer hold a left hand each over his head, and their remaining hands on their own hearts.

We stand outside the room in silence. We hear everything. Fr Jason and the lads are praying like mad, groaning and running through the whole repertoire. Mixing up Our Fathers, Hail Marys and Rosary Best ofs, with Apostles Creeds, Eucharistic Prayers and God knows what. Eventually, like one of those wind-up war sirens, they reach a pitch where the words start to blend and they go all Jabba the Hutt on it. Wacka-chucka-wanga-bang-jee-coke-pack-nu-neet-solo-see-mi-nigh dah-teel! None of us says a word. Pilibeen starts to sniffle and blub. And then it comes. Daryl's voice, super-high-pitched now, but doing the Jabba the Hutt talk and everything. Eeeeeeeee-solo-seee-mi-ni-haaaaa-daaa-teeel-holy-mother-of-god-holy-mother-of-god-holy-mother-of-god seeeeeee-eeeek-a-chunk-cow-a-wookie!

The fellas in the corridor queue, quietly, and with some determination, start swapping places. Everyone wants to go further back.

After ten minutes of Jabba talk, it goes totally silent. The door then swings open and Daryl comes shooting out, face flushed but beaming with pride and happiness, like he's just been popped out of the best Santa's Grotto of all time. He beams at each one of us, clocking us right in the eye, and says that it was the best thing ever, totally amazing, and that we've got to try it. Blow your minds, lads, he says. Blow, your, minds!

After that it's pretty much a stampede into the green room. Everyone, even Pilibeen, abandons the queue system and goes charging down to get their fix of red-faced gobbledegook. I, however, stay last in line. And when it comes to my turn I just can't do it. It's that simple. I walk into the room, look down at the bible, and stay standing. I tell Fr Jason that it's not going to happen for me today, and that I worry that maybe I have the devil in me, and that I don't want my head to explode apart in a big high-octane super-spiritual battle between good and evil that the task of making me speak in tongues would inevitably involve. Fr Jason gives a disappointed look and says that it's a shame, because after yesterday he was looking forward to my turn the most.

But, he adds, wise to the end, there are more ways than one to skin a cat. And then he sends Jacko and Fenzer out of the room. He pulls up two chairs and we sit down and talk. He asks me what was going on yesterday, and I say nothing. He reminds me that anything I say here, in this quiet green room, is in the strictest confidence, and that he's not the police. I give him a few tasty morsels, while making sure to withhold the big guns. I tell him about Helen Macker and the ball, and how it seemed that she knew what was going to happen to me way before it did. This gets Fr Jason strangely excited, and he gives me a big lecture on how time isn't actually linear, how we don't actually move in line from 'a' to 'b' to 'c'. Instead, he says, life and time is more like a giant pepperoni pizza, just flat out there before us, totally stagnant, unmoving, and we live each event in the pepperoni slices on the pizza, occasionally pinging from slice to slice, but not actually traversing the pizza with purpose. Time, he says, is the great illusion, and God is both the pizza maker and the pizza.

Helen Macker, he says, was probably one of the gifted few who can see the entire slice of pepperoni all at once. In the olden days she would've been a mystic, a prophet, or a witch. Or a god? I ask. Never, he says, reminding me that there is a difference between being able to see the whole slice of pepperoni at once and being able to survey the entire pizza.

He then asks me, leaning close, if I've heard about the multiverse? And when I look at him as if he's still speaking in tongues, he says that there's a million million universes going on right now. And God created them all. And in every one of those universes there's a me and a him going about our daily business, only this one here is the only universe where me and him are actually sitting in a quiet green room having a chat about the multiverse. In all the others we are doing all the other possibilities that could ever happen in every choice we ever made at every step along the way in our lives. And so, he says, in one universe he's probably still an alkie. And in another he mightn't even be living in Ireland at all. He might've gone to America to be with his sisters. And you, he says, meaning me, you mightn't be on the retreat in one, you mightn't even be going to St Cormac's in another, and your parents, in yet another, might not have even had you.

I tell him that it's mad, and that it's hurting my head to think about, and he says that it's God's truth, and just the way the universe, or, ahem, multiverse, works.

I tell Fr Jason that this is all new to me, and dead interesting, and that I think he's one of the best priests I've ever met, and that I want to hear more. But instead of answering me, he looks me in the eye and says, dead serious, and totally out of the blue, 'Who is Father?'

In my head I go, Oh, for feck sake!!! Not him again!!! Because it was like I had almost forgotten everything to do with O'Culigeen at that moment. And I was almost enjoying it all, and thinking about life, and time, and pizza slices and the multiverse like any of the fellas jostling and messing in the corridor outside. Fellas with normal problems, that is. Like being force-fed table-scraps in front of full-length mirrors. Normal fellas who had normal lives ahead of them, with chatty wives and squeally kids, and days where they drank a bit too much and cursed the givers of childhood scars but nonetheless had happy gatherings at Christmas and Easter with all hatchets buried. The very mention of 'Father', on the other hand, is like pulling the chair right from under me. I get a bit of a pukey feeling in my stomach, like I've a better chance of throwing up right now than mentioning that abominable fecker's name, so I just shoot up in my place, tell Fr Jason that I can't tell him anything, and then run out the door, like how Carl Lewis would've run if he was being chased by the dog in that film about a dog that only bites black fellas.

I know Fr Jason isn't going to leave it at that. He's been to Africa after all. He's seen cannibals in action. He's not afraid of anything. And I know he's on my side. He won't rest until he finds out about 'Father'. At least, I think that's the plan.

6

Unhappy Birthday

My fourteenth birthday arrives at something near an all-time low-point in my life. Drudgery in school, me getting worse and worse, and falling out of favour with every teacher on staff, and getting pucked in the arm on a daily basis by Jack Downs. Elsewhere O'Culigeen's post-rape chats have gone completely off the scale. Sometimes, in fact, I think he's raping me just so he can have the post-rape chat. He gets me to lie beside him in the sacristy, on a DIY mattress made of rough red cushions pushed together and covered in a purple picnic rug, and he lights up a fag, or a 'sneaky smoke' as he calls it, the big prat, and starts banging on about all his plans and dreams for the future.

His passion, he says, is travel. He's never been anywhere but he wants to go everywhere. He sucks on his fag and goes on about sunsets over the Pacific and what it must've been like to be a Polynesian tribesman in a little leather boat sailing through giant thirty-footers. And then he tells me how the Polynesians discovered America before the Americans, and how you could sail today from Tahiti to New Zealand by using the stars alone as signposts. Imagine that, he says, tossing the hair on my forehead lightly, and pointing his fag-tip upwards, as if we're lying back and looking up into some gorgeous galaxial vista and not just the dirty yellow ceiling of his own private rape room.

Every now and again it gets really bad, and he asks me to come away with him. He says that he's going to get a transfer out of this dump, all the way to Papua New Guinea. And that'll show them, he says. By 'them' he means his brothers back home in the bog in Sligo. He says, hugging me tightly, that they were mean bastards growing up, and that they made his life miserable and did terrible things to him. Unspeakable things, he says, half crying and kissing me on the temples.

At this point I always ask a few questions. Because this is the danger zone. This is the moment where he could be thinking about having a double-dip, and so you have to be careful. You go a bit silent, and his mind wanders, he starts to heavy breathe, and before you know it, you're screwed. Literally. So a few choice questions, nothing too heavy, just enough to pull him off target, is always the best option.

I ask him what his brothers do now, and he tells me that they never left the farm, and that they run it together. Bastards. Shagging sheep all day, eh? he says, giving me a nod that says we know what these bogmen perverts are really like, don't we? I say, yeah, quietly, and add, none too convincingly, 'Feckin sheep shaggers.' Then before I know it, O'Culigeen is back up on his feet, trousers tightly locked around his waist, business as usual. He gives me a hug and a kiss, and ruffles my hair again. Mission accomplished.

The questions, of course, don't always work

on O'Culigeen. And if they don't, and if he's still getting a bit breathy, I've learnt that my best bet is to leap up and flick on the telly, and hope that something will catch his easily catchable attention. A news report. A GAA match. An old film. I got him once with an old John Wayne cowboy flick on UTV, where Wayne's son, called Matt, who's a real softie but a nice fella, takes over the cattle drive, and sends Wayne himself off on his own into the desert. But Wayne survives and comes back to fight the softie son in a big final punch-up that goes on for ever but is stopped by a woman with a huge gun who tells them both to stop fighting and explains to them that they love each other deeply and that's why they're fighting in the first place. O'Culigeen was hooked from the minute it blurred into focus on the screen. But it wasn't because it was filled with big hairy men punching each other and saying that they loved each other. No, it was a bit in the middle that got him, just before the softie son called Matt sends John Wayne off into the desert, to face certain death. John Wayne is standing by his horse, getting ready to meet his maker, when he suddenly turns to Matt the softie son and, instead of saying, 'Oh Jaysus please, don't do this, spare my life! Please!' he goes even tougher than ever and does a big huge speech about how his softie son better spend the rest of his life looking over his shoulder, because he's going to survive this particular crisis, he's going to get back on his feet, then he's going to spend his own life tracking down his softie son, and then, finally, when he finds him, he's going to kill him. He ends the speech by looking away from his son, and hissing quietly into the distance, 'I'm gonna kill you, Matt.'

O'Culigeen was mesmerised. I could see his little head nodding on his neck, like he totally got it, like this was touching him on only the deepest possible level. Or like he and John Wayne were the only two men on the planet who knew what was what.

At home, I try to act as if the coming of my fourteenth birthday is the most brilliant thing ever to happen me since getting my first pube. I have pubes now too. Not like the big bushy cavemen in the Natural History Museum, where there's so much hair that you can't even see the mickey, but enough to make a difference. O'Culigeen, who is the only person, funnily enough, who gets to see me that way, makes all sorts of snarky comments about me becoming a big filthy buck, now that I've got pubes. But then he adds, real creepy like, that he won't have to start shaving me just yet.

I don't let anyone else see them, but in the house they nonetheless know that the times they are a-changing when I say that I don't want any toys for my birthday. Mam can't believe it, and keeps saying in panic, 'And what about all your *Star Wars* figures?!' As if I had signed a contract to agree to play with *Star Wars* action figures until I was fifty, and now all the neighbours are going to find out when the police come to arrest me for abandoning Han, Chewie and Luke in Hoth costume. My new suggestions for presents are very precise. They range from the twelve-inch remix of 'It Ain't Necessarily So' by Bronski Beat, to a pair of sunglasses, with or without mirrors, but with the same shape lenses as the cops wear in *Chips*. Plus I ask for my first bottle of aftershave — not that Old Spice rubbish that Dad wears, but the new stuff, Kouros, that Sarah came home reeking of recently, and Siobhan said was from Philip O'Malley who'd been necking her all evening against the ping-pong tables in Mount Merrion Youth Club.

I also ask for my first two proper books, real books that adults read, and not the teen guff that Mam always leaves on my bed, featuring action men from the RAF on the front, holding women with busty blouses in one hand and a sub-machine gun in the other. No, these two are corkers, and have come straight from the source. *The Zen of Physics*, first of all, is a Fr Jason recommendation. He passed me on the bike, going through the mucky shortcut behind the brothers' monastery a couple of days after the retreat, and asked me what was my favourite bit. When I said it was the multiverse chat his eyes lit up and he said he was thrilled to have found a fellow convert and promised that he'd lend me his OTHER bible, called *The Zen of Physics*.

Talk about molecules and atoms! Jaysus wept! he says, adding with a nod to the sky, Bless me, Father! He then tells me that it's all in there. The multiverse, the pizza theory and much more. Like? I ask. Like how we can be in two places at the one time, he says, beaming now. Like how there are dimensions in the world that we can't even begin to see or comprehend. And like how we can use our minds and our thoughts to change the nature of the reality around us.

That's it, I'm hooked, and I can't wait. I whack *The Zen of Physics* down on my birthday list, and it gets all sorts of snooty comments from the girls. Mam tells them to leave me alone, and is clearly impressed, hoping, I guess, that this one book will witness a sea change in my plummeting performance at school. The other book is called *The Story of the Eye*. I have no idea at all about the exact contents of this one, but I know that it's got to be a bit mad, considering it's the one book that O'Culigeen has in the sacristy that isn't a Goddy book. And it's one that he's always teasing me with, toying with it, flicking through it and cooing and laughing and chuckling to himself, and then telling me, no way, it's not for little eyes as pure as yours. Then he sticks his nose back inside, and starts gurgling happily away to himself. He says he's read it hundreds of times and never gets bored of it, but he wouldn't dare show it to anyone else. They might get the wrong idea. But because me and him are so close now, there's no reason to keep anything hidden from me. And then he adds, real smart arse like, Except what's inside the pages.

He makes such a song and dance about the book, and he seems to get such pleasure from not letting me read it, that I decide to completely sicken him by putting it, smack bang, on my birthday list, right above *The Zen of Physics*. I know, for a fact, that Mam isn't going to read it anyway. Because I know, for another fact, that she'll barely have time to buy it, wrap it, and stick 'from Claire and Susan with Love' on the gift tag. I know this because she's been organising little family meetings recently, where she stands up against the countertop and tells us that she's reaching breaking point with the amount of housework she's handling, without a tumble drier! (she says this last bit while glaring at Dad). Looking after six all-eating, drinking, clothes-wrecking, money-sucking monsters is a nightmare, she'll say, at her lowest point, with the bottom lip wobbling. And that's not including his nibs! (Again, another dagger.)

We'll usually end these meetings by agreeing to do more housework, and sometimes we even write out a rota for dishes and hoovering. It never lasts long, though, and Mam always ultimately slips back into pole position on the chores front. Which means, for a fact, that she will not have a single minute before my birthday to even flick through the contents of *The Story of the Eye*. The birthday itself, unfortunately, is a different matter.

No one normally cares about my presents. I open them, pile them up in the corner near the green-topped flip bin, and then get ready to cringe at the cake, candles and chorus ceremony. Here Fiona will have made something dry, hard and chocolatey in Home Ec, which will be loaded with all fourteen candles, and there'll be whoops and cheers, and even Dad, head out of his hands for long enough, will join in the chorus. So I'm as surprised as anyone when I see Susan rifling through the pile, flicking through

The Zen of Physics and then settling on *the Eye*. Her face drops in seconds. She does the opposite of the O'Culigeen face, which is all smiley, licky-lipped and excited. Hers, instead, is a bit sicky. She passes it to Sarah, who also does the anti-O'Culigeen face, but reads even more furiously than Susan. At this stage Mam is up on her feet and fussing around Dad, making sure he's got sugar for his tea, and a fork for his cake — although he never uses it, and prefers to just ram the whole slice, no matter the size, right through the wide open mouth until the front of the piece hits the back of his throat and his lips close down over his fingers.

Sarah, the big cow, after five or six pages, has read enough, and promptly hands the book over to Dad. Now Dad — who has been out selling office furniture all day, all week and all his life it seems, and has barely enough energy to keep his eyes open at teatime — often gives the impression of being a man who is out of the loop on his home turf. Though he jokes, at parties, with a glass in his hand and a contented smile playing on his lips, about being surrounded by women and being all on his own in a female fortress, in other quieter moments, when he has no one to impress, this is in fact exactly what it seems like for him. He'll often walk in the door, just as everyone's scraping through the last bit of skin on the rice pudding bowl, and give us this one big collective look that says, Who the feck are yiz all!? Or else he'll play the poor-me card, when he finds himself a stranger to his own children in thoughts, words and deeds, and he'll say, mock hurt, Oh yes, tell your mother everything and tell me nothing! As if Sarah and Siobhan are going to jump on his lap the moment they reach the table and say, Guess which fella I snogged in Blinkers last night?

So, naturally, when he reads a couple of pages of my birthday present, he nearly has a seizure. I will discover later, when I fish it out from underneath the gravy-stained muck in the grey garden bin, that the book is unsparing in detail. Typical O'Culigeen, the big filthy pervert, to fall in love with a tale that's non-stop mickey action. I get a particular chill when I read the bit about the priest getting strangled to death while he's being friendly raped by the girl — I can't help feeling that this is where O'Culigeen got the inspiration for his choking habit. I don't know what pages exactly Dad landed on, but whether it was the mentaller being raped by the horny fella and girl together, or the gang bang in the drawing room, or the girl shoving a castrated testicle into her fanny, it is safe to say that this was not what he was expecting to read around my birthday table, and in front of a dry brown chocolate sponge with blue candles and 'Happy Birthday Jim' written across it in pink icing.

The biggest surprise, however, is that he doesn't go bonkers. He doesn't lash out at me, or chase me around the table and up the stairs (although I've sneakily pushed my chair five inches backwards and angled it away from him, just to give me a head start in case). No, this time, he simply looks up from the book, then slowly over at me. But instead of anger, his face

206

is riven with sadness. He stands up, with book still in hand, and quietly leaves the table, head bowed. Like a man defeated. We all, me and the girls and Mam, pass glances to each other in silence, as if to acknowledge that we have witnessed a man who has truly, and literally, buckled under the burden of the last straw.

Now, the girls have theories about this. And later, much later, if they're feeling a bit mean, and thoughtless, and if they're tracing aloud the arc of Dad's illness, and pinpointing the moment when he finally gave up on life, when he began to sink back into the sadness of sickness, they will point to this moment. Him, walking out of the kitchen, clutching a copy of *The Story of the Eye*, with his heart broken, his wife ignored, his daughters alienated, and his son a sex-obsessed nutjob.

The birthday tea ends with me going quietly upstairs with a slice of Fiona's cake and *The Zen of Physics*, while Mam and Dad argue in the garage about whether I'm a pervert or not. The girls have all given me filthy looks, as if it was my ingenious plan all along to ruin my own birthday tea. I've only been on the bed about twenty minutes, and have just had a chance to look up 'multiverse' in the *Zen of Physics* index, when Mam appears at the open door, all red-eyed, puffy and crying-faced.

I say nothing and just kind of shrug. She sits down beside me, still snuffling back the tears and mucus from the fight with Dad. She's got that look on her face — an awkward half-smile — that tells me there's something to do with mickeys coming up. She gave me the same look before the unfinished 'babies' chat on the way back from Kilcuman.

This time, though, she comes straight out with it, and asks me who told me about the book. I practically wet myself. Not ready for this one. No, sir. I say that I just heard, ye know. But from who? she says. I say, again, that I just heard about it, but she keeps pressing. Like a Rottweiler. 'From who?' is her mantra. I decide I'm going to choose a fella from school, but I have to be careful. Has to be someone credible. Someone mad enough to be a reader of sex fantasies. Mam tells me that she knows I'm protecting someone, but she wants to hear the truth. The doorbell goes as she's saying this, and I'm hoping that I can sit in silence long enough until Mam has to go down to deal with the visitor. Only she's having none of it. She bangs on a bit more about the truth, and tells me that all families are sacred, and our bodies are sacred, and how she doesn't want this kind of filth in the house. So tell me, where did it come from?

Now, of course, I should've been a bit cool about it, and named one of the lads from the retreat. Say, Daryl McDonagh. That would've made sense. In between gulps of burnt potato skins in front of a full-length mirror, his dad might've forced him to read *The Story of the Eye* to see if he could hold his food down while simultaneously reading about a castrated testicle humper. But Mam's voice is getting a bit strict towards the end, and there's anger in there too, so I kind of panic, and just say the first name that comes to mind. Gary!

Mam goes, Gary?!! As if to say, Are you out of your fecking mind? Little Gary with the gadgets?!! But, yes, I say it again, Gary! Gary knows all about it. In this cunning trick, I am picturing O'Culigeen in my mind, but actually putting Gary's face on O'Culigeen's body, which makes the lie easier to spin. Mam, though, wants more details. She wants to know where he got the book from. She says she knows Maura Connell like a sister, like she knows herself, and she just knows that she wouldn't have that filth in her house. This is about to get dead complicated, because I know I have to make up someone else now. Some other luckless character is going to be drawn into the web of nasty sex. And yet, just as I'm about to land it all on the head of poor little Pilibeen, and say that he's way mature before his time, Fiona suddenly sticks her head into the room. She looks at me, and casually says, right at that moment, one of the sweetest sentences I've ever heard in my life.

It's Saidhbh, for you.

7

Saidhbh Returns

Saidhbh comes shuffling into the room before Mam has had a chance to leave. She's gorgeous. A vision in the snow-washed denim of Jon Bon Jovi and Madonna's white 'Borderline' lipstick. She doesn't even look me in the eye, but instead clocks Mam full-on and asks her if it's OK to take me on an outing tomorrow to Knocksink Wood. There's a whole gang of us going, she says. It'll be a grand ole hoolie, wading in the river and marching through the trees, and we'll get some fresh air into those lungs of his! Mam has always been a fan of Saidhbh's because Saidhbh is young and glamorous and religious and not her daughter. She agrees straightaway, but again, gives Saidhbh the serious look, woman to woman, that says, You'll be his mam for the day!

Saidhbh then looks over at me, but not into my eyes, just somewhere above my forehead, and with her own face fixed like a robot, says, blankly, All right fella. Ten a.m. On the dot.

And then she's gone.

My sleep is rubbish that night. I can't imagine what's going to happen. Worst-case scenario, it's another beating from Mozzo, who's probably back to being her boyfriend again, and who's heard about my kissing effort. Best case, she wants to go to a brand-new Hollywood comedy.

As it turns out, it's beyond best. Yes, we meet at ten in the morning. But by one o'clock that day, the day after my fourteenth birthday, me and Saidhbh are snogging like mental all over the fallen brown pine needles in the Wicklow mountains, just eight or nine feet from the main path in Knocksink Wood. It feels as if we're deep deep inside the forest and magical miles away from the track. But that's the effect of the Stag extra-strength cider. And when we eventually sober up later, before we get back, we're a bit embarrassed to see that we were actually doing everything, the works, just feet from the main sun-dappled drag. We cringe when we imagine all the dog walkers and families tottering on by, and seeing us, gripped and entwined at the foot of the trees, faces stuck together like glue, arms locked around each other, for ever. And ever.

So, yes, safe to say that, contrary to her yarn in the bedroom, there was no one else invited to the Knocksink trip. Instead, Saidhbh just grabs me when I round the corner from The Rise and gives me a big smacker on the lips. She says that she has been thinking about us for months now. And that she can't make sense of it all, but she can't make sense either of life without us being together. She then says that, once she had decided to be with me, she had to wait until I turned fourteen before she could act. Because otherwise, she says, dead seriously, because she's four years older than me, anything we do would have been a sin in the eyes of God himself. A mortal sin. Just think of it, she says, a woman of her age, and a boy of my age. It's unholy.

She says, in Goddy mode, that it's taken her months of prayers, and petitioning the Lord, and asking for his permission, and begging him to let this be the right thing in her life. She even did an extra Rosary before bed for fourteen days on the trot. She fasted too, without anyone at home knowing. Skipped three evening meals in a row, and offered them up to the souls, and waited for a spiritual sign to proceed, or not, with our loving relationship.

She said she was already feeling faint, on the last day of the three-day fast, when the sign finally came. It was her period. Came gushing out in Sister Veronica's French class, at least a week early, and sent her fleeing from the room, with her sports bag under her arm and a big wad of school bog roll in her pants. She came bursting into the home kitchen and found her mam at the table, eating a bowl of monkey-nuts and staring into the unassembled hand-cranked meat grinder that she uses for shepherd's pie, and on her first sherry of the afternoon.

They had a chat, she said. Their first real heart-to-heart, about being women, and having periods and what it means in the world to have babies and families and to be the cornerstone of everything that society, even the world itself, rests upon. Sinead Donohue even poured Saidhbh out her very own glass of sherry. Saidhbh said it was a mega-deep chat, and a sign in itself. Especially when, at the end, her mam went on a big rant about love, and how nothing made sense without love. And she looked into Saidhbh's eyes and told her never to give her body up to anyone without love because without it she'd be screwed for the rest of her life. Like a cracked monkey-nut shell, without the nuts.

But what about God? Saidhbh said, in the midst of all this, surprising her mam, yet again, with what a holy moly she could suddenly be when the mood took her, and making her wonder, I guess, even for that split second, how she ended up with a little Maria von Trapp against her best efforts. Well? continued Saidhbh, confused by all this talk of Mr Right and love everlasting. Where does God figure into all this?

Apparently, Saidhbh's mam just smiled, went all knowledgey and wise, took a swig from her sherry, and said, 'God is love.'

Saidhbh said that she wasn't sure if all this meant that her mam had been very careful in her romantic life to pick herself a fella, Taighdhg, who she loved truly and thus had avoided, as she said, being screwed for the rest of her life. Or if she meant that she didn't actually love Taighdhg at all and was, speaking from bitter experience, truly bollixed for ever and warning Saidhbh not to make the same mistake as her. Either way, the nod from God was all that Saidhbh needed to hear, and with spiritually sanctioned love on her mind she hatched her plan to make her move on the day after my fourteenth birthday, which would be, according to her reckoning, the beginnings of my manhood.

★ ★ ★

213

We get the bus to Knocksink, with a huge Deveny's Off Licence bag clinking away at our ankles. Saidhbh has bought all the booze. Twelve small bottles of Stag. Which, for me, who's only ever had two cans of HCL and some straggly bits of party booze from other people's sloppy seconds, will be more than enough to do the job.

It's a cold February morning, and we're wrapped up well, me in a grey duffel over the grey grandad shirt, her in a black bomber with badges over a denim, over a polo, over two T-shirts and a bra. It's sunny, though, too, and as we sit, as is our style, in silence on the top floor as the Saturday-morning bus winds its way up through Kilcuman, Sandyford and into Enniskerry, we sweat from the effect of sunlight mixed together with the smoky bus heater, and so we take off our layers, bit by bit, in a quiet, half-embarrassing striptease.

We mostly hold hands, though, all the way. God, I love her hands. So soft, and so warm, like a dreamy five-fingered skin-plug into the flex of her soul. We squeeze tight, sometimes knuckle-breaking tight, all the way. It's like everything in our bodies, our hearts and our minds are rushing into our hands and all we can do is squeeze for all we're worth, and hope our fingers snap and break and our hands meld into one big sloppy gory mess of blood and passion.

We kiss a bit too. Just little pecks on the lips. Saidhbh is gorgeous up close. I've never smelt her face before, at this distance. And it's heaven, a dizzying mix of make-up, stale coffee and old ladies' lipstick. And even when we get so close

214

that she goes cross-eyed, it's still kind of magic.

We start drinking the booze the minute we get through the forest gates. We drink and walk as we go, along the smaller brown footpaths near the start, and the bigger wider sandy ones halfway up. The goal of the walk is to go from the Glencullen river right up through the trees, along the side of the valley, until we peep out at the top and get some sort of majestic view of Dublin below that will make us feel proud to have made the effort. But we're not that fussed. We've both had about two and a half bottles of Stag by the time we reach the wide sandy path, and that's when our kissing gets a bit crazy and we detour into the trees and the beds of fallen needles.

We lie together on my open grey duffel, taking turns at being on top of each other, and we kiss. And that's all we do. I run my hand over her bra at one stage, but that's only because I'm guessing that it's the right time for that. But Saidhbh nudges me away, just to let me know that this is going to be a kisses-only day, and that no matter what I think I saw her do with Mozzo she's actually a serious woman, a religious woman, with beliefs and convictions and is not going to go to hell because of any mistakes she makes with me.

We kiss for ages. We do this thing called shifting. Which is, Saidhbh tells me later, like Frenchies without the tongues. So we just kind of clamp down on each other's mouths, breathe through our noses and go open and shut, open and shut, open and shut, with our mouths for ever. A bit like we're both eating a very chewy bit

215

of steak at the same time, only without using tongues, and with no steak.

During all this I'm totally loving it, and it's like the best day in my life by a million miles so far. But there's nothing really happening in the mickey department. I'm not all flushed and randy, like I used to be when James Bond got it going with the back-stabbing Chinese spy-girls who were hiding behind his fold-up bed in the downtown hotel room. My heart isn't beating madly, and I don't even feel like tearing off Saidhbh's clothes. Which is probably why she swiped my hand away during the bra feel — she could tell my heart wasn't in it. I even have time to think about lots of things while we're shifting. It's that relaxing. Open and shut, open and shut, open and shut. My mind wanders, and I decide that I must warn Gary about *The Story of the Eye*. I decide too that I'll try to concentrate more in school. And maybe get better grades in my exams because of it. And who knows, I could eventually go to college and study architecture like Mam has always wanted for me, so I could become a famous designer and build skyscrapers in New York and build a nice retirement home for her and Dad down in the country. That last bit was her idea, but I kind of felt the pressure nonetheless. I even wrote 'Architect' on the back of my maths jotter, to remind me what I needed to be when I grow up.

We pull back from the shifting briefly, and look into each other's eyes and smile. Saidhbh calls me Jim the madser. I call her Saidhbh. It's mental, just to be able to say her name so close to her face, and to kiss her. And for those kisses to turn into another fifteen minutes of shifting.

After about an hour of solid shifting, no joke, we take a break. Both of our mouths are wrecked. Our lips are swollen and red, like Ronald McDonald on a bad day. Saidhbh cracks open some more Stag. We slug it down, rubbing the cold glass bottles carefully over our mouths, and lie back underneath the trees, staring up at the branches from below and making chit-chat. This is clearly the best bit, and I can see why O'Culigeen is so into it. Only we don't talk rubbish about travelling the world and getting revenge on our sheep-shagging brothers down the bog. No, we do dead intimate stuff, like stories from our families that we'd never have said before on the bus into O'Connell Street.

Saidhbh, especially, can't wait to tell me about what goes on behind closed doors at Donohue Towers. Says that her dad has nervous breakdowns the whole time, because he can't stand the pressure of being top dog at Coláiste Mhuire ni Bheatha, and because his own dad, her grandad, died in a midnight farm blaze when he was still tiddly, leaving him to be raised alone by a useless alkie mam. This meant that he had to grow up imagining that the whole country of Ireland and all its history was his mother and father combined, and that he belonged more to old gobshites like Michael Collins and Eamon de Valera than the real flesh-and-blood bodies that brought him into the world. She says that half the time her mam is like a nurse to him, taking the booze from his hands, stuffing food into his mouth and cleaning him up before the school day begins. She says the whole thing has turned brother Eaghdheanaghdh into a mute. He doesn't know what to say about it all. Just listens to his constant thrash metal upstairs, head-banging alone in the corner of his bedroom, and biding his time until he's old enough to flee the nest.

Saidhbh tells me that the worst bit is the way people talk about her dad, and gossip behind his back. She says that it's a nightmare in school, and that she's forever crashing into conversations about how her dad is a real-live IRA supporter, and has plenty of no-joke IRA friends, and how he has turned the family home into a safe house for escaped IRA prisoners. Last year, she said, was the worst. The very day after the Maze breakout she couldn't go into a single class without hearing someone whisper about her dad, and her family, and how there was a whole gang of 'RA men sleeping on the floor of their sitting room and the only reason that the guards hadn't been called is that nobody wanted to have their kneecaps blown off in a punishment shooting. It got so bad that she had to leave school for nearly two weeks. And so did her dad. Just until the story died away, which was around the same time that the two lesbian nuns went on the *Late Late* and distracted everyone into hysteria for the rest of the year with a what's-the-nation-coming-to? scandal.

Saidhbh pauses for bit, and I say, Well? And she goes, Well what?

I ask her if there really were IRA fellas on the

218

floor of her sitting room after the Maze breakout. She smiles and says that it's for her to know and me to find out, and then she rolls half on top of me and we start shifting like mad. Really fast this time. Open-shut-open-shut-open-shut-open-shut. Jaw-breaking stuff. It gets really slippy too, which is good this time, because it stops our mouths getting totally wrecked beyond recognition.

We take a breather after ten minutes, and Saidhbh rolls off me and asks about my family. I tell her that it's totally nuts. And that my dad's a bit like her dad, only without the breakdowns, the booze, the songs, and the IRA buddies. I tell her that he acts like he hates us all most of the time, especially me, and just can't wait to fall asleep reading the *Indo* in the evening. I go, 'Bastard!' But I can tell it's not that impressive a story. So I tell her about last night, and the big birthday blow-up over *The Story of the Eye*. I describe it brilliantly, and Saidhbh is in knots as I'm telling it. She strokes my face as she's laughing, and lets her head fall fully forward on to my shoulder in between the chuckles. And as she does I breathe deeply her neck smell, and the light downy hairs behind her ear rub against my lips and I want to die with happiness.

And who *did* tell you about the book? she says, out of the blue, still chuckling as she hits me with it. It was feckin Fr O'Culigeen, I say, laughing my Stag-addled head off, thinking that this is the best bit of the joke so far. Saidhbh stops laughing immediately and says O'Culigeen's name again, with a mixture of disbelief and disgust. The joke

219

is over, but I try to make light. Yeah, I say, the mad ole fecker. I tell her that he had it floating around in the sacristy and I thought I'd check it out. I'm trying to be casual, but everything about Saidhbh changes before my eyes. She starts acting like I'm the enemy, and goes dead quiet, and retreats into her own head. She barely says a word for the next ten minutes, and instead just toys nervously with the neck of her Stag bottle. I'm thinking that this is our very first lovers' tiff, and I start to stand up and suggest that maybe we should be heading back, when Saidhbh suddenly, as quickly as she left, returns to normal. She half trips me up, pulls me to the ground and says, 'Come here, ye madser!' Naturally, we start shifting again.

Later, on the way down the dirt track, Saidhbh apologises for being a bit weird back there, and tries to explain, saying that O'Culigeen, since the day he arrived in Kilcuman, has been the Donohue family confessor and a bit of a favourite with her mam, and that she just can't imagine what a straight-up soul like that, a man of God, is doing with such a filthy book. We walk along in silence for a while, with me saying absolutely nothing, but thinking everything, and not knowing how I could start, what I could say, even if I wanted to say it. Saidhbh breaks the stand-off with a squeeze of the hand, a peck on the lips and a solemn order to forget about it.

8

Dad's Bad News

It's also around this time, just over a month later, in fact, that Dad's tiredness disease gets a name. And the name is cancer. Which isn't as bad as it sounds. For a start, me and Saidhbh are going through a belter of a time ourselves, first love and all that. An unstoppable honeymoon period of passion and abandon that coincides neatly with a first hint of spring in the mid-March breeze. Which takes a certain amount of edge off the blow from Dad's news. In fact, it probably sandwiches us even closer into one inseparable super-romantic unit, slammed together for hours in clingy hot hugs of unspeakable sadness, mixed with slow and slightly mournful shifting.

And Dad, fair dues to him, plays down the whole cancer thing like it's just a very very long and serious life-threatening cold. He doesn't even use the word 'cancer'. Ingeniously, he calls it, 'my neck thing' — which is where the cancer started. Fiona tells me at night, during the first week, from underneath my bed, that it's called lymphoma, and that he'll most likely be dead by the end of the decade, and certainly won't get to see the 1990s in. She's brilliant like that, Fiona. No bullshit. Straight down the middle, but with loads of tears on top. I can hear that she's gagging thickly on her own throat pain as she's whispering up through the mattress.

They don't know where it came from, but Dad suspects it might be because of the new microwave. Mam was one of the first women in the street to get a microwave, and for weeks all the neighbouring mams, including Maura 'tumble-drier-eat-your-heart-out' Connell, used to file in and watch cold coffee go scalding hot, and frozen rolls go squishy in an instant ping. No one could believe it, and everyone kept eating lots of unnecessary rubbish just to be able to say that they knew exactly what food that had been super-heated in fifteen seconds tastes like. But on the days when *Benny Hill* wasn't on TV, Dad was a documentary man. And it wasn't long before he learnt about the possible dangers from cheap Chinese microwave ovens, and what could happen to the human body if the microwaves accidentally escaped and started cooking you from the inside out.

So when the relatives visit, and he comes downstairs for a few brief moments in his scratchy grey dressing gown, with his hair all squashed to the side and his face ghostly and puffed, like he's been sleeping for ten weeks in a row, but in the bowels of hell instead of on a bed, his voice drops to a whisper and he half covers his mouth — as if he doesn't want to offend the oven itself — and announces that he blames the microwave. I blame the microwave myself, he says. He also whispers this because he doesn't want Mam to hear, because in some ways he's worried that this is like blaming her too. The microwave is her one beloved gadget, purchased after yet another failed family meeting, and designed to lighten the workload involved in looking after us lot of savages. She never tires of getting frozen scones from the deep freeze and popping them in the microwave for ten seconds and then announcing to anyone in the vicinity, whether they've heard it a million times or not, 'Would you look at that!'

So blaming the microwave is like blaming Mam, and even Dad isn't thick enough to do that out loud. But still he has his theory. When he walks through the kitchen after that he kind of half ducks when he passes the microwave. Just in case it's still spewing out cancer-causing rays that might start cooking his few remaining healthy cells. Mam knows how he feels about the microwave, and she should get rid of it. But she doesn't. Sometimes when I look at her, flitting about in front of it, pressing all the buttons, listening to the beeps and needlessly defrosting baguettes and bridge rolls, I get a funny feeling that, on some deep and dark level, she's siding with the microwave instead of with Dad. Or that she's happy to swap the former for the latter. If it was a big Hollywood movie she'd be a woman having a love affair with the very robot assassin who tried to kill her husband. Or maybe, on the same deep and dark level, unaware at best, she bought the microwave precisely to kill him. Fr Jason says that in the quantum world intention is everything, and that the bad feelings you have towards someone are easily translated into real-life physical events.

He says that in all the big quantum mechanical experiments that they do in science labs it's the thoughts of the scientists that actually affect the outcome of the experiments. Just by expecting a result you find it. And so, if Mam was furious with Dad for being a ghostly passenger in the house, who drifts in each day and falls asleep under his paper, it was only a matter of time before her angry thoughts, with the help of a few stray microwaves, turned into actual cancer in Dad.

Dad, of course, doesn't tell us, the kids, what's happening inside of his body. And we're not even sure what details exactly Mam knows. She cries a lot, at unexpected moments. She'll suddenly stroke me on the face, burst out crying, and say, 'He just looks so weak!' meaning Dad, but staring at me.

Dad himself embraces his neck thing by disappearing off to the hospital and out of our lives for a full three weeks. During this time the house is strangely calm, and punctuated only by brief bursts of *Hart to Hart* on TV, and Mam's occasional sobs. I spend most of the time in the downstairs cloakroom, with the light off, on the phone to Saidhbh. I don't know why I turn the light off, it just makes it more magical that way. We started doing phone chats with me in the hall but it never worked, and she just got annoyed with me being all stiff and worrying that the girls were listening to my love talk. So I quickly changed positions, and dragged the phone, flex and all, into the understairs cloakroom with the coats and the old wellies, hats and scarves and tennis rackets. I sit on the hard cover of the sewing machine and talk lovey stuff to Saidhbh and tell her about life in the house without Dad, and how I miss her arms around me. She, in turn, tells me how boring it is to be studying for your Leaving Cert, and how much extra pressure is placed upon her, being the daughter of a mega-teacher. It's got to be As or nothing. Especially in Irish.

Naturally, the girls find out about Saidhbh and me during these three weeks, and thus, so does Mam. It turns out to be the best timing in the world because everyone's so concerned about Dad dying that they think the idea of me having a girlfriend who's old enough to finish her Leaving Cert and get a job, a husband and have babies, isn't that troubling at all. Mam is more confused than gutted, like she's been tricked by Saidhbh all along. And the girls go mental the day they find out — not from me, but from Julie Kennedy, whose brother is in the same class as Eaghdheanaghdh at Coláiste Mhuire ni Bheatha, and who tells Sarah all about how things are getting hot and heavy between me and Saidhbh. Sarah is practically drenched with sweat when she gets in the door, from the run home, and bursts in on the funereal atmosphere with the news that Saidhbh Donohue is now my girlfriend. Mam does her confused face, and the rest of the sisters go all squeally and chatty among themselves. Susan and Claire immediately fling themselves at Mam and say that it's not fair, because they were told they couldn't have boyfriends until they were at least seventeen, and how come I'm allowed to have one at fourteen. Especially when Saidhbh is seventeen! Sarah, noticing Mam's quiet distress, tells the girls to shut up, and that they're just jealous because no fellas are interested in being their boyfriends yet. She doesn't, however, let Saidhbh off the hook either, and instead makes repeated eeuuch faces to Siobhan and says that she always knew there was something odd about that girl, the cradle-snatcher. Fiona, meanwhile, simply sticks her head into the kitchen from the TV room, grinning from ear to ear, and gives me a big bold wink. And then she disappears back inside to complete her session with Robert Wagner and Stefanie Powers.

I visit Dad only once during the three weeks. It's the rule. He's left strict orders for us not to be brought in to see him in such a state, but Mam sneaks us in nonetheless when he's out for the count just to, well, show us the body. He's not much to look at, with his mouth hanging dry, wide open, his moustache all grey and patchy, and tubes coming out of both arms. Mam actually says, There's your father, when she shuffles us inside, as if we wouldn't know which one of the blue-skinned cadavers we belonged to. Fiona says later that Mam was doing this for herself more than for us. Because she couldn't carry the burden alone of seeing him every day like this, and so bringing us all in was a way of making it normal for her.

The house, as I say, is dead quiet during this time. Some neighbours drop by to give Mam hugs and say that it must be awful having a hubby as poorly as Dad. They occasionally come in for coffees and biscuits, but you can tell that they're going through the motions. The chat too is a bit serious and quiet, and no mention at all of the gruesome war stories that normally keep them afloat. Not a fatal accident, a drowning or a decapitation among them. It seems that when death is staring you in the face, it's the last thing you want to talk about.

Gary comes over with his mam, and we drift off upstairs and put on a bit of Bronski. Gary, like me, is a fan of Bronski Beat, and is quite happy to sit in silence and lip-synch to words about me and him fighting for our love without feeling a hint of embarrassment. We are back being best friends after Gary saved my life over the whole *Story of the Eye* thing. He was amazing. Cool as a cucumber when Mam marched me to his front door and asked to speak to him and Maura at the same time. When Mam turned to Gary and asked him about *The Story of the Eye* he didn't even hesitate, or even look to me for hints. Simply stared back at her and said, half sheepishly for effect, that it was a book he had heard about from Mozzo. That sealed it, there and then. Mam and Maura looked at each other and said, together, That fella! And then Mam came in for coffee and I told Gary that he was, officially, my hero for ever.

Gary wants to know all about Saidhbh and everything we do, but it doesn't feel right to give him all the gory details. Partly because, as Gary keeps reminding me, not many fellas my age have girlfriends, especially not seventeen-year-old school-leaver girlfriends, and partly because there aren't really many grisly details to report.

Me and Saidhbh are strictly shifting for the moment. We meet up every second night, for a spring evening stroll and a shift, even if it's only for an hour in between her packed study units. Her study timetable has been devised by her father, who has broken up her entire non-school day into hefty and continuous revision chunks — with only brief breathers for food and fresh air. I fit into the fresh-air category. We meet down by The Sorrows' canal, and we walk all the way to the college grounds in Belfield. On the walks Saidhbh will point out the different buildings on campus — the library, the students union, the bar — and imagine, and worry, and wonder about what it's going to be like next year when she's a proper adult student.

And even though her best and her favourite subject is art, she is determined to go and study history, because her father says that it's the easiest way to get into teaching, and because it's good to know everything possible about what happened to the country you live in, and about the ins and outs of Ireland's glorious past.

Sometimes I ask her, even though I know the answer, Yes, but what does she really want to do, underneath it all? Surely she wants to do art in real life, no? She says no, and adds that there's no such job as art. And then she stares at me with a scrunched-up face that implies there is no other job on the planet that anyone can possibly do that isn't teaching, so why did I ask the question? She calls me a madser and turns it round by tickling me in the ribs and asking me what I want to do when I grow up. She's teasing me here, about being a baby who's going out with a real woman, but I take the sting out of the tease by saying that when I grow up I want only one thing, and that's to still be her boyfriend. She goes a bit gaspy on this, and pulls me close. We head to our usual spot, the tiny manicured copse in between the bar and the playing fields, and start, again, to shift like crazy.

So, yes, me and Saidhbh are strictly shifting for the moment. Or rather, I'm strictly shifting. It's not that Saidhbh is trying stuff on left, right and centre, but any time she does, like the time she started to inch her tongue into my mouth, I go a bit mad and freeze up totally, and stop working my jaws and everything. I do the same thing if she starts running her hands down my sides towards my belt. I just freeze until she gets the point, and it's back to stage one.

Saidhbh is brilliant about this, and she doesn't seem to mind at all. The way I figure it is, after Mozzo's roamin' hands and rushin' fingers, she's probably thrilled to have in her arms a lover who's a little less, well, keen. I'm not sure exactly why I can only do shifting and nothing else. I'm guessing it has something to do with being a full-time altar-boy rape victim, but I'm hoping if I persist I'll eventually loosen up in the sex department. In the meantime, as a couple, we are becoming magic at the actual shifting itself. Just the right amount of pressure, the lightest hint of saliva to ease the chafing, and a near-perfect rowing speed. We lie on the grass, anywhere we can, and we get down to it. Not a word between us. And sometimes as we're doing

229

it — open-close open-close open-close open-close — it's like we reach this trancelike state of total oneness. After one of our sessions, a big one, a big forty-minuter, Saidhbh emerges with tears streaking down her face, saying that we had gone to truly deep places. She jokes that maybe it's the lack of fresh oxygen getting into her lungs, but at times she feels like, right at the climax of the lip-lock, she is truly tripping into other dimensions. She says she sees colours, blues and purples mainly, oozing before her eyes, and her mind completely goes blank in love. She says that our shifting is the best secret that any couple have ever discovered and she understands why I never want to stop.

We do shifting in the field next to the Ballydown terrace houses, just before Saturday's Mass. We must have some evidence of it still on our faces because when Saidhbh drops me down to the sacristy O'Culigeen goes completely mental.

9

The Prodigal Son

I ding on the bell just after 6.55 p.m., for a
7.30 p.m. kickoff. I'm technically late, but really,
what's he going to do? I'm pushing Saidhbh's
hands away from mine, all giggly, as I hear his
steps charging towards the door from within. He
flings it open and throws himself outside, going
'Ta-dah!' as he does. And as he does, he waves
three small coloured brochures in his hand. His
face, however, drops like a stone when he sees
Saidhbh, and I barely get a chance to read the
first line of the first brochure, which says, 'Visit
Papua . . . ' before he roughly shoves them, all
crumpled, into his back pocket.

'Oh. Saidhbh,' is all he can say when he sees
her by my side, but he can barely stop his mouth
from curling up into a snarl of disgust. Saidhbh
nods at him, calls him 'Father' but can easily feel
the bad vibes. And so she turns and says
goodbye to me, waits for a moment, to see if I'm
going to reach up and kiss her, then, undaunted
by my obvious inaction, casually kisses her own
fingers and wipes them on my cheek, as a kind of
cutesy farewell.

This makes me feel brilliant, and warm and
safe, but it blows O'Culigeen's mind. Raging, he
shoves me inside and slams the sacristy door. He
rages non-stop for the next twenty minutes,

full-on ranting, right until the moment when little Johnny Carroll, my second-in-command, pops his cheeky ginger head around the corner and we begin the processional. Johnny was forced upon O'Culigeen by Johnny's mam Carmel Carroll aka Curlywurly (she has incredibly curly hair, like an Irish African). Her husband owns half of a hoover factory and has paid for twenty-two brass plaques on the pews that say the names of loads of her dead relatives. She practically owns the church, is forever breathing down O'Culigeen's neck, and so when her boy Johnny came of age O'Culigeen just had to accept him into his flock, despite the fact that he was clearly not the kind of boy that he normally fancies.

So, I can feel still feel O'Culigeen's eyes boring into the back of my head as I'm carrying the big golden cross through the packed church, dead serious, up the aisle and on to the altar. Mrs Daikin from Clannard Close is upstairs on the organ playing her dirgy version of 'God Father, Praise and Glory' when I turn around with the cross and catch his eyes on the altar steps, and they're still kind of mad-looking. He spent the whole preamble in the sacristy calling me back-stabber, and a Brutus and a Jezebel. Not a filthy pup, or anything to do with sex. In fact, I could tell from the way he was looking at me that rape was completely off the menu. Instead, it was all about how much I had betrayed him. His language was all over the place. He called Saidhbh a bitch about a hundred times. And said she was a whore, and the daughter of a drunk. And then he said that I had shat all over him. Like the Brutus that I was. Ripped his heart right out of his chest and shat directly on top of it.

Now, normally, in moments like these, he might go a bit randy at the thought of shits and bums and stuff, but this was a different level of anger altogether. Even out on the altar he can barely contain himself. He does the First Reading and the Psalm through gritted teeth, and then he suddenly announces that he's going 'off-piste' with the gospel-reading and that everyone should turn on their missals to Luke 15:11, for an old favourite of his. At this point he warms up, and slips back into *Knight Rider* mode, and asks the congregation to join in a little game with him. He tells everyone, a full house, to listen closely to the words of Luke, to really listen to what he's saying, but then not to worry, because there won't be a test afterwards. The whole congregation hoots at this. They're the easiest crowd to please, Mass-goers. They're having such a monumentally grim time, thinking about their sins, their dead relatives, and how it's all going to get totally shit after they die, that the worst joke in the history of comedy would still get a sizeable chuckle.

The hooting, nonetheless, gives O'Culigeen a boost, and he immediately decides to go all Vegas on it. Throwing caution to the wind, he turns to me and, still leaning into his own mic, says that he needs some help from his beautiful assistant for this one. Now, on any normal day, and on any normal planet, this would be a risky statement — a bit icky. But here, in Kilcuman village, in early April 1985, during a Saturday evening Mass, it's like the biggest, funniest gag that anyone's ever cracked. More hoots from the congregation, this time half giggling at me in a kindly a-would-ye-look-at-the-poor-fella way. I step gingerly up towards O'Culigeen, aware that three hundred giggling gombeens are watching my every move, and his. He smiles at me, like St Francis of Assisi looking at a newborn lamb, and hands me his own backup bible, open on Luke 15:11. 'You can be the younger son,' he whispers, before winking at me with the eye that's hidden from the crowd. Johnny Carroll shifts in his seat, and gives O'Culigeen a needy look that says, 'And what about me?' O'Culigeen just glares back, a vicious sneer that says, 'And you can feck right off!'

The reading begins. It's the parable of the Prodigal Son, with me playing the title role. O'Culigeen does all the other voices — the dad, the older son, and, most importantly, Jesus, who's telling the story in the first place. He's actually pretty good as Jesus, and drops his voice down into a deep and dreamy 'Once upon a time' style lull that's almost as good as Robert Powell. 'There was a man who had two sons,' he says, dead slow, milking everything for what it's worth. 'The younger one said to the father . . . ' O'Culigeen nods curtly at me for this. I'm standing on the second mic, at the secondary lectern, right at the edge of the altar, where visiting priests usually hover, on big ceremonial occasions, or where the Protestant vicar stood

234

the time they had the all-faith hands-across-the-communities celebration.

'Father, give me my share of the estate,' I say, voice shaking like mad, and quiet, and with not a single bit of O'Culigeen style pizzazz. O'Culigeen almost rolls his eyes when he hears my delivery, but goes on nonetheless as smooth Jesus, describing how the father then divided the property up and handed the loot out to the younger son. Now, O'Culigeen's normal practice is to break up the actual text with little asides and footnotes, and anything he thinks will 'enrich' the gospel experience. So here he goes on a big lecture about how the estate would've been an olive-yard, and describes how olive trees take a full fourteen years to mature, and how valuable they are, and how you can get up to twenty gallons of olive oil from a single tree. Although nobody in the congregation seems that interested in olive oil. Certainly not twenty gallons of it. This is strictly a butter-only community, and they only use 'that foreign muck' for treating dry scalp, or to make the skin more glisteny when you're sunbathing. In fact, Sarah has her own baby bottle of olive oil that she brings with her any time we make it down to Silver Strand in Wicklow, or Barley Cove in West Cork. On those days, with the sun belting down and everyone sweating like dogs before a quick dip into the icy water, Sarah simply lies there, still as a corpse, and dripping with freshly applied layers of olive oil, just to make sure that every single ray of sunlight that's racing down from the fiery heavens is bending and curving towards her fresh and fragile Irish skin, nuking every single cell within, and turning her into a third-degree burns victim that will eventually, for two days, and only after the bubbling and blistered skin has flaked away dead on to the floor, look a tiny bit brown.

So the olive-oil lecture isn't one of his best, but it's nowhere near as manic as where he goes next. He looks down at his lines, and it's as if he's only just realised what's coming. Because his mood totally changes. 'Not long after that, the younger son got together all he had, and set off for a distant country and there squandered his wealth in wild living.' He says all this in a dead serious growl. Still low and deep, and Jesus of Nazarethy, but a bit angry. He goes into footnote mode and glares around at the congregation, silently nodding, before finishing up at me and saying, 'Do we know what Jesus means by 'Wild Living'?' He doesn't let anyone answer, and instead keeps on staring at me, saying the words 'Wild Living' over and over again.

'He means . . . ' O'Culigeen pauses, and scans the crowd for kids. You just know he wants to say words like 'fucking' and 'shagging' and 'arse-raping' but instead he says, super-loud, 'CAROUSING!!!'

He looks over at me, all mad-eyed and furious lips, says the word 'carousing' again, and then delivers the rest of the rest of the verse right at my lectern, without taking his eyes off me, without even looking at the page. All off by heart. He finally comes to the bit where the younger son recognises the error of his ways, after years of famine and pig scraps, which means that it's my cue again. 'How many of my father's hired men have food to spare, and here I am starving to death?' I say, this time with a hint more confidence than the last, kind of getting used to the character, and even putting a little whine into it, like the Billy Barry kids who do song-and-dance routines on the *Late Late Show*. 'I will set out and go back to my . . . '

O'Culigeen interrupts me, with a raised hand, and whips round to the congregation for another enriching footnote. This time he asks everyone, with a vicious gleam in his eye, to notice how the younger son is driven. Not by guilt, he says. Not by compassion for his father. Not even by the recognition that he has fallen from grace. No! he says, again catching me in a sidelong glance, the younger son is fuelled by selfishness, by hunger, and by the animal need to feed his own gut. He gives me a curt nod, as if to say, That showed you!

We go on like this through the whole reading, ping-ponging back and forth. Me doing the selfish son, better and better, eventually even getting the accent right, going for the Arabic guy who works in Luigi's kebab shop on Ranelagh Road and who says, 'fecking bashtar' a lot, for 'fecking bastard'. And O'Culigeen, being angry and a bit mad and explaining everything in a way that's meant to educate the audience and make me feel bad about having a girlfriend at the same time. By the last verse, however, O'Culigeen, the big ham, decides that he's had enough of punishment duty, and gets right back into the forgiving flow of his character. He gets to the bit where the older son, also voiced by O'Culigeen, is going bonkers, and can't believe that his dad has welcomed back the young wastrel with a feast of fat calves and booze and the best of Bronski.

O'Culigeen pauses dramatically here, and gives a little half-chuckle to himself. An inward smile of sorts. Something he knows that we don't know. He then addresses the audience as if they were the older son, and slowly, even as he's speaking, begins to walk right across the altar, Val Doonican style, towards me.

'My son,' he says to the crowd, who are intrigued by his showmanship, and have never seen the walk'n'talk before — certainly not in the middle of a reading — 'You — you are always with me, and everything I have is yours. But we have to celebrate and be glad because . . . '

He reaches my lectern, puts his hand on my shoulder, and lets me see up close his wild red eyes, glistening with real tears, the creepy old bollix. 'Because this brother was dead, and is alive again . . . ' He pauses once more, and actually gags this time with emotion. Not trying to hide it any more, in fact, positively showing off, he closes his eyes and raises his head heavenwards, and lets the tears stream freely down his cheeks. It's a genius move. Some of the old biddies in the front pew burst into floods in sympathy. He's got the entire congregation in the palm of his hand. 'He was lost,' he continues, and this time he opens up his arms, both of them, as if waiting for me to hug him. ' . . . And now he is found!'

He stands there, all teary-faced and puffy-eyed, his arms out wide, looking like the sorry sap that he is, and waiting for the climactic hug. I can feel the whole crowd willing me on, and at this stage I'm so beyond protesting that I let myself fall into the big stinker's filthy chest. His arms lock around me tight and the entire congregation, all fifty-six pews and the standing room at the back, bursts into spontaneous applause.

The hug goes on for ever. My face is squashed completely into his armpit, with only my left eye poking out just long enough to scan the faces of the satisfied throng. They're in ecstasy, all the old biddies in the front pew, thundering away, clapping their arthritic paws to pieces. Inside, I'm kind of having the weirdest oddest laugh in my life at the whole thing, and at the gas of it all, when my roaming eyeball is drawn to one lone worshipper, sitting deadly still amidst the grannies, wearing a bright-red coat, black leather boots, lightly dyed blonde hair, and a mildly disgusted expression on her face. I've already started saying to myself, 'What's her problem? Didn't she catch the whole show?' when I clock her closely, pull my second eye out from O'Culigeen's armpit, and recognise her fully and for the first time. It's Aunty Grace from England, and she's staring right at me, giving me a look that's saying, in no uncertain terms, 'What. The. Fuck?'

10

Aunty Grace

Aunty Grace knows everything about everything. She's Mam's younger sister and has been living in London since she was a teenager. She knows all the modern stuff that the English know and that the Irish are just learning. So when she comes over it's always dead exciting, and there's always a chance that she'll start talking, right in the middle of dinner, about sex and divorce and being gay. Not that she is gay herself. She's been married and everything, but her husband, my uncle, had too many affairs, so she left him, and now she lives alone in a big house near the Queen's garden and is married only, she says, to her work.

When Aunty Grace left for London it was a big deal. Mam said that the whole family was crying and weeping for weeks, as if Aunty Grace had gone off on a coffin ship, never to return again, instead of just a ferry to Holyhead. Although Mam says things were different in those days, and that the Irish in England had a worse time than the niggers, the pakis or the kikes.

Aunty Grace says that it's actually worse now than it was when she first went over, because of all the bombs, and the IRA. And that every time some horse gets blown apart in Hyde Park she gets weeks of death threats and heavy breathers, phoning her at all hours and telling her to pack up and get out of the Queen's own good country. 'Go on, you Irish bitch!' is the usual one, she says. It's hard too, she says, when you're on your own, and it's night-time, and every creak in the house could be one of the mob, sneaking up the stairs to tar and feather you and chuck you out the window. It was different when her husband, Nigel, was around. They never threatened him, because they thought he was English in the first place. Mam said that all of her family thought Nigel was English too when he came courting with Aunty Grace way back in the day.

She was only seventeen, and he was already deep into his twenties, and had a dead flash job working for the civil service. Mam's parents loved him at first sight, and practically gave him a free pass to have his way with Aunty Grace whenever and however he wanted. He had a curly moustache, and wore his hair slicked to the side, and Mam said that her dad, my grandad, used to call him 'King George' behind his back. They only found out later, after he and Aunty Grace left for London, that he wasn't actually English but from Carlow, and had always fancied himself something of an English rogue ever since his mother told him, at a young age, that his father wasn't actually his father but had been an English sailor on leave up the Liffey for one night only.

So Nigel became his own dandy, and became his own dad in a way too, a great lover of women, and with a posh English accent to boot. Mam told Fiona that Nigel never actually wanted to go to London, really, but that getting Aunty Grace in the family way was the last straw. So the two of them left from Dun Laoghaire harbour, amidst much weeping and wailing, with Mam, Grace and Nigel alone holding the real reason for the departure close to their chests. It was Nigel's decision. He was too young to be a father, he said. Too young to be tied down. But he'd do the right thing, and pay for it all, and take his chances in the UK. Mam told Fiona that it was a mad old farewell, with everyone hugging and kissing King George himself, and telling him he was a great man to be taking Grace on such a serious life adventure, and everyone telling Grace to take care of herself and of her fella, and all along Grace would be just staring at Mam, sharing the quiet and hard secret that she was going across the water to kill a baby, nothing more, nothing less.

Fiona says that the abortion was pretty rubbish, and that Aunty Grace nearly died because of it, lost her womb and everything. But on the upside Nigel agreed to marry her and to change his woman-loving ways right then and there while kneeling at her almost-death-bed. However, Fiona says that Mam says that Grace changed after that. Became hard as nails. Only married Nigel because why not. Got a job herself as a secretary at a law firm. Had loads of affairs for a while, totally turned the tables on Nigel and even used to bring her fellas home while he was in the house. She made all the cash too, while Nigel scrounged for jobs, which didn't come easily, especially when he found that his posh English accent wasn't actually that convincing in England itself, and rarely got him further than some labouring work on a building site, or shuffling cupboards for a removal firm.

Aunty Grace eventually calmed down and made a new name for herself as a recruitment boss who hired out secretaries to the very randy lawyers that she used to go with herself when she was feeling all angry about having no womb. She gave up on men altogether, even on Nigel himself, who she eventually kicked out of the house. He went back to being a ladies' man, and began running his own wine wholesaling business and got his accent down pat. Fiona says that they'll never get an actual divorce, even though they don't see each other from one end of the year to the next, because once you've almost died with someone, it kind of cements you together for ever, even if you hate each other. Aunty Grace had an idea, briefly, that she might even adopt some children on her own, but Fiona says that the part of her that would've done it was too long dead inside her and she didn't have the right equipment to bring it back to life. Instead she concentrates on being brilliant in work, and living in a huge flash house in the Queen's own private park, and having amazing leather clothes, and being a brilliant aunty to all of us.

You wouldn't have a clue, when she's over with us, being the life and soul of the party, getting everyone up dancing, and talking all modern-like about sex and gays, that she is, as Fiona says, hard as nails. But when you think of all the phone calls she gets in the middle of the night, telling her to feck off back to bogland for being a big Irish bitch, and how she doesn't give a feck about everyone knowing the story of her life and how she got here, then you get just a tiny hint of how tough she must really be deep down inside.

I get a bigger hint when she grabs me by the shoulder outside the church and tells me she's hauling me right up to the sacristy to confront O'Culigeen, and to ask him to explain, in plain English, just what sort of godforsaken abomination had occurred right in front of her eyes on the altar of a holy fecking church. She says that she's hot off the plane from London, here to help Mam on cancer watch, and was going to surprise me with a lift home in her hire car, but now can't believe what she's just seen in broad daylight. I plead and beg with her, big time, not to do anything, not to cause a fuss, because O'Culigeen, I warn her, will only make it worse for me if she does.

Worse for you? she says, with mouth agog in disbelief. What do you mean, worse for you? Now, there's a moment here when I could answer her. I could explain. And of all the people who had looked for answers thus far, be it Saidhbh, Fr Jason or even Fiona, it was my Aunty Grace who was mostly likely to get a real answer. But I don't. And I don't know why. I only know that I can't. And so, instead, in my silence, and via the power of a vaguely

244

constipated expression alone, I try to let her know that she has, perhaps, momentarily forgotten what country she is in, and that this just isn't the way we do things over here, and that her English attitudes might actually upset the apple-cart completely, rather than shake the bugger out of it.

She doesn't buy it. She grips my shoulder even tighter and drags me round to the sacristy door, telling me that we'll see right now who's worse off at the end of all this. She barely gets a finger on the brass knocker before O'Culigeen's there in person, vestments off, and back in his man-in-blacks, and with the madness in his eyes. 'There you are, ye little scamp!' he says, reaching out and grabbing my other shoulder, with barely a word to Aunty Grace. She holds tight on her side while O'Culigeen's own fingers dig deep around my clavicle, curling up under, and into, my armpit. He hits Aunty Grace with a barrage of information, about what a chancer I am, about what a good actor I am, how I should be on the stage for life, how I've been begging him, O'Culigeen, to do more performance readings on the altar, and how the whole thing is my idea, and how he humours me because I'm a terrible fella and because of my poor father, and wanting to give me some sort of enjoyment, and some kind of outlet for my pain in these sad and terrible days.

Aunty Grace tries a few 'buts' and 'yets', but she's no match for a horny priest with a hefty dose of rape on his mind. Because as he's talking and mentioning me, again and again, he's looking at me like I'm the best fecking blancmange in Clery's café that he's ever seen, and his eyes are bulging and telling me that, if he can work his magic on Aunty Grace, he's going to finish what we started so romantically on the altar. And it's not going to be pretty.

He's like a battering ram. Doesn't draw a breath, tells her that I was out of order for skipping out this evening without hanging up my surplice or anything, and that there was a good half-an-hour's worth of work to be done back there before I could consider myself a free man, ho ho. He winks at Aunty Grace and tells her that he's sure that everyone back home could do with as much breathing space from the young 'uns as possible, considering my dad's condition and everything, and that he'd be more than happy to drop me off later in the car, once my chores are done.

I can feel Aunty Grace's grip loosening on my shoulder and I think, feck! And shit! And all the words that mean I'm in for something that might finally push me over the edge tonight. O'Culigeen can sense it too, and he's practically got his trousers down as he pulls me momentarily free from her grasp. It's all going hunky-dory for him, and Aunty Grace has pretty much given up the fight, when she says to O'Culigeen, harmless as anything, 'I'm his Aunty Grace, by the way.'

Now the big thick country bigot had a million ways he could've played this. A million ways. Most of which would've meant a glorious result for him, and a hateful, possibly fatal night of pain for me. But instead, his own worst enemy, the little small-minded, spud-munching gobshite had to go and say, 'Oh, I know all about you!' And he says it in such a way, all pointing downwards with his nose, that means in no uncertain terms that he is referring to Aunty Grace's past life as a fallen woman in London.

Bam! Her hand is plunged back into my shoulder like the spear of Satan itself. She pulls me so hard out of O'Culigeen's grip that she nearly takes his own hand with her, and makes him give a little yelp of agony as the tops of his fingernails are suddenly snapped backwards with the jumper jolt of it all. 'The boy needs to see his father,' she says, cold as graveyard stone. This was tough Grace, hard-as-nails Grace, in action. She then turns on her heels and drags me behind her through the darkening Saturday evening churchyard. The last glimpse I catch of O'Culigeen is of him standing there in disbelief, angrily sucking on his damaged fingernails, and giving me a look that lets me know, without a doubt in my mind, that the next time we get together in private, I am as good as dead.

Aunty Grace drives me home in total silence, and doesn't mention another word about O'Culigeen. She spends the weekend in our house whispering to Mam over coffees and wines in any quiet corners they can find, about big plans and big changes that need to happen, and fast, in order for Dad to stay alive and Mam to stay sane. I catch snippets of their chat, and it mostly revolves around sick-pay, and how we're running out of money, and how Mam can't afford, in both financial and energetic terms, to

247

run the household and to play nurse to a dying man at one and the same time. Aunty Grace's flight back to London is Monday morning, and thus Sunday night ends with a climactic meeting in the sitting room, kind of like the results section of the Eurovision.

Here, while Dad's upstairs, lying on his bed in his dressing gown, we three youngest are sitting round the fire with toast crumbs in our pyjamas, after eating bananas on toast and watching *Glenroe* and *Murphy's Micro Quiz-M* back to back. We are told by Aunty Grace, who's basically leading the meeting, like the spokesperson for Mam, that it is time for the family news. Fiona, Sarah and Siobhan come shuffling into the room, all red-eyed, like they've been crying for ages, and with Mam following close behind them, and actually crying, and before they have a chance to speak a word Aunty Grace announces that Sarah and Siobhan are going to move out of the family house to their own flat, which they'll pay for with a handsome donation from Aunty Grace together with the dole money they get now but spend mostly on fags and fellas in Blinkers — the total monies, all considered, aren't a lot, and might only get them a poxy little place in Cabra, but will hopefully encourage them to get better jobs so they will eventually be able to afford to move south of the river.

Before we have time to process this, she turns to Fiona and speaks directly to her and to us at the same time, saying that Fiona is being taken out of school and coming back with her to England on Monday morning, to work with her

248

in the recruiting business. Fiona gives Aunty Grace a half-nod of thanks in return, but doesn't dare look around at the rest of us. And that means that the little ones, continues Aunty Grace, meaning Claire and Susan, will have to start pulling their weight around the house from now on, with extra housework and less time gadding about with their friends. And me? I say, perhaps a little foolishly. Aunty Grace just looks over at Mam, who's kind of glassy-eyed and zonked through it all, and then back at me and tells me, solemnly, that I'll have so many things to do around the house, manly things, like fixing the central heating, and cleaning the chimneys, that I won't have time, from this very night, to partake in altar-boy duties ever again. Ever.

11

The Next Two Months

The next two months are the best in my life. Really. Turns out that having half your family taken away from you and looking after your dying dad is a bit of a breeze after all. Sarah and Siobhan have got a deposit down within a week, and are out of the house before the fortnight is up. They share a tiny one-bedroom flat in a grim three-storey tip on Hamilton Street, just off the North Circular road. They say, on Sunday visits, that the move was the prod they needed to fulfil their futures as bright young independent women in an emerging Ireland. Within the month Sarah has a job as a cashier in Allied Irish Bank, while Siobhan is working in the men's fashions section of Dunnes Stores.

The Monday-morning farewell with Fiona is pretty gruesome, everyone all weepy at the front door, as the taxi man puffs on his John Players and we get a taste of the real Ireland from hundreds of years ago when you were born to leave home before your time. She gives me the biggest goodbye of all the siblings and squeezes the feck out of me, telling me always to check under my bed for ghosts and ghoulies and to keep my precious Saidhbh safe from harm. I love that last bit, because it makes me forget about the hard and tight lump of sadness that's stuck

250

in my throat and concentrate instead on the feeling of manliness glowing in my stomach.

Once the door shuts behind Fiona, Claire and Susan almost instantly go into seventh heaven mode. They each grab a room for themselves, and are happy, as per the new rules, to exchange a daily routine of washing up, hoovering, and even making a tray of brown scones, bran buns or German apple slices for the privilege. They can't quite believe their luck, in fact, and they secretly treat Dad's cancer as the best thing that ever happened to the family.

Me, I'm told to buckle down at school and am given a new roster of home duties that include lots of manly stuff, like using Dad's prized hatchet to chop blocks of wood into kindling for the fire. Or filling the coal bucket up from the bunker out in the back garden. It's mostly maintenance related stuff, and the central heating is the biggie. Dad himself makes a big deal of it, and shuffles down, grey scratchy style, and announces over sodden Weetabix that it's time to teach me a few things about the house. 'Because I won't always be around, ye know.' He says this last bit without a drop of feeling, like he's reading from a manual underneath the table that gives you handy hints on what to say to your son when you're going to die but don't actually want to talk about it.

Sometimes, when he's being like this, all deathy, but not, I want to run up to his face and scream, 'Cancer, cancer, cancer, cancer!' a million times, just to see what he'd do. My top guess is that he'd stand up, reach for the cane in the corner of the kitchen, give me a belt on the backs of the legs, and then run into the sitting room, flop down on the couch, drape the *Irish Independent* over his face and fall asleep.

Although he pretty much stopped using the cane when the cancer came along. Fiona said it was because he was discovering his inner humanity, and the senselessness of violence, and how we are all connected everywhere by love alone. But, looking at him wheezing through the kitchen, on his way upstairs to take another dose of secret pills from his sock drawer, you only got the feeling that he was too exhausted to cane anyone, but that the minute the strength returned to his arms he'd be back in action, whipping and thwacking with the best of them.

So, I learn lots of manly stuff, and I try my best to knuckle down at school — although there, I'm given special kid-glove treatment the minute they find out about Dad. Most of the students, except for Gary, stop talking to me, in case their dads get cancer too. While the teachers offer to let me have days, weeks and months off class, as long as I want. Fr Jason is especially good about it, and is forever cornering me in the yard, telling me about his brother who died of leukaemia when he was only a child, and how a tremendous calmness descended upon him a couple of weeks before he passed away, a knowingness and an understanding of the preciousness of every minute of life. Fr Jason says that his door, up there in the monastery, is always open if I need to drop by and talk over anything. My father or, well, you know yourself, anything.

The central heating, as it turns out, is dead easy, and I can do the whole job in under ten minutes. I use Dad's smallest Phillips screwdriver to unscrew three tiny screws from the ignition casing, after which I slowly and gently remove the entire ignition housing unit from the body of the central heating boiler itself, then dip a paint brush in some white spirits, and finally clean the spark-plug free from heating soot, replace the unit, and the casting, and press ignition, and nine times out of ten the whole system fires into gear without a bother.

Saidhbh is dead impressed with my new role as man about the house and, as a joke but not really, she sings the pop song 'So Macho' whenever I come to her with grease on my knuckles or stories of how Dad put his stainless-steel vice-grips in my hand and made me slide under the car and change the oil. She sings it sometimes right into my ear, when we're spooning in bed together, up in her room, or my room, and messing about in the quiet mid-morning after having real-life honest-to-goodness sex.

Yes, things go completely mental in the physical stakes with me and Saidhbh. Once I'm free from O'Culigeen's grip it's all systems go. It's only a matter of days, in fact, after Mam's made the call to O'Culigeen, announcing my retirement — she said that O'Culigeen was furious, and tried every ruse in the book to keep me in the job, even offered to pay me, and at the last minute insisted, fruitlessly, that he be given a chance to say goodbye — that me and Saidhbh actually start using tongues during shifting.

253

It's amazing how quickly it gets out of hand. It's tongues one night. Down to pants the next. And before we know it, we're both bunking off school, waiting till our respective houses are empty, then sneaking in upstairs, pulling the curtains closed and having complete and uninhibited nudey-nudey action. It's totally brilliant, like a combination of playing doctors and nurses, and feeling like you're exploding with excitement from the inside out, and then, occasionally, just very occasionally, feeling like you're going to burst out crying and be physically sick with sadness as you look at the other one and realise that you can't actually melt into them and become one big huggy-kissy-weepy bed-bound beast.

And we do everything too. Saidhbh can't believe it, and neither can I. She says the whole time that she's definitely going to hell for this, and she sometimes says it like she really believes it too, but that only adds to the atmos. In the thick of it, she sometimes whispers out quiet little prayers of mercy, like 'Lord have mercy on my soul' or 'God forgive my heathen actions,' but it doesn't actually stop us doing what we're doing.

She says that the priests in Kilcuman church and the nuns at Coláiste Mhuire ni Bheatha would collectively string her up if they knew what she was doing. And she can't believe how quickly we've gone, in a matter of weeks, from breathy shifting to the works. And we didn't have lessons or anything. She goes on top, or I go on top, or she goes on top again. And we just get on with it. Like naturals. Our favourite, which is a bit of a cogger from the films, especially *An Officer and a Gentleman*, which we watched together on UTV's Friday Night at the Movies, is where we don't stop staring at each other as we're doing it. Right from the beginning to the end. Real slow-like, and just staring. Eyeball to eyeball. Which makes us giggle like mad at first, and then pull our heads in even closer, clunking our foreheads together, as if we're trying again, hopelessly, to become the one big huggy-kissy-weepy beast. We usually end that one with loads of groaning and ooh-ing and aahh-ing.

We're pretty good at controlling the noises, though. We even do it while Dad is in the house. In the mornings he's normally knocked out in bed on cancer medicine, and so doesn't really have a chance to hear anything, even though we do it in total silence. But just in case, when we sneak upstairs and into my bedroom and we put a load of school books on the floor in the unlikely event of him waking and shuffling towards the room to see who's there — at which point we plan to leap out of bed, fling open the curtains, rip on some trousers and tops, and assume the manner of two very curious if slightly sweaty students.

We don't go in for the kinky stuff, though. We tried once. Saidhbh asked me if we should try doggie doggie, and I said why not. But it was all too weird in the end. We couldn't do our eyeball thing in any decent form, although Saidhbh did try twisting her head backwards, and I managed to lean myself forward and clunk her forehead

255

once before she spasmed away from me with the pain of all that heavy twisting. Otherwise the whole thing gave me creepy flashbacks to O'Culigeen, and his teeth gnashing, and his grippy hands and his curses and his hate, which killed the mood in the mickey department and sent me flying down on to the bed beside Saidhbh for some old-fashioned cuddles and kisses.

It's during one of these sessions, in mid May, just after ten in the morning, when Mam's doing the weekly shop in Quinnsworth's, and the girls are at school and Dad is passed out asleep, that I first tell Saidhbh I love her. I kind of get all upset, nearly crying and everything, and tell her that there is something welling up inside me that I just have to get out or else I'll be sick all over her. She beams excitedly, because she has an idea of what's coming, and then I pull her close to me under the *Sesame Street* covers, stare at my parked Porsche poster and say the words, 'I love you.'

Funny thing is, I don't know at all how the words make her feel, but it's the most amazing thing on the planet to say them myself. Like fireworks going off in my mouth and depth charges in my soul as the words come out. Saidhbh doesn't say 'I love you' back. Which is cool. And at that moment I know that we'll have a whole lifetime left together when we're married for her to tell me that, and besides it was about what needed to come out of me, not what I needed to hear. She does, though, go all coy, and pulls the sheets up to her eyes, so that Ernie's chin is just poking out under her nose, turning her face into half-woman, half-muppet, and tells me that she has something to say too. Go on! I say, a bit nervously, hoping that she's not going to say she's expecting a baby, although she has totally got that sorted and says that she can tell exactly when she's in the danger zone by the pain she gets in her side and will be able to keep us safe from babies for years to come. What she does say, however, is that I'm the first person ever to have sex with her. This seems to be a huge deal for her. Bigger than it is for me. She says that she knows what people say about her, that she's kind of mad, and half-nun, half-whore. But the last bit isn't true, and up until now, she's been all nun in that department.

I ask her about Mozzo, and remind her of all the groping that I saw at her family hoolie. She says that it was nothing, and that Mozzo was always trying it, but never even got beyond her underwear in those days. Not like you, sending me straight to hell, ye dirty madser, she says, reaching down and giving my mickey a right yank, and in a way that's supposed to be funny but is actually a bit painful. At which point she cuddles even closer and goes, casual as anything, And you? I should feckin hope that I'm your first! And then she laughs at the very thought of anything else.

Now, maybe I'm still a bit sore from the yanked mickey, or maybe the way she giggles, like I'm the baby and she's the mother, just rubs me the wrong way, but I think of her question, then I think of O'Culigeen, and I go and say the words, 'You were. Kind of.'

Kind of?!!!!!! Bam! She's out of the bed like a bullet and reefing up her jeans, face flushed, eyelids instantly brimming with tears. What the feck do you mean, Kind of!!!??? I tell her to be quiet, because her screaming is going to break through the cancer medication, and Dad'll be in here in seconds! Kind of!!! She says it again, this time followed by the chant of 'Who was she? Who was she?' I start pulling on my trousers too, as I realise that she's actually having a full-blown fit, and is moments away from storming out of the house.

Her last words, as she slams the front door, and as Dad eventually stirs in his bed, are, 'And you can forget about the fecking Debs!'

12

The Debs

The Debs is the highlight of the school term, of the school calendar, and of the school social scene. In fact, it's the highlight of just anything that happens in school, from the first nervous steps you take through the front gates with your mam in hand to the final walkout from the final exam. It's the climax, in other words, of the whole life that you have lived, and the person that you have been, while you were there, under that roof and inside those gates. And it takes the form of a big dance at the end of the last summer term, a bit like the American Prom, only with extra doses of booze and vomiting, that symbolises the end of your life as a young childish student with no cares in the world and the beginning of your adult existence as someone who drinks too much and feels slightly sick all the time.

It happens in snazzy and not so snazzy hotel bars all over the country, and Fiona says that it's like a mass disease where for one night only the entire nation covers its eyes and sticks its fingers in its ears, and pretends that there's nothing odd at all about tens of thousands of seventeen-year-old darlings hitting the hard stuff till the wee hours, and mostly ending up in broken bedraggled heaps, with clothes torn and stained, faces smudged and stomachs turned inside out on the pavement before them.

It's a release, isn't it? Mam says to Gary's mam, when they're chatting over soggy bickies, and talking about Seamus Kennedy's Debs, and how he got his nose broken down in the docks when he tried to get an early morning chaser from a tough city boozer while still in his monkey suit. He was with his Debs herself, Fianna Malarky — because you call the girl and the dance the same thing. She was standing by his side in a purple chiffon dress, and the bar owners, dead scuzzy Dubs, allowed her to come in but not him, and then they knocked him about, left him unconscious down a side street when he called them knackers.

Gary's mam agrees that it's a great big release for the children of the nation, and their one chance to get whatever it is they've had knocking around inside them for thirteen school years out of their systems via a pre-dance drinks, a sit-down meal, a jazz-band performance and an after-band disco followed by an early morning fry up and a shame-faced taxi-trip home.

The subject is foremost on Mam and Gary's mam's minds because of me. Everyone knows I'm going to Saidhbh's Debs, which is a huge thing, especially because I'm way underage, and because it's the only piece of good news to ping through the front door of our house in months. Saidhbh, of course, had to ask Mam's permission to take me, and it was a big scene, with Susan and Claire banished upstairs, while Saidhbh and Mam waited by the fire for Dad to appear and nod his bleary-eyed approval too. Saidhbh and Mam then half hugged each other, like they'd agreed on the wedding date and everything, and then Mam let Saidhbh run up to my room and tell me the good news — this was all, of course, before the big bust-up over me not being technically a virgin.

The word gets out in school too, courtesy of Gary. And before long it's Debs this, and Debs that, and everyone calling me Finno the Madser for being the first fourteen-year-old bender ever in the history of the school to get to go to a real live Debs, and with a girl too. Gary tells me that some of the teachers have said that it's a disgrace, but that they understand why I'm allowed go, considering my dad's dying and everything.

Naturally, I'm absolutely bricking it, in case Saidhbh has really called it off. I won't know where to start with the explanations. Tell Mam first and hope it spreads out from there, via the coffee-morning mams' information service. And then how to face everyone, and take their triple and quadruple doses of pity, knowing that I'm the only guy in the country for whom not a single sliver of life ever goes right. And so, out of a combination of worry, loneliness and just the sheer gut-wrenching agony of being on the other end of Saidhbh's huff, I send her this huge mad letter — written in biro on jotter paper, with spirally doodles all round the edges, and done right through the night, that says everything about how much I love her, and how afraid I am to lose her, and how I held back on the virgin thingy because I was unsure of what sort of man she wanted, and wasn't sure if I could be that man, or if I was even a man to begin with. You know? I write. 'So Macho', and all that.

I stick it through her letter box, with an 'eyes-only' stamp on it, from one of Gary's gadget collections, at seven in the morning, under the pretext of nipping out for an early morning jog, because I'm allegedly trying to get fit for the Big Day. Although Mam gives me a dead confused look when I arrive back in my black-and-red tracksuit, as if wondering what exactly I plan to do on my Debs that will require tip-top physical fitness. I tell her all the fellas are doing it, just so we'll lose a few pounds and look our best in a monkey suit, and she seems satisfied enough.

Either way, the letter does the job, and Saidhbh arrives later that morning, just after Mam dropped Claire and Susan to The Sorrows, full of huggy-huggy sadness and a renewed belief that we are the one couple on the planet who are destined to be together for ever. There is only one thing, however, she says. And that's the sex. She thinks we were wrong to get going on it so quickly, and considering my age and everything, she wants us to stop it. She's even contemplating going down to the church and begging for a clean slate in confession, from the PP himself, Fr O'Culigeen.

I panic at this, and tell her not to be an eejit, and in a big rush of words I add that love is good and God is love and love is sex and sex is love and if love is good and God is good and sex is love then God is sex and sex is good is God.

And that no priest is going to understand that unless they've had sex, or love, or both. And I add, just for good measure, that O'Culigeen is the last person on the planet who's going to understand any of this, because he's a lifeless old stiff, and not qualified to talk about anything other than the bible, the price of olive oil and prodigal fecking sons! She hugs me some more and tells me not to be such a blasphemous little hot-head, and that she can't confess now, anyway, because O'Culigeen has had to go down to the bog on family business — a funeral of one of his brothers — and that she wouldn't dream of confessing to anyone else but him.

In the meantime, though, she says, tweaking my nose, no sex for you.

* * *

We have sex three times in a row on the morning after the Debs, and it's a hoot. Slap bang in the middle of the Donohues' sitting-room floor. We're both bleary and blotchy from the night before, Saidhbh in a great big purple dress with stiffened felt breast-plate and soft puffy shoulders, and me in the monkey suit and extra-gelled hair. We can see from the toilet mirrors in Abrakebabra on Dame Street that we look wrecked, and we've been drinking so much and dancing so much that we're kind of just hovering in a shaky blur rather than walking or standing. Naturally, Saidhbh promised my mam that a drop of drink wouldn't cross my lips all night, considering my age. But that was scrapped the minute the taxi dropped us off into Jury's car park in Ballsbridge, and we bashed around with a load of Saidhbh's Mhuire ni Bheatha buddies who all had naggin bottles of spirits because the price of the drink inside was wicked. I took enough slugs to floor me in the first ten minutes, and then got chatting to some of the older Debs fellas, who were pretty decent, and elbowed me a lot and treated me like I was a mascot for the night — I always got first drinks at the table, and a big punch on the shoulder whenever I finished a pint. Saidhbh got them all calling me a madser, and before long I was one of the gang, boozing and joking and flicking peanuts at the bar girls with the best of them.

Saidhbh and me did snogging and sexy stuff in the loo during the jazz band. But I was basically numb from the eyelids down. One of the older fellas, Fergus, a big rugby type, came hammering on the cubicle door, saying that he needed to get in there with his mot, meaning his Debs, Barbara, and he kept yelling for whoever it was, meaning us, to get the feck out. But when Saidhbh told him to feck off with himself, and that this cubicle was booked for the long term, he leapt up on to the door frame and, staring down at me half undressed, and Saidhbh's gear all hitched up to God knows where, he just burst out laughing and shouted out to everyone that the little madser was busy at work in the loo.

Naturally, we didn't dream of coming back to mine in the morning. Mam would've been horrified to see the state of me, to smell me, and to know that all sorts of sacred trusts and truths

264

had been broken during the night. And besides, it would've been too much for Dad, to briefly break the fog of drug-addled isolation at the crack of dawn, to find his only boy bleary-eyed and banjaxed to the world.

No, instead we crash into Donohue Towers at 8 a.m., just as Taighdhg and Sinead are on their way out the door, with Eaghdheanaghdh following silently behind. They're much cooler than my folks about booze, the Donohues. Especially coz their dad's an alkie, and is hardly going to start lecturing them all on the evils of drink when he can barely get his brogues tied in the morning without a bracing shot of Jameson.

Saidhbh says that even if her dad was anti-booze, or if he became anti-booze overnight, like the way my mam did when she took the pledge, he wouldn't do anything about us, because he was far too busy with all the political stuff to care about something as trivial as teenage boozing. Being a teacher means that he is practically running the country, and always at union meetings, and urging people to form community groups and strike and march and vote on this, that and the other. Which is part of the reason why his nerves are shot, because he's so exhausted from trying to fix the country.

At the moment he's knee-deep in 'RA prisoner rights and the fallout from the Eighth Amendment, says Saidhbh. The first one is all about making sure the British Government don't get the 'RA boys beaten up in prison just because they ruined Christmas for everyone in London by blowing up the English version of Clerys. And the second one is about making sure that our country isn't overrun with West Brit heathens who want to turn all our women into sluts and make them kill their unborn babies with broken vacuum cleaners and sledgehammers against their will. She says it's dead important, and one of the biggest battles that the teachers have ever got involved with, and a chance to show the world that in Ireland we recognise that babies in the womb are just as important to us as adults on the street, or in the pub.

And she's right. Because Taighdhg barely says a word to us as we stumble in his front door, looking like zombie tramps from a black-tie horror film. Instead it's up to Sinead, who's all dressed up in big earrings and bigger hair, in high-glam tour-guide style, and busy trying to give Eaghdheanaghdh a side-parting with a bit of spit and the palm of her hand, to say that she hopes that we had a smashin time at the hoolie last night, and that there's fresh Brennan's in the bread bin for toast. The three of them bundle themselves past us through the door and into the car and, after some false spluttery starts and wheezy engine whines, scoot off noisily into the early morning work rush.

Saidhbh leads me inside, straight into the sitting room, where she lifts up all the fallen newspapers and makes a clean space in the centre of the floor, by the gas fire, and pushes the coffee table into the corner, right against the record player. We then, without a word, get stuck into each other, like animals. It's completely mad, and if we hadn't had our jumbo doners thirty minutes earlier in Abrakebabra, I'd say it was almost like we were devouring each other for once and for all. There was eatin and drinkin in it, as Mam says about the best soups she makes. Although I'm sure she's never thinking about Dad's mickey when she says that.

The session goes on for hours, upside down, back to front, inside out, and all around the garden. By the end of it we're sprawled out across the carpet, laughing and panting and giggling and half crying at the sheer lunacy of two people being this happy, and sweaty and naked and slightly nauseous all at the same time.

I have a shower, and get back into my manky monkey suit, and tell her, joking yet testing the waters all the same, that she's going to have to do some major confessing to O'Culigeen when he gets back from down the bog. She holds my face and kisses me tight, sticking her tongue, real tough like, right into my mouth and licking the roof like she's proving that we've moved beyond sexy and can do things now like licking each other's tonsils in a friendly way, and then she pulls back and says, eyes rolling, 'You're telling me!'

★   ★   ★

I skip on home up The Rise like a fella on fire with happiness. There's no car on the slope, which means that Mam must already be up at Mass. Which is handy, and also means that I won't have to do the big post-party chat until I've got my story good and straight, and have carefully removed all the forbidden bits about

267

boozing and feeling and getting hot and heavy on the carpet down the road.

I swish through the garage doors, and have already got my hands on the Weetabix box when there's a shocking rumble down the stairs and none other than Dad appears at the kitchen door with a mad look in his eyes, the last few clumps of hair on his head poking up with rage, and spitty fury firing out of his mouth. He calls me a corner boy, and wants to know who in blazes hell gave me permission to stay out all night? I tell him that it was the Debs, and that everyone stays out for the Debs, but he just shouts Debs Me Arse and lunges at me with his dressing gown trailing behind him. He says that although Mam may have been born yesterday down the bog somewhere, he's a Dub and Dubs aren't thick, and Dubs know exactly what I've been up to all night. He says, again, that he's not thick and that just because he's lying in bed upstairs every day doesn't mean that he can't hear me and Saidhbh doing 'the filthy' whenever we get the chance. He says he knows exactly what's going on, and right now, this is the last straw. He says all this with his hands now holding the collar of my monkey suit. He stinks something awful. Like morning breath, pee, and a bit of death all mixed up.

He says that it's an absolute disgrace, at my age, and he gives me a shove. His hands, however, are weak as anything. And it's a bit like being shoved by a dizzy scarecrow with no hair and bad breath. I shrug him off with ease, drop the Weetabix box on the table, and dart up the stairs before he's had time to steady himself against the cereal shelf.

Normally, he'd give up now, and stumble into the sitting room, and spend the rest of the morning on the couch, sweating and trying to get his breath back. He hasn't chased anyone up the stairs in months, maybe even a full year. Because of his condition. But something's flipped in him this time. And sure enough, I'm hovering outside the bedroom door when I hear him, in a mad half-pelt, shooting out the kitchen and up the stairs, bamboo cane clattering the banisters as he goes. It's like he's channelled every last pulse of energy in his weedy body down into his legs.

Feck! I dart into the loo and lock the door. He's on it in seconds. He bangs hard like a bastard, and roars at me. He tells me that I'm a disgrace, a disgusting disgrace, and that I'm no fecking son of his. He bangs hard on the door for a good half an hour, calling me a disgusting disgrace whenever he has the breath. He kind of collapses eventually, and sits on the floor, propped upwards against the door.

Mam comes home from Mass and gives a right yelp when she sees him there. I eventually emerge and help her to drag him into bed and she calls the doctor. Dad gets given more painkillers, and a huge bottle of Lucozade, and is told, from now on, to get out of bed only twice a day. He never mentions the Debs again. Not to me. Not to Mam. And, wherever possible, from this day forward, he avoids talking to me, or looking me in the eyes, or generally acknowledging my presence at all.

13

Preggers

Saidhbh tells me that she's pregnant just under three weeks after the Debs, on 21 June 1985. It's like that book says. The best of times and the worst of times. And at these times, me and Saidhbh are stronger than ever, and back doing the nudey-nudey full-time. And she's even stopped threatening to go to confession about it. We're like real adults, and we go to the movies, and we study together, and we kiss, and I quiz her on her upcoming Leaving Cert biology papers — aqueous and vitreous humour, all thirty-three vertebrae, the venal and the renal, and so on. And she tests me on my Peig, and on next year's history and geography books, all in the hope that I can pull myself up by my bootstraps, and not be such an embarrassment to my family and my dying dad.

And in these times too, and in that department, and despite all the gloomy words from the doctors, Dad stays in a permanent state of dying without, thankfully, actually dying. He still doesn't ever get out of the grey scratchy dressing gown but, despite the new orders, he leaves the bedroom whenever he feels like it, to come downstairs to make a bit of chat with Mam, and to eat some dry toast, and very occasionally to get riled up and furious when

Gay Byrne has a whole show devoted to divorce. This has a positive knock-on effect on the whole atmosphere in the house. And even though he does his very best to ignore me, and barely passes a single glance in my direction from the morning of the Debs meltdown onwards, the general mood around the place becomes much less like a funeral home. Mam, for a start, seems happier, and she goes back to calling Dad a terrible man, and boasts about how every cloud has a silver lining and how she's not doing half as much cleaning up any more now that she has her 'little maids' to help her.

At this Susan and Claire usually chirp up and do a version of a song they learnt in Sister Maureen's English class, where they go, with hands together under their chins, 'Two little maids from school are we!' And anyone who's listening laughs, even Dad. They boast too that becoming maids was the best thing that's happened to them, and that they can now change the hoover bags, and make an entire tray of German apple slices without Mam's help. Meanwhile, Sarah and Siobhan come home every Sunday, with exciting tales from the worlds of banking and typing. They hand over cash to Mam and they eat the big Sunday roast, and they can even, depending on his form, drag an old argument out of Dad — who pulls his hands away from his face long enough to say that they're both dirty Jezebels now that they're living on their own and going to nightclubs and staying out till all hours and doing God knows what in the back of heaven knows whose car.

Things are going well for Fiona too, over in England. She sends over typed letters, from Aunty Grace's electronic typewriter in London — one to Mam and Dad, one to the girls, and one to me. And in them she describes her working day in the recruitment firm, and how a lot of her job is about calming all the young girls down when they get to reception, and helping them to fill out their forms. Because some of them, she reveals, are from way down the darkest parts of the bog, and have only just made it, by the skin of their teeth, all the way over to London. The poor little things, she says, they try to hide it from her, but after ten minutes of shape-shifting on the reception sofa it's obvious to see that they can't read or write.

Aunty Grace, however, is apparently brilliant with them, and always manages to calm them down, and give them a little lecture on being a bit of a gobshite for never going to school, but then she still manages to find them some sort of work, even if it's just day here or a day there, making coffee for some big-city flash boys with red braces and cigars. Fiona writes that it's brilliant living with Aunty Grace, who has always wanted a daughter, and that even though she seems tough on the outside, the two of them get on amazingly well and spend most nights, till the wee hours, drinking red wine and chatting about fellas, specifically about this bloke called Deano, who works in the recruitment office and has his eye on Fiona. In her letter to me Fiona says 'wink wink nudge nudge' after the word Deano, but to everyone else she just calls him Deano.

It's her code for saying things are going very well in the shifting department.

At the end of her family letter she asks how everyone's doing, each by name, and she even includes Saidhbh when she mentions me. This kind of thing would normally get a big oooooooh from the girls, especially during Sunday roast, with Sarah and Siobhan there, but the best thing of all that's happened recently is that me and Saidhbh have become so normal that no one says a thing, and just lets it flow past them unnoticed. In fact, the subject of me and Saidhbh is so old that no one even flickers any more when it's mentioned. No child-snatcher jokes, no me-and-my-granny jokes, and no sneers about k-i-s-s-i-n-g up a tree. It's just dead normal, and in fact is more than normal and makes me seem brilliant in the eyes of Mam at least, who is forever rubbing my head and telling me that I'm a very mature boy for fourteen, and that Saidhbh is a very lucky woman.

Of course, Mam initially couldn't help herself, and one day on a casual walk in Castle Mount Park, she gave me a good grilling about what me and Saidhbh actually get up to when we're alone. There was no excuse in the world at all for the walk. It was around four in the afternoon, the girls had just got in from school, and Dad needed to be woken for a shower, because his old work chums Jack and Aoife Madigan were coming over to visit tonight, and Mam thought he looked a state with the old white stubble growing goodo all over his face. He'd have to hook the shower pipe up because a bath would just wreck him completely for the rest of the day, she warned. So she was in the midst of all that — of giving Dad a lecture about not being dead yet, and needing to find some gumption and clean himself up, and also preparing tea for the girls — when she suddenly asks me if I want to go for a walk. I knew, straight away, from the way she wasn't looking at me, that it was going to be just like our sex-talk walk. So I kind of agreed, like the way you do when Spits McGee asks you to come up to the board even though you know he's going to thump you when you get there.

So she waits until we hit the gates of the parks, and then she leaps all over the subject, saying that she'd been listening to Gaybo's radio show this morning, and it was all about the young people today, and what they get up to when the parents aren't looking. And what they do at Wesley and Bective discos, and how the Gardaí are always finding girls and boys feeling each other's mickeys and fannys in the stands at Lansdowne Road at midnight. And she knows that I'm way too young for any of that, and that Saidhbh is more like a big sister to me, replacing Fiona, she guesses, but with a little bit of kissing, because she's heard that from Claire and Susan, but she just wants to check that there's nothing else going on but kissing.

Naturally, I act all Don't be stupid, Mam, sure I barely know what kissing is! I'm totally over the top with how rubbish me and Saidhbh are with anything other than holding hands. In fact, I don't even admit that we kiss, and instead make an eeuurrghh face whenever Mam uses the

274

word. I let her bang on with her theory that Saidhbh is the new Fiona, because it seems to make her happy, and makes her feel that some element of her life, at least, isn't falling apart at the seams.

She chats away by herself for a while more, and we round the basketball courts, and go through the tiny bit of the park that's vaguely woody and would definitely hold perverts, rapists and abusers at night-time. And then, finally, just as we start to turn back towards the main gate, Mam goes all weird, and her voice goes a bit throaty and snotty, and she tells me that if we had divorce in Ireland she would've divorced 'your father', meaning Dad, years ago. She doesn't say why, but I guess that all the talk about couples and kissing and what to do and what not to do has started making her think about the beginnings of her love life, and all the fellas that she used to kiss in the porch when her own father would bang down on the floor from above. And maybe she was thinking of one fella in particular. Because Dad always slags her off about Tim Coolan, this awful bald eejit who calls once every three months to the front door, and brings chocolates for the family, and a snooker statistics book for Dad, but is really here to see Mam, because they used to be boyfriend and girlfriend back in the day. Tim is widowed, but Dad jokes that he killed his own wife because he couldn't get over losing Mam to a handsome whizzkid salesman like himself.

These slaggy joking sessions usually don't last long, with Mam either joking back at Dad,

275

telling him that she chose the wrong one there, clearly, or else just sharply telling Dad to shut up, and making all of us take a special note of that one, because it definitely struck home. And anyway, as I say, after telling me that she would've divorced Dad if the country wasn't so backward and full of finger-pointing bogmen, she goes really quiet and snuffly, and without looking up at her once I can tell that she's crying like mad. Part of me wants to ask her, Are you thinking of Tim Coolan? But the rest of me knows that it must be totally rubbish being married to a human dressing gown that's inches away from dying every day, and comparing that to when you look back at the first time you kissed a fella, or he held you in his arms, or the first time you told a fella that you loved him, it must be like comparing the world's sweetest and lightest and creamiest pavlova to a plate of shite.

Either way, she has a big weep, and by the time we get home it's all over, and she's ready to get going again as World's Number One Mam, to lift Dad out of his dressing gown and hoist him into the shower, and maybe even shave him at a push. Plus she'll do the girls' tea, make them eat their potato-cakes, and listen to their stories about who is a fecking cow, and which teacher is picking on them, and about how much money they'll need for the school trip that Mam can't quite afford to send them on. But most of all, Mam will be content in the knowledge that, no matter what's happening around her, and how the world is falling apart, at least her son, her only son, her precious son, isn't like one of them kids on the Gaybo radio show, and actually doing real-life rude stuff with his girlfriend.

★ ★ ★

Naturally, I don't tell Mam about Saidhbh being pregnant. I don't tell anyone, in fact, not even Gary. I'm in shock mostly, for a whole day after she tells me. She just phones up ours on a Sunday morning, speaks to Mam and asks her to tell me that she needs me to come to hers urgently with the biology notes she left up in my bedroom. This is a mad message to leave, and clearly rubbish, because her Leaving Cert biology exam is already over, and she screamed and whooped last Wednesday evening about how she'll never look at another biology note for as long as she lives.

Nonetheless, I gather up a load of old papers, some of my history mixed with her biology and geography, flash them at Mam and the girls, who've come back from Mass, and tell them that I'm on an important mission to save Saidhbh's Leaving Cert. Secretly, I'm dead excited, and I'm imagining that the entire Donohue clan have just whizzed down the driveway and Saidhbh is already lying flat out on the big double bed upstairs, waiting for her man to arrive and do all the good stuff that makes us both so brilliant together.

Sadly, that idea gets rubbished the minute Eaghdheanaghdh opens the door with his big bored puss on him. He looks at me and shakes his head and tells me I'm in big trouble, because

Saidhbh's been crying all morning and their mam and dad know that it's my fault. I can hear Taighdhg from the sitting room shouting out, Is that him? But another voice, Sinead, quickly silences him, and tells him to mind his manners. He says that manners is what it's all about, and as the two start snapping at each other, and deciding just whose business all this actually is, Eaghdheanaghdh flicks his head backwards, towards his left shoulder, meaning that I can slip past him and up the stairs.

I can barely imagine what in feck's name is going on until I burst into the bedroom and find Saidhbh lying in a heap on her covers, and holding her tummy with cupped hands, like she's either trying not to fart or she's hiding a newborn kitten behind her fingers. I know straightaway. I just know. I don't even have to ask her. And she doesn't have to say. Instead, she does a big snuffle, wipes her red ruffled face, pulls back the pillow she's been lying on, and then flings three white plastic sticks at me. The sticks, she later tells me, were purchased at the Dublin Well Woman Centre, in Ballsbridge. She had to make the trip into town, last Friday, especially for them. She says she got the brain-wave, like a bolt from the blue, during PE, when everyone started moaning about their periods and she, suddenly, realised that she hadn't had hers in yonks. She bunked off school that very afternoon and flew into town on the 62 bus. She said they were nice in the Well Woman, but a bit too nice. Very chatty, and trying to ask her to sit down and tell them everything about

278

her life. They were good-looking women with kindly eyes, and nice jewellery, but Saidhbh was having none of it. Just the sticks, please, and nothing else.

The sticks are home pregnancy testers, and they work through the magic of piss and windows. She peed on all three of them, and each of their tiny glass windows told her the same thing — preggers.

I ask her if she's told her parents, and she says that she's not a complete thick. Though, she adds, she must be pretty stupid to let me do this to her. I say, hurt, and still not sitting down on the bed beside her, that I didn't 'do' anything, but she doesn't listen. She's off wailing and ranting, asking me how the hell she's going to become a teacher now, and what's her life going to be like as a mam at seventeen? I tell her not to panic, and that there's a way out of this, because there always is. She gives me a look. I'm thinking on my feet, but I'm remembering Don Cockburn on telly, and the news stories, day in and day out, during the Eighth Amendment debates, and the girls they interview in shadows who've gone over to London on the ferry, and sorted themselves out. Hard shaky voices of women whose souls are now as black as their shadows and can never have a public face again because they've killed the babies in their tummies.

I tell Saidhbh that I have thirty five pounds saved in my post office account, and that could easily get us to London and back, if we got a cheap ferry. She goes bonkers, and bursts into floods, and tells me never to say what I've just

279

said again, and asks God to forgive me for what I just said. And then she cups her stomach even tighter and cries some more, and says sorry to the baby inside her, and curls up into her own baby position, and tries to pull her own hair out in frustration at the fact that two days ago everything was perfect — she was in the middle of her Leaving Cert, and perhaps only inches away from becoming a happily married teacher, and now the boy she once loved is talking about using his life savings to pay to have her baby killed.

She mentions God about ten more times and I roll my eyes with frustration, and tell her that God has already done his bit in this crisis. Saidhbh sneers back at me and says that 'He' said I'd be like this, and 'He' said that I'd try and persuade her to take care of it, and, most of all, 'He' said that she'd have to be strong, and keep the baby no matter what.

And 'He' is? God?

No, she says, calling me a smart arse, and adds, casual as anything, that 'He' is Fr O'Culigeen. Yes, she says, that's why it's all kicked off today. She did the test on Friday, and has known since then, but couldn't think straight about it until she went to confession this morning after Mass. She says that O'Culigeen was brilliant, and closed up shop just for her, and took her into the sacristy, and gave her a one-on-one session, and said that I was a bad penny, and that she must keep the baby at all costs, but end the relationship with me at once. Hence the crying and the confusion.

I tell her that O'Culigeen is full of shite, and she asks me to leave. And not by the front door either, she says, pointing to the window. She tells me that her dad wants to kill me with his bare hands, because I hit his only daughter right across the face during an argument after Mass. I give her the 'What?!!!' face, and she tells me that her dad came up with that one all by himself, when he saw her falling in the door in tears. And because she was still in pregnancy-shock, and couldn't think of anything reasonable to say in my defence, and ran upstairs into a heap instead, the story just kind of stuck. Him shouting, He hit ye, didn't he? He hit ye? The little bollix! He hit ye!!

I climb down from Saidhbh's window, monkey style, by holding on to the heavy metal drainpipe and scraping my knuckles, both hands, against the hard yellow pebbledash of the paint job. I run home, up the long grey arch of The Rise, with my fingers scraped and bleeding, and my head cocked around my shoulder, just in case mad Taighdhg Donohue has revealed his true face and already sent an active IRA flying column in hot pursuit to kidnap me and teach me how to behave around women by blowing off my kneecaps and knocking out my teeth. And all the time I say words like feck and shit and bugger to myself, and I can't quite believe just what in shit's name has happened to my life.

I think about Fr Jason's own story, and wonder is it too late to take a detour to an inner city church and fling myself on to the hard marble altar, and wait for the glowy man from

281

heaven to appear from nowhere and take away all my troubles with a magic abortion-tipped thunderbolt from the palm of his hand. I feel sick at the very idea of me and Saidhbh heading off, some manky Monday morning soon, to catch the ferry at Dun Laoghaire with my life savings in my pocket, and Saidhbh looking like the living dead beside me, and all the stories and all the lies that we'll have to tell, just so we can both ruin our lives, our minds and our souls for all eternity, without anybody finding out.

I'm thinking about all this, and about how right Mam is, and all the coffee morning mams, when they tell you with serious faces that life changes in the blink of an eye. One minute you've got your fur coat on, and you're crossing the road from Castle Mount Church, the next you've paused to wave at Margaret McDonald from number 40, and you've tripped on your own heels and fallen smack against the approaching kerb, and split your head in two right down the middle, dead. The fur coat. Totally useless now, they'd say. Because you can't bring it with you. No, you can't bring it with you.

I'm thinking that I wish I had smashed my own head against the kerb instead of ruining the life of my only love and becoming enemy number one on the hit-list of a known IRA big shot — and it's not as if I can say, No, Taighdhg, I didn't hit her across the face, I got her pregnant instead! And that's not even mention-ing Mam and Dad. The news will definitely send Dad to his grave for good. The last few healthy

cells will just shrivel up and die of embarrassment when they hear. The girls will go bonkers,
Gary will flip, and I'll probably get expelled from
school for unnatural animal behaviour.

So, as I say, I'm thinking about all this as I put
my key in the garage door and clock, straight
away, what is by then an extremely unusual
sound coming from the sitting room. Yes, it's the
thum thum thum of *Hooked on Classics*. For a
moment I get a flush of happiness, and dart
inside the house, instantly giddy in the knowledge that Dad, for the first time in for ever, is
feeling well enough to crank up the record player
and fill our home with the loud, consistent and
strangely clappy electric beats of Tchaikovsky,
Mozart and Mendelssohn.

I even picture Dad in his suit, clean shaven,
armchair back against the wall, elbows out, paper
folded in his lap, feeling good enough and smart
enough to crack jokes at Mam's expense. And
the girls, Sarah and Siobhan, back from the flat
for the day, and feeling happy enough and homey
enough to tell Dad, with a smile and a giggle,
that *Hooked on Classics* is rubbish. I whizz through
the empty kitchen, and straight into the sitting
room, expecting nothing less than the no-holds-
barred restoration of familial bliss as it once so
briefly was, but what do I get?

Fr O'Culigeen himself, sitting on the couch
like an evil vision in black, clutching a cuppa and
a German apple slice, with his feet tapping to the
music, and a big broad beamy smile on his face
that he instantly flashes to me, as if to say, You,
my friend, are a fucking dead man!

14

The Plan

Of course, what he actually says is, Hello there, stranger! And gives me a big wink and a smile. He's sitting alone with Mam. The girls have been sent upstairs to play with their Sindys. Dad is asleep. Mam, who is also clutching a German apple slice, has put on the record especially for O'Culigeen, so that the 'Dance of the Swans' with a beefed-up drumbeat can provide the perfect bash-bang background music for their Sunday morning heart to heart.

O'Culigeen, Mam says, right in front of his face, is here for the family. Here to see how Dad's doing and everything. She says that he's very encouraged by Dad's progress and hopes to see the whole lot of us back together for the 10.30 family Mass very soon. She adds that O'Culigeen even blessed Dad while he slept. Leaned over him and asked the Holy Spirit to come down from heaven through his body, along his right arm and into Dad's body, and to finish off the last bit of medical work that was needed there, and to bring Dad finally back to the land of the living. And do you know what? Mam says, leaning forward with a giddy grin on her face. Your father woke up at that very moment and said that he felt hot!

And feeling hot, O'Culigeen told her, is a sign

that the Holy Spirit is fully entering the body and working its magic. Mam opened the bedroom window for some air, and Dad fell back to sleep again, but Mam was sure he looked more peaceful this time, because he had the power of God inside him. And then she says, Thanks to the Father here!

O'Culigeen puts on a holier than thou expression and nods solemnly, like he's the best priesty in all Ireland but doesn't want to admit it. I say nothing. I just look at the two of them, blankly, and wait for the famous O'Culigeen trap to spring. And then it does.

Oh, and the Father has a surprise for you! Mam says, half spitting out a few pastry flakes with nervous excitement. He is bringing yourself and a whole rake of young boys up to Three Rock Mountain for a camping weekend, next Friday. And before I can say a word about how completely mad this is on every possible level, she tells me not to bother, that O'Culigeen has told her everything about us, and about how I had become too friendly with him, and too close, and started treating him like an older brother in my time of need, and not like the respected pillar of the community that he is. And because of what was happening at home, with Dad, O'Culigeen didn't want to come down too hard on me, so he indulged my obsession with him, and said nothing when I stole some pennies from his wallet, disrespected him when he was going live, on the altar, and drank a half-pint of communion wine in the sacristy. No, she said, O'Culigeen was prepared to wipe the entire

285

slate clean, forget all past indiscretions, and to start off anew, with a bit of healthy bonding all weekend long, out in the midst of mother nature.

O'Culigeen smiles. A real greasy one. Game over, it says. You're a dead man, it says. The moment I get my hands on you.

We look at each other, me and him, for what seems like an age. He's got a seriously demented look in his eyes, and a light covering of sweat on his forehead. It's like that short ten minutes with Saidhbh in the confessional this morning, and the news that she is preggers with my baby, has totally pushed him over the edge. Like it's driven him instantly out of the sacristy and into his car and right up to our front door, with a head full of impulses and a rashly hatched plan, just because he can't stand it any longer and wants to make some sort of angry point. He wants to show me who's boss, and what I'm missing by not being by his side, in his life, in his dreams and in Papua New Guinea, holding hands in the bush, spotting rare species of monkeys, dodging flesh-eating tribesmen, and then kissing and screwing together all night long under the South Sea skies.

I don't know what my eyes say back to him, but Saidhbh's news, and the baby in her stomach, and the world that's warping all around, has changed me too. Changed me utterly, as Spits McGee would say. Because in my heart, and for the first time ever, perhaps the first time in my entire life, I tell myself, No!

I have five days to sort this fecker out. If not

286

for me, for the sake of my unborn and soon to be dead child.

★ ★ ★

The journey all the way up to Three Rock Mountain passes in near total silence. Neil Hennessy, a little blond ten-year-old twerp from Kilcuman scouts whose mam died last year, is the only one who says anything. He's never been away from home ever, so this is a really big deal and, for a while, he can't stop asking stupid questions. Are there going to be bears on Three Rock Mountain? Will there be wolves? How do we go to the toilet in the dark? Will there be potties in the tents? How will we keep the sheep away from our food? And so on. No one answers him anyway. And otherwise, in the back of the rented HiAce, it's total silence. The other three boys, all hard-bitten altar-boy stock from the church, have nothing to add. I'm guessing they've each already had a taste of O'Culigeen at his worst, and so are either dreading what sort of unimaginable and perverted nature-hell might be facing them over the next three days, or are just numbed into wordless silence by the very prospect.

O'Culigeen, meanwhile, in his black leather *Knight Rider* gloves and painfully sour-puss grimace, is gripping the steering wheel and fuming himself into a simmering angry silence. His jaw nearly hit the floor when he saw Fr Jason toddling towards the van beside me, with a huge blue rucksack on his back. Fr Jason played it dead cool, though, and said that he'd be no bother to the gang of us, and that he had his own tent and everything, but that he was dying for a bit of company, and thought it would be a hoot to tag along with us lads and do nothing but men things for the few days.

O'Culigeen could barely get a word out. He opened the back doors of the van, and as we all climbed inside, single file, passing him dutifully, one by one, he grabbed hold of my arm roughly, and gave it a right yank, as if to say, This is your doing! And, I want my two hundred pounds back! I say nothing and squeeze right through, and find my place on the floor next to Hennessy. We sit cross-legged on a false plywood bottom, without seats, seatbelts, or anything. The van has been inherited from O'Culigeen's dead brother, Padraig, and it is, according to its new owner, very useful indeed. You can only imagine.

The two hundred pounds in question is delivered directly to my door the day before. It was technically a bribe. I say bribe, but it was more sort of a teasing kind of flirty threat. The note I left in the sacristy simply read, 'All is forgiven. For £200. Cash. In this envelope. By Friday. Or I'm not coming. Deliver it by hand. Your pup. Xxx.'

The cash is for the abortion. Turns out the buggers are a lot pricier than I thought. Fiona's done all the research from Aunty Grace's office, and after giving me a major bollocking over the phone about the fecking scandal of getting someone pregnant when I'm only barely out of nappies myself, she tells me that the B&I Line

288

ferry tickets, return to Holyhead, will be thirty pounds each! The train fare to London, on top of that, will be a fiver each, and then there's the abortion itself, which won't be cheap, but will have to be sorted out with the good people of the Marie Stopes Clinic in the West End of London. Two hundred, she says, off the top of her head, should probably cover the lot.

Persuading Saidhbh to even think about it is a nightmare. I barely see her the whole week, because the Leaving Cert is now in full swing, with written French, parts one and two, and oral French, and both Maths papers and all three Irish papers all crashing in on top of each other in the space of four days. When she does eventually agree to see me, for a private emergency meeting by the lake in Belfield, I kind of ruin it by spending all my efforts trying to calm her down while, at the same time, working up the courage to tell her that I've got the entire abortion trip sorted, and that all she has to do is say the word, and we're on the Monday morning ferry to Holyhead, straight after my weekend of camping hell with Fr Feck Face.

She goes completely mental the first time I say it, and starts shaking all over and everything, and says, as serious as she's ever been in her life, that she's going to throw herself into the lake and end it all now if I keep going on with that. She looks over the concrete ledge and into the water and I can see by her sad, tired, red-rimmed eyes that she's not joking. She pulls a piece of paper out of her pocket and tells me that she's been writing poetry. It's about a depressed grizzly bear that she once saw in Dublin Zoo, she says. And it's called, Insanity Follows.

★ ★ ★

Setting the perfect trap for a filthy evil rapist priest is, it turns out, easier than convincing the love of your life to go to London for an abortion. All it takes is a bit of shaping outside the monastery after school, and a game of long-distance donkey with Gary — it's like normal donkey, where you spell the word D.O.N.K.E.Y with every drop of the ball, but you do it over a huge distance, like eighty yards, or, the whole length of the driveway up to the monastery front door. Anyway, I'm catching the ball really loudly on the grass outside the two front prayer rooms, and the next thing I know Fr Jason appears and starts patting me and shaking my shoulders and telling me that he hasn't seen me in ages and what's going on in my life, and how's me dad and how am I getting on with the theory of the multiverse and so on.

I tell him nothing much, and I show him that Gary's there, and I have to go. But I tell him just enough, mainly that I'm going to spend the weekend camping up Three Rock Mountain with Fr O'Culigeen and a rake of boys, and was wondering if Fr Jason had ever done anything like that. At first he doesn't get it, and just tells me that he hasn't gone camping in years, since his wild and crazy pre-priest days, and he hopes that I have a blast, and isn't O'Culigeen a great man to be taking on such a challenge. I tell him that he is, and I say his name again, this time banging out the word 'Father' louder for emphasis in the hope that it'll trigger Fr Jason's usually laser-sharp brain. But nothing.

Gary does the 'what's going on?' gesture with his upturned hands from eighty yards away, which tells me that we either need to continue playing long-distance donkey or go home for the day. And so, with no time for niceties I pretty much spell it out for Fr Jason and tell him that O'Culigeen is the big 'Father' in my life at the moment, and that it would be great if Fr Jason himself could pop along to Three Rock this weekend for a bit of gas and a laugh with the boys. I don't even wait to hear his reply, and just run off and pelt the tennis ball in a massive swinging arc that sends Gary flying backwards over the bicycle racks and right into 'donkey'. I know that Fr Jason has twigged. He gave a sudden sharp insuck of air as I was speaking, and I could almost hear him whisper the words, Oh God no, as the O'Culigeen penny dropped. It is enough for me. I know he'll be there. Because, in my heart, he is a hero to me.

15

The Honey Trap

Pitching the tent is dead tricky. It's not raining exactly, more misty wind than anything else. But all five of us boys are useless at it, even Hennessy with his scouts' experience. Plus O'Culigeen has decided that our first lesson in outdoor survivalism will be how to pitch a tent in the mist without any printed instructions on paper or spoken advice from the mouth of the one adult who knows how to do it. I can tell he's still fuming at me for bringing a real priest with me, because he keeps looking at me and gritting his teeth. He can't hide it from the other boys who are now officially terrified, and snatch nervous glances from him to Fr Jason to each other, and try not to contemplate the kind of god-forsaken sex circus that's going to kick off once the sun goes down.

Fr Jason, though, is playing it dead cool, and has pitched his tent a good fifteen feet away from ours. His is a tiny nylon one-man jobby, like a navy-blue triangular coffin, or a Toblerone made out of rain jackets, just big enough for him to lie on his back, as he does once he's finished, and read a small paperback and look over at us, winking, and saying, This is the life, eh?

O'Culigeen, of course, just paces distractedly in wide circles around the spot he's chosen for the tent — a small flattened clearing on the lower slope of Three Rock, fifty yards of huffing bags and camping gear inland from the winding gravel road that runs all the way up to the radio mast at the top. He chose his spot carefully, and kept saying out loud as he was driving, Hmmm, now let me see, let me see, as he pretended to scour the road ahead for the right place to park. But anyone could tell that he'd been here a million times before, and so when he said, Would you look at that! as he pulled into a deserted and tree-shaded lay-by, it was almost a joke.

You can't see the van from the road. And the camping spot, equally hidden in a weedy overgrown field, looks like it is strictly an O'Culigeen find, and not visited by actual normal human beings with real-life camping on their minds. It kind of makes me feel a bit sick and sad at the same time, when he stops us there, and we look around at the big empty green space, and the patch-work of empty green fields beyond that tilt slowly downwards into the distance, getting greyer and darker until they merge into Dublin city itself. And, even if only for a moment, we listen to nothing up here but the sound of the wind in the leaves and the long grass, and I think of what these things — these fields, these sounds, this emptiness — are supposed to mean to normal people who go camping for fun, rather than raping.

And it makes me think of Saidhbh's favourite story about her mam and dad's honeymoon in Galway, and how they really wanted to go abroad but couldn't afford it, so they settled on

Connemara instead. It made them a bit moody for the first few days of the honeymoon, and it felt like a bad beginning, to start off their married life on a penny-pinching drive rather than living the dream in faraway lands. But then, on day four of the honeymoon, while they were out strolling aimlessly across one of the region's many famous dirty great patches of rocky brown and barren scrubland, the sun suddenly came out and turned everything all warm and gorgeous and it made Saidhbh's parents hug each other tightly. When Saidhbh's mam, Sinead, looked into Taighdhg's eyes she could see that he was crying, and when she asked what was wrong he said nothing, but asked her to look around her at the beautiful landscape of rocks and muck that was Ireland at its best. At which point in the story Taighdhg says, Why? Why would a person from Ireland ever ever ever want to go and visit any other country in the world when they have this kind of beauty on their doorstep?

And after that, and for the rest of their married life up to now, Saidhbh's parents never left the country and always holidayed in Ireland, the most beautiful country in the whole wide world.

Saidhbh finally cracks on the Thursday night, after her Irish oral, just as I'm packing for the camping trip. I'm up in the bedroom and I've covered the duvet with three pairs of clean everything, which seems a lot, but it's mostly for smells, and in case it rains. I've a heavy four-mongo-battery torch for doing midnight slashes. I've got a toothbrush and a bar of Lifebuoy soap for the

294

usual. Plus I've a woolly bobble hat for the early morning hours when it gets bonkers cold, and a Nevil Shute book with boobs on the cover to impress the lads in case we're supposed to read before lights out.

Mam pops her head around the door to tell me Saidhbh's just been on and it sounds serious and she doesn't want to speak to me but wants to meet down by The Sorrows hockey pitch. Right now. Lovers' tiff? Mam asks, and then doesn't even wait for an answer but says, You two! I mean, really!

When I skid up to her on my bike she's a mess. Hair lathered to her face with tears, and half hiding everything else deep inside Taighdhg's big brown duffle coat, which she's gotten buttoned up to the neck, even though it's as balmy a night for early June as you'll ever get.

She says, OK, OK, about a hundred times, and tells me I've won, I've won, and am I happy now, and that she wants to do it, the abortion, but she wants to do it now, as soon as possible, no messing about. She wants it out of her body, right now! She says that she's had it with everyone, including me, and including the baby inside her. She says that the last straw was O'Culigeen, who, this very evening, shooed her away from his door like a common alley cat when she called in for some life or death advice. She said he was totally distracted and crazy looking, and barely recognised her face at first, and when she mentioned the fate of her unborn baby he just told her to do what she thought was right for everyone and to leave him alone

295

because he was a busy man. Saidhbh, who'd never seen O'Culigeen's true colours, and had generally regarded him as a semi-saint, decided that he was just fecking about, and tried to take a step over the threshold, but O'Culigeen shut the door on her foot. When she yelped he told her he was sorry, but that she really needed to feck off with herself right now, and stop looking for answers from everyone else but herself. The last thing he told her was not to worry about me, and what I'd done to her. Because I was a cute whore, but he was going to put some manners on me this weekend. And then he slammed the door for good.

Saidhbh takes ages to sniffle up all her tears, and get back to breathing normally. When she does, she tells me that she'll go with me to London on Monday, and she'll have the abortion. She'll stay with me and Fiona and Aunty Grace on Monday night and all of Tuesday. At this point she says, real cold like, that she doesn't know what exactly is going on between me and Fr O'Culigeen, and she doesn't want to know either. But what she wants to make violently clear is the fact that when we get back to Dublin on Wednesday afternoon she never wants to see me again. Ever. Ever. Ever.

★ ★ ★

The first night in the tent is pretty hairy. There's all five of us lads squashed elbow to elbow, on one side of the tent, with our heads all jammed up against the side, noses against the damp saggy

296

yellow canvas that'll be dripping wet by the quiet cold of morning. The other side is left entirely free for O'Culigeen. There's buckets of space over there, and in fact you could've fit a fella each, easy, on either side of him, but none of us are completely thick. Although Hennessy, the new boy, does make a move in that direction, squeaking away that he doesn't mind snuggling up to a priest. He gets a savage puck in the arm for his troubles, courtesy of Ronan Duignan, who's a bit of a toughie and yanks him back over to our side of the tent and squashes him in between the rest of the altar boys, without a single word of explanation.

Our voices are wrecked anyway, coz of all the singing. Here, after we've barely got the tent going, Fr Jason, with just a set of spoons, gets us doing 'All God's Creatures Have a Place in the Choir' over and over again, until we can do seconds, harmonies, the works, totally mixing it up, singing low for a laugh as the words say, 'Some sing higher' and then singing high, for another laugh, when the words say, 'Some sing lower.' O'Culigeen is a bit annoyed at first, coz he can see that Fr Jason is hijacking the night, and turning it into a major sing-song, but it isn't like he has any choice. With his booze bag hidden in the corner of the tent, and all his devious plans on hold, he eventually peels off the driving gloves and starts slapping his right hand on his thigh a couple of times, just to show that he's enjoying the tunes.

And then there's the cooking part, which is easy, and we all get a big kick out of using sticks

297

and twigs from the ground around us to fish our very own burnt-on-the-outside-and-raw-on-the-inside flame-cooked potato out of the fire itself. O'Culigeen then splatters huge spoonfuls of baked beans on to our plastic plates, and all over the poor blackened spuds, while Fr Jason makes some jokes about cowboys farting in the old days. We laugh at this, all the boys do, but O'Culigeen keeps quiet. He barely says a word throughout the whole meal, other than to correct Hennessy for using his fingers as bean-scoopers. He calls him a little pup a few times for doing it, and adds that he's being a disgrace to his dead mother and his poor widowed father, which seems way over the top for getting a blob of tomato sauce on your hands, and Hennessy is getting a bit wobbly-lipped about it when Fr Jason bursts in again in sing-song mode. This time he tells us to stack up our plates near the fire, and to get ready for the best of Neil Diamond.

We do 'Sweet Caroline' for nearly an hour, until the summer sky gets purplyblackyblue and some of us are singing, Bam, bam, bum, with our eyes closed. As suddenly as he started, Fr Jason stops, chucks down his spoons and tells us that it's time to clean our teeth and put ourselves to bed, and leave the night hours to the grown-ups.

We brush our teeth in a tiny basin by the side of the tent, all at the same time, pigs-in-the-trough style, just so we can get a good dunk of clean water on our brushes before it becomes filled with stretchy white spit and froth.

O'Culigeen stands above us for this and, like a right ponce, explains to Fr Jason that he's supervising our ablutions, and then says something that sounds like he read it off a Christmas cracker, about how God likes clean boys just as much as he likes holy ones. Then he leads us round to the back of the tent, near the nettle bushes, and tells us that it's time for our pee-pees. We look at each other, and no one wants to be the first, and O'Culigeen says, Well?! as if it's the most natural thing on earth, to be staring at five boys with their mickeys out at the same time. I'm thinking of holding mine in for a midnight effort with the torch when Hennessy starts it off with a tiny jet of his finest. We all join in after him, but we end up half-slashing over each other in our shuffly full-bodied and swervy-shouldered attempts to do it straight into the bushes without letting O'Culigeen get a good goo for himself.

After this, we go shooting into our sleeping bags, like five nervous bullets, and we roughly whip off our jeans and pull up our pyjamas while remaining safely deep in the darkness of the bag. We, nonetheless, keep peeping our heads out above the top, with the thick bronzey zips rubbing against our chins, like a little pack of jittery African animals, hiding in the long grasses of the Serengeti, but always keeping twitchy eyes out for the local lion.

Within seconds, our worst fears are confirmed. We hear the two priests saying, 'Night then, Father' to each other, like two total gobshites who don't even realise that they sound completely thick when they call each other Father. O'Culigeen then sticks his ugly mug into the tent and tells us, with a fake yawn, that he's too tired for grown-up talk tonight and is going to join us here in the boys' tent instead. He squeezes himself in, bodily, and grins like a mad man as he climbs over us, petting all our bags individually, and telling us that we did ourselves proud tonight, with our lovely sweet voices, and that we're the Palestrina Boys' Choir in the making. He lets his hand rest on my bag, and under the same purply blackness of coming night, gives me a secret squeeze, a real vicious one, that tells me I'm still in the most super-dooper trouble of anyone on the planet.

He sits over on his side of the tent, cross-legged, and starts sniffing and taking deep deep breaths and muttering under his breath the usual rubbish about us all being dead filthy and trying to ruin him. It's like he's building himself up for the big one. Getting into character. Quiet as a mouse, he untwists the cap of a small spirits bottle from his booze bag and takes a monster slug. He then grabs his black priesty jumper and pulls it over his head, followed by his black shirt, and his white vest, before reaching down roughly for his own belt like a man possessed.

Knock! Knock! Are you still awake, Father?

It's Fr Jason, the living saint, hovering inches away from the main zip outside.

O'Culigeen flinches, freezes, and tries to play the dummy. Ronan Duignan, seizing the moment, does a pretend yawn and a roll over that sends a leg flying right into O'Culigeen's bare stomach. It winds him and makes him say Ooof and Shite out loud. Fr Jason asks him if he's all right in there, Father, which forces him to say, Grand, Father, which is funny, when you think of it.

Turns out, after lots of toing and froing from either side of the main zippy door, that Fr Jason can't sleep and feels like having a fireside chat to Fr O'Culigeen about life and the universe and all the deep things he has on his mind. O'Culigeen tries to think of a million excuses not to go out there, but Fr Jason is so brilliant at describing his own situation — a bit sad, a bit lonely, a bit confused — that there's just no way O'Culigeen can stay in here without seeming a complete and utter bollocks.

Fr Jason also says that he's a fierce thirst on him, but not a drop of drink in his rucksack, and is wondering if any of the clinking clanking noises he heard earlier from O'Culigeen's bags might be the cure. O'Culigeen does a million little silent curses to himself, and reefs his black jumper back on, reaches over to the booze bag, pulls out a fresh naggin of Powers, and scrambles out of the tent, pucking Ronan Duignan and me as he passes.

The two fathers, funnily enough, have a great ole night by the fire, and they do, as Fr Jason promised, talk about the big stuff. It starts out vague enough, with Fr Jason doing most of the talking, and banging on breathlessly about the days when he was an alkie, and all the bad things he'd do for booze. He says about ten times, during this bit, that he doesn't have a problem any more, and that he saves his boozing for special occasions like tonight. O'Culigeen stays silent during this whole bit, but we can tell he's drinking too, coz Fr Jason keeps saying, Amen, in the middle of his own sentences, and each time he does he clinks his whiskey mug against another mug, which must be in O'Culigeen's hand.

After barely thirty minutes Fr Jason has moved on to feelings and moods, and how lucky they are to be priests today, in this day and age, and yet how no one understands the burden that comes with the gig.

Amen to that, says Fr O'Culigeen, speaking for the first time. His voice is like a clap of thunder in the darkness, and shakes all five of us, even the sleepy ones, into a state of bug-eyed awakeness.

For me, he says, it's all about the man upstairs, and has been my whole life.

He gives Fr Jason a big spiel about the role that God has played in his life, always watching him, through thick and thin, and worse, on the farm. Always there at his shoulder, showing him what's wrong and what's right, always there to comfort him when others that he knows, mostly his brothers, have strayed sadly from the path. He says that it's just like that footprints thing, where the fella is dead and finally meets God, and God says, 'See that beach back there, that's your life, and those two sets of footprints are me and you walking through life together, side by side, me always watching you, keeping you safe!' And the dead fella says, 'Oi! But what about those bits there, the big gaps, where there's only

302

one set of footprints, what happened there?' And God says, 'They were the worst times of your life, the absolute pits!' And the dead fella says, 'Well, what the feck were you doing when I was having the worse time ever?' And God just smiles and goes all Goddy on it, and says, 'I was carrying you!' And the dead fella's like, 'Ah, Jaysus! That's brilliant! Tanks a million!'

O'Culigeen finishes his little speech by saying that God is his real father, and not that ole fella down the bog, and that all his life has been about his love for God, and trying to get God to be happy with his behaviour, and happy with the path he has chosen for himself.

Fr Jason clearly isn't happy with this, and launches back into his version of God as not being a man with a beard in the sky but a big floaty thing that wound up the universe billions of years ago and just let it go to see where it went. He goes straight into the pizza theory of time too, and the multiverse, and tells O'Culigeen that they only think that this camping is happening over this weekend, whereas it's happening on a giant and unmoving moment in their lives, and yet it's not happening at all, while simultaneously happening in every possible way in every possible universe.

We can hear nothing from O'Culigeen, which means he's either drinking or thinking, but either way Fr Jason continues and suggests to O'Culigeen that God is really someone who is kicking back and admiring his own multiverse unfolding, and not some old bossy git, staring down at everything that's happening to every person in the world, with a black notebook and pen by his side and a score-chart of who's done what to whom.

But mostly Fr Jason, three sheets to the wind now, tells Fr O'Culigeen, three sheets also, that God at his best is simply love. And there is love for everyone, he adds, before saying slowly, Even you.

O'Culigeen, slurring now, tells Fr Jason that he's right, and that God is good and God is love. And for a moment, all of us in the tent dare not look at each other in the darkness, because we're all thinking the same thing — that maybe Fr Jason had this planned all along, and that his lecture is getting to O'Culigeen, who is realising, on this one mild summer night, in a tiny patch of grass low in the Dublin mountains, on planet Earth, that God is love, and love is the only way to go, and that it's not too late to turn his back on his wickedness, and embrace the beauty of the universe in the for ever now of the all non-time.

The fathers say goodnight to each other in a jokey way, using foreign accents and different words that all seem to mean See you in the morning. Within seconds, O'Culigeen comes crashing into our tent, almost taking the central supporting pole down with his shoulder. He stinks of booze, and is struggling so much with his belt that he falls forward and decides to bed down with his clothes on. He pads about the groundsheet for his sleeping bag, now scrunched up in a ball near the top canvas, and as he does he starts pawing us all in the process. Right then, it's like as if a light bulb suddenly goes off in his drunken head, and he remembers that there are five youngfellas wrapped up neatly in presentation sleeping bags, like fecking Ferrero Rocher, and arranged around the floor of the tent for him to feast upon as and when he wishes. For then he starts leaning over us, one at a time, on all fours like a family dog inspecting a series of food bowls. He hovers over each one of us, coming in real close with his stinky booze-breath, and sucking our air in, with a real shake in his throat, as he decides how to proceed.

He stops at me, of course, and lets his big horrible head fall fully down on mine, forehead to forehead, with a solid clunk.

Wake up, pup! he whispers, all spitty and wet. Wake up, pup! as he pokes me firmly but quietly in the ribs with his open finger. I keep my eyes shut, and play dead, even when his finger-pokes turn into full-fisted thumps. Still nothing. He drops his head down beside my face and viciously bites my earlobe. Still nothing. He calls me pup once more, and says that he's had enough of my horseplay to last him a lifetime, and has just started to unzip my sleeping bag when a last-minute bark, here-comes-the-cavalry style, of Knock Knock! is heard from outside the zippy door.

It's Fr Jason, who has spilt, he says, an entire two litres of lemonade over his sleeping bag, and all over his groundsheet, and would O'Culigeen mind, just for the night, if he bunked in here? O'Culigeen groans as he pulls himself together and drily welcomes Fr Jason inside. The two men are soon lying side by side in the darkness with Fr Jason up against the side canvas, and Fr O'Culigeen against the middle poles and against the tips of five different pairs of boy feet. Fr Jason falls asleep in seconds, but I can tell that O'Culigeen's still awake ages after that. I can almost hear his gummy eyes blinking open and shut with frustration. I then stretch forward with my left foot, and give his thigh a right good and sexy rub, just to let him know that I'm still here, and to give him a seriously decent taster of what he's missing.

16

England

The ferry to Holyhead is brilliant. Dead exciting. Me and Saidhbh are having a hoot outside on deck. And for some of the trip we even forget that we're going over to London to kill a baby. There's Irish all around us, and they're all doing loads of drinking, even though it's nine in the morning. There's some English too, but they're easy to spot, because they mainly have families and are sitting down in neat clothes reading the papers, and hoping that their Peugeots and their Rovers are safe in the car deck below, and not getting bopped about into each other's bumpers by the waves.

The Irish, meanwhile, are in brilliant mood, packing out O'Kelly's Sea Lounge, full of fun and cracking jokes, and doing the country proud. If you were an American on the boat, or say a Chinaman, you'd look at the Irish and then you'd look at the English, and you'd know straightaway what nation was the biggest laugh. You'd be straight over to the Irish, saying, Give us a pint, lads, and let me sit among you and watch you all be a bit mad and funny and drunky.

And they're here, the Irish, mainly in three different and easy-to-spot groups. There's fellas on their own, on the small tables, with pints and

307

huge rucksacks, and all looking sad about being on the boat, and having to leave the homeland for good, to look for work as builders and sweepers in London town. One fella near us has a book called *Dubliners* out in front of his pint. Saidhbh's done it for her Leaving, so she clocks it straightaway. The fella isn't reading it at all. It's more of a sign to let everyone know, and himself, that although he may be waving goodbye to his homeland, possibly for ever, he's still a salt-of-the-earth fella who reads books called *Dubliners*, and not something called *Ireland's a Bit Rubbish and Has No Jobs*.

The second type of Irish on the boat is gangs. Gangs of builders happily cradling their pints, glad to be going back over to the mainland, to continue their construction work after a break on the Auld Sod. Gangs, too, of fellas, loud and shouty, drinking and singing, heading to England for God knows what, with all sorts of hopes and dreams and imaginings in their drunken heads. And more gangs. Gangs of red-haired tinker kids, running riot in the bar, far away from their gangs of tinker parents, some of whom are already face down on the table, calling out the names Jacintha, Shane, Frankie, Concepta, and yelling, Get yir bleedin arses over here before I burst yiz, yiz little bollixes.

The third and final type is us. Young people, in twos mostly, his and hers, bog-standard looking, with a few shifty expressions darting about on their faces, no pints in front of them, and dark and strange unspeakable plans in their hearts. Coming to London to get it out, to make it happen, to do it. Consequences be damned. God not allowed. Young couples, his and hers, who walk around outside on deck a lot, and hug each other every now and then, with him saying it'll all be fine, and her choking back the tears when thinking about the bigness of it all.

As I say, Saidhbh is in dazzling form, considering. She's dressed in patent Docs, dungarees, and another of Taighdhg's sports coats — navy blue this time — and she's even wearing big black sunglasses and a leopard-print hair bow, like Madonna in *Desperately Seeking Susan*. She says that she feels lighter, and kind of giddy, knowing that we're going to split up at the end of this awful business. And that we were mad to rush into it to begin with, and that she always looked on me as a kind of lovely little bender friend, and that's the way we should've kept it. She asks me if I think we can be best bender friends after the abortion, and I tell her that I don't see why not. She gives me a big bender kiss on the cheek, and bets me that I can't catch her as she springs away from me, and darts around the thin metal corridors of the upper deck. I find her eventually, at the back, and we spend ages there, near the engines, standing in the smoky diesel-brown air and looking deeply down into the churning white water. We don't say much. Instead we watch in silence as Dublin slowly disappears into the dirty horizontal haze in front of us.

Saidhbh does give me a few titbits, though. Says, with a shrug, that her folks barely noticed when she said she was off out the door for a three-day post-Leaving Cert blow-out with Finula Sweeney in Malahide. Her father especially, she explains, was up to his neck with a new march, Teachers Against Internment, and was happy to see the back of her for now. Her mam had to shout in his ear, like he was a deaf aul wan, and say, Taighdhg! Your daughter is going now! To Finula Sweeney's! What do you say? And even then he just looked up and grunted a goodbye, but without words. Although Eaghdheanaghdh, she says, gave her a pretty wicked look as she walked out the door, swinging a hefty brown suitcase by her side. It was an I Know What You're Up To face.

I tell her that mine were a breeze too. And that a few frantic phone calls between me and Fiona was all it took to get Aunty Grace involved, and before I know it I've got an urgent invite to go across the water to visit my favourite aunt in London, no questions asked.

Saidhbh asks me about the camping weekend, and I tell her that nothing much happened. Just a load of boys, eating beans and farting. She pulls the sunglasses down an inch or two on to her nose, and looks at me, eye to eye. And what about you and O'Culigeen? she asks. Well? Did he beat some sense into you?

★ ★ ★

By the second night of the camping trip I have O'Culigeen right where I want him. Gagging for it. I've been flirting like mad with him all day, brushing by him during the morning ablutions,

310

accidentally rubbing against him during the lunchtime puck around, and even suggesting that we all go stream swimming in our pants to cool down, the whole lot of us, just to wind him up into a boy-hungry frenzy. But I never leave Fr Jason's side. I'm not thick. I even stand behind Fr Jason, by the riverbank after the swim. And when he's busy struggling to pull up a pair of dry socks over wet legs, I give O'Culigeen a real Hollywood stare, and touch my towel a bit, like I could whip it off at any minute, and just might.

O'Culigeen, of course, is getting madder and madder by the minute, like a frothy rabies case, and doesn't know what to do with himself. The hunger too is making him reckless, and he starts showing his hand, in a way, to Fr Jason. He rushes us, for instance, around the rubbish orienteering course that he and Fr Jason cooked up after lunch, and he then rushes us through our tea too — baked beans again, this time with burnt sausages. He cuts Fr Jason dead in his tracks, when the idea of another sing-song is suggested, by saying that the demon drink has given him an awful headache and he's going to crash out 'with the boys' instead. Fr Jason's a cute whore, all the same, and brilliant at trumping O'Culigeen's plans, and comes clattering into our tent with a broken pole in his hand, saying that you can never trust a British-made tent, that he should've bought an Irish one, and that he was going to have to bunk in with all of us again!

No one sleeps. Everyone's pretending in their own way, except for Hennessy, who's really out

311

of it, and doing a kind of half-whiny snore, like he's having a dream where someone's called his mammy a big cow. The rest of us, we're all lying there, eyes shut tight in the darkness, listening to the grass blowing in the nettle bush behind us, to the odd passing car in the distance, and to the far faraway hum of Dublin life wafting its way bravely up into the Three Rock air.

It takes me ages, but I work up the courage after an hour. I start rubbing O'Culigeen's leg like mad. Like he's turned into Saidhbh and I'm trying to work my way into her fanny. I'm rubbing so loudly that the whole tent can hear it, the slippy slippy of two sleeping bags sparking together. Up'n'down'n'up'n'down. I can feel the little bodily trembles coming from O'Culigeen. He's gasping for air, and letting out these tiny light whines every twenty seconds, like Hennessy in his sleep. I can tell that he's biting his own hand too, with the whole fat thumby side stuck good and deep inside. I can hear his exhaled breath 'fffff'ing out through his teeth with each deeper thigh rub. I go rub crazy until it's almost embarrassingly loud, and just as I'm waiting for one of the lads, or Fr Jason himself, out of sheer awkwardness alone, to ask what in feck's name is going on, I suddenly stop. Just like that. I kneel up in my sleeping bag, with my navy-blue Dunnes Stores pyjamas all loose and hanging off me, like the Mexican housemaid in *Down and Out in Beverly Hills*, and I walk straight out the door, as if I'm going to do a slash, or to take a long romantic stroll in the moonlight.

Naturally, Fr O'Culigeen comes racing out

312

behind me with the maddest grin I've ever seen on any human being ripped across his crazy face. He's already got his mickey out when Fr Jason rugby tackles him to the ground. He gets punched once in the head by Fr Jason who, instead of going all tough, and beating O'Culigeen to a pulp, merely hugs him tightly in a bear-like grip, and tells him that it's all over, and that he's safe now, and that he can give up the struggle. There's no more hiding, he says. It's all over. You are saved.

O'Culigeen bursts out crying and lets his sore, punched head fall on to Fr Jason's shoulder. He moans a lot and keeps it buried there for ever, unable, it seems, to lift it out and to face the world ever again, or to look upon the eyes of boys who are no longer filthy young pups but real-life children with their own mams and dads, or men in the making, with cares and fears in their own hearts, just like his. Instead he sobs, and clings. And Fr Jason strokes, and pats, and says, There there.

None of us sleep for the rest of the night. And O'Culigeen is made to spend the few hours of darkness on his own, in the broken Toblerone tent. Fr Jason does all the driving the next morning, and drops us off, each one of us, to our homes, without saying a word. O'Culigeen doesn't say anything either. He just sits in the front seat, hands on his knees, sulking like a baby throughout. He's obviously had time to think it all through in the Toblerone tent, and to pull himself together, and to put the sobbing and the sad O'Culigeen far far behind him. Because

313

when it's my turn to get out he simply shifts in his seat, tosses his head towards the open side door and, just as I slip past him, out on to the footpath and to freedom, he hisses and spits in the maddest most vicious tone, like John Wayne times a million, 'I'm gonna kill ye!'

★   ★   ★

Fiona meets us in Euston station. By then we're not so cocky. We've gone all *Buck Rogers in the 25th Century*, the first episode, where he wakes up from space sleep, and mostly spends the whole programme trying to deal with the fact that everyone five hundred years into the future wears leotards to work and has little metal midget helpers who don't really do anything useful apart from chatting to you and saying beedley-beedley-beedley. Or at least Saidhbh is Buck Rogers and I'm her little metal fella, tottering along beside her, as we stare with wonder renewed at the world around us.

London's massive. We spend the train journey down from Holyhead thinking that England is very much like Ireland, with green fields everywhere, and walls and houses, and a few giant chimney things every now and then, to let you know where the factories and the power stations are. It only starts changing in the last hour, as we get closer and closer to London. From then on the voices of the Irish on the train, all the usual gangs, still drinking tinnies of beer and chatting, get quieter and quieter till they disappear altogether. And yet, what's completely

314

bonkers is that the Irish voices get quieter in exact proportion to the amount that the English voices get louder and louder.

It's mad, as well, if you haven't heard that many English voices together and up close before in your life. Because mostly you know the sounds from *Minder* on telly, or *The Professionals*, or even *The New Avengers*, or *The Good Life*, or the presenters from *Blue Peter* who say that the telephone is ring-ging, or the children are sing-ging. But if you've only ever seen no more than a few real-life Brits in person, say holidaying in Ireland, and asking directions from the windows of the camper vans in West Cork on a sun-splitting-the-rocks kind of day, then it can totally blow your mind.

Because up close, in that train carriage, with buckets of them, black, white, brown and yellow, all rammed together, and getting more rammed with every passing station, closer and closer to London, it's like someone grabs your head and sticks it right into a great big noisy English voice machine, one that's on turbo spin and boom bass, and pumps out all this deafening chatter that sounds like everyone's teeth are showing at once and they're shouting out words like, free hundred and firty-free and a fird, and talking about how much they're finking about their muvvas, and their bruvvas, and how it's all a lot of bovva.

That's why the Irish go quiet. It's like *Invasion of the Body Snatchers*. You don't want anyone to know that you're not the same species, or to know that if you opened your mouth you

315

wouldn't go free hundred and firty-free. Instead, it would give your position away in a second if you took a big breath and said, Tree hundred and tirty tree an a tird. They'd be on to you with their dead alien faces, and their hungry flesh-eating teeth showing, with just the sound of finking, finking, finking, echoing in your ears as they chew you to pieces.

As I say, by the time we get to Euston station Saidhbh and me are pretty quiet. She's also realised that although it's going to be brilliant to split up from me once we get back to Dublin, we still have the small matter of an evil God-bothering baby murder to get out of the way in London. Of course, we don't actually mention the subject to each other. We just sit in silence, and look out at the big chunks of grey concrete and graffiti that go whizzing by the windows until we slide to a halt on platform number 8.

Fiona picks us up, right on the concourse, but she has to wave at me, up close and into my face, before I recognise her. She's gone totally English, and has her hair cut dead short at the sides, like a boy, and floppy on top, and wears mad baggy trousers that go in at the ankle, and an orange *Miami Vice* jacket with huge square shoulders. She looks at me and Saidhbh and says that we're a state, like two knackers from a tinker site, and tells us to hurry up because Deano's double-parked.

Deano is now officially Fiona's boyfriend. The minute I see him, pacing by the Peugeot, just past the croissant stand, I nearly fall over my suitcase with the shock of it. He's practically a

316

hundred. Fiona knows this, and I think that's why she was snappy with me in the station. She knows that I'm going to be like, What the effing hell is that ole grandpa doing with my sister?!!! And worse than that, he's called Deano! And he works for Aunty Grace! He offers to lift me and Saidhbh's suitcase into the Peugeot's boot but I tell him not to bother: in my head I imagine his back exploding with the effort of it all, like the cartoon robot guy on the telly health-information ad who instructs you on how to lift heavy things because otherwise it can-cause injury, can-cause injury, can-cause injury, can-cause injury.

He's dressed in baggy trousers, like Fiona, only his are a bit manky dirty. And he's wearing a white collarless shirt and a black waistcoat. He's mostly bald but has scraped a load of white hair from around his ears into a ponytail at the back. And his face is all craggy, like he was crumpled up and left in space sleep for five hundred years and then finally unfolded only last week.

He's very smiley all the same, and hugs me when he sees me, and looks at both me and Saidhbh together and smiles kindly and calls us poor children from the homeland. Fiona later tells me that Aunty Grace only hires Irish, because they're brilliant workers, they're great craic after hours, and they don't phone you with death threats every time a bomb goes off, or throw rotten eggs and human shit at the front window of your business, or stop you on the street and tell you to fuck off back to Paddyland you piece of shit Irish bitch.

Aunty Grace's house in the Queen's park is much smaller than I imagined, and not actually in the Queen's park. Instead, it turns out that we've been misunderstanding her for years and that the house is actually built in an area of London that's simply called Queen's Park but is nowhere near the real Queen herself, which is not surprising, given the amount of rubbish on the roads and the hundreds of old drunken bent-over fellas with tangled beards and spitty coats stumbling around in the doorways. And that's not the full of it either, because Fiona tells me later that Aunty Grace's house, which is bang in the middle of a small narrow street called Glengall Road, is not even in the official Queen's Park area, and really belongs to the next-door neighbourhood, which is called Kilburn, and is where all the Paddies from all four corners of Ireland end up when they first come to London — and it must also be the place where they get the beards and spitty coats, and strict instructions to go and fall about in each other's doorways.

Aunty Grace, though, is very concerned about making the right impression, and doesn't want to be seen in the wider business community as any old immigrant just off the boat, so she puts Queen's Park as her address, instead of Kilburn, and no one — not the water company or the electrics or the post office itself — has ever bothered to make her write the truth.

The house itself, unlike the one we always heard about in letters and in chat, is tiny, and squashed in between two other tiny houses on

318

Glengall Road. It's teatime when we arrive, and Aunty Grace greets us on the kerb, smiling but swinging a big bunch of keys, and making a point of telling us that she had to close up shop early for this, which is something that she hasn't done since they blew up them horses in the bandstand. Her next-door neighbour, an old dear called Jackie, comes tootling out on to the street in slippers and housecoat the minute we arrive. She's dead English, has orangey brown smoky fingers, a real deep husky voice, dyed yellow hair and thick milk-bottle glasses. It takes only two seconds to spot that she's mad as a bag of hammers. She asks Aunty Grace if we're from the CIA, and when Aunty Grace, dead patient like, says, no, we're from Ireland, Jackie says that her parents once owned a castle in Ireland, near Galway, but that her brother-in-law, the bastard, cut her out of the will. She then says that any time she goes to Dublin she always gets free drinks in the pub, because she's related to Daniel O'Connell, hero of the nation. She chats away like this, for another ten minutes before Aunty Grace nods and does a polite little laugh, and then tells Jackie to go back indoors before she catches her death. Jackie tells us that she's watching us, and warns us not to drink the water, because it's filled with poison from a reactor-leak in the Brecon Beacons. Aunty Grace says that Jackie's an old dote, and that the street here is a mixture of old eccentrics and new up-and-comers like herself.

The atmosphere around the tea table, once all the hellos-and-great-that-you're-heres are done, is pretty rubbish, because everybody knows why we're here and nobody's allowed to say anything about it. We eat meals from amazing space-aged packets that come boiling hot, nuclear style, straight out of Aunty Grace's massive cancer-making microwave. She jokes that she's a working woman, with a business to run, and doesn't have time to be doing all the fancy food, like Irish Stew and spaghetti bolognese, that Mam makes for us back home. And so we eat like astronauts, holding our white plastic trays in front of us, and dipping two slices of brown meat-like stuff from one wide shallow bath in the corner of the tray into another smaller yet deeper bath of brown sauce-like stuff at the centre, before topping it all off with some white mash-like stuff that lives in the biggest bath in the other corner.

Deano, who's still with us at dinner time, and seems to be a bit of a permanent fixture at the house, jokes that this is exactly the sort of grub them boys ate when they went to the moon. And then he adds, If you believe that sort of thing. Fiona says, Here we go! just before Deano begins a brilliant explanation of why nobody has ever been to the moon and that it was all just a big joke played on the world by the Americans, to make us feel that they were masters of the universe. And then he says, But there is only one master of the universe, before looking directly over at me. I'm expecting him to say, God, or Jesus. But instead, he says, The Source, and claps his hand quietly in front of his smiling face as he does so. Fiona sighs again.

She tells me later, sitting on the edge of my bed at midnight, that Deano's a good sort, and really brilliant with her, but he sometimes gets carried away with all the hippie-dippie stuff. She says that he had no parents back in Ireland when he was young, was an unwanted baby, and has had an awful time, all his life, trying to find out who he is, and why he's here on Earth. She says he's brilliant at the guitar though, and is always the most popular fella at any party. And he's magic at his job, which is sort of like a career guidance counsellor, a priest, and a head doctor all rolled into one. All the youngies who come over from Ireland, broke and banjaxed, make their way straight to Aunty Grace's office, hoping for the best from a top-flight career as a note-taker, typer and occasional coffee-maker. And while she does all the professional stuff, and gets them up to speed on their Pitman shorthand and words per minute, and pays for new haircuts and business suits, which means that she gets a nice chunk of their pay packet for her efforts, it's Deano who does all the other stuff. Tells them that they're special people inside, and unique, and that whatever they're doing over here is part of their life's journey, and not to be ashamed about leaving home but to look ahead at the opportunities that England has to offer. Fiona says that Deano's taken lovely care of her, in the nicest way, since the day she arrived, as part of Aunty Grace's emergency efforts to fix our family fast.

I sleep in Deano's bed, which is in a spare room with a single giant framed Beatles poster called *Rubber Soul* on the wall, and a tiny window that looks out on to a back concrete courtyard filled with rubbish bins and old ladders. Saidhbh has to bunk in with Fiona. We didn't ask or discuss it with anyone, it was just obvious that you wouldn't want to be rubbing Aunty Grace's nose in it, even though we haven't bothered to tell anyone that me and Saidhbh are finished as boyfriend and girlfriend, and just in bender-friends mode for ever more. Deano tells me not to worry about him and his bed, because one of his friends from 'Community' has agreed to put him up for the night. I don't ask, but he starts to tell me about Community anyway, saying that they're a great bunch of punters, real searchers, every one of them. If it wasn't for Community, he says, he'd be in rag order. Still, I say nothing. He begins the whole story of Community, and of how they bought the old church spot up in Islington, when Fiona stomps in and cuts him short, saying that it's my bedtime, and that little boys need their beauty sleep. Deano calls me 'Little Man', and skulks out of the room, saying that he'll go help Aunty Grace put the bins out.

We chat for a bit, me and Fiona. About home, about Dad, and about how mad everything's got recently. And even though it's just like old times, and all I'm missing is the parked Porsche poster on the wall above me, I'm pretty quiet for most of it, and don't really have the stomach for it. Fiona, who's still totally brilliant at looking straight into the heart of me, shuffles up closer on the covers and tells me not to worry about

322

anything, and that everyone makes mistakes. She strokes the side of my head, around my ears, and calls me her little boy. I melt on the spot, and have to use superhuman strength to stop myself from wailing out loud and flinging my arms around her and asking her, please, right now, to take me home to Ireland and lock me up in my mam and dad's house for ever and ever.

Instead, I tell her that I'm tired and just need some sleep. I roll away from her, towards the wall, and she nudges me sharply in the back. Oi! she says. Haven't you forgotten something?

Oh, I say, and lean up to kiss her goodnight.

She flinches. Not me, ye eejit! What about her!

She tilts her head to one side, indicating the next-door bedroom. I stand up automatically, without much feeling, like a beedley-beedley robot, and plod across the room, out the door and rest against Saidhbh's door jamb. I knock. No sound. I open the door.

Saidhbh is already in darkness. She's lying, curled up, on a mattress on the floor next to Fiona's bed. I flick on the sidelight on the chest of drawers and Saidhbh barks an annoyed, Jesus! My eyes dart around the room, from Fiona's Duran Duran posters, to her neatly folded piles of Ton sur Ton sweatshirts, to her enormous collection of make-up bottles, powders and pads, and finally to her three neatly arranged and handmade Miss Piggy dollies that she brought with her from Ireland. I turn off the light again and kneel down beside Saidhbh. It's like she's dying, and I'm the one praying for God to take her soul swiftly and painlessly.

Big day tomorrow, eh? I say, finally.

She says nothing, but in the darkness snuffles quietly to herself.

I reach out to find her hand. It's up around her mouth. My fingers are like spiders running up along her forearm and over her wrist. I'm expecting her to tell me to feck off, but she doesn't. She opens out her own fingers and lets me slip mine in and squeeze. She squeezes back. Nothing happens for ages, and it would seem really calm if you were watching us from the outside, but inside I'm actually racking my brains for something to say. Something to make it better. A joke, maybe, about Deano or Jackie, or mad people in general. Or about what they'd say at home if they could see us now. About school, about the nuns, about Mary Davit or even about Fiona's new hair, or Aunty Grace's space dinners, anything to take away the dark thoughts of this thing we have to do in the morning. My brain tells me to go light, to go funny, but my body has other ideas. It sends up a wave of feeling, right from my stomach, that just lurches out from my throat and into the room.

I love you so much, I say to Saidhbh. And as I do I feel my eyes go stingy, my throat go supertight, and tiny little tears form right inside the nosey part of my lids, like I've just said the saddest thing that anyone has ever said in the history of the universe or the multiverse, and of time, linear, non-linear and otherwise.

Saidhbh gives my hand another squeeze, and she whispers in the darkness those three little words that are everything to her, and bring her

324

back to the safety of home in moments of fear and need.

God is good, she says. Yes. And then she repeats them. God is good.

I go to bed. I know, for sure, that we are truly fecked.

THREE

1

The Terminator

Saidhbh goes a bit nutty after the abortion.
Although I say abortion, we never actually got
through with the whole shebang. They were dead
nice and everything in the centre. It was a huge
old building with high ceilings and massive
doors, from the times of Sherlock Holmes and
the like, and with four floors all dedicated to
abortions, right in the heart of London, just
north of Oxford Circus. I know the name Oxford
Circus well, and so does everyone in our family.
It's the name of the tube station that nearly
swallowed up Sarah and Siobhan for good, when
they were in London, as girls, on a holiday trip
with Mam and Dad, while Fiona, Claire and
Susan stayed home with Aunty Una. I wasn't
even born yet, but I've heard the story a million
times: about how Mam and Dad got separated
from six-year-old Sarah and Siobhan in Oxford
Circus tube station, and how they ran up on to
the street, sure that they'd never see their darling
twins ever again, until the two girls suddenly
popped up with guilty smiles on their faces at the
other side of the crossroads completely. Mam
and Dad screamed, Stay right there! And then
they ran right across the busy intersection and
slapped the hell out of the girls for giving them
the worst fright in their lives. After that they went

to Wendys for a burger.

It only takes us fifteen minutes to get into Oxford Circus from the Kilburn tube station, although Aunty Grace tries her best to persuade us to walk backwards away from Kilburn and leave from Queen's Park station. She says that the platforms there are much cleaner and the trains that leave from there go much quicker. But Fiona makes rolly-eyes and shaky-head faces behind Aunty Grace's back, so we go to Kilburn instead.

The journey in is pretty quiet, even though it's slap bang in the middle of Tuesday morning rush hour. And me and Saidhbh, on a London tube train for the very first time in our lives, can't quite believe how you can get so many people into such a small space and have them make so little noise. Just a couple of dry coughs, followed by the rattle-rattle of newspapers, punctuating nothing but the metal moan of the train rails. And nothing else. If you shut your eyes tight you'd swear you were all alone in a very hot and very empty carriage, instead of one that's wall to wall with bodies and suits and skirts and jeans and jackets and bags. I'm guessing it's because they're all tired, and it's first thing in the morning, and the last thing they want to be doing is getting ready for a big sweaty work-day in the heart of the London metropolis. But Fiona says later that it's because they're all English, and the English don't talk to anyone they don't know. And even when they do know you, she says, you'd be hard pushed to get some decent chat out of them, unless you're all sitting around a big banquet table or at a posh dinner somewhere, and you're elbow to elbow with Lord Whoo-Haw Ponkington Smythe, and he's only talking to you because it would be dead embarrassing and against the rules not to, and the English never break the rules.

The abortion people are totally different, and dead friendly. And they even have a special Irish woman to deal with all the girls from the homeland who come over in the family way. And she's called Noreen and has super-short hair, like Fiona's, and is probably one of the friendliest people you're ever likely to meet in an abortion clinic. The others are nice too, but they mostly stare down at forms, and run through really embarrassing questions about how many sexual partners have you had, and at what age did you have your first sexual partner, and is this the father? The woman who says that has blonde hair, and amazing *Top of the Pops*-style make-up, dead glam, but when I say Yes to that question, she kind of looks at me from above the clipboard with an awkward smile that seems to say, I wasn't talking to you, baby-maker!

Most of Noreen's questions, however, are all about back home, and who knows, and what help have we had, and do we have tickets, or enough money to get back over the Irish Sea. She gives Saidhbh a full glass of water when her lips start wobbling after looking at the leaflet that shows an artist's impression of the Y-shaped abortion seat with the stirrups up in the air and a cartoon doctor kneeling dangerously close to a cartoon woman's cartoon fanny. And then she tells Saidhbh that she's going to be a grand girl now as she leads her by the hand into the abortion room. Me and Saidhbh don't say anything to each other at this stage. We don't even look at each other. I was going to say, Good luck now with it all, but that feels a bit thick. And Saidhbh seems to have gone into such a mad trance-like state that anything other than actually putting one foot in front of the other and eventually pushing herself up into a half-seated position in the dangerous man-made stirrupy contraption is totally out of the question. She disappears behind the abortion doors, with no sign yet of the doctor and his tools, cartoon or otherwise.

I'm waiting outside in the holding room — the only fella, surrounded by four nervous-looking women — reading my *Peig* notes, hoping to get back on track with some super-early swotting for the next school year, when she comes out, sooner than expected, literally ten minutes after going in, with all her paperwork half scrunched up in her hands, a funny stare on her face, and Noreen clinging on to her arm. Noreen glares at me when I stand up. She says nothing, but just shakes her head and shuts her eyes at the same time, as if to say that it's a sad thing that Saidhbh has come all this way from Ireland, only to fail the Oxford Circus abortion experience. She slides Saidhbh towards me, like she's handling an ancient Chinese vase, and I receive her gently, using the same under-arm grip as I shuffle her out of the reception room and out into the daylight, through the massive wooden doors of Abortion Towers.

We celebrate the no-abortion in a flash Mexican restaurant called Border Town in Oxford Circus, with a late breakfast of chips and chicken fajitas. I've never had fajitas before, and my eyes nearly pop out of my head when I see them sizzling and smoking towards me through the restaurant, swooping down like an Airfix spaceship from telly's *Flash Gordon*, leaving a vapour trail of thick black cloud as it goes. My fajitas are being carried on a black iron skillet and small wooden holding tray by a very relaxed waiter who looks like he's done this a million times before, so isn't bothered at all by the impressive special effects set-piece at the end of his wrist.

Saidhbh's cousin had fajitas once before, on holiday in Benidorm, which is why she made me order them. They come with their own round box of pancakes, and Saidhbh has to show me how to eat them, rolled up with red and green sauces poured down the middle, on either side of the chicken strips. It's a complicated process, and Saidhbh gets a bit of a kick out of teaching me to eat and calling me a dummy at the same time. It's fun enough, in fact, for us both to forget, even for a few minutes, where we've just been, and for us both to feel like we're in the most strange and faraway place on Earth, and eating the craziest smokiest sparkiest food imaginable. I even decide then and there that when I'm old enough to work I'm going to come back to England and ask Aunty Grace to do her best, and to use all her work connections in her contacts book to get me a job in Border Town in Oxford Circus.

On top of all that, we drink virgin pina coladas, which are like liquidised Bounty bars, and there's music blaring, real country style, and there's a blonde girl wandering around in denim shorts and a cut-off shirt that shows her tanned belly while her whole torso is wrapped in a Mexican bandit's belt that's full of little glasses where the bullets should be. She stops at every table and mostly talks to the men, offering them a drink from the two spirit bottles sitting in her hip holsters. A lot of them say no, and point to their watches, but two fellas in suits next to us take a shot each. The bandit girl clanks the glasses down on the table, then spins a bottle in each hand, real cowboy style, before splashing booze into the two tiny glasses and taking a pound each from the lads. She then spins round to us with a big gorgeous grin, and tells us that her name is Sandy. She turns her whole body towards Saidhbh and offers her a shot, winking towards me and saying that she's sure that Saidhbh's son, meaning me, won't mind!

Saidhbh shrugs, a kind of what-else-have-I-got-to-lose shrug, but I take a risk and lean right over the smoking fajitas, put my hand on top of Sandy's shot glass, and tell her that Saidhbh is expecting a baby. Sandy gives a little smile, which tells us that we are both creeps, and then she moves on. Saidhbh says nothing. She looks at me. Although I say, she looks at me, but it's more kind of in my direction but not really focusing.

It takes the whole meal, right to the last fajita, and some shared bites of key lime pie, to get a few words out of her. I tell her that everything will be fine, and that once we get back home, and the folks have had a chance to get used to the news, it'll be the best thing ever. She can still do her teacher training, and I can crack on with my schooling. And the baby will be the best thing that's happened to both our families. It'll make Saidhbh's parents slow down, and stop her dad doing so many marches and things. And it'll probably bring my dad out of his cancer slump, and give him something to live for. He'll be like, Damn this whole dying rubbish! And he'll round up every healthy cell in his body and tell them that he's not giving in, no, sir, not while there's a grandchild on the way, and the prospect of new life, of rebirth, and of happiness everlasting.

Now, the truth is, sadly, that I don't think, and I don't feel, any of this. I am lying, because I am in cat-nurse mode. It's the way you go when you're faced with a fluffy Burmese kitten that could be about to die right there in your arms from crusty snot block and wheezy lung breaths, and all that you can do is focus every drop of your energies into cleaning out that snot with cotton buds, and softening those breaths with shower steam as quickly and carefully as possible. Because to do anything else, anything else at all, like even daring to think about how your swollen heart feels for this precious little love bundle before you, would simply destroy you right there on the spot — take the legs from under you with sadness, and leave you in a weeping paralytic puddle on the floor.

It's been happening between me and Saidhbh, slowly but surely, ever since she found out that she was preggers. It's a look in the eye. A word here. An expression there. The crusty snot and the wheezy breaths of the soul. And I am scared.

Saidhbh grunts at me after lunch, and tells me that she wants to go home. Although she gets the exact same upbeat lecture treatment from Deano after tea. He tells her that what she's done is a truly magical thing, and that the step she has taken towards the universe in not killing her baby will mean that the universe will take two steps back towards her, to meet her and supply her emotional needs with everything she could possibly want. She is a good person, he tells her, over and over again. And the universe will reward her. He follows her around Aunty Grace's house all night, even when she's packing our suitcase, whispering top tips into her ears, telling her that she should be taking folic acids for the baby, and not eating shellfish, but drinking a glass of Guinness a day for the iron.

He makes her lie down on the bed, in her pyjamas, and puts his hands over her womb. He's not touching, just hovering. He says that he's giving her a healing, and that it's something that he's learnt in Community, from a group of crack professionals called the School of Astral Sciences. It's all natural, he says, and all about harnessing the existing auric energies of the cosmos. And so, after fifteen minutes of heavy breathing, during which time he says that he is grounding himself into the Earth and feeding off the energy in his Hara line, he tells her that the baby's life force is enormous, and unstoppable, and has given him one of the largest Human Energy Field readings he's ever experienced. Literally, his hands were being pressed back away from Saidhbh's womb by the force of the tiny being inside. Our lives are about to change, he says, calling me into the room, while leaping excitedly up from his knees. Because this baby is the living manifestation of a benign and all-powerful universe, he says, reaching down and touching Saidhbh's tummy properly now. This baby, he says, will not take no for an answer. Because this baby is life itself made flesh. It is life.

★ ★ ★

Saidhbh starts cramping in the small hours. The baby arrives in a tiny little globule of red-coloured mucus, by morning. She flushes it down the loo and stomps back into Fiona's bedroom and slams the door behind her. She pushes Fiona's wardrobe along the floor and in front of the door, sending a hundred make-up bottles tumbling to the ground in the process. She climbs back into bed without saying a word. We miss the train. And the ferry. And the rest of the summer in Ireland.

2

More Fajitas?

On the downside, all hell breaks loose at home when we don't come back. The Donohue clan go bonkers when they find out that Saidhbh's been lying to them, that she's with me, and that she's just had our miscarriage, and that, worst of all, she's in England. They can't believe it. Taighdhg especially is heartbroken and has to take two weeks off work just to let it all sink in. Gary sends me a massive letter, eight foolscap long, giving me a blow-by-blow, real serious like, of everything that happened since the news broke. He says that my mam and his mam and all the usual gabbers had a mega-coffee meeting over at his, and they went through two packs of malted milks, and a half-jar of Maxwell House, not to mention all the John Players, and that practically every word on the table had some connection to me and Saidhbh, and to all the trouble that we'd caused. We were like bandits, he said, like his and hers lovers on the lam like you see in movies, and Maisie O'Mally said that we had scandalised the whole Rise and most of greater Kilcuman itself.

The big coffee morning was called mainly to see if there was anything that the women of The Rise could do together for the Donohues who, apparently, had taken it all much worse than my mam and dad. They said that Taighdhg had been in shock from day one, when Saidhbh called and broke the news and said she wasn't coming home. Taighdhg told her that she was talking rubbish, and that if she wasn't going to come back he'd have to do something about it. And that even though he didn't have a passport and didn't agree with international travel as a rule, he was going to get one first thing in the morning, and go right over to fecking England and bring his daughter back.

Saidhbh told him that if he dared attempt to come anywhere near London town, or specifically Glengall Road, she'd kill herself on the spot. She was up in Aunty Grace's bathroom at the time, and had locked herself in, with the cream phone flex sticking out under the doorway, snaking its way into the bedroom socket. It was during the first of many of her locking-herself-in phases, and she was just mad enough to scare Taighdhg into taking her seriously, especially when she warned him that she had a fistful of Fiona's Lady Shaves blades in front of her, and that she'd slit her own throat if he even thought about coming over, or about sending anyone over in his place.

He got the message, put the receiver down, and hit the bottle good-o. Gary's heard that there were huge fights in the house after that, with Taighdhg Donohue cursing my name, blaming me for everything, and threatening to call in his contacts with The Movement to take care of me once and for all. It took Sinead Donohue hours of reasoning and gallons of coffee to calm him down, and to convince him, even to the slightest degree, that his own daughter might've had a part to play in the entire unfolding drama.

And yet, even then, and such is the man's love for his only daughter, he blamed everything else but Saidhbh. It was the TV, he said. It was the movies. It was the music. They'd brain-washed her with their insidious Englishness, and plucked her right from out of his arms, and from the all-embracing love of Ireland. And now look at her! In London! For God knows how long! He knew, he said, from the very first day that she started listening to Boy fecking George that nothing good would come of it.

Of course, he'd held his tongue for too long, because he knew that nobody would listen to him, and they'd all call him an old fogey and a square and a bogman. But he said that he knew what he was talking about, because it was called Post-Colonial theory, it was on the teachers' syllabus, and it meant that all those episodes of *Minder, Grange Hill* and *To the Manor Born*, plus all those songs from Kajagoogoo and Spandau Ballet, had made Saidhbh see the once proud Irish people in the same negative way that the Brits see them. She had become the star of her own Irish joke, like the bit in the *Kenny Everett Show* where the Irish farmer, with a pig under his arm, runs straight into a wall because he's so thick. And everyone in the audience, all the Brits down at the BBC Television Centre, laugh not just because he's run into a wall, but because he's run into a wall and is Irish too. So

Saidhbh, because of all her telly and music, had started to think, and against her better instincts, that England was the cool place to be and Ireland was just for old fogeys with cloth caps and pigs under their arms and an inability to tell the difference between brick walls and open doors.

Sinead Donohue was a harder nut, they all agreed, and hadn't shed a single public tear since this whole debacle broke, and hadn't missed a single day at the Book of Kells or Kilmainham Gaol. Gary says that everyone at the coffee morning kind of agreed that Sinead was a bit of a cow underneath it all, and deserved all the trouble she got anyway, and her lack of crying and collapsing had proved what they thought all along, which is that she was too into herself, and her role as a famous super guide, and a mini-hero to tourists from all over the world. And if she'd only kept her eyes on what was happening a little closer to the hearth then none of this would've happened and poor Devida here, meaning my mam, wouldn't be left frantic with worry for her only son.

Gary says that Mam didn't seem that worried at all, and told everyone to shut up when they suggested that she was still in shock. And when the biddies asked her if she was having trouble sleeping at night, she said that everything was grand, and that what was done was done, and that she trusted her sister Grace to the bitter end, and knew that I couldn't be in a safer place on Earth. Some of the women thought she was putting on a brave face, and asked her about the

341

scandal of it all, and the shame that her son had brought down upon their house, and told her that they wanted to call the new Parish Priest, Fr Murray, on her behalf. But Mam just shot them down straightaway and said that she had lost a lot of faith in the Church since Fr O'Culigeen left for the missions. Didn't have a going away hoolie or anything. Didn't even come up to the house to say goodbye. Just finished a week of Masses with a quick communal confession on Saturday evening and then headed off to the South Seas first thing in the morning, on a top-secret mission to turn the little savages into altar boys.

No, the real one Mam was worried about was my dad. He didn't do anything dramatic when he heard the news. And, in fact, he barely reacted at all. He was shuffling round the house in his slippers and scratchy dressing gown at the time, on his morning lurch around, after taking the pills and carefully running a comb down and around all the balding patchwork of hair clumps that have become his head these days. Gary's seen my dad recently, and knows what he's talking about. He says the medicine's taken out another big chunk of hair, real weird like, in a strip right round the back. Says he looks like a new baby who's rubbed himself a special baldy spot from lying on the flat of his back, and turning left and right for ever.

Mam had to lure him into the kitchen, pretending there was a freshly baked scone with jam and cream waiting for him when he got there. But instead she made him sit down, and told him the whole score about me and Saidhbh, and the baby, and then the no-baby, and then us being stuck in London for the moment until Saidhbh stops being a bit mental. She said he looked around the kitchen, turned his stubbly jaw to the side, and just rubbed the light pink surgical scar on his neck. He stroked it weakly, running his finger along its path through the prickles, and asked Mam for the scone she had promised him. It seemed on the surface that nothing had happened at all, and that he had nothing to say about it. But Mam told the coffee girls she could swear that another precious light had just gone off in his eyes.

Gary wrote that my mam cried for a bit at this stage, but that all the mams gathered and clucked around her and told her that Dad would pull through, and they decided, being positive, that it was probably better that I was over with Aunty Grace until Dad fully kicked the cancer. Just so Mam could handle it in her own way. They said there'd be plenty of time for me when Dad got better. And then they chuckled and giggled together as they dreamt, with some excitement, of the big day when Dad's strength returned and he could effortlessly grab the bamboo stick and beat me black and blue for my sins.

Of course, it's hard to tell exactly how mental Saidhbh had really become, because, thanks to the toll the whole experience has taken on her, she has mostly given up talking.

We barely saw her at all in the first few days, thanks to the bedroom lock-in. And she broke that only for quick sobby calls home to her mam, and some rapid-fire trips to the kitchen for some toast, or an apple. She did these during the day, when the others were out, and I'd often try to catch her on the stairs. I'd be sitting with a bowl of Frosties on the brown denim beanbag in Aunty Grace's telly room, with the door to the hall wide open, and reading *The Ladybird Book of London* and learning all about how the Great Fire was started in a baker's shop on the funny-sounding Pudding Lane, or how Dick Whittington was a real-life actual mayor and not just a fairytale fella, or how there was nothing more delightful than a trip to St Paul's or a visit to Madame Tussauds, and how you had to be careful when you spoke to an attendant in Madame Tussauds because, or so the book warned me, they might be made of wax! Which made me feel a bit weird. But not as weird as the sound of Saidhbh thundering down the stairs in her bare feet, with her thin Mickey Mouse nightie flowing behind her as she swooshed by the open door, like a particularly tormented breeze, on a sudden snack break between quick pees and sobby calls.

On these occasions I'd drop the book and fling myself out of the beanbag, and make a dash for the door. But I'd end up just standing there, frozen within the door frame, a hand tentatively reaching out to her as she passed, like trying to catch a ghost. And me with a million unformed words on my lips. All blocked by fear, and by cat-nurse mode, and by the need to say, and to do, exactly the right thing that would bring her

344

back to me, and to us, and to all of our lives.

Eventually, Saidhbh was talked out of the room by Deano. He sat at the door for a whole weekend, and didn't say much at all, other than the fact that the universe had a plan, and that Saidhbh could relax now, because she was surrounded by goodness and light. He told her a whopper on the Sunday lunchtime shift, and it was probably the one that did the trick, about how he had accidentally blinded a man once, in his dark days back in Ireland, with a broken bottle and everything. And how he thinks about that blind fella nearly every day, in the same way that Saidhbh must be thinking about her baby. But the difference is that Deano says he's managed to forgive himself for blinding the bloke back home. In the same way that Saidhbh needs to forgive herself for almost going through with an abortion that somehow led to the death of her would-be first child. And yes, he says, piling it on thick and fast, pulling no punches, maybe the child did sense the negative energies that were directed against it in the abortion clinic. And maybe that child then decided to absent himself from humanity, and disappear that very evening, back into the ethereal realm, leaving Saidhbh with only mush for memories. But even if the child did all this, and brought the end of his corporeal form upon him or herself, it was clear that this was not Saidhbh's fault. The child, says Deano, putting some much needed icing on the cake, will only come into a world that's ready to have him. And you, my sweet darling girl, were not ready to have him. But take

345

heed and know that he's out there, in the heavens, waiting for the right moment to come back to you. To feed at your breast. And to live in your heart.

Naturally, Fiona and Aunty Grace are in floods at this, listening closely from the bottom of the stairs, with me in between them. Fiona rubs my shoulders too, as if to say that I must be hurting deep deep down inside for the tragic loss of my baby that never was. And that I must be imagining all the winter bike rides that we'll never have, me and the little one, or how I won't ever be able to teach it to throw *Top of the Pops*-style shapes to Bronski Beat in the bedroom. And I know what the nuns say, and I know what the brothers say, and the priests, about the sacred life of the child pinging into action from the very minute the girl gets preggers, and I know that Aunty Grace has been here before herself, in painful times gone by, and so I point my head down to the carpet, like a good boy in church when the communion bell rings, and I play along. But somehow, and somewhere inside, I'm guessing that this is all wrong, and that feeling totally rubbish for the sake of a little red blob of mucus just doesn't seem right when we should really be thinking about the brilliant girl at the top of the stairs who's worth more to me than all the overflowing buckets of blobby red mucus in the world.

Of course, we're not surprised at all when the door clicks open and Saidhbh suddenly appears looking a bit red-eyed and bedraggled but otherwise not like a woman emerging from the

346

depths of despair. She glances at Deano, and then down at us, and acts like it's any normal Sunday, where you've just woken up from a jammy afternoon kip only to find your friends and family surrounding you on the landing and the stairs below. Oh hi, she says, casual as anything, addressing me, Fiona and Aunty Grace. She then says that she's hungry, and that she wants to go out for some food, and for a change of scenery.

We all agree that this is an ace idea, and practically fall over each other, grabbing coats, keys and shoes, in a helter-skelter attempt to get kitted up and out the door before Saidhbh has time to change her mind and dash back upstairs for another lock-in.

Aunty Grace takes us to the Crown and Anchor on Cavendish Road, near the Kilburn mainline station. It's her local, and she gets a big wink, and then a hug, from a big fat fella from Offaly with a huge pink turnip head and rolled up sleeves, navy track-suit bottoms and brown shoes. He's on his knees when we arrive, fiddling with a plug at the back of a sparkly, glowy, Space Invader machine. His name is Larry, and he's the boss, and Fiona says that Aunty Grace's nickname for him is the Last Port of Call. Which means that when the girls at work can't get real jobs as secretaries in offices, and when they can't even get backup jobs as waitresses in restaurants, and, in fact, when they can't get any sort of paying job at all, at all, Aunty Grace gives them a wink and a nod and drives them over to Larry, the last port of call. Because Larry, says Aunty

347

Grace in a jokey way, is always in need of more girls because he's a desperate man for the women, and doesn't know where to put his hands. And most of her girls go blemming out the door by the end of their very first shift. Oh yes, says Aunty Grace, he's an awful fella, meaning that it's gas the way fellas are always grabbing at girls' boobs and bums.

Larry leaps up and calls Aunty Grace 'Your Ladyship' and, after a few mumbles and whispers between them, plus a few nods in Saidhbh's direction, he promises to give us the best seats in the house. He leads us to a raised platform at the back of the building, where just three tables are arranged, looking down over the entire pub, like a theatre balcony on to the stage. Larry serves us himself, for the rest of the night, and doesn't once let a bar girl give us anything, or take anything away from the table. He does lots of the usual chat. Asks us where we're from in Dublin and wants to know what's happening back there in the Auld Sod these days. Me and Saidhbh both shrug our shoulders and say nothing much, because we don't really know what he means. Aunty Grace tells him to leave us alone, especially when Larry starts asking us about old pubs in town, and if we knew about this fecker or that fecker who used to sit in the window of Davy Byrne's all Saturday afternoon.

The music blasts into gear at around ten o'clock, just as the ice-cream sundaes are hitting the table. It's not a real disco, but there's space downstairs, in the middle of four or five low tables, to have a bit of a dance. Larry kicks it off from a hi-fi machine above the pint glasses, and sure enough three girls at the bar, and one fella, are the first to start shaping. It's Culture Club, 'Karma Chameleon', and I can see Saidhbh's leg bobbing up and down under the table like she's dying to get up for a boogie. We both, me and Saidhbh, have glasses of Guinness in front of us too. Aunty Grace is brilliant like that, and just gave Larry the nod during the drinks order, and it was Guinness all round. No one even looked at me, or mentioned my age. I was just part of the gang.

Saidhbh's Guinness glass, now her third, is empty by the time 'Karma Chameleon' ends. She's only picked at her sundae, and has hardly said a word all meal. She clings tightly to the empty glass and taps it nervously against her thigh as she waits for the next song. I'm wondering how exactly, without sounding too greedy, can I make Aunty Grace order Saidhbh yet another drink, just to dampen down all the nervous tapping, when it kicks off. It's 'Smalltown Boy' by Bronski Beat. The slow ghostly intro sends shivers down my spine, and I get that rush you feel when the best song in the world comes on, and you know that everything in your life has never-ending possibilities just for those few gorgeously roaring moments. It's magical. And for the first time since I've put a single foot on English soil I get the tiniest whiff of the sense that everything might, in fact, be about to play itself out for the better. And maybe it's also the effect of the bitter black booze slowly eking its way into my system, or maybe it's the combination of the booze with

the dreamy high-pitched purr of Jimmy Somerville at his best, but for the first time too I begin
to drop my guard, and to step out of cat-nurse
mode, and to look around me and to see that
Saidhbh is still brilliant, and that Aunty Grace is
brilliant, and so is Larry the Last Port of Call,
and that pubs themselves, and London itself, just
waiting there outside the dirt-streaked windows,
with all its rubbish and traffic and busy people
and nutty neighbours and beardy Kilburn tramps,
it's all, all of it, brilliant!

The drums kick in, and I'm in heaven. I start
to nod and sway in my seat, doing some of my
best bedroom dance moves from the waist up. As
the beats get louder I'm tapping the table and
shifting shoulders, left to right to left to right
again. Fiona and Deano are down on the floor in
seconds, and doing brilliant forward and backward moves, a bit Dollar, a bit Legs and Co, like
they'd planned it all night. Aunty Grace is just
looking on, smiling. When the music goes bonkers
high and says, 'Run away turn away run away
turn away run away!' I feel flooded with happiness and nudge Saidhbh in the shoulder and
point my nose hopefully towards the dance floor.
She scrunches up her face and gives her head a
tiny shake, which is not a definite no, but certainly not a yes. I lean my chin sideways on to her
shoulder and am just about to plead, directly into
her ear, when she whips her head round and
says, Look at this!

At what?

She pushes her chair back, just a couple of
inches from the table and, with a triumphant

350

smile, reveals to me, and to me alone, that instead of tapping her thigh, she has actually snapped her Guinness glass apart into handy razor-sized chunks, and is currently working her way right down, deeply down, through her hand, from the tip of the middle finger all the way to the start of the wrist, cutting and jabbing away, while a heavy and messy Ribena-red flow gushes out over both hands, both thighs, and on to the floor.

★　★　★

With one word from Aunty Grace, Larry leaps into action and whizzes us out the back door. He insists on taking Saidhbh and Aunty Grace to hospital himself, while Deano walks me and Fiona the couple of hundred yards back to Glengall Road. We stay up for ages, with Deano and Fiona at first going over the night a million times, and wanting to know every gory detail, about when I first saw the blood, and did I have any inkling of what she was up to under the table, and how did I manage to wrestle the glass from Saidhbh's hand with the help of Last Port of Call Larry? They cool their jets, however, when they see that I'm shaking so much that I can hardly bring the cup of milky sweet builder's tea to my lips without splashing and scalding myself to pieces. They change tack and tell me that Saidhbh will be fine. And that it's just a blip along the road to her eventual recovery. Deano even says that it's a good thing, and that if he has learnt anything from the School of Astral Sciences it's that the path of healing is a mysterious one, and that tonight was an energetic release for Saidhbh, as well as a blip. But I'm not so sure. Jack the cat didn't have blips. And he died.

Saidhbh gets back in the wee hours. She lashes upstairs without saying a word, and keeps her bandaged hand hidden under her coat. She slams the bedroom door three or four times in a row when she discovers that Deano's taken off the lock. And then she flops into bed and doesn't get out of it, pretty much, for the next entire month.

On the upside, I get a job at Border Town!

3

Awakenings

Border Town is totally brilliant. Aunty Grace pulls a load of strings and calls in a million favours to get me in the door. She tells me exactly one week after Saidhbh's hand-slashing night, during which time I've mostly been staring zombie-like into space or learning the *Ladybird Book of London* off by heart while keeping loyal watch outside of Saidhbh's bedroom door like a cross between a heartbroken puppy and one of the Queen's very own Life Guards (who daily sit, I recite, on patient glossy horses and wear splendid uniforms). I know that everyone's worried about me, and they think that maybe I'm going to go the same way as Saidhbh, which is why I'm not expecting much joy when Aunty Grace sits me down on my own in front of another space-age dinner and says that we need to have a serious conversation.

She says that it looks as if I'm in Queen's Park for the long haul, until Saidhbh stops being mental at least, so I might as well earn my keep while I'm here, and help pay for some of the lovely grub that I'm eating and the bed that I'm sleeping in. I give her a look, and say nothing, and she continues, telling me that she's spoken to my mam on the phone and she agrees that it will be good character-building stuff, and that after bending a lot of rules and calling in a lot of old favours, particularly from a randy old Italian called Giorgio, who runs an employment agency exclusively for busboys, she has finally managed to get me a paying job as a table-clearer, floor-cleaner and general mopper-upper in none other than, and at this point she pauses for ages, just to make it even more impressive, Border Town in Oxford Circus.

Gobsmacked, I practically throw myself out of the chair and fling my arms around her neck. Border Town?! You're fecking joking! The big time! Aunty Grace dismisses me and tells me that I'll have to lie to everyone I meet and tell them that I'm sixteen and must never admit my real age, or else she'll get into lots of trouble with the British Government. I tell her that her secret's safe with me as I dash out the door and run straight up the stairs to tell Saidhbh the good news. I know that this is weird, and it's selfish, and it's probably the last thing on Earth that she wants to hear, but more than anything I want Saidhbh to return to being normal, and she'll only be normal if I'm normal right back to her too, and treat her like the old Saidhbh, the one who wants to listen to, and laugh at, any old rubbish that I have to say, especially the good kind of rubbish.

I catch her awake with the curtains half open, sitting on her bed, and holding a copy of *Jackie* magazine right up to her face with her big bandaged hand. Not mental at all in my eyes. I flop down beside her on the bed and tell her the news. She gives a little half-chuckle from behind the mag and says that it's great to hear something good for a change. She calls me a lucky madser, pulls the mag away from her face for a split second, and gives my nose a right comedy tweak, before going straight back to reading. It's the problem page, she says. Below-the-belt issues, she says, making a real meal out of the words, below the belt. And then she chuckles again. A dry chuckle. Not really laughing.

★ ★ ★

The job itself, it turns out, is dead easy and mostly involves me and two little Italian fellas called Marco and Luca — all three of us dressed in real flash uniforms of black trousers and blue denim shirts — whipping all the empties away from the table-tops as soon as we spot them, and rushing them into the kitchen. We clean up the spills too. And we even mop the vomit into buckets. That happens, I quickly discover, mostly on Saturday nights, when too many crazy fellas in rugby shirts have had too many tequila slammers from Sandy the shooter girl. Mix all the tequila with some spicy tomatoey and peppery foods and tons of beer, and you've a recipe for a badly splattered trip to the jacks, and multicoloured upchuck all over the back stairs.

I take to it like a duck to water, and everyone treats me really nice, from Trevor the English manager with the shaved head to the Arab fellas in the kitchen right through to all the gays out on the floor. Yeah, there's gays everywhere. The bloke at the front, who takes you to your seat, the tall blond fella behind the bar who makes the cocktails, and all three of the main waiters, are all super gay. It's a big change from Dublin, where you never really saw a gay, because they all must've been in hiding together somewhere, but these gays are brilliant about it, and dead funny, and always cracking jokes to each other and acting a bit like posh women who are on a break from having afternoon tea in huge mansions, and just doing waitering for a laugh. Billy, the head waiter, is the nicest, and he's always calling me his little Irish helper, and telling me I'm cute as a button, and stroking me and hugging me. It's the best thing ever, and it's not at all like O'Culigeen. Not a bit. Not dangerous at all. It's lovely and warming. Like the touch of a mam. And it makes me want to be near him, and listen to him, and make him happy with me whenever he's on duty.

I'm not the only one though. Everyone loves sitting around Billy after shift, listening to his stories. When the customers are gone home and the vomit and tomato is all cleared up, it's staff beer time, and the bar stools are usually arranged in a little semicircle around him, and he can just go on and on all night, till dead late, right into the morning, with funny stories and sayings and expressions that he's collected from years of being a top London waiter. Telling you about the early days in Soho, and the fights in Greek Street, and the rude sex-related things you'd see on the turn of every corner. One of his stories is about a girl running down the street with no pants on. And when he gets to the bit where he has to describe her fanny he does loads of funny actions, as if he's about to get sick, and as if the very thought of a fanny is enough to make him feel faint. We all burst out laughing at this, me and the other busboys and all the gays, because we know that it's dead funny when a fanny makes you want to puke.

At first Aunty Grace doesn't allow me to stay for staff beers. Partly because I'm too young, and she says that the after-hours chat would be unsuitable. Although Fiona sticks her head into that argument and reminds Aunty Grace that after everything that's happened me, well, really, come on?! But it's mostly because she doesn't like being called out at one in the morning on cold car pick-up duty, to drive all the way to Oxford Circus wrapped up in two heavy dressing gowns, woollen socks and slippers, and with eyes full of sleep and a head full of half-dreams. When Billy hears about this he goes mental in front of Trevor and insists that I get a staff taxi home every night that I work, just like all the girls do. Which isn't a big deal, because the British Government says that I'm only allowed to work two shifts a week, on Friday and Saturday night, on account of me being a pretend sixteen-year-old.

I plan to stay at home for the rest of the week, on Life Guard duty right next to Saidhbh's bedroom door, but Aunty Grace won't hear of it. Not least, she says, because there's boxes to be lifted, shelves to be stacked, and files to be numbered down at The Business. I begin to tell her that Saidhbh needs my help, and my attentions, but Aunty Grace just waves me away and says that the greatest help I can give to that poor young wan is to lead by example, and to show her that I'm not a moper, like she is, and am out instead and helping with The Business. This seems like the sort of thing that adults say when they want to get their own way, like when they go, I'll time you if you run down to the corner shop and buy me a packet of fags, or, I bet you can't empty that dishwasher by the time the titles for *Dempsey and Makepeace* are over? But I go with it anyway. Because I don't have a better plan. And because I know that, when it comes down to it, the idea of being at home alone on the brown beanbag when Saidhbh eventually finds the courage to stab herself with another broken glass — successfully this time, and right through the neck — freaks me to Jaysus and back.

★ ★ ★

Aunty Grace calls it The Business, but the official working name is *Grace's Angels*. It's the name typed on the rusty metal buzzer panel outside the door that leads you up to the office itself, which is really two huge rooms knocked into one above a chemist's shop in Ladbroke Grove, just opposite the tube station.

I walk down there after ten most mornings, way after everyone's started, and after I've finished my Frosties and had a chance to stick my head into Saidhbh's room and tried to get

358

something, anything, out of her. I usually do this little song-and-dance routine that Mam used to do to me when I was a tiddler, and it goes, Good morning! Good morning! You slept the whole night through! Only you're singing it, and you're shuffling from side to side as you do, and you're moving your hands around, both of them open and flat, in front of your body in little circles, as if you're washing a window pane in front of your face with two separate cloths.

When Mam used to do it back in The Rise she'd go from bedroom to bedroom in the early mornings, patiently performing the whole routine from scratch in each room, and getting totally different responses each time. Sarah and Siobhan would be all like, groggy and, Shag off with yourself and your good mornings! Whereas Claire and Susan would squeal with the thrill of it all when Mam got to the you, you and you bit, because then she'd be dancing closer, step by step, to the bedside, and she'd poke you in the armpit with big tough tickly fingers every time she said the word, you.

When I'd hear her coming towards me and Fiona's door I'd get instantly giggly, and hold the sheets right up to my face for the whole song, and work myself up into a hysterical high-pitched fit at the pokey, tickly, you, you and you climax.

Of course, I don't do the tickling bit with Saidhbh. But I do go through the whole routine, right there in the dark, and even manage a couple of shuffly left-to-right dance steps most days. Sometimes she answers with a groan.

Sometimes she giggles very softly under the covers, and sighs to herself that I'm Finno the Madser. And sometimes she says nothing at all. On those days I leave straight away, slipping quietly out the door, and feeling like a right berk — which is a new curse word that everyone in England uses, especially Aunty Grace, and it means prat or wally.

The walk down to Grace's Angels, from Kilburn through Queen's Park and into Ladbroke Grove, helps me remember that I'm in London, and that my life is mad, and that you can get used to anything when your girlfriend's life is depending on it. And anyway, London is pretty much the same as Dublin, except for the amount of people, the bigger streets, the faster cars, the deafening noise, and the blacks. In Dublin, besides the Shilawehs, we don't really have any blacks, whereas there's millions of them here. Although Fiona says that this is because of the particular part of the city that we're living in, and because the blacks and the Irish are always thrown together in every city in the world, because they're the lowest of the low. Everyone hates the blacks, she says, because they're lazy and they have big mickeys and are desperate to have sex with all the white girls. And everyone hates the Irish because they're lazy, and are always drunk and they don't use their mickeys for anything other than peeing up against your doorway in the small hours of the morning on the way home from the pub. So, together, the Irish and the blacks are a lethal combination, like one big lazy, drunken, stumbling sex-machine, and are best kept hidden in the darker corners of any city.

Fiona's brilliant like that. She's become really wise since living in London, and she knows loads more than she did when she lived in Dublin. And she's serious too, about her job, and about being all successful and everything, like the women on telly with the shoulder pads. She charges around Grace's Angels all businesslike, and gives me a potted history of the story so far, and of how there's a quarter of a million Irish living in London, but most of them are women, because Irish fellas usually get given the land down in the bog back home, and because even if they don't get the land the fellas are usually mammy's boys, whereas the girls are always a bit tougher and more full of adventurous spirit thanks to all the crucial early years that they spend being beaten up by angry nuns and being told by everyone to shut their fecking faces and go off and make the tea.

She says that it's boom time for Grace's Angels because of the amount of Irish girls that turn up in Kilburn every week. Although it's getting harder and harder to get the really thick ones into jobs, because the jobs themselves are changing and everyone has to be able to type at best, or at worst be able to read and write. Which is why Grace's Angels now has a full line of typewriter desks next to the windows, and is like a school most days, rather than a job centre, with nervous-looking girls getting rapped on the knuckles by Aunty Grace's ruler every time that they try to type with one finger instead of using the whole hand. Yes, says Fiona, sounding like a real old pro, it's all about the FIBs now — which is, she says, looking at me like it's the most obvious thing in the world, Finance, Insurance and Banking. Because ten years ago, according to Aunty Grace, you could get a girl into anything. Working at a biscuit factory, or in a furniture makers or at a car plant, you name it and there was a gig for a girl there, as long as she had two arms and half a brain. But now everything's gone upmarket, and there's no factory jobs any more, and all the city fellas with the red braces and the big cigars will only think of hiring great-looking women with brilliant typing skills and *Dynasty*-style suit jackets.

But then, of course, there's always restaurants, says Fiona, handing me a fresh pile of envelopes to stuff, and giving me a sisterly smirk. It's nice that being this successful hasn't changed Fiona at all, and she still knows how to be jokey and friendly-mean, without being hurtful. She thinks it's great that Aunty Grace snagged me the Border Town gig. And that I'm dead lucky to have an actual job, while most fellas my age are running around playing with Action Man, and *Star Wars* figures and scabbing pocket money from their mammies on a Sunday morning after Mass. And in London too! she says, beaming broadly, which makes us both instantly give each other the look that says that London's brilliant, without a doubt, yes, sir.

And besides, she says, it's good to keep your mind off of you know what. She nods at this, as if agreeing with herself, before I have a chance to

362

say anything back. I nod too. And then we sit for an age in awkward silence, while a gang of hopeful girls from Kerry bash away eagerly at the line of electronic typewriters that Aunty Grace has set up for them in the mid-morning sunshine.

⋆   ⋆   ⋆

I feel a bit of a spare tool when I get into Border Town on Friday evenings. Because I know that everyone's been having the time of their lives all week, and having brilliant battles with the customers, and listening to amazing stories from Billy during staff beers about the woman who ordered the tomato, bacon and mozzarella salad without the bacon or mozzarella, or about the time that he scribbled 'Tipping is not a village in China' on the receipt of the tight-fisted guy who left nothing at all for the waiters.

But Billy's the best. He clocks me immediately, and gives a little whoop of delight. He never makes me feel like I'm not one of the gang. And he's real protective over me too, especially because we can talk all night about Jimmy and Bronski Beat. He's hugely impressed that I know all the words to 'Smalltown Boy', and he even gets me to sing the entire song, without back-up, all five verses, in the staffroom one evening before Saturday shift. The staffroom is like our own private place, where no public can go, in the middle of all the madness. It's right down at the back of the restaurant, through a lone bright-red door with a slim window of shatter-proof glass and a big Strictly No Entry sign on it. It leads out to a manky back street next to the stage door of the London Palladium, but it's a special place in itself, with open lockers and wooden benches where you can sit down and have decent chats, and laughs, before the shift begins. And if you feel like it, you can sing too.

And this time it just happens, with everyone squeezed in and changing, that Trevor the manager's watching and everything. And half the kitchen staff. And normally I wouldn't do it, and would be far too embarrassed about my Aled Jonesy voice, but Billy's so convincing and tells me that I sing exactly like Jimmy, that I go for it. I get a huge round of applause at the end from everyone, including Faizel, the strict Arab sous chef, who normally hates anything to do with anything other than his mother or God.

Later that night Janus, the tall blond barman with a huge bottom jaw, who's from Denmark, corners me during staff beers and says, Come on, out with it, are you gay or aren't you? Billy comes rushing in and tells him to shut his faggot mouth, and reminds him that I'm only a kid. After that I always get Billy's tables, which drives Marco and Luca mad, because Billy's the best tipper of all. And I clean them super-fast for him, without even waiting for the nod. Sometimes he'll come blemming out of the kitchen, all panicked that the mains are on the way to a table of fifteen and he hasn't even begun to clear the starters, and he'll see that I've already cleared and set the entire table, right down to the steak knives and pancake holders. At which point, he'll stroll back in and pinch my shoulders and call me a *dolly filly*, which is part of an ancient and secret language of the gays, and it means a good good child.

Billy has a boyfriend, who's also gay, called Soz. Soz is from Turkey, where everyone's really strict, and they chop off your fingers for picking your nose, so being gay is totally out of the question. He's been in London for ever, and has worked his way up from the post room in a big City law firm to being his own man, and an accountant to boot. Billy makes loads of jokes about gay accountants that I don't understand, except the ones about sticking your pencil in the sharpener and stuff like that. Soz is nice too, though not as nice as Billy. He's quieter, for a start, and a bit fatter, and always looks a bit tired, like he's been up all night, and up to no good. The stubble doesn't help, which is super thick, and shaved in perfect straight lines all around his face, like Action Man. And he's real gruff sometimes, when he comes in for a late-night Saturday drink. Just plonks himself down at a table near the bar, and growls at me to get Billy over to him pronto, and to get the first of his Long Island Iced Teas on the go. These are drinks that taste like Coca Cola but have loads of booze in them, and are secretly made by Janus and hidden behind a box of straws at the service entrance of the bar for any of the waiting staff who are dead stressed and want to get a bit buzzy for the night. I never take one myself, because they're too strong, and because Trevor says that he'll fire anyone that he finds drinking on the job. But I happily bring them over, one after another, to Soz, who drinks them down like nobody's business and then gives a big wave and a nod of thanks over to Janus, who waves back with a big twinkly grin because they know each other, and are friends through Billy, and through being gay.

Soz is the one who asks me, out of the blue, if I'll come over to dinner at theirs on a Sunday night in August. It's just before the Friday shift starts, and he's rushing out as I'm rushing in, and we clatter right into each other. He looks like fury, and I'd swear he's going to hit me so I kind of duck and wince, but he only reaches down and pulls me to my feet and says that him and Billy have decided to go dinner party crazy and would love to have me over some night for a bite, and how does Sunday suit? I pause for a good few seconds, because dinner to me is a middle-of-the-day thing, with roast potatoes, gravy and everything, and the idea of having it at night-time, and with a party on top of it, seems a bit weird. But I trust Billy, so I say why not, and Soz smiles and says Fabulous, darling, and for the first time ever acts real girlie-like in front of me, and does a little bum wiggle as he spins around and disappears out the doors.

4

Lucky Star

The dinner party, it turns out, is actually brilliant, and Billy and Soz couldn't be any nicer if they tried. For a start they move the whole thing forward so that I can be dropped off and picked up by Aunty Grace, without making anyone miss too much sleep. They live in Earls Court, which isn't, they say, too far away from Queen's Park, but takes Aunty Grace forty-five minutes of effing and blinding through inch-by-inch traffic to get there. She's dead suspicious, and she first has to have an epic phone conversation with Billy where she gives him the sob story about me and my dying dad and my mad girlfriend, about how she's effectively my mam for now, and how she wouldn't hear of it if I was to come home with even a hair out of place, and how in fact, she corrects herself, she'd hear of it one way or another, and there'd be hell to pay. Billy, from the other end, sounds like he's being all charming, jokey and funny rude with Aunty Grace, and telling her that she's got a wicked imagination and that fellas like him and Soz are good as church-mice, and normally get up to nothing more exciting than a bit of good nosh and a quick bop-about to Madonna.

Billy ends the conversation, smooth as eggs, by turning it all back on to Aunty Grace, and having

367

a big chat about Grace's Angels. And it sounds like he's telling her that she's the best businesswoman in the world, to have come from where she's from, and to have nonetheless built an empire of recruitment around her. Aunty Grace says that it wasn't easy, and talks about pulling herself up by her bootstraps, and she wags her finger a lot while she's talking. She eventually sits down firmly on the kitchen stool, and smiles quietly to herself, and looks like a woman who's finally getting a prize for doing something lifelong and monumental, like raising war orphans, or nursing someone with a terminal disease.

Even so, on the night, Aunty Grace scrumples up around ten pieces of paper with her home phone number on them and shoves them in all of my pockets and whispers to me, as I leave the car, right in front of their flat, that I'm to make sure to remember to lock the toilet door each time I'm using it. I tell her not to be mad, but she says that she's been around their sort for years, and she knows what they like, and that I've got three hours, tops, and if I'm not back down on the street by 11 p.m. she's coming up herself to get me.

The dinner itself, as I say, is brilliant. And Soz, as well as being a gay accountant with Action Man stubble, is also an ace cook. We have lamb chops with little chef's hats on them, and home-made chocolate brownies for dessert. And it's not just me either. Billy and Soz have invited two of their best buddies, Roger and Jamie, around to share in what Billy predicts will be an evening of *fantabulosa dishes*! Roger immediately tells him that he's awful when he says that, and looks down at me unsure and asks Billy, while using only the ancient language of the gays, if I'm an *omi palone*. Billy rolls his eyes and tells Roger he's got a one-track mind, while Soz moves in behind me and tells me to ignore Roger, and says that all those sweaty men, with their big sticks and their balls, must've turned his head.

This is a joke, I find out later, about baseball. Because Roger is American, and him and Jamie have been playing baseball all day in an amateur London weekend league organised by a load of working fellas called expats, who are mostly American, with some German and some Japanese too, and all united by their love of baseball. And even though Roger's at least fifty, he's dead competitive, and a bit of a home-run king, and doesn't tell anyone at Sunday baseball that Jamie's his boyfriend, just in case it distracts them from everything that's going on in the strike zone.

Roger's easily the oldest in the room, and with the wrinkly face and baldy head to prove it. But he's also the chattiest, and is an even better storyteller than Billy. Roger sits at the head of the table and goes on for ages, telling me and the group at one and the same time about how he met Jamie, who's a tiny little fella, and from Italy, and doesn't speak much English but seems to be having the best time of anyone in the room because he can't stop laughing. Roger, whose job was very important back in the day, and was all

369

about importing and exporting, was on a business trip to Rome last year, when he found Jamie living rough on the streets and swallowing swords for a living down on the Piazza Cavour. At this point he says, No jokes please, ladies! But no one laughs, except Jamie, who's in hysterics. Roger finishes this whole long and epic story about sweeping Jamie off the streets and cleaning him up, and getting him off the drugs and generally making him shipshape again for a new life in London, by his side. And then, at the very end of it he just bursts out laughing himself and says that he was only joking, and that he met Jamie in the bar of Hilton on Park Lane, because they were both at the same conference. At which point Jamie laughs even louder than before and says, through snatched breaths, over and over again, Same conference! Heeheehee! Same conference!

We have wine too, which is a first for me. I have tasted it before, in the concoctions at parties that you'd collect at the end of the night, mixed with the dregs of gin and vodka, and you'd have a sip that would make you want to retch but get you buzzy enough to dance to the hoolie section of the hoolie. But this is different. This is a full glass of red wine, ruby red, sitting there in front of me, like a real person, in a wine glass, with no rush, and no need to slug it all down because someone might see me and tell my mam that I was shaming the family. In fact, it's the complete opposite here, because whenever I've barely a sip taken out of the glass Soz whizzes over to my shoulder and fills it right up to the brim again.

I totally lose track of how many sips I've had, but I know the evening's going well because at one point Roger gets everyone to listen as he calls me his Celtic companion, and asks me to tell him my story. I've been sandwiched in between Roger and Jamie all night. This is, says Billy, to stop them gossiping like a pair of dizzy *riah shushers*, but I've mainly been listening to Roger tell me about anything and everything to do with his life. He started with the easy stuff, about baseball, and about all the London galleries that he'd brought Jamie to in the past twelve months, and how he was educating this little Italian brute in the cultured ways of the English and the sporting ways of the Americans. At which point Jamie peeked his head round my shoulder, gave Roger a nice firm puck in the shoulder, and burst out laughing again, saying, Little brute! Heeheehee! Little brute!

By the time the chocolate brownies arrive, however, Roger's gone all serious. He's telling me about his bastard dad, and his childhood in upstate New York, and how there are two types of gays in this world — those that are born gay, and those that are turned gay by someone else, which is a bit like being a vampire, or a Jedi from *Star Wars*. The 'someone else' who turned him to the gay side, as it happened, he says, was his bastard dad. A bastard rapist who ruined every night of his childhood until he found a way, when he was barely a teenager, to break free, and flee for good, into the waiting arms of the big city. Just like you, he says, giving me a wink as he does.

I've had buckets of wine at this stage, so I tell him that I'm not gay myself, but that I know a gay man back in Dublin. Although, I say, straightaway correcting myself, he's actually more of a rapist than a gay man. A bit like your dad, I suppose. Roger looks hugely hurt for a second, as if it was OK for him to say rude things about his dad, but not someone like me. He runs a hand slowly over his smooth bald head, and then grabs his glass and thwacks it with a fork and asks me, in front of everyone, to tell the table my story.

This creates a bit of a weird atmosphere, and Billy tells Roger to leave me alone. Soz snaps at Billy, and tells him not to be such a mother hen, and joins sides with Roger, saying that he wants to hear my story too. The effect is immediate on me, and it's like someone instantly turns me upside down and empties all the red wine out of my body, and I sober up. I take ages, but when I see that I'm not wriggling out of this, I eventually choke out the words, Well, I'm from Dublin. This gets a huge round of applause and cheering, and Roger does an impression of someone going flying backwards off his chair due to the sheer excitement from hearing such a sizzling piece of info. And, I say, after another age, calling up the one detail that's never far from my mind, I have a girlfriend, and she's not very well. Everyone goes Booo at this, and throws crumpled-up paper napkins at me. And Soz says, Rubbish! Tell us your real story!

I look over Billy's shoulder, and think about dashing for the door, but either the remains of the red wine, or something about the kindness in Billy's eyes brings me back to myself. Inside I say, Feck it, and I think about confession back home, and how Mam always says that confession works the best when you don't know the priest that well, and how Maisie O'Mally would drive halfway round the whole city of Dublin in order to find a faraway church in godforsaken nowheresville with a priest that she'd only visit just this once in her life and never again if she ever had anything really serious to tell. So I look around the room at the lads, and I know that this kind of thing is totally up their streets, and even though I feel mad with nerves at the prospect, I close my eyes for the night that's in it, take a deep breath and give it a go.

Well, I say, there was this priest back home. Everyone cheers at this. Soz says, Now we're cookin! And Roger leans in very close. I say that the priest gave me a rude book once, and then I stop. My leg is twitching again, real fast like. I can feel the energy bubbling up inside me. I have to shut my mouth tight, coz I swear I'm going to start speaking in tongues. And the book, I say. And my dad, I say. And the camping. And Saidhbh. And Saidhbh.

I'm suddenly pouring sweat, and these are the only words I can get out. Little short sharp barks. All my strength goes into holding my jaw wire-shut, because I don't want to freak everyone to Jaysus. If I let go, I have no idea what sort of gibberish could come spewing forth. And for a moment I'm completely stuck, with my mouth stretched wide in this madly frozen grin, and my panicking eyes staring out around at four increasingly confused faces.

Deano says that it's all about energy control. He says that if the School of Astral Sciences has taught him anything it's that we are all energetic beings who are constantly absorbing power from the Earth's core, and that if we have a block inside us, or if we don't let it out, we build up energetic steam, like a human pressure cooker, that can become monumental in strength if properly directed. And if we don't explode it all out away from us we'll end up re-directing the energy around the insides of our bodies and giving ourselves cancer and terminal illnesses. I wonder if that's what happened to Dad. Was he blocked because of a life spent selling office furniture and paying for six kids when all he really wanted to do was hang out and tell breastfeeding jokes with Mam? Or did he just get cancer?

Either way, Roger and the boys are not impressed with my rubbish story and sudden stutter. Soz slowly pushes his chair back, and stands up on the spot. He says, returned to gruff man mode, that he's had enough of this shit, and rips off his shirt. Oh yes, he then says, beaming at the others, it's that time of night! Jamie too leaps up in his seat and gives a whoop of excitement, just as Roger unbuckles his belt and lets his trousers drop to the floor, revealing a pair of navy-blue baseball shorts. Holiday time! he says staring over at Billy, who looks in my direction and gives me an apologetic shrug. Soz reaches down behind the table and fiddles with the stereo. The hiss from the speakers tells me that he's gone full volume, for the benefit of us lot, and all of Earls Court.

Ignoring me completely, all four men march into the middle of the sitting room, which is the same as the dining room and the telly room and the kitchen, because it's all one flat, so they move to a part of the carpet that's furthest away from both the couch and the table. The ceiling light goes down, and Billy puts on a side light that has a red bulb that makes the room look all ace and disco-y. Madonna suddenly blares. She's singing 'Holiday'. The men dance. They do dead professional, *Top of the Pops* style moves. I watch for ages, right through 'Dress You Up' and 'Into the Groove', without making a move. Just watching, and smiling, and feeling relieved about the fact that we've stopped telling stories. By the time 'Borderline' comes on I get up and join them on the floor. I copy some of their moves, but mostly I throw in my own special shapes, from the Gary bedroom days. They love this, and they do a lot of woo-woos, even once making a little circle around me while I do my stuff in the centre. I do a bit of mock-acting-dancing too, so when Madonna sings that it's the borderline, and that she feels like she's going to lose her mind, I hold my hands to either side of my head and pretend that I'm pulling my hair out. For the slower bits of the song I make it interesting by doing some of the high kicks that Madonna does in the video.

When 'Lucky Star' comes on we break up into groups. Me and Billy do face to face, while Soz,

Roger and Jamie form into a little dancing triangle. Me and Billy hold hands too, but in a jokey way, like the way aunties and uncles dance with kids at hoolies, or like he's the disco-king instructor and he's showing me what to do with my arms, when to pull, when to push, and when to wave them around in giant alternating circles. And while all this is happening, and while Madonna is singing about watching the very first star that makes everything all right, Billy leans into my ear, still dancing and bopping and wiggling my hands, and shouts full blast, like you do in a real-life disco, So this priest, yeah?! He diddled you, yeah?!

I don't stop bopping either, but I nod like mad, making sure, nonetheless, to keep my nods in time with the beat of 'Lucky Star'. It's my way of saying, yes, yes, God and Jesus, yes, but through the power of disco nods rather than words. Billy doesn't ask anything else. He just shakes his head, side to side, still to the beat, makes his eyes go slitty in anger, and then mouths the word, wanker. We dance in silence until the end of the song, and then 'Burning Up' comes on. Billy gives my hands a right squeeze, followed by a huge arm swoosh left and right, and then he spins me sideways, right into Soz, Roger and Jamie's triangle, which is where I remain for the rest of the bop.

★ ★ ★

Aunty Grace breaks up the fun at 11.30 p.m. with some heavy thumping on Billy's flat door

376

and a furious face on her when she eventually steps inside. She glares at me for keeping her up so late, but Billy works his magic, and after a small glass of red wine and chinwag about the highs and lows of the employment business all seems to be forgiven. In the car on the way home she tells me that Billy is a lovely fella, and one of the best gays around. She says too that she knows I've been drinking loads by the smell of me. She says that it doesn't bother her, but that I'd better drink plenty of water, and wash it all through me before tomorrow morning. Wouldn't want it wrecking your vibes, she says, half joking to herself.

That's the other brilliant thing about working at Border Town. It gives me plenty of time to practise my healing.

5

Community

Normally I wouldn't be into healing, or anything binjy-banjy like that. Actually, Fiona calls it binjy-banjy. It means that it comes from India and other faraway places, where everyone speaks all binjy-banjy with their heads wobbling on their shoulders and everything about them is a bit funny and not funny at the same time. She says that the fact that Deano's into all the binjy-banjy stuff is why she loves him. Because he's a trier, and he never says that anything is rubbish, and God loves a trier, and if it wasn't for the fact that Deano was in her life right now, over here, in this England, and in this London, despite all the brilliant bits about working in Grace's Angels and being in the biggest and best city in the world, she probably wouldn't be able to breathe. Because, when it comes down to it, she is the opposite of Deano, and so many things are rubbish and thick to her, so together, she says, they make the perfect match. Plus, she adds, after all that, that she finds the healings very relaxing. Like having a super-long massage, but with heavy breathing on the side.

It takes Deano ages to persuade me to go to Community. He doesn't use the word 'the'. It's just called Community, on its own. That's the way. And it's meant to symbolise the bigness of it all, and the fact that it's not a lone, single idea. But everywhere. When I ask Deano about it, we have our first genuine argument, because he tells me that there's no 'I' in 'We', but when I answer that there's an 'I' in 'Community' he goes mental.

Anyway, the building itself is a converted church in Islington, which is nearly an hour away from us by the regular overground train. So it's a big hassle to get there in the first place, even if you're not being dragged by your ears. Deano, from day one, was forever shoving leaflets into my face, brochures that featured photos of healers, who were mainly beardy fellas with ponytails and smiley eyes, or else mammy-aged women with grey hair, chunky wooden necklaces and multi-coloured tops, and all of them, men and women, looking into the camera with their best Jesusy faces on. Or else they were wearing baggy vests and track-suit bottoms, and standing with their legs apart and half bent beside massage tables, and leaning, arms outstretched over their seemingly sleeping healees, and with their own eyes shut tight and their heads tilted upwards to the sky.

At the top of the leaflets were the words, *The School of Astral Sciences*, and on the back page they had a photo of the School's big boss, a woman with jet black witch's hair and big white American teeth. She was called Serenity Powers, and she had a little printed speech below the photo, where she said that she was originally a top-secret scientist working on all sorts of cutting edge stuff for a huge American corporation when

379

she discovered that she had the gift of seeing auric fields, and being able to manipulate the many subtle energy pathways within our bodies. And that she now wants more than anything to share this gift with the world, and that's why she's opening up schools of Astral Sciences everywhere she can. And she wants you, meaning me, to enjoy the gift, and finally feel what it's like to have the power to heal.

I thank Deano for the offer, but tell him, copying Fiona, that it all sounds a bit binjy-banjy to me. He doesn't gives up though, and comes back to me again and again with a million different arguments for why I should join him at Community. He says that since I'm doing nothing during my weekdays other than mooching around The Business and stuffing a few envelopes, it's time that I started thinking about school again. But with his plan, he says, a couple of sessions in Community will give me more than I could possibly learn from a lifetime of lessons in any real-world schooling system.

I tell him that it sounds brilliant but the main thing for me, I say, coming up with a winning escape clause, is the money. At thirty pounds a session, it's nearly my entire weekend's wages, minus tips. Which means I wouldn't have any left for Aunty Grace's rent. Deano tells me that money is just energy, and it's irrelevant to the School of Astral Sciences, and that they only charge a lot because the service they provide is so specialised and has come, essentially, from the highest ranks of the scientific community. You wouldn't ask the biggest corporations in America to hand over their best products, their chemical advances and their scientific weapons for free, would you? Well, this is just the same. It's about turning your hands into highly evolved scientific weapons, but weapons of wonder and healing.

I dig my heels in and say that I'm trying to save for a surprise present for Saidhbh — an aeroplane trip home at Christmas time. The travel agent has said that it's going to be five hundred pounds all in for both of us, so every penny counts, science weapons or not.

Deano's had enough, and he goes a bit red in the face and says that I'm missing the point entirely. What does money matter, he says, hissing furiously, when compared to the health and well-being of those you love? If not for yourself, he says, then why not for Saidhbh?

I'm not expecting that. And it kind of knocks the wind out of me. Hurt, I blurt back at him anything I can, and I tell him that Saidhbh's grand, and just needs a couple more weeks to get over the baby, and she'll be right as rain. He puts a hand to his mouth and pretends to gag and to scoff all at once, and gives me a look down his nose that means that he knows, and I know, and we all know, that this might not be totally true. Eventually, hand down, and moving in towards me, he speaks. He tells me to come on now. And he says that she's just not normal any more. Meaning Saidhbh. And, well, the binjy-banjy bastard is right.

★ ★ ★

Saidhbh is on the slippery slope. And it's not in the big dramatic stuff either, like slitting herself open with broken glasses, but in the way she is, and the way she won't look at you, and how she acts all twitchy and flinchy when she passes you on the stairs, like she's about to be hit at any minute by a big thundering bamboo stick from the heavens. And her clothes are filthy, but she won't let Aunty Grace go near them. Especially the dungarees. And her hair's a mess, all knotty not silky, and stinking of smoke, because she smokes now, tons of them, right out the bedroom window, like a secondary Glengall chimney. And at first they were the only things that got her out of the house, down to the corner shop beside the launderette, for a packet of twenty Rothmans and a pack of Hula Hoops. But then she went further afield, away from Kilburn altogether and through Lonsdale Road, across Salusbury Road and right into Queen's Park, the parky bit, itself.

She came back from that day on a high, and looked everyone in the eye for the first time in ages, from person to person, and really locked us with some killer stares, all buzzy and blinkless and super-happy, and said that what she wanted to do more than anything else, right now, was her art. She turned to Aunty Grace and made her go out to the High Road, at that very minute of the evening, and buy her a giant art pad, with huge tear-off paper pages, and a box of colour pastels for drawing lines and smudging colours. And when Aunty Grace came back with the gear, Saidhbh just grabbed it roughly from her, and didn't say thank you or anything, and instead dashed out the door again and straight down to the parky bit of Queen's Park to do her art.

She draws trees all the time, and that's all she does. And sometimes the same tree for days on end. And, depending on how satisfied she is with the drawing she's done that day, she'll be in a brilliant mood or a mad mood when she comes in the door. It's like she has a job, and it involves grabbing her art gear and two packets of Rothmans and Aunty Grace's camping stool, all at the crack of dawn, and heading down to the park to draw nothing but trees till the darkness. On her very first early riser I had no clue, and totally panicked when I popped into her room, and worked my way through the first few bars of 'Good morning! Good morning . . . ' before I realised that she wasn't even in the fecking bed. I raised the alarm down at Grace's Angels and Deano was sent out in the Peugeot on scouting duty, but he found her almost immediately in the park, stuck to her stool, sketching away like a woman possessed, smack bang in front of a bright green elm tree with huge overhanging branches.

Deano had a word with a fella wearing a bright yellow hat and jacket who is the park Keeper, and who knows Saidhbh on sight, and says that she has a nickname already, and that everyone there just calls her the Tree Woman behind her back, even some of the mams with prams. When she's not drawing, the Keeper says that Saidhbh sometimes approaches the mams with prams, especially when they roll close by her camping stool, and she asks them if she can look inside at the little ones. The Keeper thought that this was going to be a big problem when he saw her do it first, maybe a job for the cops, and he even started jogging towards Saidhbh with his whistle out, and was ready to tell her to feck off with herself and her filthy loony ways. But the mams were brilliant with her, and one of them even lifted a baby out of the pram for Saidhbh, and let her hold it and cuddle it. And the keeper said that Saidhbh was brilliant right back with the baby, all soft and stroky, and hushed, like a mam that you'd see in an advert for washing powder, who cuddles a baby with a fresh yellow towel and makes the baby beam with happiness just because she's there, looking, in that instant, eye to sacred eye. It made the Keeper feel like an awful eejit for getting it so wrong, and for forgetting that mams together are like a tribe of their own, and that women and babies is a fierce combination. He backed away slowly, and let Saidhbh alone. And never interferes any more when she bothers the pram mams.

And all of this, of course, doesn't seem too bad. Because when Saidhbh's having a good day, and good episodes, and happy with her day's work in the park, you get flashes of the old Saidhbh. With no twitching or flinching, and lots of proper looks, and even a few giggles. And in these moments, say, when we're sharing a pizza while squashed around Aunty Grace's tiny kitchen table, you'd swear that everything was back to normal, and she might even chuckle when Fiona starts telling funny stories about life back home and the things she used to do in Sister Pauline's French class, or she might seem to be listening intensely when I read out the latest letter from Gary, about how boring a summer in Dublin really was, and how much he's dreading the return of the school term and how well my dad seems to be these days. After that one she even rubbed my shoulders and said that Gary's news about my dad was fantastic, and that I must be really relieved, mustn't I? I looked round at her and touched her fingers and said yes. And as I said yes, in the moment of the yes itself, I felt that, yes, I was happy then, and with the way this was going.

But underneath it you never know. Because Aunty Grace came down one morning, hardly after seven o'clock, and got the shock of her life to find Saidhbh in the kitchen, fully dressed and ready to go, with camping stool and art pad by her side, but with an untouched bowl of Frosties in front of her, and a big plastic bottle of Domestos in her hands, and pressed right up against her face. And she was just reading it, the whole label, like she was hypnotised, or like she was only seconds away from pouring it all over her Frosties. She didn't say a word to Aunty Grace when she came into the kitchen either, which upset Aunty Grace no end, and made her have a huge discussion that night with Fiona and Deano about whether Saidhbh should be sectioned or not. I wasn't invited into that discussion, because I was working in Border Town, and because I didn't know what sectioning meant, and Fiona had to explain it all to me when I got home, and

385

said that, for now, Saidhbh was off the hook, but that the pressure on Aunty Grace was almost becoming too much to bear, and that it didn't help that the Donohue clan were haranguing her on a daily basis and kept the phone hopping off the hook with annoying questions about Saidhbh and the state she's in. And, of course, worst of all, if you mention to Saidhbh the very idea of going back, or travelling anywhere further than her beloved park, and her beloved trees, then she goes berserk and twitchy, and weepy to boot, and without actually saying it, is kind of threatening to reach for the Lady Shave or glug back the Domestos at the drop of a hat.

★ ★ ★

If nothing else, Deano is persistent. Seeing that the whole Saidhbh subject has winded me into moody silence, he says that I've no idea how much a bit of the old Serenity Powers could help Saidhbh with her issues. And imagine how great I'd feel if I could relieve some of her pain. Me, personally. From my hands to her body. It was, after all, he says, going for a bit of levity, my hands on her body, and all the rest, that caused this mess in the first place. And what about the Donohues? he asks. And the whole Finnegan family? And Aunty Grace? And everyone who knows Saidhbh? Think of what I owe them all, and how grateful they'd be if I could just ease some of Saidhbh's pain.

That night, still chewing over Deano's offer, I flop down beside Saidhbh, and she shows me her drawings. Brilliant trees, I say, as I skip through them, page after page, after page. I tell her a bit about Border Town, and how I served a beef chimichanga even after I dropped it on the kitchen floor, but mostly we just lie there in silence. She looks older, I think to myself, like a real woman. Certainly sadder, or at least like someone who could do with a good night's sleep. Her messy knotty hair is scrunched up into a bun, and there's loads of frizzy bits sticking out around the ears. Her mouth and nose are the same as always but her eyes, those magic eyes, are totally different now. Surrounded by ashy grey rims, they somehow seem to be bulging outwards from her face and falling back inwards into her skull at the same time. They're also kind of blank.

What are you looking at? she asks, after an age of me staring.

I'm looking at you, I say, careful not to mess her about.

Pervert, she says, nudging me sharply in the ribs.

I ask her what she's thinking about and she says one word. Him.

Who's him? I say, the cat's father? Trying to keep it light.

No, she says, blank as ever. Him.

I get it. She means Him, our dead baby. Our dead baby is now a boy. This is new. I don't really have a good follow-on for this, so I let the moment sit there in silence. I wonder what kind of boy we would've had, and what it would've been like to be a dad to a boy. I picture myself playing football with him, and going to rugby matches, and doing all the rough tough manly things that I don't do with my own dad. I imagine showing him how to remove the ignition housing from the central heating, and I feel suddenly sad at the speed of everything, and how life is racing and how I haven't yet had a chance to live the dream date with my dad where both of us sit at a low pub table with pints in front of us, and we go all manly and compare froth-stained moustaches, and laugh our heads off, and maybe even punch each other in the shoulder, which will be our way of saying, You're the best. No, you are. No, you are. No, really, you are.

Saidhbh breaks the silence, finally, and tells me that He is always with her. He never leaves her. I say, Right? And I act dead normal and dead interested, and even do a little scan around the room, as if I'm trying to pick out the sight of a teensy-tiny mucus blob with arms and legs wearing an even tinier microscopic nappy. There's another monumental pause before Saidhbh finally shuts her notepad with a bang and says, He likes trees.

I tell Deano the very next morning that I'll give Community a shot. He's thrilled to pieces, and says that I'll have to wait till the following night, because the School of Astral Sciences only practises three nights a week. For the rest of the time, Community is taken up with yoga, tantra, pathway work, family constellations, and a load of other binjy-banjy shite.

6

The Night

On the night, of course, I get cold feet. I think of
every excuse in the book to try and wriggle out
of it, but no luck. And it doesn't help that
Fiona's been slagging me all day, and calling me
a hippie in front of the girls at Grace's Angels.
She thinks it's hilarious that I'm actually going
to an Astral Science class with Deano in the first
place. And it's even funnier, but in an odd and
slightly disturbing way, that I think it's going to
have the added bonus of making Saidhbh
mentally stable again. She says that the best I
should hope for is the ability to give Saidhbh a
long and slightly boring massage. That is, she
adds, if I can ever manage to peel her out of
those stinking dungarees for long enough.

I go bonkers at this, and call Fiona a fecking
berk, and tell her to shut her fecking mouth,
right in front of three of the Grace's Angels who
are at the typewriters. Then I run out on to the
fire escape and have a big cry. Fiona's out beside
me in seconds, and with her arms tight around
me, and calling me Jimbo, and telling me that
everything will be all right with Saidhbh, and
that I'm a great lad for going to all this trouble,
and that Mam and Dad would be dead proud of
me if they could see how I'm taking this problem
on, like a real man. And what's more, she was

just joking with me, she says, because Deano's told her some ace stories about the Astral Science healings and the things they've done to the lame and the blind. Real miracles, she says, before pinching me on the cheek like a baby and adding, You'll do grand.

Still, I get a massive case of the collywobbles right before Deano shoves me into the front seat of the Peugeot, and I feel like I'm going to be sick. I tell Deano that Community sounds like Camp Generation down in Connemara, which is full of Goddy loo-las, and so I've changed my mind and don't want to go. But he just says, Nonsense, and drives off into the traffic like it's the most exciting night of our lives even though something deep down in my stomach is telling me that I should fling myself out the moving car door like T. J. Hooker on a good day rather than proceed any further.

I ask him if we could go to the cinema instead, and see the new Eddie Murphy flick, *Beverly Hills Cop*, but he just hoots with laughter, in a hee-haw hee-haw Eddie Murphy way, and then coldly says, No. I tell him that we could see *Beverly Hills Cop* ten times for the amount of money this one class is going to cost, but he just winks at me and tells me that this one is on the house.

The church hall is all concretey and freezing, even in the dog days of August. It still has some stained-glass windows of old, and some white church columns on the sides. But there's no actual seating left, like long wooden benches from the Mass days, and instead the whole inside of the hall has been neatly arranged for the

390

night, with five rows of five massage beds, all facing the king massage bed on the stone platform where the altar used to live. The Astral Science students begin to arrive in dribs and drabs, and gather round the herbal tea table right next to the rear double doors. They look like younger versions of Deano, all of them, even some of the girls. And they all seem to favour the ponytail style, and the smiley Jesus eyes, with clothes made out of baggy anything. Baggy jumpers, baggy T-shirts, baggy sweat-shirts, and baggy tracksuit bottoms. And they smell too, like proper stinky BO. Like the way I used to smell after school, just before I started getting hairy, and Mam had to leave a bar of Lifebuoy soap and a can of Imperial Leather deodorant on my bed with a note that said simply, 'Use!' which was a way of saying that my hormones were kicking in and that I was really stinking up the house so I needed to get washing, fast.

Deano tells me later that soap interferes with your natural electrochemical balance. And that the Astral Science students are actually dead clean, and always washing themselves with plain water. And so what I'm really smelling, in their stink, is the whiff of genuine and natural humanity at its best, and not some chemical poison that's been invented by American companies and sold by fellas running through the desert on TV so that fellas like me will spend our pocket money, or get our mams to spend their housekeeping money, on little pressurised tins of poison that will make us all smell like robots and knock our electrochemical balance right out of whack.

They mostly have funny names, the students, and mostly taken from nature. And they are names from the good part of nature, like Forest Leaves, and Sunny Day, and not stuff like Drizzly Sunday or Piranha Faeces. I ask Deano why he hasn't changed his name yet and he says that you can only do it when you've graduated from your fifth year of Astral Sciences studies. There's a whole ceremony and everything, where Serenity Powers officially hands you the name in a rolled-up document. He says that he has a name all geared up and waiting, and will be able to use it from next January onwards. He won't tell me the name, but gives me a hint and says that it's connected to fish (he tells me three weeks later that it's Swimming Water, but only because I keep tormenting him with stupid suggestions: Cod in Batter? Captain Birdseye? And so on). He tells me that I should start thinking of one now. I groan. But he says, confident, You'll see!

★ ★ ★

The students hug each other too, for ages. They come in and they go, Hi, Blue Blossom, and then fall into these huge epic five-minute hugs, as if someone had just died. Deano gets loads of them. After which he'll usually say, How are you? And then the hugger, instead of saying, Fine, and you? will actually bang on for another five minutes about how they're really feeling, and how they feel disappointed in themselves for re-enacting old patterns and giving in to the old story of their personal negativity and the very

392

idea of the ego. At the end of all this Deano introduces me to each one of the huggers, but I just nod hello at them, and am careful to back away as I do, in case they get any ideas. Although, they can probably smell my Sure extra-strength deodorant from ten paces and are worried that if they hugged me I might actually rub some of their pongy electrochemical doo-dah away.

Either way, Deano does a good twenty minutes of hugging and mutual moaning, during which time he's careful to introduce me to three different women, clearly his favourites and all Mam's age and older, in matching grey tracksuits, who are called, by their first names, Peach, Feather and White. They tell me that they envy me and that my life's about to change right now. Your first Astral Science class? they coo. You'll never be the same again. Although, says Peach, it's a shame that Mossy Bough is too ill to hold the class tonight, because that would've been a first class to remember. Instead, I'll have to make do with Winter Rain.

Deano groans when he hears that Winter Rain is taking the class, but the women tell him not to be so critical. Winter Rain, he explains to me in a whisper, is not a patch on Mossy Bough, and is, in fact, just a little upstart who's been given preferential treatment by Serenity Powers and hasn't even finished a single fecking year out of the full five yet!

Jealous! jokes Feather, making big fond eyes at him.

But I thought I was going to meet Serenity Powers? I ask.

393

They hoot, all four, and collectively explain that Serenity Powers lives in California, and only visits her Astral Science classes once a year, for the January naming ceremony. Other than that, they say, the classes are held by her brightest students, chosen personally by Serenity herself.

And they're supposed to be fifth years! adds Deano, with a loud and disappointed tut, meaning that Winter Rain is a right little rip for skipping the queue.

And, in fact, he begins, if you ask me . . .

Right on cue a ding-dongy bong-bell rings, and Winter Rain appears from behind the altar, dressed in bright and baggy white pyjamas, a red sash around the waist, but with her face completely covered in a white veil. When Deano sees the veil he sighs, and rolls his eyes. Feather turns to me and explains that Winter is going to call her guides to help us through the class tonight. A bit of a murmur-murmur goes round the hall. The guides are a big deal. Peach pinches me, and gives me a hefty wink, letting me know that I am in for the time of my life.

The guides, however, are actually a bit of a letdown, and certainly not as interesting as anything you'd see in *Beverly Hills Cop*, or *Ghostbusters* for that matter. Rain just tilts her head back and in a normal speaky voice asks the guides, who are called Waylean and Mestapheen, to come into her from the Earth, the stars and beyond and purify this room, and these people, meaning us, and help her hold this session with power and focus. At which point she goes a bit jerky, like a break-dancer, and then does a scratchy exorcist voice, totally deep, and says really thick things like, I am with you now, and My hands are your hands, and I am the light within and all around. Deano explains later that the veil is to keep the class leader, and her or his guides, completely in the healing zone, and to make sure that they're not distracted by the sight of a hall full of eager-eyed students before them. But I'm betting with myself that it's there mostly to hide the fact that she's laughing her head off while doing the funny voices.

Deano, despite the moans at first, is soon hooked by the stage show and by Winter Rain. And so are all the others. She's obviously good at what she does, and the students go crazy when she speaks in her guide voice, and Peach even gives a little miniscream, as if she can't bear the excitement, like she's one of the black-and-white girls at old Beatles concerts who just have to let it out because the very idea of being near John, Paul and Ringo and the other fella is so thrilling. I'm mostly looking at my watch, and thinking about what a big disappointment this whole night has been, and how I'm not going to get magical healing powers to help Saidhbh, and how I wish that we could've gone to the flicks instead. Winter Rain seems fine, and a very good performer, but after everything that me and Saidhbh have been through, I'm finding it really hard to get involved in the play-acting on the altar, and can't stop myself from wondering why, if all the whirling powers of the universe came pouring down into one particular person on Earth, the first thing they'd do would be to put on a silly voice?

And still, there's something about Winter Rain that I can't quite shake. Something about her first voice, her speaking voice, before she went into cosmic ghost mode. Something in the tone that won't let me go. She tells us, still throaty, and still pretending to be Waylean and Mestapheen, to divide ourselves up between healers and healees and to get on to our massage beds. Naturally, I choose to be a healee and Deano becomes my healer, and I hop up on to the bed, facing heavenward. Deano isn't even looking at me. All eyes are on Rain. She barks out words like 'ground', 'deeper', 'breathe', 'centre' and 'hold your Haras' and 'breathe deeper, louder' until the entire church is filled with a chorus of noisy hissy breaths, mostly a bit stinky also (I'm guessing that minty toothpaste is an electrochemical blocker too), from over twenty healers who are pumping themselves up, and into the zone.

We, the healees, are also given ghostly instructions from the altar. We are told to close our eyes and abandon our physical senses, and to give ourselves up to the universe. I close my eyes and wonder if there's as many f-words in *Beverly Hills Cop* as there was in *48 Hours*. We were shown *48 Hours* in our video club in school and Spits McGee went mental. He passed by the room, with just me and five other fellas glued to the screen, and he stopped immediately when he saw Eddie Murphy. Spits gave that know-all look that he does, as if to say that he knew all about the black fellas because of his time in Africa. But within seconds he had turned puce and was looking around, wanting to know who in God's name had told us that we could watch these unadulterated corner boys unsupervised. He marched up to the video recorder, bent down and let his hand hover over the big thunky buttons. But you could tell that he didn't have a clue and so he gave it a thump with his fist and charged out the door again. By the time he'd found Jack McQuaid, the careers guidance counsellor, and the one man who's supposed to be in charge of video recorders in the school, we'd already got past the final blow-out where Eddie Murphy shoots Billy Bear stone dead.

Rain warns us to be wary of our conscious mind. It is the enemy, she grumbles, before telling us that we must un-become what we have become in order to receive the energies that Waylean and Mestapheen are guiding into the hall.

Begin! she barks, and I feel Deano instantly leaning over me. He starts straight away at my mickey, and I nearly burst out laughing. His hands hover over my jeans, right at the zip, while Rain shouts the words 'Root Chakra' and explains to the healees that this chakra, this small spinning ball of internal energy, no bigger than a tennis ball, connects us to our basic survival instincts and must be restored to a healthy clockwise rotation if we want to be at peace in the world. She tells the healers not to block the flow, and adds that she can feel a lot of blocks in the room. Breathe! she shouts again. I told you to breathe! There follows more hissing, even louder, from the healers. In fact I'm sure Deano hits me with some flying spit, but I dare not open my eyes. I'm putting all my energies into not giggling, especially as Deano's hands keep bashing off my zip every time he takes a huge breath.

Sacral Chakra, orders Rain, and tells us that this chakra is connected to our sexuality and pleasure. Deano moves his hands upwards a tad along my body, but he's still basically hovering over my mickey. Rain warns us that in the Western world this chakra is usually the most damaged and decrepit because of our fear, our misunderstanding and our abuse of sex. She orders her pupils to think back to the purity of their beginnings and to unblock with all their might in order to allow Waylean and Mestapheen to get to work on these banjaxed tennis balls. More breathing. More hissing. I start to feel a bit rubbish about my Sacral Chakra, and the giggling totally stops. I can only imagine how bollixed up it is, probably not even the shape of a tennis ball at all, and not spinning in any direction either, just lying there, like the living dead, shocked, knackered, and screwed. And I feel angry with the Western world for being so crap, just like Rain says. And I'm angry with rapist priests too, and unwanted fecking babies. And I suddenly feel like saying all the curse words in the world, like shit and feck, right there on the massage table, when I notice that instead of the giggles I've now got the shakes.

I think that this must be from holding my stomach so hard in anti-laugh mode, but the funny thing is, they've started in my feet, and are now working their way up my legs. I feel dead embarrassed, because my heels start to click clack clack against the wooden frame of the massage table, and I'm sure everyone can hear. I open one eye and have a peak at Deano. He's in another zone, head tilting upwards, and I'm not even sure if he notices.

Crown Chakra! she continues, and Dean's hands shoot right up to the top of my head. This one's about connecting us fully to the spiritual essence of the universe. Normally Rain likes her healers to work their way methodically up the body, but today, Waylean and Mestapheen are detecting a block of such magnitude that they're going to have to mix and match through the chakras in order to toggle it loose.

My hips go too. Shake, shake, thump, thump. Up and down on the table, like I'm showing everyone how I used to do it with Saidhbh, back when we lived on planet Earth. I keep my eyes shut tight now and try to ride out the storm. I can't imagine what Deano's thinking. Probably thrilled that his healer's hands are finally doing the trick. Like he's Paul Daniels under laboratory conditions. And it reminds me of watching a film one summer night back in Dublin, when everyone was out in the garden chatting about the goings-on in The Sorrows, and I was alone inside with the real-life story of an American schoolkid who is actually a mentaller but doesn't know it. Then one day in class a really evil bully calls him a retard, which is the American way of saying mentaller. He comes home that night and bursts out crying to his mom, and says, 'They called me retarded, am I retarded?' Only the way he says retarded is with an accent, and dead sad. Am I retawded?

I bawled my eyes out, alone in the room. And I worried for weeks that I was retawded and no one had the guts to tell me. I think about this film, suddenly and clearly, as I'm pinging around on the table, like a mad fish, flapping for his life.

I'm concentrating so hard on controlling the flips that I miss the next three chakras. Third Eye, Throat and Solar Plexus chakras. They go by in a blur, and I'm not even sure if Winter Rain, or Waylean and Mestapheen, actually says anything about them. It's just heat from Deano's hands, and everything, every part of me, banging and bobbing, and flipping and bopping, right there on the spot.

Then she says it. Heart Chakra! Deano moves his hands down, right over the centre of my chest. Bam! I shoot up on the table, like my chest is either going to burst right open and splatter everyone with gore, or I'm going to have a massive diarrhoea attack. Thankfully I avoid both by flipping myself right off the table and landing face down on the ground. Deano breaks the trance and hoists me to my knees. There's a general commotion as all the healers around me, all twenty-something of them, snap back out into reality. Naturally, I'm a bit freaked, so I shake myself free from Deano's grasp, tell him to leave me the feck alone, and make a mad dart for the double doors by the tea table.

And then I hear it.

Jim Finnegan!

My name is shouted, bellowed even, right

400

across the hall, as loud as be damned. I grab the handle, yank it down and reef one half of the heavy wooden door wide open.

Jim Finnegan!

Again. I'm almost out the door, but I give a little backwards glance, just to see which mentaller exactly is trying to make me stay.

Of course, I almost collapse when I see it myself. I definitely don't let go of the door handle. Just for support. Because there, up on the altar, lifting her veil high above her head and bellowing out my name for all to hear is none other than old fizzy eyes and scarface herself, Helen Macker.

It's me! she says, ripping the veil off altogether. It's Helen!

7

Let the Healing Begin

Meeting Helen changes everything. I start taking my healings dead seriously from then on. She says that she can see something in me, something glowy and bright, and if I could only harness its power I could be a brilliant healer too, just like her. The limits are only your own, she says, sounding a bit Goddy, but smiling all the same, and telling me that, with the right instruction, I could cure Saidhbh in a single session. Easy-peasy, she says, clicking her fingers and shaking her head. I could heal the loss inside her biological body and simultaneously make her ethereal soul excited and motivated to face the world anew, and I could help her make pure and quiet peace with the soul of our dead baby.

Oh yes, she says, giving me a face that means that I can't wriggle out of this one. Your baby is very much a spiritual being, and ethereally alive, and tied to Saidhbh's energetic cords with a near unbreakable bond. With her, beside her, above and below. Which is a thing that I've heard before from Mass, but Helen has gone and made it her own.

⋆　⋆　⋆

We have a brilliant chatting session together that first night, me and Helen. No one in the hall can believe that we know each other. And they're totally shocked at the way Helen ripped off her veil and 'broke healing', which is basically like staring Waylean and Mestapheen in the face and then slamming the door shut on them without a word of explanation. Helen isn't bothered though, and instead runs down through the beds and tells me that she recognised me the minute she saw my field. She says that she can see auric fields with her naked eyes, and that everyone has different-coloured fields that correspond to the movement of their chakras within. Healthy Root Chakra means lots of red in the field. Throat Chakra is blue. Solar Chakra yellow, and so on. She doesn't tell me my colour but just giggles and will only say that it's very, how can she put it, distinctive.

She's still gorgeous. Even with the hockey damage. Her eyes still fizz with crystal blue when she looks at you. Her hair is shorter, but still wavy. And the scars that snake outwards from her mouth, like the manky legs of a dead spider, only make her look more interesting. As if she's got a story to tell.

She says that she never meant to get into this healing lark in the first place, and that it was thanks to the guiding hands of the universe, and to Gaia, that she ended up here. When she says the word Gaia she does a tiny little bow. Which is kind of funny, because it makes me nod too, as if I'm also a big Gaia fan. Although Deano later tells me that Gaia is just another name for the spiritual energy of the Earth, which, I suppose, actually does make me a fan, and certainly explains why Obi-Wan Kenobi clutches his heart in *Star Wars* when Princess Leia's home world is blown to pieces, because it's like the whole planet itself has just died, and since it clearly has a big giant spirit too, like Gaia, and Obi-Wan is like Serenity Powers and can see all the magic stuff in the universe, he's taking it all a bit personally. Hence the chest pains.

Helen says that things went bad after the hockey-ball accident. And that even after her teeth were done and the stitches were taken out she felt rubbish about herself and her mashed-up face and would've had a full-blown mental breakdown, and gone into St John of Gods and everything, only her mam was a dead strong countrywoman and dead practical, and immediately signed Helen up for an eight-week course in Beauty Therapy and Cosmetology in Kilcuman Tech. My eyes go a bit glazy when she says Cosmetology. I'm thinking of the old fat fella with the eye-glass on BBC2 who does the star-watching programme that Dad pretends to watch when he wants to feel brainy. But Helen says that it was all about make-up, and that for the first few weeks she was gutted, because you had to look at yourself every day in the mirror, and use your own face as a Girl's World-style dummy for a million different make-up techniques.

Eventually, and with the help of the other girls on the course, she got over it. Two of them especially, lovely young wans called Bernie and Delores, were brilliant at helping her apply tons of filler and foundation all over her scars, and by week four you wouldn't even know that she had a single mark, let alone a faceful of crooked snaky lines. They became best buddies and were instantly known around town, because of their love of make-up, and of the bronzed Caribbean Deluxe style in particular, as the three Oompa Loompas. These are the little fellas in *Willy Wonka* who have green hair and orangey faces and are great at whipping together catchy tunes about spoilt kids who've just nearly died. Helen laughs now, and says that sometimes the rugger players from Rock, meaning Blackrock school, which is a posh school for boys with rich dads, would start singing Oompa Loompa Doopadee Do whenever she and Bernie and Delores would walk into McSorely's in Ranelagh for an evening bevvie after a hard day at the mirror, and wearing the full-on Caribbean Deluxe. It wouldn't bother them, though, she adds, laughing again at the way she was then, because they'd still be all over you by the end of the night.

By week eight they all graduated with flying colours, and by that Christmas, which just happened to be my worst one ever, they had all emigrated to London, because London is where you find the best make-up jobs in the whole world, including ads, movies, TV and weddings. Bernie, Delores and Helen mostly did weddings. They clubbed their talents together and decided to call themselves The Oompa Loompas as an eye-catching business thing, and even hired a van with it written on the side, just above their phone number and a picture of lipstick and a make-up brush. They weren't fussy at all, and they did graduations too, and even naming ceremonies. And this is where Helen met Serenity Powers.

Helen gets a bit choked at this point. She's not upset, as in crying and going red-faced. But her eyes are watering all the same. We're sitting opposite each other, on two different massage beds, and I'm half lying back, with one leg kind of cocked up in the air, like Burt Reynolds when he poses for magazine shoots. I'm cold, but I don't show it. And it's gone dark outside, because the few remaining stained-glass windows are now totally coal black, and you can't see the picture at all. The rest of the class is all murmur-murmur in the background, down by the tea table at the double doors. I can tell that they're looking up at us, and making comments, but I pretend there's no one around, and I just listen, all ears, to Helen's story.

She says that she did the make-up for this little Portuguese wan with lethal acne, who asked her to drop by the naming ceremony itself, to say congratulations for five years of hard healing finally done, and to raise a glass of orange juice in her name. Helen, always with an eye for the business, and imagining raking in a shedload of clients for The Oompa Loompas, turned up at the bash, in this very same church hall in Islington, expecting to laugh her head off at a bunch of beardy mentalists, and instead met her Maker in Serenity.

She says that Serenity clocked her from miles off, from about here to the tea table. And even though Serenity was surrounded by students and

406

friends and colleagues who were hanging on her every word and generally licking up to her big time, she simply stood up and walked over to Helen and — and this is the maddest bit — she reached into her own handbag and pulled out a paper hankie and wiped all of Helen's make-up away, right in front of everyone. Helen says that she stood there, scars showing to the whole world for the first time in ages, and she cried out loud, really bawling, louder than ever before, with her whole heart in it. Serenity just stood still, smiling in front of her, and held Helen's face so softly in her hands and said, I see you. And you are beautiful.

And that was it. That was the beginning. She says that she does a couple of shifts now and then with The Oompas, just to make up the rent and her part of the weekly Safeways shop, but generally she's taken to the School like a duck to water. She says, between you and me, she thinks that the hockey-ball impact kind of dislodged some primal block in her spirit, which possibly explains why she's picked up the tools of the trade so quickly. And why Serenity allows her to take so many classes. Like tonight, for instance! She makes her eyeballs go big at this, and lifts her eyebrows high, to show that it's a funny old world.

I tell her, in return, that it's totally mad that me and her should meet again, and in London of all places. But she instantly goes all wise and quiet and just shakes her head and tells me that she knew this would happen. She says that you can't fight the forces of the universe, and of light and of energy. And then she smiles and strokes the side of my face, like I'm a lost puppy returned, or the prodigal son.

★ ★ ★

Deano doesn't know what to be doing during all this. He's mostly awkward and stuttery around Helen, especially because he's never seen her as anything other than Winter Rain, who is either the annoying little rip who jumped the Astral Science queue or else someone who just might be, thanks to the Serenity Powers' stamp of approval, the real deal.

Looking at her, sitting on the massage beds and being all relaxed and chatty and young, is odd for him. He occasionally floats over to us when he hears me talking, and butts in, adding little decorative details to my story, such as how long we've been staying at Aunty Grace's. But otherwise, and especially when me and Helen are getting down to the nitty gritty, he simply floats backwards away through the empty hall towards the other students who've long since packed up their healing towels and folded away the rest of the beds, and have gathered near the tea table for hot water and lemon juice, and wheat-and gluten-free flapjacks, and are hoping for the inside scoop on Winter Rain's sudden break with the School of Astral Sciences play-book.

Of course no one gets charged for the night's session. And Helen even whispers to me that I won't have to spend a penny for any of my lessons. She'll have a word with the boss woman herself, on my behalf. It'll be an honour, she says, to bring you out of your shell. And then she winks, as if it's all getting a bit rude. Which is funny. Because the chat we're having, then and there, is such full-on magic that a part of me starts to feel dead guilty, especially when my stomach goes a tiny bit giddy, like it does when you know that you've met someone who you fancy, or at least might fancy at some point in the future.

And I keep thinking of this jokey phrase that Mozzo used to say about birds and fannies and how he could get any bird he wanted to in all of Kilcuman but he couldn't be arsed because of having Saidhbh at home. And the jokey phrase was about him not being fecked to go out for a mouldy burger when he had a delicious steak sitting waiting for him at home on the kitchen table. Meaning that Saidhbh was the steak, and any other bird that he met out on the street on the way to Quinnsworth's or to Foley's would be a burger. Mozzo also told me and Gary that when it came to getting fanny action you shouldn't be looking at the mantelpiece when you're poking the fire, which was a rubbish thing to say, and only made us imagine some headless young wan with Christmas cards on her neck and a blazing fanny, and us with singed eyebrows for getting too close to the hot zone. But for the moment I'm stuck on the steak and the burger, and I'm thinking of Saidhbh at home right now, in her Glengall prison, puffing Rothmans out the window, or leafing through the day's tree work. And I know that she's steak, and that she'll always be steak. And that Helen, with her brilliant stories and fizzy eyes, is just a special kind of burger.

And anyway, it's only talking and gabbing and catching up. Like when Mam meets one of the aul wans from the swimming club in Bray, and she hasn't seen them in nearly ten years and only spotted them by chance as they crossed the Ha'penny Bridge on the back route to Henry Street. The pair will hoot and hug for a few seconds and then, realising that they're still going their separate ways at the end of the head to head, they have to rattle through everything that's happened in the missing years, machine-gun style, no prisoners, no mercy.

Me and Helen are a bit like that. We can see that the students at the tea table are really getting restless, and kind of tapping their feet with boredom, so everything we say has to be rushed and short and bursty, with huge big stories about life and love crammed into a few jabbed words. My stuff is mostly about Saidhbh, and coming to London, and how I got Saidhbh 'into trouble'. Helen listens to it all and nods slowly with her best Goddy smile, as if she knows everything that I'm saying already, like the way the Lord knows each one of the hairs on your head, even before you're born and have hair, or a head. She tells me that she can see it all, crystal clear, right in front of her face. When I ask her what she means, she laughs and calls me a dummy and says that it's all over my field, my auric field, and that she can read it all, like a living language, in the colour swirls and energetic

410

eddies that flow in front of my actual physical body.

I can see EVERYTHING! she says, making a mountain out of the word everything, and doing the kind of goofy nod that you do which tells someone that you know loads of secrets about them. And then she laughs, swings her leg forward, and gives me a little kick, from her massage bed over to mine, as if it's all a big joke, but not quite.

The last of Helen's stories are mostly about how brilliant her life's been since joining the school. She says that even though she's living with Bernie and Delores in a manky two-bed in Shepherd's Bush, and still does the odd few weddings and hen nights with The Oompa Loompas, she's hoping to give it all up and go full time into Astral Science, maybe work directly for Serenity Powers herself, maybe even move to California!

Go right to the source, eh? she says, while rolling her eyes to the roof and adding with a sigh, God, it's such a rush! You'll find out all about it, mark my words!

And then she suddenly stops herself and leans forward on the bed, right into my face.

You are coming back for more healing, aren't you?

It's as if the thought that I might want to scrap the whole healing thing and go back to being a non-multicoloured normal fella had only just occurred to her, and the thought's very existence was a knife to the heart.

Before I can answer, however, she jumps down

411

off the bed, grabs me firmly by both shoulders and knocks her forehead against mine while making a solemn promise that, if I stick with the School of Astral Sciences, she'll turn me into a fully-fledged healing machine before the year is up. You'll be raising the dead, she says, again with a bit of a twinkle in her eyes.

★ ★ ★

Later that night, I almost smash through the front door itself in order to tell Fiona the news about Helen Macker. Deano has been moody the whole way home in the car, and is a bit fecked off about me being star pupil on my first night, so he's miles behind me when I tear on up the stairs and into Fiona and Saidhbh's room screaming, Guess what? Guess what? at the top of my voice. It takes me a second or two to notice that the main lights are already off, and that Fiona is crouched down on the mattress next to Saidhbh, who is lying by candlelight only, and half curled under the covers with her clothes on. Saidhbh looks a bit puffy, like she's been crying, but I try to ignore it and tell Fiona instead about meeting Helen Macker and what a completely mad night it's been. Fiona doesn't say much at first, besides a few repetitions of 'Isn't that gas!' before she cuts me short and makes big bug eyes that indicate the sniffling body on the mattress and then says that Saidhbh needs her rest and that I'm not to be annoying her with trifling stories. I look over at Saidhbh, giving her the questioning eye, and she just

412

waves Fiona's protests away like the queen to a servant, saying that it's OK, for now, if I want to continue prattling.

I give them both the gory details. About Helen Macker being a make-up artist and a genius healer, and how she was asking after Fiona at the end, and how she hadn't changed that much at all since the hockey days. I talk up the scars, and make them sound more gruesome than they actually were, because it's more interesting for them and it makes Helen sound a bit grim and not as funny and chatty and fizzy as she actually was on the night.

I mention the healing too, and the many skills that Helen's going to teach me for free. I tell Saidhbh all the things that Helen said about us and our baby too, and how she can feel through my auric field that the baby's still hanging around Saidhbh on an energetic cord, and how it'll be up to me, given the right amount of healing lessons, to do the manly thing and to cut that cord and set the baby free to go back into the universe. Which will be like giving birth, only backwards.

Saidhbh shakes her head manically when she hears this, and gives the mattress such a series of jolts that Fiona has to steady her back down and hold on to her hand for calming comfort. Saidhbh says nothing for ages, but then pushes herself up on her elbows and tells me that I'm a complete idiot if I think she's going to let me take Jackson away from her. Jackson is the name of our dead baby. I find out later, during a hugger-mugger downstairs with Fiona, that

Saidhbh had taken the household record player up into the room and was listening to *Thriller* all afternoon. Fiona explains, trying not to get dead embarrassed, that Saidhbh has had her first 'curse' since losing the baby. And she seems to have taken it badly. I ask her if there was any song in particular that she was listening to, and I guess that it was probably 'Billie Jean', because that was the rude one that we weren't supposed to listen to back home, because it was about having a child and not being married. Fiona slaps me across the back of the head and says that I'm a moron, and that Saidhbh was listening to the whole album straight through, if I must know.

Even 'P.Y.T.'?

Yes, she says, and 'The Lady in My Life'.

Saidhbh says that Jackson is the best thing that ever happened to her in her whole stinking life. In all this, she says, I knew there had to be a point, and a reason. God has put us through all this pain because of Jackson. He wanted to make sure that we were ready for him. As parents. She unhooks her hand from Fiona's grip and rolls over on her side, showing me her back from under the sheets, still dressed in a lime-green sweatshirt, as she protects an imaginary space in front of her belly. She asks me, facing the wall, if I think that, after all this, she's going to let me take Jackson away from her? She tells me that they will only ever be separated over her dead body. And then she raises her damaged hand up above the sheets to let me know that she means business. She turns her face completely into the

414

pillow and whispers the name Jackson softly to herself, over and over again, with little bites of My Love, and My Darling, and My Sweet Baby Boy dropped in for good measure. Fiona gives me a look. We get the point, and tiptoe out of the room.

Downstairs, me, Deano, Fiona and Aunty Grace have a hugger-mugger. We shut all the doors, Fiona puts on the tea, turns off the telly, and Aunty Grace drinks red wine. She listens to my Helen Macker story with a stony face and then says, straight away, that she's going to put Saidhbh into a mental home up the road in Cricklewood. This causes a huge argument, with Deano basically saying 'No way, it's cruel,' and Fiona and Aunty Grace saying 'Yes way, it's for her own good.' I don't really say anything, because I'm not good at arguments, and normally have brilliant thoughts that eventually come out as nervous sentences that are actually really obvious and not brilliant at all.

And besides, the whole thing makes me feel a bit sick, like the time I sat outside the kitchen door back home and listened to Mam and Dad arguing about sending Fiona to a no-nonsense boarding school down the bog because she was being a bit wild at the time. She had only just got her first few periods and was going a bit snappy with everyone, and saying 'f' this and 'f' that all over the place. And Mam thought that it was a terrible example to be showing Claire and Susan, and she just didn't know how to handle her any more because Fiona would tell her to f-off with herself whenever she stuck her head

415

inside the bedroom door.

Dad, of course, wouldn't hear of it, and said that no daughter of his was going to be shipped off to the back end of beyond like a common criminal, packed off to a load of country savages with no questions asked. Dad talked a lot about being tough, and loving strict rules, and how much he liked to give his kids a good old-fashioned belt to show them what's what. But when it came to the big decisions, he was soft. Softer than Mam, anyway. And this time he insisted that giving Fiona a bit of a lecture, from him to her, was all that it would take. Mam scoffed, but Dad was right. Fiona got over the bad-girl blip, and was back to normal within a couple of days, and not cursing, not shouting at all. Which made Dad feel great, and like the best parent on the planet, but was probably more due to the fact that I told Fiona, the night of the argument, all about me sitting out in the hall and listening to Mam and Dad going at it, and planning to send her away for ever to a hideous and evil culchie-filled boarding school in the middle of the bog, where you'd be force-fed porridge all day by huge country girls with red faces and rolled-up sleeves and camogie sticks under their pillows, for belting you in the middle of the night for being a big angry effer and blinder.

Back then, outside in the hall, I had wanted to burst into the kitchen and hit Mam and Dad with a million different reasons for not sending Fiona to a bog boarding school. But I was frozen by the shock of listening, and by the danger of

416

what they were saying. And I was frozen too by the possibility that the wrong result would be too much to bear. And so I stayed outside, like someone trying not to breathe on a house of cards, but willing them to fall in the right direction all the same.

It's just like that here. And Deano can see that I'm rooted to the spot, so he makes a big deal about speaking for me, and saying that Winter Rain is going to help me to fix Saidhbh, and has promised to have her fit as a fiddle in no time.

Fiona and Aunty Grace go bonkers at this together, with Aunty telling Deano that he's a gullible gobshite, and Fiona insisting that he stop using the name Winter Rain, and refer to her as Helen Macker, or even Scarface. Anything but Winter Rain. Deano, in turn, tells them both that he pities them because they have closed hearts.

Aunty Grace takes a huge slug of red wine and starts crying, and tells Deano not to talk about her closed heart, and lectures him about the things she's had to endure in her life, as an Irish woman in England, in order to get to where she is today. Fiona, equally choked up, continues on Aunty Grace's behalf, and threatens to throw Deano out the door, and tells him to find someone else from one of his binjy-banjy classes with a bigger heart, maybe Helen Macker, and see if she'd put up with his nonsense. Deano starts crying too, and complains about his life, and never having a dad, and how hard it's been for him to find his place in the world.

All three of them end the hugger-mugger totally flopped in each other's arms and cuddling

417

and crying at the same time. I'm feeling dead embarrassed for everyone in the room, like every single person I know in the whole wide world has suddenly gone mental at the exact same time. And I feel bad for Saidhbh, and the way we're all talking about her, as if she's a rotten old piece of burger meat, with her steak days long gone. So I try to sneak out and up to her room without attracting any attention. But Aunty Grace, all smeared and bedraggled, lifts her head out of the hug, and barks over at me. She says that Saidhbh can stay for the moment, providing that she doesn't get any more nutty. She says that it's up to me, and Deano, and all those binjy-banjy berks in Community to fix her. And when she's up and ready, and back on her feet again, she wants us both out of here. No questions asked. For good.

8

The Grindstone

By mid October I've paid for half the flights. Me and Saidhbh are going to arrive back home at Christmas like the conquering heroes that we are. Me, with a real-life job in the best restaurant in London. And her with her head totally sorted and a massive folder full of tree pictures under her arm. I prattle on about Christmas to Saidhbh whenever I can, because I know that it's her favourite thing ever, and because it'll be like this magical glowy place far away on the horizon but almost visible that will make living her life worthwhile. You heard about that sort of thing all the time back home from the coffee mams, about some ancient aul wan who goes, Oh as long as I make it as far as little Jacintha's First Holy Communion I'll be thankful to the Lord. And at that stage Jacintha's only a baby, and everyone's secretly thinking that the aul wan is a bit greedy and a bit cocky to think she's going to live for another seven years. But sure enough she makes it right to the Holy Communion day itself and is the undoubted star of the hour, and of all the family photos and especially the big one with everyone gathered around her in the telly room like a giant multicoloured family flower with her as the ancient grey bud at its centre. She's sitting in an armchair with plastic underneath the material in case she does a pee in her pants, but she's smiling quietly to herself and happy as Larry to have finally made it, as good as her word, this far and to this day. And then, the very next morning, she dies.

Well, Christmas is a bit like that for Saidhbh. The whole she-bang. Everything. From buying the tree with her dad from the cute whore in the bus terminus in Oakfield, right through the giddy build-up of Bing Crosby records and Boney M's 'Boy Child' to the big day itself. She loves it all. She loves the 10 a.m. Mass that whizzes by because everyone's dying to get home to their presents, and she loves the way the priests know the people's mood well, and so they don't do a sermon but instead tell all the mams to get back to their kitchens and make sure that their turkeys aren't burning, which always gets a big laugh, especially from the mams. And then there's the visiting, with a million mad car trips all around Dublin to the uncles and aunties who, right up until your eighteenth birthday, always seek you out by the peanut bowls and the 7-Up, and give you a pressie and a big goozer on the cheek for your troubles. And then the big monster meal around the table, and the way the mams and the aunties always make everyone do games, like a proper family, where you stick a name on your forehead and you have a guess at who it is and I'm always Mother Teresa which is a bit unfair because she's a girl and not really someone I think about a lot except when she's on the news for being all sainty and wrinkly and covered with hungry babies.

And for Saidhbh, Stephen's Day is even better than Christmas Day, because it's the day when the Donohue family hold the famous Donohue Family Stephen's Day Hoolie. And with this one, they go and leave the front door open all day, and everyone from all around the whole of Kilcuman, and anyone they've ever met in their entire lives, comes piling in for all-day-drinks, pies and a couple of sneaky rebel songs. And they don't leave till four in the morning, till every last drop is drunk, and the voices are hoarse, and it's an official fact that this Donohue Family Stephen's Day Hoolie was even better than last year's effort.

And so I describe to Saidhbh how we'll sashay through Dublin airport, with all the other long-lost children from all corners of the globe, and we'll look at the glowy lights that offer us a hundred thousand welcomes in Gaelic. And we'll get hugs and pats on the backs from our nearest and dearest and we'll say that it's great to be back on the Auld Sod, and describe how the flight was smooth as eggs but the traffic to the airport, in London town, was mad as be damned. And then we'll squeeze into the car, and on to the roads, and to The Rise, home, and we'll keep everyone up all night with crazy stories of life in London and all the oddballs you meet and the strange things that happen to you when you're away from the embrace of your country's bosom.

Saidhbh smiles at this. Things have been rougher than ever for her lately, so she's not just being polite, for my sake. She's had two trips to

421

A&E in Paddington, one for a suspected heart attack and the other an overdose. With the heart attack it was a Sunday and we were all sitting around watching the English knackers shout at each other in *EastEnders*, and Saidhbh suddenly bursts into the room saying that she can't feel her arm and has lost the ability to breathe. She crumples to the carpet in front of us, head on to the floor, and kind of passes out. We all go mental and Deano says that it's a heart attack, and Fiona rings 999, and Aunty Grace screams that Saidhbh is too young for a heart attack. By the time the ambulance gets here Saidhbh is breathing again, and can feel her arm, but they say that it's protocol now, and that Saidhbh has to go with them into A&E to be checked up and monitored in case she has a rare genetic heart disorder that could kill her at any minute. We follow the ambulance in Deano's car, and we're allowed into the beddy bit of A&E, and we sit in silence and say not a single thing while Saidhbh's monitors blip away happily for twenty-five minutes and let her go with a clean bill of health.

The overdose was scarier, even though I was in Border Town at the time. Aunty Grace said that it was like Saidhbh was so shamed by the pretend heart attack that she decided to kill herself to get over it. Only she didn't actually kill herself, and just drank straight vodka up in the bedroom until she got knocked out, but not before munching back a whole load of Disprins that went all foamy around her mouth and made Fiona go pale with shock and call 999 again. When Saidhbh came to her senses this time, she just giggled, probably out of embarrassment. And when Aunty Grace got all rough with her and asked her about the Disprins, she just joked that she had a headache from the vodka. And everyone left it at that.

So it's nice for me, and it's real, when I see her smile about my Christmas plans. Her eyes too, they kind of kick into life, and I can see that she wants the dream. And I know that I can make it happen. For her. And for us.

★ ★ ★

I've booked the tickets for Christmas Eve itself, to be all atmospheric-y. I'm pretty sure there'll be cameras from RTE there when we touch down. You always see it on the night-time news, capturing the tears and the hugs from that afternoon's reunions. Our flights have a 2 p.m. landing, which should be just perfect for a homecoming close-up. I got them from an Indian woman on the Kilburn High Road called Gaganadipika, or Pika for short. She says her name means 'Lamp of the Sky' which, she adds, is a bit of a hoot, considering she spends her day booking people on aeroplanes. Pika runs a student travel company above a carpet shop, which means that she can get you a cheap flight or cheap boat trip as long as you can prove that you're in college. And if you can't, and as long as you're of studenty age, she'll just whip behind the counter and stick a small piece of grey cardboard through a huge hot metal machine and, hey presto, you're suddenly a student with your own plasticy student card.

I made her put the School of Astral Science on my card. Although she rolled her eyes when she did it. I told her that I was studying the chakras and the Hara line, and I gave a little hopeful nod, thinking that she'd open up her arms and say, Ah yes, in my country we all study that binjy-banjy shite, here, have your flights for free. But instead she just looked at me like she was a bit bored, and told me that I could pay the total of nearly five hundred pounds in weekly instalments.

Everyone at home, of course, is thrilled by the news. Every time Mam phones Aunty Grace she asks to be put on to me and Fiona and says that we're not going to recognise the place when we get back, and she can't wait to see what we think of the new suite. She says that Claire and Susan have been angels since we left, and that Dad's going grand with the cancer, and she'll get him to write us a card when he comes down in the morning. And usually, true to her word, a couple of days later we get a note scribbled on home stationery, letting us know just how excited they'll all be to see us at Christmas.

The stationery was Mam's idea. She copied Maura Connell, who said it was the done thing. Maura's cards had a shiny silver edge and curvy writing, but ours were the thrifty version, with no edges and no curvy writing, just name and address smack bang in the middle of a yellowy piece of stiffened paper. You were supposed to send them to people to thank them for inviting you to their parties and social gatherings, but

Mam quickly began using them for shopping lists, cake ingredients and notes to Dad — so that if he woke up when she was at Mass he'd be able to find his way from the fridge to the cooker and know what to put where.

His notes to me and Fiona are totally different. To Fiona he writes 'Dear Fiona . . . ' And to me it is, 'Well, Shithead . . . ' He has called me Shithead on paper in the past. But always for a joke, like the time I was down in Irish Summer Camp in Galway, and hating it, and in need of cheering up. It was like a private joke between him and me, and a bit rude, and just crude enough to annoy Mam something rotten, and to prove that me and him were on the same team of crude and rude boyos. But when he wrote it this time, he knew, and I knew, and he knew I knew, that it meant something different entirely. There was anger in it. And resentment. And unspoken fury at the secret cause of his collapse on the Debs morning.

After the shithead intro, he races through a rapid rundown of the girls, saying how Claire got top of her class in recorder practice, how Susan got a hairline fracture in her middle finger during the netball finals, and how Sarah and Siobhan brought up a fancy new dessert called a Viennetta for Sunday dinner last. He closes as he began, a bit hard, by saying that my mother, meaning Mam, is very much looking forward to having me back at Christmas, and that he hopes, for all our sakes, that I'm taking care of my 'friend' Saidhbh. His sign off is Your Father, Matt, just in case I thought it had been

425

ghost-written by Mam or one of the girls.

Gary also sends me a card. It's like a blank birthday card, but it has Soft Cell on the front, and a Golden Discs sticker on the back. He says that everyone in St Cormac's has stopped talking about me by now, but that he overheard his mam chatting to my mam about how Spits McGee is holding a place for me, in next year's 314. Gary thinks this is hilarious, and makes lots of jokes about how I'm going to be this big huge fifteen-year-old thicko sitting at the back of a class full of tiny thirteen-year-olds who've barely got pubes. I'll be like Kevin Doyle, he says, who was held back for two years for being dim and then just kind of gave up trying to learn and decided to beat everyone up for lunch money instead. That is, of course, writes Gary, if you're coming back at all! He says that he's watched a programme on emigration on RTE2, where they interviewed all these ancient bogmen living in the filthiest parts of London. Half of them were alkies, half of them were a bit mad and lived on their own on a diet of canned Guinness and cheese sangers, but all of them said they told themselves the same lie: I'll be coming home soon! Every Christmas, after all the celebrating was done, and the hangovers setting in goodo, they'd turn to their nearest and dearest, just as they're boarding the boat back to London, and promise that they'd be coming back for good, any day now. Ireland, they'd say, was in their blood. It had made them who they are, and they'd never leave its mystical shores.

★ ★ ★

I get my first postcard from O'Culigeen around this time too. I know that it's from him the minute I see the photo. Don't even have to read it. Just a picture of these three scary-looking fellas in the middle of the jungle with small sticks, like slim pencils, stuck through their noses, and furry hats on their heads, and necklaces that curve into tusks on their chests. They're wearing tiny pouches around their mickeys but otherwise they're naked and you can see everything. Typical.

Straight away, I know that it's him, without even looking at the back. I scoop it up off the carpet and shove it into my healing bag and drop the rest of the post casually on the breakfast table. I read the message in the loo at the School of Astral Sciences, and it says that he's been thinking of me non-stop and that we have some serious unfinished business. He signs it FOC.

It makes me feel sick on the spot. I think of *Red River*, and how O'Culigeen's 'unfinished business' clearly means that, like John Wayne, he plans to fulfil his final promise and actually kill me. The postcard is his way of telling me that getting sent out to the missions in Papua New Guinea hasn't changed a thing. And that being surrounded by a thousand naked men with mickey pouches swinging in his face every day of the week doesn't mean anything to him when compared to the thought of strangling me, for real this time, with his bare hands. And that I can run all I like, but thanks, no doubt, to some blabbermouth penpal from Kilcuman parish, I can't actually hide. It's only a matter of time, he's telling me, before he finishes what he started way back when.

I come stumbling out of the loo, pale as a sheet, and straight into Helen Macker's arms. She can see that I'm all over the place, but she doesn't say a single word. Instead, she reads me. She holds me up straight, and at arm's length, and then stands back from me a full six feet. She closes her eyes, takes a deep breath, and just lets her lids fall open. She takes me in, reads everything, all seven chakras, all circulating auric fields, and then snaps her lids shut, like clapping the covers on her magic binoculars. I see, she says, before telling me that I should be healee for the afternoon, and let her do the heavy lifting. Then she gives me a little wink, and nudges me over to the massage bed.

Helen and I are getting on brilliantly. She's like a friend and a teacher and a bit of a mam and a sister all rolled into one. And, as well as Fiona, and Billy from Border Town, she's one of the best people that I know in London. I'm all excited about her, and I try to get Fiona to meet her, or at least to drop me off at the school and to have a big girlygab about the old days when it was just them two against the world. But Fiona makes up a load of excuses about being too busy with Grace's Angels, or being too tired to make the trip all the way to Islington. Then she tells me one night, after she's cracked open a bottle of Aunty Grace's red wine, that it's more than that, and that I'll probably understand when I'm older, but that too much water has gone under each of their bridges since they were kids, too many changes in their lives to make a reunion possible. But I can pass on her love all the same, if it'll make me feel any better.

I try mentioning Helen a few times to Saidhbh too, but it comes out all wrong, and it sounds like I fancy her, which is totally not true, and we end up having a mini-argument because I say to Saidhbh, when I'm denying fancying Helen, are you mental? And she just gives me a really hurt look that says, how can you ask me that? How can you say those words when you know that every day I'm having this monumental battle with the possibility of becoming a mentaller for the rest of my life?

★ ★ ★

Helen says that she's chosen me as her permanent healing partner because I'm on a fast-track system and need to be up and operational as soon as possible. It's a life-or-death matter, she says, without mentioning Saidhbh by name, but I know all the same that she can read Saidhbh, and the dangers that she's facing, within my own field. Helen says that the auric field is like, among other things, a video camera, and it records and absorbs your emotional and personal interactions and exchanges at the most profound level. This could be anything from a sudden and unexpected slap from your mam when you were seven years old, right up to a worried look that you shared with your potentially suicidal ex-girlfriend

429

yesterday morning when you were having a mini-argument about whether you fancied your healing teacher or not. They all matter, she says. And they all leave an impression.

She says that she was particularly blessed because she was taught auric field reading directly by Serenity Powers herself. And depending on the type of person you are, and the healer you're about to become, it can either take you the full five years of Astral Science studies, or you can get it in a couple of weeks. With me, she says, not being cocky at all, but proud all the same, I got it over a single weekend.

Serenity saw something in me, and she drew it out of me just like that, she says, arcing up her arms into the air and twinkling her fingers, as if following the path of a glitter-filled fountain.

She explains that you normally start by staring at bananas and pineapples for hours on end, with no toilet breaks, no food breaks, no nothing, until you can see their auric fields. Because fruit, like any living thing, has a field. Once you're totally comfortable with the fruit, they move you on to small animals, mostly cats, because they're quieter, can sit still longer than dogs and have lots more thinky stuff going on inside them. And then finally, real people, with rainbow colours in their fields, and patterns within those colours that read like very simple books, or the strange Czechoslovakian cartoons that they show on BBC2.

Feeling the field, on the other hand, is dead easy. Baby stuff. And it's how Helen starts me off. She does a couple of demos on the old timers, and gets four of them lying down on massage beds that are arranged in a cross formation around her. She then does a little dainty jump and lets herself land, legs apart, in a sort of half-squat that allows, she explains, the energy of the cosmos to flow up through the floor of the church hall and right into your body, along your Hara line. She has a joke about the Hara line, and says that it's just like having a long electrical flex hanging down from between your legs, and that you need to plug it into the universe whenever you want to do a proper healing. The old timers hoot at this, because it's a bit funny to start imagining yourself as a healing machine, with plugs and everything.

Anyway, she gets into the half-squat and says that her Hara line is now plugged in and then she waddles over to her first healee, which turns out to be one of Deano's buddies, Feather Way. Helen does the big breaths that are so much part of the healer's tool kit, then she raises her hands high in the air before letting them fall slowly down towards Feather Way's body. Only they don't actually make contact with her body. Instead, kerthunk, Helen's hands stop around three feet above the table itself, and she mimes moving around a giant invisible egg. This, Helen tells us, is the outer shell of Feather Way's auric field.

At first it looks dead silly, and I can't help thinking of the Kenny Everett fella in black tights in the white room who's always pretending to be bumping up against walls. But Helen's miming is excellent, and she even does little bumps and creases as she moves along the field's uneven surface. Best of all, she asks us to join in, and gets us to stand in a circle around Feather, then to breathe big and loud, to plug in our own Hara lines, and to feel the field. And sure enough, if you concentrate hard enough, and imagine hard enough, and believe hard enough, you eventually find it, not quite rock hard, but certainly a resistance, pushing back against the force of our hands pushing down.

Helen pushes down hard too, and, with the aid of some more breaths and Hara energy, breaks through the outer layer, and down through six more layers until she comes to the root layer. At which point her hands just hover, inches over Feather Way's tracksuit, sensing the static crackle point where the spiritual, and the mad and the binjy-banjy meet the physical and real and the fleshy.

She breaks us into twos and, naturally, hops on to the bed before me and tells me, with a wink, to do my worst. I do the breaths, plug in the Hara line and, within seconds, I can feel her field. It's huge, and almost sparking against my hands, certainly pushing them backwards, right away from her invisible egg of energy. Helen speaks softly all the while, and tells me that I'm doing marvellous, which is just what I want to hear. She tells me to push against her field with all my strength, and to work my way towards her skin. She barks out orders to the class as she does so, and tells them that they need to harness the energy of each auric layer in order to push their way into the one below it. She tells us that we need to be open to the interplay of energies between our two fields, the healer and the healee. And we are not to be afraid, she warns us, of the things we see and the things we feel in the fields of others.

Right on cue my hand plunges right down, through six entire auric layers, until it comes smack up against Helen's root layer, hovering inches over her belly button, with my fingers splayed out towards her boobs. I feel a great big whoosh inside me, like the first time I had a sexy dream and didn't know what was happening until I woke up panic-stricken in the sticky-cold darkness of the Bert & Ernie bedsheets at midnight. It's the same here. There's a whoosh. I can barely look Helen in the eyes. She tells the class not to be afraid of any feelings that the healings arouse within us. It's just our cosmic bodies speaking to us, often for the first time.

I hold my hand over her belly, and breathe. Helen slowly whispers the words, 'Look, At, Me,' under her breath. Inch by inch, painfully, I lift my eyes up, along the stitching line of her white silky shirt and to her neck, chin, the scars around her mouth and, finally, to her eyes. I almost puke. We burn together. Our eyes on fire. It's like our souls inter-lock, madly, and for ever in all eternity. Helen smiles, dead chuffed with herself to have got me this far so effortlessly, and, without breaking contact, she whispers to me, her quietest words yet: 'This. Is. Love.'

I don't feel like saying much in the car back to Glengall. Deano blabs away and wants to compare notes about how many layers I could feel, and how hard it was to push through the outer shell. He's especially interested in the size of Helen's fields, and how firm they felt. He wants to know, once and for all, if she's the real deal? Or is she just a make-up artist who got lucky?

I grunt a bit. I have a million thoughts racing through my head about Helen, and about what she said to me during the healing, and about love, and what is love? Is it the stuff that you make together with someone after ages of going out together and turning all the giddy stomach stuff and the holdy hands stuff and the eye-staring stuff into something safe and rock solid and huge and big enough for you to want to catch a bullet for them or at least want to stay in another country and change your life completely all in the hope that they'll come back to you as the person they once were? Or is it just this magical thing that's there, or not there, and you know it when you feel it, flowing through you like a river, or a happy poison? And if love is like that, and it's just this huge blob of cosmic honey, what's wrong with feeling it, and having a taste? And can you have the rock love and the honey love at the same time, or is that cheating? What would Saidhbh say if I told her that Helen Macker had opened up a channel for cosmic love within me? I know Fiona would go mental, because she's always talking about all the old perverts who are attracted to binjy-banjy stuff because it's just a way to get free sex. She says that Deano's an exception, but mostly the fellas who are into spiritual stuff are all like, and here she does a brilliant impression of someone who's a bit hippie-ish, like the fella from *The Young Ones*, and she goes, Hey man, my energy has just totally collided with your energy, I think we should have a shag!

Or it's like Jerry Casey, who's Steven Casey's dad from St Cormac's, and who runs a cement company, is dead successful and lives three doors down from the Connells. He had serious solid-rock love with his wife Patricia, who backed him all the way, and raised their four kids during twenty-five brilliant years of marriage, and made them the envy couple of all Kilcuman. Jerry played in a band too, with some of the other dads. And when they played their four best Beatles numbers at the St Cormac's prize-giving night everyone told Patricia that she was super lucky to have landed a smasher like Jerry Casey. But then, as a result of twenty-five long years of child work and house care, Patricia got all old and wrinkly, with saggy boobs, a bent-over back and sad downturned eyes, and Jerry went out and found cosmic-honey love with a girl from the office who had lovely legs and huge young boobs. He came home and had a big cry in Patricia's arms, and said that he was so sorry but he had never felt anything like this in his life before and had decided to go with his heart this time. But then the office girl slowly became all annoying and talky, with words and everything. And it turned out that she didn't even like the Beatles, and Jerry had to look for cosmic-honey love elsewhere because when he eventually went begging back home to Patricia he found that her solid-rock love had been broken into pieces, and was useless now, lying in fragments all around her, like a Cadbury's Flake on a bad day.

Still, I wish there was some way to raise it with Saidhbh. Because it wouldn't have to be bad. And it wouldn't be harsh. And it wouldn't be like I was telling her that she couldn't even rely on me, of all people, for solid-rock love any more. No, instead, it would be all chatty like. And it would be her and me discussing, face to face, the two different types of love theory. She'd probably have some totally wacky angle on it that she got while out tree painting that day. Or she might be all interested, and chin-strokey and convinced that this is the best subject to talk about, ever. And so, while Deano's banging away about Winter Rain's field, and guessing wildly about what sort of reactions it provoked within me, I decide that, yes, I'll just play it dead honest with Saidhbh, and I'll start with, no messing about, You won't believe what happened to me in tonight's healing?!

Saidhbh, of course, has other ideas. When we get home, Aunty Grace is furious, and says that she's just back from dropping Saidhbh off at the hospital after a big dramatic Lady Shave incident.

Don't worry, she says, she didn't do any real damage, the crazy berk, although she'll need stitches.

But, more importantly, Aunty Grace says that Saidhbh's being transferred to the Cricklewood Mental Health Centre first thing in the morning. She says that Saidhbh has burnt her bridges with the folks at the hospital, and they won't allow her home. Not this time, and not until she can prove that she's not a danger to herself and not a complete loony. Fiona's with her for now, until lights out, but Aunty Grace says that she can't handle any more of this madness. She spills some wine on her mustard yellow carpet and bashes her fist down on the small brown side table next to her armchair. She pushes herself out of the chair and shuffles around the room distractedly, weeping quietly, and muttering to herself in between, about why she should have kept her nose out of everyone's business in the first place, and left Ireland well and good alone. Deano says, Listen, Grace . . . and tries to put his arm around her, but she slaps him coldly away. She tells him that he disgusts her, with all his binjy-banjy shite.

Yes! she says, suddenly turning to me, as if she's had the best idea ever. Where is your binjy-banjy healing shite now, eh? she says, with a real scary sneer on her face. Her eyes are bloodshot, her breath close enough to smell. All booze. Some fecking healer, you are! she says. Who are you supposed to be healing if you can't heal your own fecking girlfriend?!

9

No, Really. Let the Healing Begin!

The next entire month is a mad bonkers blur. Aunty Grace, of course, was dead right, and so I snap myself to my senses, and set my heart on healing Saidhbh, and curing her from all the sadness inside of her, as soon as possible. Definitely can't wait till Christmas. It's now or never. Helen isn't too keen, though. She says that I could do more damage than good if I start healing Saidhbh without mastering even the most basic Astral Science programme first. Deliberately pulsing enormous amounts of cosmic energy up and down the body isn't child's play, she warns. A wrong turn here, an anti-clockwise chakra spin there, a half-breath inhalation instead of a full-breath exhalation, and I'm liable to turn Saidhbh's inner sadness into full-blown mental psychosis. She agrees nonetheless to hurry me through to operational level, or at least to give me the basics to get me up and going, pronto. Of course, the moment she hears of the latest suicide attempt she offers to do the healing herself, but when I suggest it to Saidhbh she says that if Helen Fecking Scarface comes within half a mile of the Cricklewood Mad-house she'll stab herself in the eye with the splintered T-square that she uses for drawing horizontal planes

during occupational therapy.

She's not bothered at all by the clinic, and in fact she says that it makes a nice change from puffing fags out the window of the Glengall gaff. She says that Jackson loves it too, and that the poor little soul likes nothing better than to hang down by her legs, swinging around on the umbilical while she completes a million different masterpieces on every kind of artistic material known to man. Me and Fiona visit her as often as we can. The place looks all flash and posh on the outside, like a lovely big country house with holly running up the walls and huge gardens back and front, but inside it's pretty manky, and smells of super-strong Dettol. It's got hard marble floors and rooms as big as classrooms, with doors made of glass with wire through the glass, so you can peek in and see what the men-tallers are up to without them smashing the door to pieces with their big nutty heads and then slitting themselves to ribbons with the bladey-like shards.

The other mentallers are mostly old, and mostly men with bad teeth and old mad hair, like a big gang of tramps in pyjamas. But Saidhbh doesn't seem to notice, and instead she spends all her time at the table on the corner room on the second floor, which is the art room, surrounded by paint brushes and pastel trays, scribbling, sketching and splashing out the nasty demons that have brought her here in the first place. And she's not just doing trees either. She's doing eyes now. Loads of them. Massive ones. All in close-up. She says that the nurses have

promised to collect all her pictures into one huge folder, and that she can have it when she leaves. Then she adds with a mad grin, If I ever leave!

This is clearly a joke. Although it's hard to tell with Saidhbh. Because at times like this, when she's head down against the page, biting her tongue with concentration, drawing dark blue pastel lines, and brushing just the right amount of chalk dust away to create just the right amount of blue that's needed to make the blue bit of the eye look both real and reflecty, she seems like the old Saidhbh, back on track. And when she starts cracking jokes too, about being in the mental home for ever, well, you want to pick her up in your arms, and let her head loll on your shoulder and smell the back of her neck, and run right out through the doors and tell everyone that the world has gone completely barmy if they think that a young wan like this belongs with a load of wonky grandads in a Dettol-filled stink zone.

But, as always with Saidhbh, there's the flipside too. And the darkness. And you could go crazy thinking about it, and you could bang your head against a knotty trunk like Heathcliff in the English bog, just from the sadness and the madness of it all, and how she teases with the one hand and slaps with the other, and without even knowing what she's doing. Deano says that this is because the universe is in a state of complete Karmic balance, but he doesn't mention that when you're standing in front of the universe with your mouth agog at the madness it also crushes, and it hurts, and it

leaves you nowhere to look.

Saidhbh's new thing is that she finds the actions of breathing and talking hard to do at one and the same time. And so, in her new way of being, she will stop herself speaking by putting a hand up to her own mouth, which is both funny odd, and funny scary, but not funny funny. And then she closes her eyes, and seems to be going through some sort of checklist in her brain, and then she takes a big gulp of breath inwards and rushes out a speedy sentence before the air finally runs out, and then she stops her mouth with her hand again, and goes through the whole shebang once more.

It's pretty mental, and I know that it's something that we are thinking about, me and Fiona, on the long walk back to Kilburn. We don't say much out loud. Because I'm normally a bit wobbly after it all. And Fiona knows better. It's like when Jack Downs smacks you to blazes for ruining Fats Madigan's geography class, and then someone like Gary comes over at the end of the lesson and asks you if you're all right. And all you want to do is burst out crying, because you're still in shock from the smacks and the shouts, and because your insides are aching at the fact that there is still kindness and warmth and love in the hearts of little fellas like Gary Connell.

This is what it's like after visiting Saidhbh. We walk past all the bric-a-brac shops on Cricklewood Broadway, and Fiona says, Well, she seemed grand, didn't she?

And I say, Grand.

And that's it. And we keep walking, and keep glancing at the bric-a-brac, and I hope for hope's sake that Fiona doesn't put an arm around me, and squeeze me kindly, and ask me if I'm OK, and tell me that everything will work out fine in the end.

★ ★ ★

Meanwhile, back in the real world, the news of Saidhbh's full-time move to a London mental home has gone off like a super-directional bomb that sends killer shock waves out in only one direction — home. Gary sends me one of his mega-foolscap epics about it, and says that everyone in Dublin goes crazy when they find out, and it makes Dad and Mam have another big family-to-family meeting with the Donohues, where Mam spills the beans and Taighdhg Donohue bursts into tears and says that he'd give his right arm to go back and change the day that I first strolled into their house and into Saidhbh's life. He can't believe that Saidhbh's in a London mental home, which is for him, basically, another way of describing a British prison. He says that he always knew I was a bad egg, and a big argument follows, with Mam defending me, and Taighdhg pointing the finger at Mam and Dad, for being rubbish parents. Gary says that Sinead's job was to calm Taighdhg down, while my own dad just stands up halfway through and walks silently out of the room in his dressing gown and goes back to bed. Taighdhg shouts a load of rude things after him as he left, about sticking his head in the sand, but Gary reckons that my dad was too out of it on his meds to pay much attention. Which leaves everything in Mam's hands.

Mam, thanks to a lifetime spent at the dinner table juggling seven different personalities at once, is brilliant at calming people down, and avoiding fights. So, according to Gary, who learnt some of this from eavesdropping on his mam, and the rest of it from the gossips down at the gates of Coláiste Mhuire ni Bheatha, Mam fills the Donohues up with booze and shares stories about how hard it is to have kids these days. Then Taighdhg stops shouting at her, and everyone agrees to a ceasefire for the time being. Mam waves them off at the door, with a promise that they'll phone each other in the morning, but nothing actually happens. Mam's too embarrassed, and can't think of anything to do — other than waste all her savings on a super-expensive plane ticket just so she can see her son, who's doing grand by all accounts, and then tell his ex-girlfriend to stop killing herself because it's scaring everyone back in Dublin.

Taighdhg Donohue is wrecked the next day, and quickly falls into a deep dark place worthy of his own daughter's mental home. Gary says that he drinks for days on end, and disappears completely from Dublin and all his usual haunts. In fact, the Vice-Principal of Coláiste Mhuire ni Bheatha is on the phone to Sinead and they're just about to send for the guards when Taighdhg returns bright and breezy one morning, looking fab, as if nothing has happened at all, and says

443

that it's time to get on with their lives, that Saidhbh will be grand in London, and sure won't they see her over the Christmas break anyway?

No one can explain the change in him, but Gary says that there's a million rumours flying round. Most of them involve The Movement. It's all guesswork, but Peadar Clancy from Coláiste Mhuire ni Bheatha, who's best buddies with Saidhbh's brother Eaghdheanaghdh, reckons that Taighdhg went up the North and made contact with the 'RA. He reckons they must owe him loads of favours for letting them youngfellas sleep on his sitting-room floor back in the day. He must've asked the 'RA to send over a couple of operatives to London to get his daughter back and to do a punishment shooting on the fella that got her pregnant. Or maybe it was easier still. Just a phone call to London, to some sleeper members of a Knightsbridge Flying Column, who were on a break from blowing up department stores and horses. Just a code word and an address, and the order to bring back that poor colleen and teach that young pup a lesson about how we treat our womenfolk in the Emerald Isle.

Of course, Gary writes that all of this is guesswork, and that Peadar Clancy said that Eaghdheanaghdh told everyone that they were full of shit and that his dad was just bollixed for five days in a ditch down the bog. But then, Peadar Clancy says, this is what you have to do once you've contacted The Movement. It involves total commitment to their truth, and not

444

yours. Lying is the first skill they teach you up in the North. Peadar has a friend, Gary says, who was best friends with a 'RA man and never even knew it. The two of them were both in their first year at university and the 'RA fella was always going on trips up to the North, saying that he was visiting his aunty in Belfast. Then one day he drops out of college and it turns out that he's been arrested by the RUC for shooting a Proddy solicitor in the head. To be a real 'RA man you've got to be able to look your own mam in the eyes and be totally believable when you say, No, I never shot that fella, and I'm not even a member!

Gary ends his letter by telling me not to worry, because Eaghdheanaghdh's probably right and everyone else is full of shit. But then he tells me, on the very last line, that I should keep an eye out for anyone suspicious-looking, or at least some fellas sneaking around in balaclavas and camouflage jackets. Just in case. My best bet, he says, is to imagine that I am starring in my own Eddie Murphy action movie, and that the baddies are everywhere and trying to kill me. It will be fun, and kind of real at the same time.

★ ★ ★

I think about Gary's warning straightaway on the Saturday-afternoon shift in Border Town, when this big scruffy beardy fella, who's sitting in Billy's section like Chewbacca the Wookie in tracksuit bottoms, makes a huge deal about meeting the busboy, meaning me, up close and personal. Billy comes sashaying into the kitchen, does a brilliant impression of a headmistress sucking her cheeks in together, and tells me that the caveman on table 18 wants to have a chat with me.

At first I nearly crap myself, and wonder if it's the 'RA assassin, sent by Taighdhg to sort me out. Or maybe I'm just in normal, real person's trouble, because of the rubbish service I've given him, barely noticing him all shift, almost ignoring his table completely. I left him sitting there twice, with a dirty plate in front of him. First after the stuffed jalapeno peppers, and then with the remains of his fajitas — he even stacked a crumpled napkin on the skillet, which is universal restaurant sign language for, I've finished my dinner, thank you very much.

I decide to go out there and apologise, and explain that I've been concentrating all my energies on a big table of twelve women right behind him, in the horseshoe alcove. They are here, they say, to line their stomachs before the big night. They are a hen night. And the main thing I've learnt so far from being busboy is that hen nights are the best tippers. This is, firstly, because they're a bit messy and blurry-eyed by bill time, and happily overpay, and chuck a big plate full of notes at you, with contributions from all the girls, no change needed. And secondly, because they're in such a buzzy party mood they feel like spreading the atmos' with a big juicy tip. Either way, a big tip from them to Billy means a big tip from Billy to me. Although, to get the big tip you often have to put up with all sorts. Most of it dead rude. They usually have a load of rubber mickeys with them, all shapes and sizes, and all of them out and on the table, and often in the food, especially salsa dip. And they don't mind waving them around either, and sticking them in my face, for a laugh, when I come to clear the mains away.

Some of the other girls tell the mickey wavers to lay off me, and say that I'm only a kid. But the mickey wavers are too busy trying to stick the fake mickeys up under my black apron and give me a pretend comedy bum-rape to care. I think he likes that, they say, and then all twelve of them will cackle at the tops of their voices, with shouldn't-be-allowed laughter. I usually blush a bit, but I don't really mind. Because somehow, with all the ladies together, and the shouting, the pranks and the noise, it kind of reminds me of being back home at the dinner table. Only with fake mickeys instead of comments and jokes, and with twelve drunken women in stilettos and suspender belts and *Apprentice Shagger* T-shirts, instead of five sisters and a mam.

Billy's even better with them than me, and has a whole routine, including lines and comments that are friendly-rude, that he can hit them with at a moment's notice. Like calling them honey a lot. And saying, No, honey, in your case I'd rather have the money, when they ask if they can buy him a drink.

With all this going on I miss out on the beardy fella's table completely. It would've been a close call on the best of days anyway. But with all the Saidhbh stuff whizzing about inside me, and

Helen cramming five years of Astral Science lectures into my brain in two weeks, and the possibility that a fully armed IRA unit might leap up out of the guacamole and kill me at any minute, I don't in any way tend to him or his needs.

So, I'm bricking it as I shuffle up towards him. I'm pretty sure that he's not with the 'RA, if only because they'd never let themselves go like that, and he'd never fit all that hair into a balaclava without looking like a big dirty terrorist lollipop and being a laughing stock of The Movement. And even if he was in the 'RA, and this was just a brilliant half-man, half-monkey disguise, he'd never do anything here, in broad daylight, on a Saturday afternoon, in front of a load of drunken women with rubber mickeys in their hands.

Still, I'm wondering what he's going to say to me, and hoping that he's not going to shout me down, and call me the worst busboy in the history of London restaurants, and then demand to speak to Trevor and get me fired on the spot. It's only when I get to the table itself, close enough to touch him, that I clock him properly.

We're supposed to touch the customers whenever possible. Trevor told us all about it, and even gave the entire floor staff an afternoon of lessons. It's a trick that's come straight from America, and it makes the customers think that you're brilliant and makes them want to buy more from you and give you a big tip at the end of the night. Billy disagrees totally with it, and says it's not the way he learnt to work — and he learnt from all the old Soho pros — and it's fake

448

and phony and a bit creepy. It's dead simple though, and no big secret, and the Americans swear by it. It's a little move that you do whenever a customer wants to talk to you — which, over a whole meal, can be many times. Basically the whole sequence involves you walking towards them and, just as you reach their table, you suddenly drop down to your hunkers, slide up beside them and touch them on the arm. In this one super-smooth move, by dropping down below their eye-level you make the customer bigger than you and more in charge, and yet because you're touching them at the same time you get all connected and almost boyfriendy girlfriendy.

So, there I am, sliding down beside this big beardy bollix, looking up at him in the sweet smiley boyfriendy way, and touching him on the arm, when I see properly through the mad browny beard and the long stringy hair for the first time, and I realise, with something close to a full-blown heart attack, that it's none other than Fr Fecking O'Culigeen himself! In the flesh! And in my face!

Together again.

At last.

★ ★ ★

I stay frozen on my hunkers for ages. He grabs a right vicious hold of my hand, which was already squeezing his arm for the mock connection. He tells me not to speak, and then just blabs away in a big roller-coaster ride of words that is part confession, part apology but all lovey-dovey cuddle-up.

He promises that he's not a rapist any more. He says that he's a lover, not a fighter. Just like Jackson on *Thriller*, during the talky bits of 'The Girl is Mine'. He tells me that five months in Papua New Guinea would change anyone, and they've changed him totally. From tip to toe he says, pointing to his new hairy molly look, before adding that it's obvious for anyone to see that he's a new man. Yes, he did terrible things in the past, and yes he was once a rapist priest, and for that he is truly sorry. But life in Papua, and particularly the love of a native boy called Buassi, changed all that. Loving Buassi, he says, openly, and in full view of the other natives, showed him that there was a greater love to be had in life than loving God. Loving Buassi out loud, in front of his parents, and the village elders, showed him that the priesthood had it all wrong. Raping behind closed doors was evil. Loving out in the open was heavenly.

He says that things with Buassi ended badly when he discovered that the little liar had a girlfriend, and was only using O'Culigeen to get the fast track out of the jungle and a chance to live and work in Ireland instead. But it had been enough of an experience to show him that he could never go back to the old ways. He realised on the night of the big split with Buassi that he'd been living a lie, and that he'd never go back to the priesthood. And he realised too that, when he was totally honest with himself, on those cold nights alone in front of the mirror, Buassi was

450

just a substitute for someone even closer to his heart. Meaning me.

I whip my hand out of his grasp and run into the kitchen. Billy says I look pale as a sheet, and wants to know what's the matter, but I can't really speak. I lean against the tray stand, face down, and Billy rubs my shoulders. He asks me, softly, if it was the beardy fella. I nod a yes. He then leans even lower, with his chin just over my shoulder and whispers, Was he the one? I nod another yes. Billy turns me around and guides me gently into his arms, where he gives me the biggest, warmest, life-saving hug that a body could ever want.

O'Culigeen leaves, but scribbles a note on a Border Town napkin before he does. It says that he'll come back here every day if he has to, until I accept his apology, and until we both get on with our lives. He signs it LOC. Because the Father is gone, and he is finally Luke once more.

10

Zoo

I don't get sad when I think of home any more. One of the fellas behind the Border Town bar is from Dublin too. He's called Fergus, and he's been in London for years, so he speaks all funny, with a half-English half-Irish accent. Doesn't quite say his Ts. But also has real Dub expressions mixed in. Talks a lot about getting 'To'ally bah'erd' every night on the booze. Or for fellas that he likes, he says that he's 'Goh' a loh' a time for that owl bollix!' Fergus has been like a tour guide for me since I got here. He says that he knows all the cool places to visit in the city, and when I show him my copy of *The Ladybird Book of London* he says that it's rubbish, and that he knows more than any owl book. And so every weekend he never lets me leave without giving me a list of must-dos to get through in between healing practice and Grace's Angels, and before the following Friday.

So far, I've seen lots of old stones in glass cases, a giant statue of a nude fella with a sling on his shoulder and a tiny mickey, and a huge dinosaur skeleton that takes up nearly the whole inside of this posh old building. That was almost my favourite, and reminded me of *The Valley of Gwangi*, and lying awake in bed at night in Dublin, long before this all began, with the boombox on my chest and my own crackling recording of the film itself — done straight off the telly — playing away. And me, imagining all the roaring dinosaur bits, even as I could hear Dad's voice talking to Mam in the background, about the point of buying new school books when the second-hand ones are just as good. The music to the film comes tripping into my head the moment I see the big thing, the bronto-saurus, standing there in the hall, looking all huge and couldn't care less. I remember the cowboys on horseback, and how they chase a tiny tiny horse made of special effects, and how that chase suddenly goes bonkers when they get greedy and go from a tiny horse to a tiny dinosaur to a huge fella, the star of the show, Gwangi himself.

The music is all pulsey. And it goes, Denuhnenuh-denuhne-huh-denu! Nenunu, nenunu, nenunu! I'm humming that madly to myself as I'm walk-ing around the brontosaurus, imagining all sorts of crazy scrapes that would happen if it suddenly came to life. I look around at the kids with their mams, and the kids on school trips, and I wonder if they're having a hoot. I wonder too if Gary would like it here. Or Saidhbh. Fiona's already been, and when I try to tell her about it she does a big pretend yawn, and tells me that I'm being a bit obvious. I don't know what she means, but it must be bad, because Aunty Grace slaps Fiona lightly across the head, and Fiona apologises to me, and asks me some more questions about my day.

Aunty Grace lets me go on these trips on my own. She gets me all the right bus numbers from a timetable in the office, and says that London is safe as houses because there's so many people watching you. And that the real dangerous places are tiny Irish villages down the country where no one gives a feck if you're forced to have a baby in a field, or chucked down a well for being a mentaller. She says that all old Irish stories about fairies and banshees are just excuses for a whole lot of baby-killing and murdering that went on when the culchies drank too much poteen and woke up the next morning surrounded by dead bodies and had to blame it on something. Aunty Grace does a brilliant joke, where she describes a bogman going, Ah Jaysus, I've just killed me sister's illegitimate baby with a pitchfork! It was the fairy-folk that made me do it!

I go to this enormous church too, right next door to the dinosaur skeleton. It's one of Fergus's favourite places in London. He says that he goes there to pray, and to be close to God. Whenever the city's getting him down, he makes a beeline, goes inside, slaps the holy water on his forehead, finds an empty row and just flops down on to his knees. He talks to God, he says, like a long-lost friend. They chat, he says. He tells God about life in Border Town, and how much money he's making on tips, and how quickly he can make a Singapore Sling. And God just listens, and seems to be very happy with it all. Then Fergus lights a candle, looks at some of the amazing multicoloured windows, and heads back into the world, supercharged, and full of Godglow.

It's packed when I go. And they're doing a

Latin Mass. I sit right up at the front, and know all the responses, and test the altar boys on their timings during the prayers of the faithful. I say altar boys, but they're actually altar men. Which is strange to look at, but probably very wise. If anyone made a move on these fellas back in the sacristy, they'd get a right punch in the goolies for their troubles. I wonder if LOC has been here since he arrived in London. Although now that he's gone all anti-Church and beardy, he probably thinks that God is rubbish and only mini-boyfriends matter. He's true to his word, though, and comes into work every day during the weekend, and every day of the week too, even when I'm not on. He eats one of two things off the menu — beef chimichanga or salmon fajitas — sits quietly throughout the meal service, in his favourite four-man booth, and then leaves.

Billy kicks up a huge stink on my behalf, and tells Trevor that he simply must chuck LOC out. But Trevor says that LOC, despite the beard and the dirty trousers, is an ideal customer, and wishes they were all like him, and since Billy won't explain exactly what it is that he's got against him, then LOC stays. Every day, or all day, if he likes. This makes Billy furious. He warns Trevor that he might just take matters into his own hands.

★　★　★

My favourite place in London so far is the zoo. And my favourite animals are the chickens in zoo corner. All the other bigger cages are dead busy.

455

And everyone else goes, Wow, look over there at that big gorilla across the big concrete moat!

He's sitting totally still in the lashing rain, and looking like he's about to burst out crying or strangle himself with the rope that's holding up the rubber tyre. Whereas the chickens are part of the petting zoo, which means you can get up close and personal, every day between 11.30 a.m. and 2 p.m.

I'm normally the oldest on the petting tours, but that doesn't bother me, and usually means that I get the chickens all to myself. You're supposed to dunk your hand into a load of seedy stuff and let the chickens munch away exclusively from your outstretched hand, but none of the little toddlers with mams beside them want to try. And those few who do usually end up bawling the minute they get an accidental peck on the thumb. So mostly I have them all. I come back three days in a row, and feed them solidly for the whole two and a half hours. There's no one watching, so I just help myself, again and again, to fistfuls of seedy stuff.

By the third day the chickens are all over me. They go all giddy when they see me walking towards them and start pecking around my laces, hoping that seedy stuff is going to pour freely from me, out of my trousers and my ears, if you peck the right spot. I clock straightaway, however, and before I've barely got my first fistful out of the bucket, that one of them's looking and acting a bit poorly. She's a big red fella who's normally the first in line, but this time she just sits by the wire, tries to stand, takes a step or two, and then falls forward, almost on to her beak, before pushing herself, with a few chickeny gurgles, back into a seated slump. Her head keeps flopping sideways on to her body, and it looks like it takes a lot of effort just to yank it back up into regular chicken position.

I go over to her and she doesn't move. She doesn't even peck at me either. I'm at the end of Helen's crammer course so I seize my chance. There's a group of toddlers and three smoking mams crowded around the sheep, but otherwise the petting zoo's pretty much deserted. I crouch down and, with no one looking, my legs slightly apart, I plug my Hara line into the earth and take some fecking huge breaths. I hold my hands far away from Big Red, as I call her, and move them slowly in close to measure her auric field. It's tiny. She's very weak. I can feel too her chakras, blurry in outline, and they're a mess. Some of them not spinning at all. Others turning in the complete wrong direction. I do the final check, which is Third Eye Seeing, which involves another breath and, at the same time, staring at Big Red with my spiritual eye, and reading her field. In this, I decide that her root chakra is damaged, that she's been frightened almost to death, literally, by some other zoo animal, probably a tiger roaring, and in the process she's fled from her physical body, hence the root damage, and her inability to move along the Earth, and to exist on the physical plane.

I hold one hand above her head, and the other just below her tail feathers, and I begin to give my first healing to a real-life being. Keeping my

Third Eye open, I channel the Earth's energy and start spinning her chakras again. She's so small that it's hard to make out individual chakras, so I just use my will to spin whatever my Third Eye sees, and spin it in the right, clockwise, direction. This is the central act of healing, Helen tells us. We make it happen by wanting it to happen, believing it can happen, and by harnessing the power of the cosmos to ensure that it happens. As a last ditch, and a safety, she has also taught me how to speak to the healee's spiritual essence. You have to call your own guides and they address the healee's spirit for you, but in your words. So, it's usually Goddy things like, Oh sacred spirit of the soul, I command you, by the powers of the cosmos that flow within me, to bring your chakras back into alignment. I command you to turn. I command you to heal. Only you say them in a deep Goddy voice, like you've come from the bible times, or like you're in the film where the fella who's playing Moses splits the sea down the middle just long enough for everyone who's not on horseback to get through.

With these orders, combined with your hands holding the field in place, combined with your ability to will the chakras to turn again, combined with your faith in the goodness of the universe, you can't lose. And sure enough, within seconds of my last command, Big Red leaps up on to her feet, gives a great big cluck, and charges toward the seed bucket. I shoot to my own feet in disbelief and, dizzy from the sudden head rush, and from the thought that I'm clearly

458

at the height of my powers, I know that I am ready. The time is right. I scatter the seeds all over the ground and head straight for the exit. There's no time to waste. Saidhbh is next.

11

The Strike Zone

Healing Saidhbh is total rubbish. She's come back from the mental home a changed woman, and is all cocky and full of herself. It's just before Christmas week, and it takes me a whole five days to persuade her to let me even try to heal her. And even then she spends most of the time looking at her watch, and asking me to hurry up.

I've got the bedroom set up and everything. Good and dark, and with three candles, and some Indian binjy-banjy music playing in the background, one of Deano's tapes. I don't yet have a massage table, although I'm saving up for one, which I'll buy after I've paid the full whack on the flights — although I'm in serious trouble there, and getting nervous calls from Pika at Kilburn Student Travel, telling me that I've only got two days left to cough up the balance on the tickets or else the flights get cancelled, and I'll have to find another way to get back to Dublin for Christmas. Which, with only one week to go, is a tall order indeed.

So, anyway, I have to do the healing on the floor, on a lilo mattress, and me on my knees, shuffling round it as I move along the body. Saidhbh, meanwhile, is dead distracted and says that she has oodles left to do for her portfolio, so she asks me to make it a snappy one. She's facing into a super-tight deadline for her course — which is to learn painting for a whole year in a school called Chelsea, where you study nothing but drawing and painting and doing arty things. She says that Toby, one of the occupational therapists from the mental home, who has a skinhead haircut and big loopy earrings, is also a part-time teacher at Chelsea. And he's going to put in a word for her, to get her on the one-year course, with a view, she says, to doing three more years after that. Toby, she says, believes in her drawings. He says that they are raw, and real, and speak to something utterly painful about a woman's experience in the modern world. And if she just fills up her portfolio with another twenty top-class pics, then it should be a cinch to get her in the door.

She'll have to move house though, according to Toby. She can't be travelling right across London every day when there's oodles of squats near Chelsea, filled with oodles of painting students who'd love to hang out with Saidhbh and compare pics all morning and then smoke drugs and talk about the Great Masters and be a bit angry about the way that Maggie Thatcher and the businessmen in red braces are making everyone selfish. Toby lives in a squat too, she says. He doesn't believe in having your own house and needing piles of money. Everything he has goes on painting gear and earrings. He's definitely mad about Saidhbh. He's already met Aunty Grace, only the once, but even from that short meeting out on the street, next to his bicycle, she said that he was 'the business'. After he's gone, Aunty Grace comes running into Saidhbh's room — which she shares again with Fiona since she stopped trying to kill herself — and she tells her, in front of Fiona, that Toby is a real keeper, even with the skinhead haircut, and that she should hang on to him at all costs.

Fiona tells me the whole story that night and I feel like shooting myself. I don't think that it's fair, that people can do that. That an aunty could choose an artistic skinhead on a bicycle over her own nephew in the blink of an eye, despite all the things that she's seen me do, and the things I've been planning for Saidhbh while she was on the inside. All the healings I've been practising. All the training. And I don't think it's fair either that Saidhbh could walk out through the gates of a mental home and leave her entire old self behind, like a rubbish bomber jacket that you wouldn't mind losing at a New Year hoolie. Or that she could suddenly start acting so grown-up and adulty, and treat me like we're just best bender buddies again, or like I'm back to being this little fella who runs around his sister's parties in Spider Man pyjamas. Like it's all been a rubbish dream, everything, from then until now. World without end.

You could go mad. You really could. Or at least you could do some serious damage to a knotty tree trunk with the action end of your skull. As it happens, I don't have a tree trunk to hand so I use my pillow instead. I have a right old tantrum, alone in the room, underneath the *Rubber Soul* poster, and I whimper through tears and scream into the bed linen, and occasionally think to myself that this is what it must've been like for Heathcliff in the English bog, going, Ah Jaysus, women are fecking mental and they're driving me crazy!

When Fiona comes into the room it only makes things worse. I'm all sort of sweaty from the tantrum, but the way she looks at me is so kind, and makes me feel so young and so small that I don't know whether to take a running jump straight into her arms and let her hug me into heaven for the rest of my life or to tell her to feck off with herself because I'm not a big fecking baby any more. I do neither, and decide to bury my head into the pillow goodo. Fiona's brilliant though, and just strokes the back of my head and tells me that I'm to try and be happy for Saidhbh, because of everything she's been through, and because this is the best that we, or anyone, has seen her in for ever.

I do some more whimpering, and Fiona does some more stroking, and in the silence she tells me not to worry about Toby, and that even though he's three times my age and has a brilliant job in Chelsea, he's only half the man that I am. This makes me sniffle slowly back to life again, and straighten up on the bed, like a teary toddler who's just realised that he is getting a second scoop of ice-cream after all.

I look fully into Fiona's face.

But what about the healing? I say, desperately needy, needing to help, and wanting to prove.

You show her! says Fiona, not missing a beat, not a second's delay. And you show him too! Meaning Toby.

She then holds my hands tightly, and says, no joke, that I'm to clean myself up, and go down there to Saidhbh, and I'm to show her exactly what these things, meaning my hands, are made of!

★　★　★

Saidhbh giggles a bit during the start of the healing, and she keeps on peeking out at me through squinty eyes when I'm trying to find the outside of her field. It's almost impossible to concentrate, and I end up, a bit angry, skipping this part, and skipping the chakra testing too, and going straight for the Third Eye Seeing. This is rubbish too, and I can't see anything other than Saidhbh lying out in front of me in dungarees and Doc Martens, gripping both sides of the lilo mattress and biting her lip with how funny it is to see how mental I've become while she's been on the inside. She smirks and giggles every time I do a big breath. And she says things like 'Easy, tiger' any time my hands hover near her root chakra or her heart chakra. I try to tell her to stop messing, and to take it seriously, because it worked brilliantly on a sick chicken in London Zoo. But she's not interested.

I get no readings at all from her being, physical or cosmic. I replug my Hara line about ten times and with each new deep inhalation from the soul of the universe I get nothing. Not a single flicker. Not a vibration. Not a colour, a glow, or a spin. Nothing. Helen warned us that sessions like this exist. She said that if you ever found yourself in this situation — and pray you don't — it means only one of two things: that the person you're healing is dead, or that you, to put it bluntly, are simply not a healer. You don't have what it takes.

I wonder, for a second or two, if Saidhbh is dead. Perhaps she killed herself for good in the mental home and this is nothing less than her ghostly memory in front of me. It's unlikely, though. For one, we would've got the call-up from the mental home in the wee hours. And besides, the body in front of me is now sweating lightly all round the mouth and forehead area with the effort that it's taking her to hold in the giggles.

We finish the session early. I don't even bother calling my guides for the direct conversation with her spiritual essence. Saidhbh can see that I'm upset, and tries to make it better by saying that she feels amazing, and so relaxed and calm and like a new woman. She's almost halfway out the door when she turns and says she'll definitely have another one of them, in a month or two, and that I've really got a genuine gift in them there hands of mine.

★ ★ ★

I go to work feeling sadder than I've felt in ages. Sick with myself, and with my life. My head feels like it's sitting in a bucket of glue, and I'm about to burst out crying again at any minute. Aunty Grace was right. Helen's a nutter. All that binjy-banjy shite for nothing.

The place is all done up, Christmas style, with tinsel wrapped around the Mexican hats, and fairy lights running the entire length of the restaurant. Naturally, O'Culigeen's already there when I arrive, staring up at me from his booth like the toilet-paper puppy on telly, and it makes me so furious that I feel like tipping a whole skillet of boiling fajita oil over him. I shuffle down to the end of the restaurant and into the staffroom, where Billy's having a sneaky ciggie and, to make matters worse, is in a right grouchy state. He's a bit snappy with me when I tell him that my locker's empty, and that I've left my second busboy outfit at home and can I please borrow one of his spare aprons. He gives me a mini lecture about being a big baby who can't stand up for myself, and should know by now how to keep track of my aprons. So I feel even more useless. And yet immediately, just as quickly, Billy waves his arms about in front of his face and apologises for his mood, and says that his dinner party buddies are coming in tonight, so his nerves aren't the best. I don't ask why. He hovers round his own locker, and makes sure that it's shut good and tight by banging it closed around five times in a row.

Sure enough, within the hour, Roger and Jamie arrive, with Soz in tow, all in denims and tight white T-shirts and Santy hats, looking super clean and fresh, and all kind of polished. Billy sits them right opposite O'Culigeen, which makes him look even beardier and trampier and them look even more like three giddy snooker balls biffing and bashing each other happily round the table. They

466

do funny gay men things like ordering a huge jug of margarita, and clapping quickly when it comes to the table, and then making jokes about the chimichanga, asking each other if they'd like some hot beef inside them. They're having a great time, and if I didn't know any better I'd say that they were being even louder and gayer than ever. Roger, for instance, grabs one of the Mexican hats off the wall display next to them, and starts doing this big loud act, like a Mexican man. Only it's not just for the other fellas, but for a lot of the other tables too, and definitely for O'Culigeen.

I'm still a bit of a zombie, and gutted about the fact that I'm rubbish at healing, despite having a bright glowy light within me. I mess up loads of orders too. I bring a lone plate of enchiladas to a family of six in Billy's section when they were supposed to be a starter for two girls sharing near the bar. Then I main-away one of Billy's tables while they're still on the nachos and waiting for their first round of drinks. And I take two orders for extra coffees from a family who are going to the theatre and then forget to tell Billy about it. They get into a big huff, and the dad says, as he's walking out the door, that if they're late for *Les Mis* because of my forgotten coffees they'll be back to ask Trevor, in person, to pay for their tickets.

You really have to be strong not to cry at times like this, and if it weren't for Billy and everyone around me telling me that the customers are fecking berks, and that I'm doing fine, I'd be in floods. But what really pushes me over the edge is these two fellas in rubbish Irish jumpers and grey pleated jeans who come in and sit down at the bar, but right at the edge of Billy's section. They stare at me through the whole pre-theatre service and they barely touch their food. Every time I whizz past them I catch snatches of their conversation, and I'm pretty sure from their High-Nigh-Brine-Kigh accents that they're from the North, probably Belfast.

I bravely face facts, and decide that they're most likely two IRA hitmen sent to kill me by Taighdhg Donohue's connections in The Movement, and the very idea gives me a sudden shot of nervous diarrhoea. I run to the loo and sit in the cubicle with everything spinning around my head while trying to remember a joke about diarrhoea that Mam used to tell which said something about the bottom falling out of your world and the world falling out of your bottom.

I don't come back on the floor for another half an hour, but when I do it's all change. The IRA fellas are still there, and still giving me the evil eye but feck me if O'Culigeen hasn't gone and joined Roger and the others on the gay table. They're all gathered around O'Culigeen, and have put one of the Santy hats on his head, and are filling his tumbler high with margarita, and pawing him and laughing wildly as he tells them about the funny things that happened to him while he was on the missions in Papua New Guinea. As I approach the table he's telling them about the time that he pretended to the savages, for a laugh, to mistake a native headdress for an exotic fruit cocktail, and they're hooting about the place at the wackiness of it all. I try to duck past them but O'Culigeen's arm shoots out and he drunkenly grabs me and pulls me to the tableside. He asks me to order a fresh jug of margaritas for his new best friends, and then tries to surprise everybody with the fact that he and I are buddies of old. From the old days, he slurs, while making a deliberately goofy sign of the cross in the air. The lads laugh again, and don't seem too interested in our story, but instead ask O'Culigeen to tell them some more stories from his priesty days. And confessions! Yes, tell us about confessions! Don't hold back! The grisliest? The dirtiest? Yes. Tell us them all!

The night goes on like this, with the gays and O'Culigeen making the biggest noise of any table, even as the music kicks in for the home stretch. This is the last two hours of service, when they clear a tiny space in front of the bar, and turn the restaurant into a half-disco. You can drink as much booze as you like if you stumble in at this point, but the catch is that you must order food with your booze, which proves to everyone that it's not a real disco and still a restaurant.

After midnight, even with three Bronski Beat tracks in a row, the place is cooling off. The whole bar area is practically empty, except for a table of sleepy-looking Hens, and the IRA fellas. While the gays and O'Culigeen, who can barely see straight, are the only ones left in Billy's section. And so, that's when it happens.

★   ★   ★

469

You'll want to see this.

That's what Billy says, serious and whispery, as he whooshes past me and towards his section, in a mad manic march. I follow at a distance and watch him skim by the gays and give Roger the nod before disappearing into the changing rooms at the back. Roger, Jamie and Soz suddenly stand up and, still half joking, knock O'Culigeen's Santy hat off, lift him up from his seat and tell him that they've got something very special to show him down the back. O'Culigeen laughs out loud, and says that he knows all about what London boys want and makes a big joke about grabbing his own belt and pulling it tight, as if to protect himself from a big three-man mickey attack.

The gays do more laughing and pull and half grab at him. O'Culigeen laughs and wriggles and half smacks back. And then, somehow, at the exact same moment, all four men, with faces dropped to granite for the first time, have the very same idea. O'Culigeen tries to leap backwards away from the table but he's easily pinned down by Soz's heavy bulk. O'Culigeen doesn't say anything at all, just struggles madly as they drag him, all three of them, towards the changing room. Again, I follow at a distance, and by the time I get to the big red door with the slim rectangular window, they've already got the blanket over his head. I don't dare go inside, but I watch through the window as Roger hands out the baseball bats from Billy's open locker and the men, all four of them now, get busy belting.

They make the maddest sounds, those hard

wooden baseball bats, on O'Culigeen's body. All clunky and thonky, from the meeting of wood with bones where O'Culigeen's arms and legs are flinging and kicking about, up and down beneath the rug, hoping to block the blows, hoping to protect. But every now and then, when they make full contact with his head, there's a loud and hollow thwock, almost like a pop, that lets them know it's the jackpot spot, and to keep going. Roger mostly leads by example in the bashing department, and gets the most hits on target in the shortest amount of time. He says motherfucker a lot too, while he does it, and suddenly sounds real American. He gets at least three whacks in to everyone else's one. But they get a rhythm going in the end, like four fellas from the old days driving in a giant wooden fence post into the ground down the bog, taking turns with their sledgehammers, while one of them says motherfucker.

O'Culigeen says nothing at all while it's happening. Not a peep out of him, from underneath that blanket, which is actually more of a picnic rug. It's like everyone knows what they're here for. Even him. By the time Roger moves to the side, and I, through the toughened glass, get a decent look, I can see that O'Culigeen has already collapsed completely into a surprisingly small heap on the floor. He is just a hand, already bloodied, sticking out from underneath a rug. The hand isn't doing much, but I'd swear it was reaching out for forgiveness, and in my direction too. As it does I get a flash of O'Culigeen as a boy down the bog, getting picked on and beaten up by his older brothers, getting dragged to the back of the hay shed, getting punched, getting bashed, and getting this.

Billy collects the baseball bats and bundles them into his locker in a big nervy rush. The men then gather up O'Culigeen, all floppy now, but still in the picnic rug. Billy kicks open the back door of the staffroom, has a quick peek up and down the darkened alley, and then signals for his friends to leave. As they do, Billy leans into the rug and whispers something angry, something that makes his teeth flash, to the bones of O'Culigeen, who will be whisked out, and eventually dumped, somewhere, anywhere. A hospital doorway if he's lucky. A Soho side street if he's not.

★　★　★

I step away from the changing room before Billy has the chance to find me and ask me, in the nicest way, for a sign of my thanks. I walk, quicker than ever, through the restaurant, right past the IRA hitmen, and straight through the front door, still in my uniform.

I don't wait around for the staff taxi either, but instead walk the whole way home myself, through drunken Christmas London. I'm in a walking trance, like yer man in *Kung Fu*, and move with the breeze along the outskirts of Hyde Park, in and out of the office parties stumbling around Queensway, past the late-night Notting Hill bars, and straight by, without even looking, the front doorway of Grace's Angels, and up

Ladbroke Grove, across the Harrow Road and eventually into Queen's Park, Kilburn and to the end of it all in Glengall Road.

It takes me nearly an hour and a half of blank, mindless foot-falls, and by the time I push my way, robot style, into Aunty Grace's hallway all the lights are on, and everybody is awake and waiting for me. Everybody, that is, including my biggest sisters Sarah and Siobhan.

They stand silently in the sitting room, surrounded by Grace, Deano, Fiona and Saidhbh. Like the world's quietest surprise party. They look at me with strange shifting expressions. Their faces, it seems, are torn somewhere between, 'Bet you never thought you'd see us here?!' and 'Feck!'

It's Dad, they eventually say, after an age of mad stares. It's his time.

12

Home

Me, Fiona, Sarah and Siobhan hardly say a word to each other on the whole flight home, even though it's my first time on a plane. They let me sit by myself, by the window, and I spend most of the flight with my face pressed right up against the clear plastic bit in front of the glass. Inside I want to scream out loud, and go woooo-wooo during take-off. I want to laugh at the tiny matchbox vans in the airport car park, whizzing underneath us. And I want to go Jaysus Fecking Hell when the whole wing starts going bendy bouncy as we pass through the clouds. But I don't dare break the silence.

Fiona, Sarah and Siobhan all order gin-and-tonics from the air-hostess, who's dressed head to toe in green — in case, I suppose, she gets lost in Heathrow and they have to point her towards the Irish area where all the green planes live with their green engines and green pilots. Gary says that his dad was always getting slagged by the British pilots because he worked for an airline called Aer 'Lingus'. He said it was one of the biggest and longest-running gags in the international pilot's joke-book.

He often heard his dad talking about it, and not finding it funny at all, and telling everyone how the pilots' union were going to vote to force the board to change the name to Aer Ireland, or Aer Eire, or just plain Eire Planes. Anything, they used to argue, other than Aer Lingus. The Brits used to fall around the place laughing every time Gary's dad and his pilot mates would walk through the terminal building. Aer Lingus! Can you imagine it? they'd say. And then Gary would turn to me and go, Aer Lingus! It's pretty embarrassing all the same, isn't it? And neither of us would have a clue about which bit was supposed to be embarrassing. We decided once that Lingus was the name of a disease of the mickey that you get when you've been in bed with a prostitute. But it didn't seem that funny. Of course now, because I know what it means, it gives me a giggle when I think about it the way the English would. Which is, to them, a bit like calling your national airline Aer Suck My Mickey. I guess that they think the Irish are so rubbish at sex that they didn't even know Lingus was a sexy thing when they decided to name the company. Which is part of the joke. And maybe it was even an English company advisor, who was brilliant at doing sex, who whispered the name in their ears and they thought, Brilliant, yes, Lingus has a real planey ring to it. A bit like National Gaelic Titty Trains or Bus Bollocks of Ireland. Either way, I find it funny when I think about it, but only with my English head on. With my Irish head on it's just what it is. A name.

Sarah and Siobhan's eyes are red around the rims and the girls sniffle while they drink. Every now and then Fiona puts her arm around them in turn, and tells them to stay strong. And to think of what it must be like for Mam.

I want to tell them that they're missing it all. And that they should look out over my shoulder at the sky, and the way that the winter sun is laying a pinky and orangey cloud quilt right across the horizon. And it makes me think of Mam too, and how she came back, after one of her first trips to Aunty Grace, with magical stories of the plane flight, and how the clouds looked like big candy-floss things, good enough to touch, if not to eat. No, she said, correcting herself, always a stickler for foodie details, in fact they were like a big ocean of whipped cream on the hugest pavlova in the universe, just before you grate the cooking-chocolate lightly over the top.

I look down too through the cloud gaps, far below, into the Irish Sea and do a bit of boat spotting. Tiny dots are trailing ribbons of white on a blacky blue carpet. Trawlers, I suppose. And goods ships too. And I'd swear I see the B&I car ferry, chugging slowly in the opposite direction. And I wonder, by all the laws in Fr Jason's physics, if there's another Saidhbh and another me, heading out across the water, with another baby on the way, and another bucketload of choices to make, to go right, to go wrong and to bring us to another place, far away from the now and the here.

Of course, we've barely been up twenty minutes when I feel the plane tipping down-wards again. The world's shortest flight. The girls hand over their empties. My can of fizzy is done too. It's Cidona, sent over by Mam especially for the trip. Sarah and Siobhan would go totally mental if they knew that I had been having booze whenever I wanted at Aunty Grace's table. And Fiona's certainly not going to tell them.

We find out later that Gary's dad organised all the flights for free. When he heard about Dad he just said to Mam, leave it with me, Devida. And he popped the tickets through the door the very next morning. I didn't have a chance to talk to Saidhbh about it, or about our Christmas flights, or about how much money I still owe Pika. She was gone by the time we left for the airport. Out with Toby at the crack. I shuffled in towards her bed. I wasn't going to do 'Good morning! Good morning!' or anything like that. But I would've said something. But her sheets were kicked back, and she was gone from me already. In every way.

★ ★ ★

There's no one to meet us at the airport, and we have to get a taxi home. This is serious, and it makes Sarah cry, because it means that everyone's gathered round Dad's bedside, on the final watch.

When we pull up to the house the signs aren't good. The taxi man's been talking all the way from the airport, comparing Dublin to London and telling us which one's better at what, and why. He says that Dublin is full of great 'characters', and you don't get that in London. He says that he's a bit of an aul character himself, and gives us lots of stories about his time in London, working on the building sites, and going mad on the Kilburn High Road. He jokes about me and Fiona coming home because we missed our mammy's cooking, and tells us that he could never get used to cooking for himself, alone, in London. And that, swear to God, is why he came back. And sure it didn't take him long to meet a grand Dub woman too, and she's responsible for this old thing, I might add. He pats his belly when he says, this old thing. He's still blabbing away as we leave the taxi. Fiona shoves a wad of notes into his hand and the girls race up the driveway.

I'm the last one to move, and not even out of the back of his taxi when there's this big mad groan from the front door. Like Mam has just run out on to the welcome mat and stuck a great big carving knife into her own stomach. Sarah and Siobhan start going, Oh Mam, Oh Mam, and they pull Fiona into their big teary hug and Mam tells them all that the ventilator's been switched off. Whatever the feck that means.

Mam sees me over the heads of the girls and she shakes her own head madly, and holds her hand out like a stop sign, like it's all too much, and there aren't things you can do, let alone words to find, that can tackle this level of pain. The three girls half carry Mam back inside, over the threshold, and they plonk her on a chair that sits alone between the Christmas tree and the low phone table. She tells the three of them to hurry, to be strong, and to say their goodbyes.

★ ★ ★

The house is already full of friends, relations and sad people. Some of them are crying. Some of them gather round the tree in the hall and stare silently at the shining decorations and flickering fairy lights. Claire and Susan have been taken to Brenda Joyce's in Ballinteer to play with her Girl's World, because they're too upset, too confused and too young to understand death in the way that everyone else is supposed to. Tim Connell the pilot has taken charge for the moment, and he gives me a hug when I step through the door and tells me, like he's only meeting me for the very first time in his life, that he's sorry for the way that this has all happened. He drags me past Mam into the kitchen, where the coffee women have made loads of mince pies and have put slices of Christmas cake out on a plate, just in case all this approaching death gives us a fearsome appetite for Yuletide snacks. They all call me a poor pet, and pat me on the shoulders and tell me that I'm the man of the house now.

Tim tells me that Dad's been going this way for weeks, for months even, and that it has taken a terrible toll on Mam, but nobody wanted me and Fiona to be too worried, knowing that we were over there in London, and unable to do anything about it. He says that everyone thought that Dad would last until the holidays, but unfortunately it's not to be. He says that with the ventilator off, my dad's only got a couple of hours of breathing left in him. And he certainly won't make the night. And then he tells me that the fire's going down and so he better leave me and get some more briquettes from the garage.

Mam appears at my shoulder. She's in bits and is handed over to me by the coffee mams. She finds the strength to call me her love and stroke my face, and then she falls into a big floppy hug on my shoulders and says that these are terrible times. Terrible times. She looks about a hundred. Her face is red, with a million lines, and wet with tears. He'll be free soon, she says. Free of it all.

She tells me to say my goodbyes, and says that Aunty Una is with him upstairs, keeping watch. She then grips me firmly by both arms and asks me if I'm sure I'm ready for this. Are you strong enough? she says, and then she warns me that it'll test me, and it won't ever leave me.

I nod yes, and shuffle quietly up the stairs. It's mad, that in this house where I lived nearly all my life with my family, I am about to do this thing, this final farewell. Fiona, Sarah and Siobhan are standing outside, staring wordlessly at the carpet, with the big bulgy eyes and red slap-in-the-face cheeks. I knock on the door to the bedroom, and Aunty Una appears in seconds, with a crazy calm smile on her face, super-chuffed to be doing the most important job in the house. She goes all wincy when she sees me and tells me that everything is just awful, and then hugs me close while yanking me inside the room.

I'll leave you alone with Matt, she says, and kind of rolls me towards the double bed, while nipping out of the room in the same slinky movement. I come to a halt right beside him, and stare down. He's pale as feck, and skinny too, skeleton skinny, with his mouth half agog, and barely a puff of breath going either in or out. His head hair is in tiny wisps, and he's still wrapped in his beloved scratchy grey dressing gown. The bed covers are pulled up to his stomach, but the dressing gown is open wide, showing a tiny bony body-cage with three shaven circles scraped into the skin where the ventilator suction pads would've lived. The ventilator itself, which is a big white box with a row of eight buttons and a smaller white TV-style box on top of it, sits uselessly by, on the top of a bedside table.

Dad's eyes are shut.

There is no one at home.

I nod to myself. I know what I must do.

★ ★ ★

Calmly, I move away from him again, walk towards the door and turn the key in the lock. I shove a bedside chair under the handle just in case. Aunty Una is on it like a shot and starts knocking quietly on the door, asking if I'm all right in there and do I want her to get my mam and my sisters. But I've already got my legs open at this stage and have plugged my Hara line right deep into the very core of planet Earth itself. My breaths are fecking huge, and with each intake I feel my whole body tingling and filling up with all the crazy and unthinkable and unknowable energies that span all the realms of life, space and beyond.

I raise my hands out above him and I know that this is right. I let them fall towards him, but his field is gone completely. Just an echo of the life that was there. I try to sense his chakras, but they're gone too. Not a single spin in sight. Undaunted, I grab another huge breath, and go for some Third Eye Seeing. I'm trembling all over, but there's still nothing in front of me.

The knocks on the door get louder now. It's Tim Connell, with the girls behind him. He says that I should open the door now, because I'm freaking the family to Jesus. He wants to know what in feck's name I'm doing in there.

I'm in the zone. My body's rattling like mad. But this time I'm using it. Like every maddening spazzy trembly fit I've ever had is welling back up inside me like a massive mental volcano, but in a good way. I tell myself that I'm just a vessel, that Helen was right, and that I'm an aerial for the entire cosmos, that there is no me, there is no time, there is no before and after, and there is no life and death. Just energy.

Dad doesn't move. Nothing. But I haven't lost hope. I will speak to his cosmic essence. I try to use the stupid Goddy ghosty voice, complete with bible-style commands, but it's not right. Nothing. Instead, with my arms outstretched, my Hara line on fire, and the cosmos pumping through me, I speak in my own voice. I say, Dad, how are you? I say, Dad, I've missed you all my life. I say, I am your son, your best boy, and you have my heart so completely that I sometimes don't know where to look. I tell him that it's all for him. That, all along, everything, all of it, was for him. And that my life is his life, my soul his soul.

I give sacred thanks too, for what he has been to me, and I tell him that I miss his arms, and his strength, and how he made the world feel when he was in it. I miss us together watching *Benny Hill* on the couch, I say. Me looking up to your huge body, your legs crossed, your hands over your stomach, and your whole form rocking on the spot from the laughing at Benny doing the A-Team. I miss the looks you'd give me at the dinner table when the girls were being crazy loud. The looks that said that we were in this together, just you and me, for the long haul, and made of the same stuff. And I miss our walks most of all, Dad. I miss me asking you questions about sharks, about space, and about life. And you patient as ever, quietly, softly, having all the answers. I miss my hand in your hand. And I miss knowing deep down inside that the world was safe with you in it.

The knocking gets even louder. Sarah's at it too. She says Mam's panicking downstairs. Wants to know what in feck's name is going on.

I tell Dad that this is it. Still using my normal voice, I say that it's shit or get off the pot time. My body goes into super spazzy mode, and I feel my heart chakra spinning like a mad man. I take one last breath, crack open my own auric field from the inside and boom — a super-directional energy bomb is blasted right into Dad's body, point blank. No mercy.

The effort of it takes me off my feet completely and makes Sarah shriek outside. I pull myself up to the end of the bed and have another look. At first it's nothing. Just the same skeleton, not for this world. But once I steady myself, and get the Hara plugged back in, I notice just the tiniest flicker of green in the heart chakra. I nearly crap myself. Instant diarrhoea. I leap into action, place my right hand directly over his heart chakra and my left hand over mine, and start channelling the energy up through the Hara and into Dad's auric field.

Within seconds I see a definite green spinning motion around his chest. And within seconds after that I see yellow for the solar chakra, red for the root, and purple for the crown. Time freezes, and the knocking seems to stop. And for what could be ten hours or two minutes, I work like fury to get all seven chakras spinning fast enough to allow Dad's auric body to jump-start his physical essence. It works, of course. And is less dramatic than it sounds. Dad just opens his eyes and takes a huge manly breath. And then, casual as anything, he props himself up on his elbows and says that he's fecking starving.

It takes me longer to get the actual bedroom door open, because I have to make Sarah and Aunty Una and Tim Connell all to promise on a billion bibles that they're not going to spaz out when they see what I've done. Sarah's howling at this, and sure that I've done something completely sick and mental, and probably expects to see Dad hanging upside down from the light fixtures. But they all agree eventually not to spaz, and I slowly crank open the door to reveal the figure of Dad, sitting quietly upright at the edge of the bed, with the sweetest, softest smile there's ever been on a human face playing gently across his lips.

★   ★   ★

We have a late-night supper, the lot of us. And we sit around the table shouting and laughing for Ireland. Mam sits on Dad's lap for most of it, although he jokes about the weight of her on top of him, like a big heifer. The two of them are on cracking form, and fire out breastfeeding gags, one after the other like there's no tomorrow. Claire and Susan arrive too back from Brenda Joyce's, which is the signal for the neighbours and the relatives to finally go home, and to leave us there, just the family, alone and together.

Sarah strolls quietly into the sitting room, dips below the line of Christmas cards hanging in front of the folding doors and puts *Hooked on Classics* on to the record player, while Mam makes extra sangers with brown-white bread. The thum-thum-thum beats in the background, and the chat goes up to ninety for hours on end. Me and Fiona tell everyone brilliant stories about life in London. Though it's Fiona who does the lion's share of the talking. Most of the time I just sit there and lap it all up, taking in the vision before me, and knowing right there and then that there are no secrets left. I am everything and I am nothing. I am in this world and the next. I am the universe and I am the multiverse. I am the splitting of moments into millions, and the living of those same moments in all their possibilities of all their times. I am alive in the kitchen with my beloved family, sharing in their hopes and their dreams for a new and inconceivable future. And I am back on the floor of O'Culigeen's filthy study right now, with the blue walls and with the smell of old socks, and with a gash on my forehead and no air left in my lungs, at all.

* * *

Stuff like that never happened around our place before.

Not right in front of our eyes.

Acknowledgements

For their support, encouragement and assiduous attention to detail, a big thanks to the Little, Brown massive, including Victoria Pepe, Richard Beswick, Susan de Soissons, Stephen Dumughn and Reagan Arthur. Especially, though, to my editor, Clare Smith, who truly has the eyes of a hawk, the patience of a saint and the instincts of an impeccable storyteller.

Thanks also to my agent Jim Gill, for his consistency, enthusiasm and humour, and for the calming assurance of his ever-present baritone burr.

For the gutteral stuff of daily life, and the fuel of loving kindness, thanks to the wider Mahers: Anne, Tom, Catherine, Lucy, Sheila and bold Diarmaid Ferriter.

And finally, thanks to my three favourite teachers: Liberty, Sky and Sylvian. Everyday, you learn me.

And to Rose. There's no book, no words, and no breath without you. You're it.

We do hope that you have enjoyed reading this large print book.

Did you know that all of our titles are available for purchase?

We publish a wide range of high quality large print books including:
Romances, Mysteries, Classics
General Fiction
Non Fiction and Westerns

Special interest titles available in large print are:
The Little Oxford Dictionary
Music Book
Song Book
Hymn Book
Service Book

Also available from us courtesy of Oxford University Press:
Young Readers' Dictionary
(large print edition)
Young Readers' Thesaurus
(large print edition)

For further information or a free brochure, please contact us at:
Ulverscroft Large Print Books Ltd.,
The Green, Bradgate Road, Anstey,
Leicester, LE7 7FU, England.
Tel: (00 44) 0116 236 4325
Fax: (00 44) 0116 234 0205

GOODBYE FOR NOW

Laurie Frankel

Imagine a world in which you never have to say goodbye, a world in which you can talk to your loved ones after they've gone — about the trivial things you used to share; about the things you wished you'd said while you still had the chance; about how hard it is to adjust to life without them. When Sam Elling invents a computer programme that enables his girlfriend Meredith to do just this, nothing can prepare them for the success and complications that follow. For every person who wants to say goodbye, there is someone else who can't let go. And when tragedy strikes they have to find out whether goodbye has to be for ever — or whether love can take on a life of its own . . .

THE NIGHT RAINBOW

Claire King

During one long, hot summer, five-year-old Pea and her little sister Margot play alone in the meadow behind their house, in a small village in Southern France. Her mother is too sad to take care of them: she left her happiness in the hospital, along with the baby. Pea's father has died in an accident, and Maman, burdened by her double grief, has retreated to a place where Pea cannot reach her. Then Pea meets Claude, a man who seems to love the meadow as she does. Pea believes that she and Margot have found a friend — maybe even a new papa. But why do the villagers view Claude with suspicion, and what secret is he keeping in his strange, empty house?

THE COLOUR OF MILK

Nell Leyshon

The year is eighteen-hundred-and-thirty-one when fifteen-year-old Mary begins the difficult task of telling her story. A scrap of a thing with a sharp tongue and hair the colour of milk, Mary leads a harsh life working on her father's farm alongside her three sisters. In the summer she is sent to work for the local vicar's invalid wife, where the reasons why she must record the truth of what happens to her — and the need to record it so urgently — are gradually revealed.

THE TWELVE TRIBES OF HATTIE

Ayana Mathis

When Hattie climbed from a train, her skirt still hemmed with Georgia mud and the dream of Philadelphia sitting round as a marble in her mouth, she couldn't guess that two years later, aged seventeen, she'd be fighting to keep her baby twins alive. Saddled with a husband who will bring her nothing but disappointment, she raises nine children with grit and monumental courage, but no tenderness — she knows the world will not be kind to them and wants to prepare them as best she can. And as her sons and daughters buck against their fates, she feels every one of their triumphs and heartbreaks, for they are all bound together . . .

PHILIDA

Andre Brink

It's 1832. Philida is the mother of four children by Francois Brink, the son of her master. The Cape is rife with rumours about the liberation of the slaves and Philida risks her whole life by lodging a complaint against Francois, who has reneged on his promise to set her free. His father has ordered him to marry a white woman from a prominent Cape Town family, and Philida will be sold on to owners in the harsh country up north. Unwilling to accept this fate, Philida continues to test the limits of her freedom, and with the Muslim slave Labyn she sets off on a journey across the great wilderness on the banks of the Gariep River, to the far north of Cape Town.

ONCE UPON A RIVER

Bonnie Jo Campbell

After the violent death of her father, in which she is complicit, sixteen-year-old Margo Crane takes to the Stark River in her boat in search of her vanished mother. But the river, Margo's childhood paradise, is a dangerous place for a young woman travelling alone, and she must be strong to survive, using her knowledge of the natural world and her ability to look unsparingly into the hearts of those around her. Her river odyssey through rural Michigan becomes a defining journey, one that leads her beyond self-preservation and into deciding what price she is willing to pay for her choices.